THE MOT
HOWDAH OF

At the dawn of independence in India, in a small *sattra* in South Kamrup in Assam, the Gossains, its religious and spiritual heads, grapple with a palpable threat to their traditional authority. The *sattra* soaks in opium fumes, taxes challenge their ownership of land, the emerging forces of communism strike at the debilitated roots of feudal power. The author holds up a powerful picture of change and transition, of degeneration and decay, which finds suitable expression in the central metaphor. Interwoven with the main story is a poignant tale of the tragedy of widowhood—the plight of Brahmin widows encased in the *sattra* and their responses to a fate worse than death… This is a novel remarkable as much for its depth of observation as its narrative power.

Indira Goswami is among the best-known names in Indian literature today. Her works stand out for their evocative prose as well as their compassionate delineation of suffering humanity—widows in Vrindavan, migratory labourers and riot victims. She has been honoured with a number of literary awards—the Sahitya Akademi award in 1982, the International Tulis Award and the prestigious Jnanpith award for the year 2000. Rupa has earlier published her first collection of short stories in translation, *The Shadow of Kamakhya*.

THE MOTH-EATEN HOWDAH OF THE TUSKER

Translated from the original Assamese 'Une Khowa Howda' by the author.

Indira Goswami
(Mamoni Raisom Goswami)
Winner of Jnanpith Award 2000

Rupa . Co

First Published 2004

Second Impression 2005

Published by

Rupa . Co

7/16, Ansari Road, Daryaganj,
New Delhi 110 002

Sales Centres:
Allahabad Bangalore Chandigarh
Chennai Hyderabad Jaipur Kathmandu
Kolkata Mumbai Pune

Photographs on cover courtesy Indira Goswami

Printed in India by
Rekha Printers Pvt. Ltd,
A-102/1 Okhla Industrial Area, Phase-II,
New Delhi-110 020

To
my revered teacher,
Prof. Maheshwar Neog
And
my lifelong friend
late Kaikous Burjore

A Few Words from the Author

The novel *Une Khowa Howda* is a nostalgic memory of my *sattra* in Amranga in South Kamrup. Almost all the characters have been picked from this *sattra,* but there have been close brushes of imagination with reality.

As the original novel was written mostly in the *Kamrupi* dialect, it would have been difficult to get it translated by any other person except the author herself. Not many people from Assam are conversant with this dialect. Besides, many words of this particular dialect have now become obsolete.

The novel was included in the list of classics by *Sahitya Akademi* and was translated into many Indian languages. An Urdu translation has been recently published in Pakistan by Mashaal Publishers—the first book from the Northeast to be done so. The film *Adajya,* based on this book and directed by Dr Santwana Bordoloi, was very well-received in film festivals in India and abroad, and won national and international awards.

I will remain ever grateful to Prof. Hiren Gohain, the renowned scholar and the former Head of the Department of English, Guwahati University, for sparing his valuable time to go through the translation and brush up the language, wherever necessary. I am also grateful to the well-known academician Prof. Harish Trivedi, professor and former Head of Delhi University for taking great pains in going through the manuscript and giving valuable suggestions regarding the translation.

Finally, the translation of *Une Khowa Howda* into English would not have been possible without the help and dedicated efforts of the late K.B. Satarwala.

Indira Goswami
New Delhi

One

1948

Indranath stood watching the card players at their usual gambling joint. The air was calm and silent. The only sound that could be heard was the rattle of the bullock-cart wheels over the newly laid gravel path. Even the women, playing *golokdham*[1] in the privacy of their room, were quiet.

The familiar trader from Borihat, Boloram, who sat leaning against a cushion, noticing Indranath standing, caught hold of his hand. "Listen Sir, why do you want to leave so early? It is the night of the full moon." Indranath glanced at the lantern hanging from a tripod of bamboos. The glow of the lantern looked pale in the bright moonlight. The soft fragrance of *sewali*[2] flowers floated on the still air.

Indranath sat down and the game was resumed. An actor from Banshi Gopal *Jatra*[3] troupe and an officer from Rani's elephant mahal were also playing.

Boloram's famous card-playing and gambling joint attracted many well-known figures of this southern part of Kamrup. Actors from various *Jatra* parties, from Sadilapur, Kharapara, Medhipara, Dakhala, Tongapara and others gathered here. Intrigue and plotting was always afoot on the part of the managers of rival groups to lure away popular actors from each other. Sometimes they came to blows and there was even bloodshed.

In the dead of the night, emaciated figures, almost skin and bones, appeared suddenly from nowhere and fell at the feet of the card players, begging for money. They were the opium addicts, once respectable farmers and villagers but now pitiful wretches. They would beg in shrill and tenacious cries, and would not let go of the feet of the card players until some coins were thrown to them.

Indranath, the would-be successor to the *adhikar's* seat, was a greatly respected man in these parts. Tall and muscular with a crop of thick curly hair on his head, he was a picture of dignity. His complexion was the colour of ripe figs, like that of the old British Forest Officers residing in these parts. His temper was widely known and feared. He would never forgive an untruthful person.

In the local *panchayats*[4] holding court in the portico of the Gossain's house, if a person was found guilty, he was publicly flogged. Indranath himself wielded the whip and beat him up so mercilessly that the victim often had to be carried away bodily. But he was a friend of the poor, though he could not do much for them as his father was still the *adhikar*. His anger had, however, lately mellowed down, especially after the death of the husband of his only sister, Giribala, who was very dear to him.

Indranath stood up from his seat. Boloram glanced at him and thought that it would be futile to try to detain him any further. All the other players also rose from their seats as a mark of respect. Bolaram shouted an order to the two servants standing there, stirring up a breeze with their fans: "You two there! Go with the Gossain! But first, wipe the dust off his bicycle."

Indranath took out his teak wood pipe from his *punjabi*[5] pocket, held it to his mouth and lit it, inhaling the smoke. Then he got on his bicycle and slowly pedalled away homewards. The night was clear and crisp. The bright moon played with the languidly waving leaves of the *jatti*[6] bamboo groves. To Indranath, it seemed that the moon was a golden fish trying to escape from the net of the tangled bamboo leaves. A *fesuluka*[7] bird flew close over his head crying its sweet notes *coo*! *coo*! He could now hear the sweet sound of the Jagalia river, so much like the rustle of the *muga mekhala*[8] of young girls. The elusive sadness in the note of the bird touched his heart. It always did when he happened to pass this particular way at night. He felt a strange feeling of sadness somewhere in his heart. Once it had known peace and rest. This feeling, this thought, reared its cobra head only when he rode on this lonely stretch of road. Otherwise it remained dormant inside him.

Indranath reached the wooden bridge over Jagalia, leaned his bicycle against the parapet and stood there. He could see the thick wood on his right. One narrow path led to Khatiamari. People from Borharamdo had spread a fresh rumour that a ghost haunted these parts of the wood and came right up to the wooden bridge. That ghostly skeleton had hovered around this bridge for a month now. It was midnight and Indranath peered here and there trying to catch a glimpse of the spectre. He had also heard that on one market day, the ghost had snatched away the clothes of some fisher-women passing by, leaving the villagers frightened out of their wits. Indranath chuckled softly to himself. Poor souls! They could not even describe clearly what it looked like. Some said it was like an old opium-eater from the village. Others asserted that it looked like the ravaged body of a cholera patient.

The pungent odour of elephant dung entered his nostrils. The *hathi bandha bakari*, the field where the elephants were chained, was not very far away. He could hear the flapping of the elephants' ears.

He searched his pocket. His fingers found a Wimco matchbox and a pack of Cavanders with the picture of a sailor on it. He lit a cigarette and thought happily about Bolo, his old friend, who had put them in his pocket without his knowledge. Bolo had won a scholarship from Palasbari High School. This scholarship was the one donated by Gilmil Sahib. Fortune has been kind to him. He is a rich man now. All the *firingis*[9] who come to Bordowa Tea Estate present him with these Wimco matchboxes and Cavanders cigarettes.

Indranath took his cycle and rode in the direction of the *sattra*. The tyres of the cycle made a crunching sound upon the gravel like a grindstone.

He reached Dibakar Bhagwati's hut. Here he turned left to enter the *sattra*. Dibakar was a contractor of the Base Camp during the war. He used to supply pigeons, ducks and rice to them. The clicking sound of the Negro soldiers' boots coming and going through his house had given many a sleepless nights to the inmates of the *sattra*. The thatched roof one saw now, was then made of galvanised iron sheets. Indranath remembered that Dibakar used to supply one curious and odd commodity to the soldiers. Leeches! Accompanied by two workers, he used to visit the river banks where elephants were bathed. When the huge beasts came out of the river with hundreds of leeches sticking to their skin, they were plucked and gathered in *dulis*[10] and sold to the Negro soldiers. This fetched him a fortune. In exchange, he, as well as the *mahouts*[11] of the elephants and the *Kaamlas*[12], used to get sometimes saucepans, sometimes tinned frogs' legs and other *firingi* delights preserved in tins and bottles. From then on, he was called "Jokram" Bhagawati (Bhagawati the leech). Now all that is no more. The roof of the house resembles an old camel skin. The walls have caved in. The haystack in the countryard has almost vanished. It is said that Jokram was ruined after coming into contact with a man from Cooch Behar who traded in opium. This man grew opium-bearing poppy plants clandestinely on the slopes of Mikir hills. After the partnership of these two men started, the sale of government opium on the banks of Jagalia under permit to the opium-eaters began to decline. It came down from two maunds per month to a mere ten seers of opium per month. When the revenue from opium suddenly declined, the excise department became suspicious, Bhagwati got entangled and finally he was caught . . . . Here many incidents connected with opium have taken place. After all, in the government budget, the revenue from opium held the second priority. Only a few years back had licences been given freely for opening opium shops at intervals of a mile or one and a half. It is said that the smuggled opium from Assam flooded even the Rangoon market in those days . . . Indranath's glance was drawn to the backyard of the house. The small heap of straw lying there looked like a crouching baby camel . . .

He remembered clearly how Jokram had fallen at the feet of the *adhikar,* his father, pleading with folded hands to save him from the net of the excise police. His father had brought from Gauhati a copy of the Opium Prohibition Act (1947) and had gone through it minutely. In Section 39, he had noticed a new addendum to the Act, which ran as follows:

Notwithstanding the provisions of Section 497 of the Code of Criminal Procedure, 1898, no person accused of non-bailable offence under this Act shall be released on bail by any Court without . . . prosecution of which due notice shall be given, provided that all orders shall give reasons for which bail is given . . . .

And Section 5 was even more significant—

Provided that an accused who is found on evidence to be a smuggler of opium or seller of opium shall not receive a sentence of less than two years rigorous imprisonment and fine . . . .

Bhagawati had collapsed in the portico of the Gossain's house. All the disciples of the Gossain had gathered, raising a hue and cry, protesting that it was a great sin to put a Brahmin into prison, that a Brahmin had never been imprisoned before in this manner. They warned the Inspector that if he threw this Brahmin into prison, he would surely fall into a deep pit of sin so heinous that he would never be redeemed . . . . But why should the Inspector heed such talk? Higher the number of opium offenders he would catch, greater would be his prospects for advancement.

Indranath's father, somehow, managed with great difficulty to get Bhagawati released on bail.

Indranath could see a *baduli chaki*[13] through the worn out frontage of Bhagawati's house. He heard the sound of a dry racking cough somewhere from the interior. It was most likely a *kaniya sabha*[14] assembled inside surreptitiously. The odour of areca nut leaves being fried wafted towards him and tickled his nostrils. That wretched man had spent many days in the camp for reforming opium addicts, but could he change? Indranath cycled around a bend in the road, crossing a huge banyan tree. Suddenly he heard a feeble voice like the cry of a sick eagle:

"Young master, so you are returning from the game of cards!"

Indranath peered under the dark shadow of the tree and saw a man crouching there with hunched shoulders, like an old eagle, an outcast from the village suffering from the hideous disease of leprosy. This man always accosted him when he passed by at this hour. His screeching voice never failed to irritate Indranath. As usual, the leper reminded him—"Can you not provide a thatched shelter for this poor suffering soul? Flies and mosquitoes tear my skin and torment me without end! Before your very eyes, my skin will be eaten away bit by bit and vanish till one day you will find me a ghostly shadow!"

Indranath thrust his hand into the side pocket of his *punjabi* and took out some coins, which somebody had given him at Bolo's card game after respectfully touching his feet. He threw the coins at the leper and walked on. The characteristic alkaline odour of elephant dung was now in the air. He hastened his step. If he rounded the next bend, he would soon be at the *batghar*[15]. The jagged outline of thatched huts in the dim moonlight looked like a painting of a ravaged village, laid waste by war. Out of the three hundred inmates of this village, nearly two hundred and fifty had succumbed to the snare of opium.

Indranath reached the *batghar,* kept his cycle in the portico and went towards the well. On the verandah, he saw his mother and his aunt Durga, waiting for him. His paternal aunt, Durga, had lost her husband and was now staying in their house. Indranath's mother had started spending sleepless nights. Ever since the sudden death of his only sister's young husband, she brooded incessantly about her young widowed daughter. She wondered whether it would be wise to bring her back to this house from her in-laws' place. Durga's plight was very much in her mind—it was agonising to think that they might refuse to take her back or cut her off from her rightful share of property, as had happened in the case of poor Durga.

Every night she waited for him and his aunt gave her company. The two women got up as soon as they heard Indranath's footsteps. His mother, while on her way to the kitchen to fetch his meal, paused for a moment and said, "When will you stop this bad habit of coming home late? Nowadays you don't even care to look after the land. There, in Marabhitha, the communists are gathering strength. They may eat up our lands like a horde of locusts. But what is it to you? Your father can hardly sleep, worrying about it."

Indranath did not reply. Durga said, "That dreadful ghost has again started haunting the roads in the dark. Your poor mother sits here waiting for you, consoling herself with her *hookah*."

Indranath burst out, "You old cats! Who asked you to sit up and wait for me? If you go on nagging me like this, I will stop coming home at night. You mark my words."

The two old women were at a loss for words.

* * * *

After finishing his dinner, Indranath sat down on a low wooden stool by the side of the two women. At this hour, the Gossainee[16] usually entered a small room adjacent to the kitchen and changed for the night. Though she had many servants, she always did the cooking herself, and for this task, she wore a red *mekhala* (she had never worn a blouse or sandals in her life. When she went out of the house, she wrapped a big *chaddar*[17] around her shoulders and chest). In the small room, where she changed, she would often take a puff or two at her hookah. But tonight, she did not enter the small room at the usual hour. She spoke softly to Indranath,

"Saru Gossainee[18] has gone to visit her disciples. Even the raging waters of Jagalia river did not deter her. In the olden days, when the boat used to return laden with offerings, it would take six to eight *bandhas*[19] to unload the boat. Now only one or two can manage it between them. I told her not to go out in such a foul weather. But she would not listen and replied, 'these are bad times. If I don't save a little for the future, I will face starvation'. Really, son, Saru Gossainee is awfully brave, so courageous!"

Saru Gossainee was the widow of Gossain *Mahaprabhu's* brother. Her husband had died in a firework display during one of the annual festivals of the *sattra*. He used to make his own fire-crackers for the festivals from gun-powder and other explosive material. After her husband's death, the land, along with the disciples, was divided and she was allotted her share by the Gossain. Saru Gossainee had gained some respect because of the way she managed her lands and the tactful handling of her disciples. But now she was gradually being thwarted and buffeted by the winds of change blowing over the *sattra*.

Indranath said, "Both of you always speak of Saru Gossainee and the Communist menace. Why don't you two go and rescue our land and look after it? You know everything about these lands and the disciples!"

Both of them exclaimed in unison: "Good gracious! We are ladies of the Gossain family! Go out there and expose ourselves? Saru Gossainee gets things done through her disciples. She has never set foot on the land herself. That is why she is respected so much by everybody! She did not even go to Gauhati to fight the land litigation case.

Everything was done by her disciples. She knows how to keep the dignity and honour of the family intact!"

Indranath interrupted, "I know what is what! But the old days are gone now. Grandmother died in this house without ever stepping outside into the *batghar.* Her ghost still haunts the four walls of this house. She wanted so much to visit Jagannath Puri. But her desire remained frozen forever in her heart. She had to peep through the curtains to catch a glimpse of the annual *sabha*[20]. You are nothing but ghosts pretending to be human beings ...."

Gossainee was annoyed: "Be silent, no more of this foolish talk! The reverence that the ladies of this house earned in life and death is worthy of Gods and cannot be turned into a ghostly emptiness. That Bolo's unholy gambling den has eaten up your head and heart. You forget about your caste and even take tea with them. Do you know that all sorts of low caste people go there?"

Indranath yawned and stretched his arms, looked at Durga and said, "Durga aunty, leaving your husband's house at Chikarhati was a serious mistake. Now you won't get even a single penny of your share of the property. Just you wait and see! They won't even come and take you back! I have heard way down at Dakhala that a part of the land has been sold off. Have you received your share?"

Durga retorted angrily, "Be quiet! I will get my share and they will also take me back! I shall never have to die here, take it from me!"

After this outburst, Durga rested her head on her knees, mute and withdrawn, hurt by Indranath's words.

Beyond the backyard, the jackals started howling from the bamboo clumps. Gossainee stood up and hurried towards her small room for her usual quiet smoke before retiring to her bed. Indranath too rose and went inside the house. Only Durga sat motionless, her head resting on her knees. It has become a habit of her to sit thus, sleepless, besieged by anxieties, oblivious to sight and sound; in winters, before a woodfire, the dense smoke going up in the still atmosphere from green branches, staining her *mekhala* with the colour of ash. Sometimes a prowling cheetah or a leopard, attracted by the warmth, would crouch there! A blur of colour would catch the corner of her eye and Durga would sit up startled, as the wild cat bounded away and she would return to her brooding . . . .

Her mind has become a graveyard. Day after day it is a tortuous task for her to find something tangible to hold on to, to hold on to her sanity. All those customary rituals of widowhood that she performed till a few years back without much effort, are now a source of fear for her. *Amoti*[21] is soon approaching. A wave of annoyance mixed with fear passes through her body. She will have to remain on a bed of bamboos for three days. Her feet should not touch the ground. For answering calls of nature, she must cover the soles of her feet with bark from the areca nut tree. She will not be allowed to eat cooked food. Her daily fare for three days will be raw vegetables and fruits. . . .

Her mother-in-law always thought she, Durga, had brought the shadow of death to the house and killed her son. She accused Durga's father, the Gossain of Amranga, of manipulating his daughter's horoscope to get her married to her son. She suspected that Durga's real horoscope had three *papagrahas*[22]. Durga was never invited for any auspicious occasions in her family or elsewhere. She was considered inauspicious because of her so-called *papagrahas*—not one but three of them! Gradually these accusations and pointing fingers seeped into her mind and she really began to believe it herself. Indranath's words again flooded her mind with anguish. She felt helpless. Her 'in-laws' had never even enquired about her welfare, let aside taking her back. Days, months had passed, waiting, waiting by the fireside, hoping against hope, but only her skin became darker, her *mekhala* more ash-coloured. There was nothing more left in her life to do . . . What does she do day after day? Early morning to the open air toilet, then a quick bath by the side of the well. Her clothes still dripping with water, she would go to the room where the wooden sandals of her forefathers and her husband were kept and she would offer prayers. After her prayers, she would take out the day's portion of boiled rice and jaggery for the servants. Sometimes she would cut vegetables for the Gossainee, squatting outside the kitchen door, but only when both were in a happier frame of mind . . . And intense abhorrence for life had cast a shadow of melancholy . . . She is childless . . . Her nature always had a tinge of pessimism, which had now become darker, more frightening . . . She has become almost a ghost, sitting darkly by the fireside . . . .

Durga's mind probed the past . . . going back to Indranath's visit long back to Chikarhati. He had come to discuss terms with the Gossain of Chikarhati about a *dohar*[23] for catching some wild elephants and making a deal with Jamatollah's Asia Company . . . She had come out on the verandah with an oil lamp in her hand. In the pale glow of the lamp, Indranath was shocked when he saw the emaciated figure, the sunken features of his aunt's face. Taken aback, he had asked, "My God! Is it you, aunty? You look like a skeleton! What's wrong with you?"

Durga replied, "Nothing, come inside."

"No, no! I must know what has happened. Come with me to Amranga."

Her in-laws were only too happy to see her go back to her father's house.

Durga's father-in-law said, "After the *Jatra* festival, I will send the bullock-cart to fetch you back."

So many *Jatra* performers, not only from Amranga, but also from Saruharamdo, Borharamdo, Barihat, Medhipara,Tallapara and the far-away Dakhala, had come and gone, but where was the bullock-cart?

After her depature, her father-in-law's elephant had captured a wild tusker of high value. He made a huge profit out of it. Then a disciple from Mayang had come and built a temple in Chikarhati with donations of abundant gold and jewellery. He had given away seven *bighas*[24] of land too! Rumours floated . . . now that the inauspicious woman had gone, good luck and prosperity flooded the *sattra* to enrich its soil. All this she heard in silence. These rumours had crossed over to the other side of Jagalia too. . . . From beyond the *bijulee*[25] bamboos, a jackal howled again . . . other jackals took up the cry and the sound shattered the silence of the night.

Durga raised her head and peered into the night. The countryside was drenched in white moonlight. She could see the dim outline of the palanquin lying in the old ramshackle *dhekal*[26]. She saw herself in the mirror of her mind attired in her wedding dress, being carried in that same planquin to Chikarhati, her husband's place.The pole of the palanquin, once resplendent with silver-plated engraving, now seemed to her, in the pale moonlight, more like a sinuous snake. Tears welled up in her eyes. Indranath was right. She would not get any share of her right, she would have to go to the court at Gauhati. She shuddered. The very thought was repugnant to her. As far as her memory went, she had never heard of a lady from a

Gossain's household stepping across the threshold of a court. Could she go to Gauhati to demand her share of property? Impossible! Impossible! She spent the whole night there sitting alone, head resting on her knees . . . The eastern sky gradually turned the colour of old *pat* silk. The fragrance of *kagji* lime[27] blossoms permeated the air. Durga stood up, her stiff knee joints protesting against the effort. She walked with slow steps towards the well . . . .

Two

Indranath, walking across the *batghar,* heard Kaltu, the mahout, sneezing three times in quick succession. He was annoyed. Undoubtedly the wretch had spent the night in the opium den of Bhagawati.

Kaltu was short-statured, hunchbacked and squint-eyed. Indranath, greatly vexed, berated him. "You, good-for-nothing! I know where you have spent the night! I'll give your worthless name to the reformation camp. Those home-guards will catch your filthy neck and drag you there like a rat!"

Kaltu tried to suppress with great effort a fit of coughing and sneezing. His eyes ran with water. Slimy mucus dripped down the corners of his lips and covered his chin. Indranath glared at him with loathing for a moment and strode away with quick steps.

Indranath was clutching an umbrella under the armpit. He wore an old *endi*[1] silk *punjabi* with a *Shantipuri dhoti*[2] and leather pump shoes. He was on his way to Bongara where he had to attend to a dispute about the sale of paddy. He had waited some days for the *mohura*[3]. But that wretched man had not come. Why would he keep the appointment? After all he was the one responsible for the confusion about the paddy sale and now he, Indranath, had to go himself to sort it out.

The sun was rising beyond the fringe of *bijulee* bamboos, the long tapering leaves rusltling in the sharp breeze of the morning. The sun's rays had woven among the cloth. In some places the sunlight poured through the holes in the cloth, elsewhere dark patches still lingered. Indranath glanced around him. He saw old, dilapidated huts on his right and left. The colour of the mud walls seemed to him the same as the dull, brownish-grey colour of a vulture's feathers. The pulp of red pumpkins with their seeds lay rotting and drying on the tattered thatched roofs like blotches of dried reddish-brown blood. He could smell the odour of *pan* leaves being fired over a fire. Inranath had a feeling of walking down a graveyard. Only a few years back, as a schoolboy studying in Palasbari High School, he used to play and run down this path. At that time, the air was full of the fragrance of new *ahu*[4] paddy. Now it was replaced by the odour of opium and nothing but opium. A sense of deep frustration engulfed him. The *pan* leaves, reminded Indranath of dried up human intestines, trailing down those trees.

Indranath walked on. He came to the place where three roads converged. Under the old banyan tree, the outcast leper was lying on the ground. He had not greeted and called out to Indranath in his usual fashion. Was something wrong? Was he dead? Indranath wondered. On closer inspection, the man appeared to be in a semi-coma. Lying there, away from his torn rags, he had become almost one with the colour of the earth. His dirty, formless pots and tins were scattered here and there. One saucepan, old and battered, with a long handle caught Indranath's eye. He had seen similar saucepans being used by the Negro soldiers in the army camp at Mirza. The sight of the saucepan suddenly reminded him that he had seen one of these things in Saru Gossainee's house too. Many times he was on the verge of questioning her about it. How and where did she get it? She was so conservative, an extremely orthodox, ritual addicted widow! Did she not know for what purpose the Negro soldiers used these pans? How could she use such leftover things from the army camp? Indranath realised the truth with apprehension. Was it true perhaps that the shadow of poverty had also touched her? Perhaps her tenants had also woken up from their age-old darkness. But where from did she get that sauce-pan? No doubt that Brahmin from Haramdo gave it to her. What was his name? Ah, yes! Mahidhar! There were rumours floating around—about a relationship between her and this Brahmin, Mahidhar....

A filthy, vermin-ridden dog sniffed here and there, found the saucepan and started licking it. Indranath picked up a clod of earth and hurled it at the dog. It yelped and slunk away. Still thinking about Saru Gossainee and Mahidhar, he turned and resumed his journey; whether the rumour was true or false—what did it matter, one way or the other? It did not draw any strong reaction from him as from other ignorant, orthodox persons. In fact, he was not too unhappy about it. Why should she not have somebody she could rely on, to give her company? He did not care much for those old-fashioned ideas about widows. He had seen the intense suffering and abject misery of some of these tragic women, made widows at too young an age by callous fate, who took root and died imprisoned within four walls....Again that odour of roasted *pan* leaves from the huts! It conjured up in his mind a vision of flesh being roasted. Decay, death, destruction. A sense of something ominous came upon him.

Indranath turned off the main road and struck a path winding through the tall *kachindariya* grass and *bankuhun* plants with purple flowers, towards Jagalia. On the river bank, in the mud and slush at the edge of the water, he saw young village belles, groping in the soft mud and picking out, with their bare hands *turi* fish. Long-necked storks were hovering around the girls expectantly. Seeing him, they cried "Young master! Don't cross the river from this spot! Go a little ahead, there, where you see the bullockcart wheel marks!"

Indranath gazed at them for a moment, then closed his umbrella and thrust it under his arm. Taking off his pumps, picking them up in his left hand and gathering his *dhoti* with his right hand, he stepped into the shallow water. Hitting a depression in the river-bed, his foot slipped and he almost lost his balance. Peals of laughter rang out from the girls behind. They started singing—

Bridal horse is washed with
Twenty-five potfulls of water;
His back is smeared with
Holy Narainee oil;
He wears a gaily decorated
Bridle on his head;
Marigold garlands adorn
His sharp ears;
Bismillah! Cries the bridegroom
And jumps on the horse.
Down he falls with
A thum and a thud....

Indranath cursed silently, "Bitches! bitches!"

He waded through knee-deep water and reached the other side. Shaking off water from his legs, he wiped his feet clean on the soft grass and put on his shoes. He started walking briskly towards the *sal*[5] forest, and gradually disappeared from view in its thick greenery.

★ ★ ★

His work over at Bongara, Indranath returned by the same path and stood on the banks of Jagalia. His face wore a sullen, baleful look. On the Gossain's lands, back there, the Communists were creating trouble, plenty of trouble. He did not like it. They were stirring up the tenant farmers. They had the insolence of declaring that the Gossain should plough the land with his own hands if he wanted to retain his domain. Contemptible rabble rousers! He, a gossain, an *adhikar,* work on the land with his own hands!

The sun was sinking behind the fringe of *bijulee* bamboos. A golden hue shimmered and danced on the surface of the flowing water like shoals of fish swimming in and out, gambolling. A hazy, silken curtain of mist and smoke from the village fires, languidly gathered its folds over the dusky landscape. Through this haze, the sun seemed blurred and golden brown as if it was covered with the skin of golden iguana.

Indranath was returning with a heavy heart. Sounds of someone shouting and cursing reached his ears. He turned and saw a bullock-cart stuck in a muddy patch of the river. The cart-man was pushing at the cart with all his strength and exhorting the bullocks with his shouts and curses. He heard him crying. "*Maichana! Maichana!*[6] Jump out, jump out!" While the cart-man was trying to get hold of the nose-ring of the bullocks, his foot slipped and he tumbled into the water. Indranath removed his shoes as fast as he could, threw down his umbrella and shoulder bag, and went to the aid of the cart-man. In no time at all, he had the man and his bullocks out of the water, on dry land.

The ladies travelling in the cart got down, one by one, and began rinsing their soaked clothes. At the same time, annoyed with the cart-man, they berated him, saying, "Can't you see and follow the cart-wheel ruts even in broad daylight? You fool! Have you gone blind?"

An old woman, hunch-backed and with a big goitre under her chin, remarked while adjusting the folds of her *mekhala,* "He has lost his sense with too much opium. That's why this has happened. This dog's eyes are clouded with the hot steam of boiling rice! If the Gossain's son had not come to our help in the nick of the moment, we would all have been drowned in the water by now! The bullocks have swallowed too much water. See, water is flowing out of their nostrils even now!"

The old woman turned sharply and looked at Eliman, the vivacious young daughter of the *pujari*[7] of Rajapukhuri. She was squeezing water out of her *gatala*[8]. She shouted at her, "Oiyee, Eliman! Don't you have any shame or modesty? The Gossain's son is standing there and you have spread open all your clothes?"

On hearing the old woman's strident voice, Indranath suddenly noticed the girl, standing about five yards away.

In the scattered golden rays of the sinking sun, as if dancing off the skin of a golden iguana, the shapely, youthful legs of the girl glinted and dazzled his eyes. (He would remember this pair of legs the rest of his life.)

.....Yes, what a pair of legs they were! Those legs were like the tender shoots of *bijulee* bamboos......

All the women and young girls climbed into the cart,

the bullocks were tied to the yoke and the bullock-cart started moving through the thorny bushes on the river. The old woman realised with great alarm that Eliman had not joined them in the cart but had gone forward to the Gossain's son. She heard her saying to him: "Young Gossain! Do you recognise me? You often come to our place with a double-barrelled gun to shoot wild ducks.....If you come again to kill those ducks, I will be there on the lake among them sitting like a duck!"

.......What is she saying? What is she babbling about? Can a Brahmin's daughter talk so shamelessly! But when Indranath looked again with some attention he saw a kind of radiance emanating from her body.

"Haven't you recognised me?"

"No."

"I am the daughter of Bahinram Bhagawati, brother of Jokram Bhagawati, who washes the family deity of the Gossain of Rajapukuri. Don't you remember? Once there was a big storm when you came to our village. You know me now, don't you?"

Indranath looked at her reflectively. Yes, many storms had greeted him on his frequent shooting trips. He had also entered many houses in the village. A circle of wide-eyed naked children would gather round him, gaping at his formidable double-barrelled gun. But this girl.....no, he could not remember her!

She said again, "Wild ducks have flocked again to the lake. We hear the guns of those Sahibs from Jamatollah Company booming now and then across the lake."

A hoarse voice interrupted her flow of words. "Your face and your shameless manners have scared away the grooms, soon it will be time for your *Tulani*[9]. Who knows? Your father may yet be thrown out as an outcaste? Then he will have to jump into the well with a pitcher tied around his neck!"

Eliman retorted, "You old hag! Keep quiet! You should have died in the last cholera epidemic. Can't you see that the Gossain is talking to me?"

Yes, Indranath was talking to her. He had never ever seen such a radiant face on the South Bank. He had come across many pretty faces among girls, who came to pick firewood, with complexions resembling the moonlit brightness of Jagalia's rippling surface. On his duck-shooting trips, he had met those Bangara girls with skin as smooth as the silky soft mud of Jagalia. Their bodies looked so soft and delicate as if a mere touch would shatter them into pieces. When he had gone to Dakhala to attend to a land dispute, he had beheld those bewitching girls with skin the colour of white mushrooms and breasts like tender white melons. Again he had seen the girls at Rani of North Kamrup when he had gone there to make the final arrangements for elephants caught in *dohar.* These girls brought fish for selling to the *mahal*[10]. They would watch the young elephant being trained by the *mahout.* The trainer would use his *khurpi*[11] to make the elephant obey his commands, sometimes most cruelly. An intense feeling of sadness would cover the faces of the young girls as they watched. The shadow of sadness on their dusky complexions created a mystical impression that Indranath found strangely attractive....Yes, yes! He remembered those girls very vividly, crouching below the cool shadow of the *machans*[12] watching the elephants with a mixture of fascination and sadness in their eyes....The roundness of their bodies reminded Indranath of the curving motion of a python gliding round a tree. Their faces had the freshness of the leaves of the *arum* plant after a shower of cool rain....

Indranath cast his mind back....In the *Shari*[13] festival, when all the deities of the nearby villages and *sattras* were brought in palanquins to the bank of Jagalia and worshipped, a small, bustling, colourful fair would spring up and people thronged round the various shops and stalls, laughing and talking loudly. Indranath had seen many village lasses, clad in thick, hand-woven cotton clothes, in this festival....Was she, Eliman, one of them? Had he seen her there?...He could not recollect....Yes, of course, this *Shari* festival attracted girls from most of the surrounding places like Tallapara, Medhipara, Borharamdo, Saruharamdo, Majkuchi, Chikarhati....The memory of the odour of old jaggery stored in earthen pots, wafting from their bodies, still lingered in his mind....Indranath was shaken out of his reveries by a rude voice. He saw the girl run to the cart, lift the bamboo-mat screen at the rear and disappear inside....Did she say something? He had only a vague recollection....But he could remember distinctly the fine beads of perspiration on her pretty nose....

The dusk was slowly merging into the darkness of night. The fading light, blended with fine dust in the air, gave the appearance of a dark grey animal skin being drawn over the landscape. The bullock-cart wheels gave out a creaking sound...krr. krr. krr...

Indranath thought again about the girl...She must be nearing puberty. He had hazy memories of what he had heard about her father, the *pujari*, long ago. It was said that at the time of *Basanti puja*[14] festival, a crowd of Brahmins, all opium-eaters and addicts, used to gather in his house, each bringing a part of the opium smoking paraphernalia. Somebody would bring *hookahs* and pipes, others would provide the utensils, frying pans and earthen pots, for frying *pan* leaves and preparing the opium for a long smoking session. In short, the *pujari's* house resembled an opium den during this *puja* festival. Most of these opium-eaters seldom observed the rites as laid down in the *Vaisnava Ahnic Puthi*[15]. Some of them used to take not only garlic but also the unclean flesh of iguana and even house sparrows. They set up wood fire ovens in open air and cooked their own food. Indranath had a vision of Eliman, running about among the opium-eaters, helping out with a *dona*[16] here or a *khanti*[17] there....And he could imagine those opium-smokers sitting round the well, conversing and gossiping in low voices....They would talk about their host's daughter. One would say, "The girl's father will soon be made an outcaste if he doesn't get her married fast......"

Another man would nod his head in agreement.

"Right you are, my fellow! See how her body has shot up, like a sturdy palm tree...."

A third opium-eater would add with a shy wink and boorish laughter, "Have you noticed her breasts? They have become like those female doves swollen with egg!...."

.....And they would all glance at the girl's body with gleeful, vile looks.

Indranath could very well imagine the wave of desire for this girl in their minds. Tut-tut, how could he think about it? Those worn-out addicts, eaten up by opium—what could they do with this young vibrant girl? They had lost their vitality and vigour long back.

Indranath now realised why they had come this day, across the river! The *pujari's* brother here must be hosting a *kaniyar sabha.* Now, all night long, the *baduli chaki* would burn in the court-yard of the ramshackle house. All the opium-eaters would gather around the dimly-lit lamps. The only sounds would be those of bubbling *hookah,* puffing pipes and the dry raucous coughing of the opium-smokers......The girl's image again rose before his eyes. Her body, her soft flesh! It was like the soft, silky and sticky pulp of the *ou*[18] fruit. Her body was as fresh as the saturated, wet ground around the newly dug well....Yes, probably the girl would visit this *sattra* more often to escape from those prying, ghostly women, mostly crones, back there in her village. These women would prowl in the night, haunting the spacious backyards of houses, to poke and probe the washed dirty cloth pieces hanging out there, for the tell-tale marks of menstruation, hoping to find some signs so that they could get their vicious pleasure in denouncing the girls as outcastes....

Krr, krr, krr....The ox-cart reached the ramshackle *batghar* of Bhagawati's house. Indranath saw some persons come out to receive the travellers, holding earthen lamps in their hands. In the dim light of the hanging lamps inside the house, some portions of the bamboo matting walls, where the mud plaster had peeled off, looked like the carcass of a dead cow. Suddenly a voice called out—

"Young Gossain! Oh! Young Gossain!"

Indranath was startled, turned round and saw the same old leper, cast out by the village, sitting below the big banyan tree.

"Young Gossain, have you anything for me to eat or at least a *bidi* to smoke?"

Indranath searched his pocket, found a crumpled packet of Sunlight brand cigarettes and threw it to the leper. He turned round and started walking towards the *batghar* of his house with quick steps.

Three

It was the month of May. Time for the observance of the *amoti* ritual. It is said that Mother Earth menstruates at this time. The doors of the famous Kamakhya temple are closed for the duration of this trial. The ox-cart that had gone to bring Indranath's youngest sister, a widow of tender age, was coming back along the path. One could hear the jingle of the bells tied round the necks of the bullocks pulling the cart. A trailing crowd of naked and half-naked children, young and old women with only *mekhalas* covering their bodies, some with babies in their arms followed the covered cart with a curtain at the rear end, curious to know who were the travellers and where they came from. Some of them shouted, "Oh, ho! Young *maichana* has come back!"

"Have you come back forever?"

"Did you wind up your affairs there at your late husband's place?"

"Is it true that the baby in your womb also died in this torture. Is it true?"

There was no reply from the cart. Her shoulders were covered with a white *chaddar.* She shrank back in apprehension from such public attention. She abhorred these crowds following her. Once long back, from such a trailing crowd, a voice had cried out, "Don't touch her! Don't touch her! You women with *sindoor*[1]. She's a widow now!"

The bullock-cart increased its speed and, with the wheel creaking *krr... krr...* and the bells ringing loudly, it soon reached the backyard of the Gossain's house. These were many women already assembled on the verandah. They rushed towards the cart and pushed aside the curtain. One of them said. "Have you come alone all the way from Bangara? Didn't they send anyone with you? Why? This has never happened before! That *jatar katar burhi*[2]. Wasn't she sent with you this time?"

Giribala jumped out from the cart and went towards the right-hand side of the verandah. She saw her mother, sitting on a wooden stool, weeping quietly. She did not look up at her daughter. Giribala stood for a while near her. Then she took a step towards the kitchen. Durga, from the middle of the assembled women, cried out. "Don't go there! The stove for cooking fish is kept there!"

The other women heaved a sigh. Giribala now went to the well. It was plastered inside. There used to be a guava tree by its side. She asked. "Where is it now?"

Durga replied. "Dried leaves would fall inside the well and spoil the water. That's why it was cut down."

There was a pònd beyond the courtyard. Giribala wanted to go there but Durga caught hold of her hand and said. "Now things have changed. You are a widow. Come, wash your face and hands. There are so many people waiting to see you."

Someone from the crowd whispered. "She has remained the same. She has never done any weaving or household work. How will she cross the mountain of days ahead?"

Durga drew water from the well and poured it for Giribala. She washed her face, then her hands and feet. Later she whispered to Durga. "Tell these women to go away."

Durga whispered back. "They have all come for your sake. They are unhappy at your suffering."

Suddenly the Gossainee got up and went to the group of ladies. She took them to the left side of the verandah, the *pathamara kathi*[3]. Durga gave a towel to Giribala. Wiping her face, she uttered. "Let those women leave. I want to be alone."

Durga did not reply.

The women now surrounded the Gossainee and fired volleys of questions at her.

"You have brought her back from Chikarhati. What will be her fate? She'll be like another Durga...."

"What will happen to her share of the property?"

"Haven't you seen the example of other Gossainees of South Bank? How those wolves snatched away their properties?...."

Gossainee retaliated, saying.

"It is only one girl! I can keep four or five other girls like her! God has given me more than enough!...."

She had uttered these words but inside her heart, she felt a tremor of apprehension. Times were changing. Communists were raising their heads in Rangamati. On two or three occasions, when the *mohura* had tried to collect taxes, he was beaten up....Those Communist rascals had even threatened some Gossains of South Bank. They would seize their lands if the Gossains themselves did not plough their lands with their own hands....

...A Gossain made to work on land?....

...*Hari, Hari, Hari!*[4]

...Is it ever possible?....

...*Hari! Hari!*....

She probed the faces around her one by one, carefully and said in cold, stern tones. "There are courts of justice! There are *kacheris*[5]. We Gossainees of South Bank will not remain silent! We will go to court!..."

There was a shrill outcry from the women. "Oh, God! My God! A Gossainee of South Bank will take her stand in the court? The Lord save us! We have never heard of such an atrocious thing...."

Many of them started heaving deep sighs.

"Ooh! Ooh!!...."

"Court!! *Kacheri!* A place for thieves and low caste ruffians and such people! Can we Gossainees stand in public among them? *Chee, chee!* What a shame!....*Damodariya*[6] Gossainees do not even look at the sun in the sky above!"

A dark, tall, thin-lipped woman sitting on a low stool, pounding betel nuts with an iron pestle, said, "Listen, Gossainee! You keep her for a few days and then send her back. Her husband's place is like heaven for a woman. If she runs away from her husband's house, she is like a naked woman loitering on the streets. Even if she tries to cover herself with clothes, people will snatch them away from her body!"

Two daughters of Haramdo's schoolmaster, Nanichampa and Bhoomichampa, were there among the women surrounding the Gossainee. One of them said, "I have heard that Chikarhati's Gossain is very orthodox and observes all the rituals very strictly, like those Vaisnava heads of Shankari *sattras.* They immerse themselves five times in the river while taking bath and bring Brahmins from Coochbehar to perform *Chandi Puja*[7]. It is said that they are the followers of Chaitanya Deva. When they take oil and water on their heads, they utter the name of Aswathama."

Now Nanichampa joined in, "Her mother-in-law's torture had crossed the limit. I heard that this is the reason why her unborn child was destroyed in her womb.......Why, she was not even allowed to go to the latrine during *amoti!*....And she could get down from her cot only after wearing betelnut bark sandals on her feet!...."

Bhoomichampa said, "Two or three Gossainees of Chikarhati died without even having a glimpse of the *batghar*....One Gossainee used to creep to the courtyard to see the *Basanti puja.* One day she was caught and...my God! the horrible punishment inflicted on her!...

There were shouts from the other women. "What was the punishment? What was it?"

Bhoomichampa remained silent. The women looked at each other with fear, mixed with inquisitiveness in their eyes.

All the women had come with the sole purpose of hearing the harrowing tales of woe from Giribala's own lips but she did not give them a chance. Like a streak of lightening she headed straight for the door of the room where the sandals of their ancestors were kept for worship (there were four pairs in this room), opened it with a jerk, entered and bolted the door from inside with the crossbar.

The Gossainee and all the rest rushed to the door. Bhoomichampa pushed and rattled the door for some time. She gave up and said, "She has jammed the door with the crossbar! She hasn't changed at all! The same *Ranchandi*—goddess of wrath! All those calamities haven't affected her a bit!"

The Gossainee spoke with a broken voice. "She never wanted this marriage. She behaved like this even on the day of the wedding."

The women who had been engaged to pound the rice reminded her: "But, *Aie* (mother), you were also not very happy with this marriage."

"How could I be happy? You know all about it. That boy did nothing but roam about with Chaudhary's *jatra* party. No other son of Gossains has squandered his life in this manner...."

"Yes, yes! We have heard all about it. He used to sling a harmonium round his neck and waste his time playing loudly on it. We have also heard that he was friends with a woman opium-seller who was being trained in the *jatra*...." Another woman chimed in, "But that bitch was not allowed by the public to dance in these *jatra* parties...."

"Really, it is a shockingly scandalous story! It is said, he even took *pantabhat*[8] and liquor in the woman's house...."

Another interrupted loudly, "Stop! Stop this disgraceful talk! How dare you say all this in Gossainee's presence?"

Bhoomichampa said, "I have seen the two-storeyed wooden house at Chikarhati. Good gracious! It is a graveyard of elephant tusks, tiger skins, deer horns, iguana skin and wild boar's heads!"

Nanichampa joined in. "The Gossain had an ornamental gun exactly like the one used by officers of Muslim kings. The wooden part of the gun had a creeper design inlaid with ivory. He used to remove the cap of the bullet with his teeth before inserting it into the gun. Ugh! God alone knows whether it was pig's fat or cow's fat smeared on those bullets!"

Another woman added, "And that Bolo Gossain just pushed aside the skins, the horns and bones and sat down with his harmonium for rehearsals......Believe me! I heard that even the skin and bones made sounds in tune with the harmonium's notes...."

One more woman had her say. "They say that, in the *batghar* with its carved tin border, many bicycles used to pile up. Even that opium-seller woman, the wretched bitch, dared to show her face in the two-storeyed house! Her ears used to blaze with large *phutis*[9] presented to her by Bolo Gossain...."

Bhumichampa said. "That evil slut died last year in the cholera epidemic. Served her right! It was divine wrath visited on her for entering the sacred sandal room of Bolo Gossain's house...."

The two fat women, wearing only *mekhala* tied tightly round their bosoms, engaged for pounding rice, now said, "People said that the belly of that filthy woman had become heavy with a child. Hai, hai! She then went to a *mahajan*[10] to get rid of her unwanted baby! She was caught by somebody in the *sattra* and many people spat on her."

The Gossainee was stunned by this open exchange of gossips. She did not know that these stories were common fodder for gossip among these women. She had thought rather naively that all these scandals had been locked up in a secret compartment of her mind.

Dham! dham! dham!....all the women were startled by these sounds coming from the sandal room. Giribala was kicking at the door with rage and fury. The Gossainee hurried to the door and knocked repeatedly. But the door remained firmly shut. The Gossainee wiped her eyes with a corner of her *gatala*, turned round and looked at Bhumichampa and Nanichampa. Their faces were plump and they were wearing clean *gatalas*. These daughters of a *jajman*[11] Brahmin were the same age as Giribala. No doubt poverty had robbed them of their health but still the round shining marks of vermillion on their foreheads made them look happy and contented. Looking at them, she cried out abruptly. "You snooping, meddling women! It was you who spied on my daughter stealthily from behind *bijulee* bamboos, whenever she went to the pond to take bath. Your prying, curious eyes were always on the lookout for the first signs of her menstruation. Don't you think you are all responsible for this?"

"First signs of her menstruation.....?"

"Yes, yes, even before the sun came up, you used to hide behind those bamboo clumps like leopards and peer at her clothes for marks of menstruation."

"*Ai chikau! Ai chikau!*[12] Don't make us the sinners!"

"You women were after me, goading me to get her married off. And again you would have gone to the Gossains of Garoguli and Tuhbhakeli and declared that the daughter of Amranga Gossain had become an outcaste......"

All the women cried out in unison. "Oh God, save us! God save us!"

An old, hunch-backed woman in torn, dirty clothes, one of those engaged for pounding rice, came forward and asked, "Isn't it true, mother, that the girl had already menstruated when she got married?" The Gossainee, without uttering a word, turned aside and spat on the ground.

Durga was making tea for Giribala. When she heard this question from the old woman, she came out like an angry lioness and cried out scornfully, "Have you ever heard of any Damodariya Gossain's daughters being married off after their menstruation? Such things never happened in our lineage and it won't ever happen in the future!"

Bhoomichampa said with disdain. "What do you mean? Times are changing. Two or three girls of South Bank

Gossains have already become outcastes!..."

Durga replied heatedly. "That may be so! But at the time of Giribala's first menses after marriage, it was you who came as *ayati*[13] and placed the auspicious basket on the pounding stone."

Bhoomichampa had a streak of cruelty, mixed with vanity, in her nature. She derived a kind of sadistic pleasure from the tragedy and suffering of Giribala. She had all the time taken second place to Giribala in beauty and accomplishment. Now her wounded vanity had a triumphant sense of achievement. A rival's downfall is always a source of happiness for someone like her.

Bhoomichampa now asked "Isn't it true that Bolo Gossain had dragged Giribala to the first floor of that wooden house and had tried to force her to take part in the *talim*[14] of the *jatra* party? I also heard that there was a great tussle in that house between Giribala and Gossain and her in-laws....Isn't it true? And..."

With an explosive sound, the door of the sandal *puja* room burst open and Giribala rushed out like a tigress in rage. Her hair had come undone and flew wildly. Her *gatala* had come off and her clothes were in a disarray. Her eyes blazed at the group of women, she screamed.

"You came here to see me, didn't you? You have seen me now. I am still alive! I will live on and have a better life than all of you...."

The words were cut off abruptly and hung in the air. She fell like a severed branch of a tree on the breast of her mother....

Four

Opposite the *haveli*[1] of the Gossain, another house shone like a bright coin. The tin sheets on the roof sparkled as if coated with silver. It was the house of Hari Mahajan. In his backyard, a granary stood bursting with grain. His courtyard looked clean and bright with fresh cowdung plaster. It appeared as if somebody had laid out to dry several goat skins, side by side. From a distance, his *bhakheri*[2] resembled an old elephant sitting curled up, quiet and covered with mud.

When Indranath emerged from the *haveli,* he saw a few opium-eaters sitting on the wooden bench outside Hari Mahajan's house. They belonged not only to his locality but also distant places like Garodhuli, Chikarhati, Majhkuchi and other villages. Their eyes were glued to the ground. They had unkempt, tangled hair. They were sitting there as if some skins and bones had been arranged in various shapes and postures. Indranath averted his eyes with disgust from this spectacle.

Their thumbs were smeared with ink used for fingerprint impressions on their opium ration cards. For them, they were just black stains on their thumbs which would wear off with time but they could not imagine that these same black stains bound them inexorably to a frightening, dark future. No, they were not concerned at all. They were in a state of drugged euphoria.

The foul smell of opium and *pan* leaves being fried assailed Indranath's nose. He removed his handkerchief from the pocket of his *punjabi* and covered his nose with it. He observed that, on both sides of the village, the *pan* leaf creepers round the betelnut trees, were completely denuded of their leaves and were hanging like dried up arteries. The thatched huts, on both sides, looked drab and grey with neglect and desolation.

When Indranath came to the bend where the path joined the main road, he suddenly realised that he was passing by the house of Bhagwati. Yesterday while returning from Bolo's gambling den, in the soft light of the *baduli chaki,* he had caught glimpses of her body through the chinks in the flimsy wall, like the vision of silvery fish darting about in water. Now not a single soul was visible there. The bullock-cart with the curtain of flower design was not there either. Indranath felt a twinge of pain. But she had come only the other day. Probably she had gone to visit her *kurmas*[3] nearly. He peeped into the backyard. Yes, he could see two chemises (made of *markin*[4] cloth). Hanging out on the clothesline. The colour of the chemises merged with the late sunlight. The wind buffeted the chemises to and fro against the nearby lime tree....

Indranath was lost in thought....Only the other day, his mother had hinted about proposals pouring in from the parents of Damodariya Gossain girls, nine or ten years old. A couple of persons had come from the Mahara *sattra* of Banamati Dev with *naksa* and *kushti*[5]. Another pair had come from Dipholu bearing *kushti* and *sidha*[6] with a basketful of rice, oil, potatoes, jaggery, vegetables and a big fat *rohu* fish. Indranath himself had seen these things in the *kharam thowa* room[7]. His ancestors never married ordinary Brahmin girls: his mother, grandmother....all came from established *sattras*....

Indranath took the main road. He looked back once and saw that one of the chemises was hanging like a flag in the branches of the lime tree....As he walked on, he could now smell the odour of elephant dung, in addition to that of opium and *pan* leaves being fried....His mind was in turmoil. Disappointment and frustration were always evoked by all that he saw around him. In the midst of the dark gloom the face of the girl rose again and again before his eyes. He felt as if he was in a cremation ground. He was watching the corpse burning on the pyre, its last rites being performed. But his eyes flew, again and again, to a rose plant nearby blossoming with flowers!....

A truck loaded with *sal* logs roared past, covering Indranath's face and hair with dust. He had now come to the part of the road going through a *sal* forest. This part of the road looked like a hill road. Ahead there was a brook flowing under a small wooden bridge, which eventually joined the Jagalia river. Indranath saw a cluster of people near the bridge. He recognised most them. They were from Borharamdo, Soruharamdo, Tallapara, Medhipara and even from the other side of the Jagalia river. They were all hard core opium-eaters. In the middle of the group, he could see a man, wearing a khadi cap and canvas shoes, addressing the opium-eaters in earnest tones. He was a volunteer of the Congress Party who went from house to house collecting statistics about opium-eaters.

He was standing on a tree-stump. Indranath drew a little nearer and standing near the wooden bridge, he listened to the volunteer's speech. The man was covered with dust from head to foot, but his voice was firm and clear. He was speaking on the poisonous effect of opium-eating. Indranath could hear him clearly.

"You are perhaps not aware that this poison of opium has struck deep roots into the people on both sides of the Jagalia. The Non-Cooperation Movement of Mahatma Gandhi opened our eyes to the evils of opium eating. We have to uproot and discard this hundred-and-fifty-year old problem. You are the followers of Mahatma Gandhi. Many of you have even gone to jail during the British rule."

Somebody from the crowd stood up and said. "No, not many of us from this side of the bank went to jail. Only four went to jail and came out in no time at all...."

The volunteer bowed low in a gesture of apology.

Another man stood up and shouted. "No martyrs from this bank of the river! Can you give us the exact number of prisoners of the freedom movement from this place?"

The man on the tree-stump bowed again and said, "All the figures are available in Government records. When the time is ripe, I will give you the information."

The assembly fell silent and he continued.

"During the revolution, under the inspiration of Mahatma Gandhi, many volunteers from all over Assam had gone to prison and in the fight against the evils of opium, the overall trading was reduced by 602 maunds within one year!"

Another man got up from the crowd.

"But here, in our place, the opium trade hasn't decreased at all. On the contrary, it has prospered!"

Indranath remembered that under the presidentship of Dinabandhu Andrews, a committee on opium had been constituted and it was proposed that the opium trade should be abolished within the jurisdiction of Assam Council. But the British Government was reluctant to lose its revenue from opium trade and had promoted and increased the opium sales considerably. Indranath heard the voice of the speaker again.

"I think you people don't know that some amendments have been made to the Opium Act....."

Many opium-eaters shouted in unison. "Tell us, tell us! What are these amendments?"

The volunteer took off his cap and dusted it. He continued. "The second amendment is very long. One new clause has been added to the tenth amendment......"

He fumbled in the pocket of his *punjabi* and took out some crumpled papers. ".....it is in English. First, I will read out to you the contents in English....."

With a peculiar Kamrupi accent, he started reading in English.

"Amendment section 10 of the Assam Opium Prohibition Act, 1947—whoever knowing or having reason to believe that an offence has been committed under this act, causes any evidence of the commission of the offence to disappear or gives any information respecting the offender with the intention of screening the offender from punishment under the Act or with that intention gives any information regarding the offence that he knows or believes to be false, shall be punished with the punishment provided for the offence."

There was a hoot of derisive laughter from the crowd. One of them, who was smoking a *bidi*, threw it away and spoke mockingly. "Volunteer *babu*, were you telling us about tigers and bears, or was it something about the battle of Rama and Ravana? We could not make head or tail or it!"

At this, there was another outburst of laughter from the assembled men. But it sounded more like the rattling of loose dry bones collected in a gunny bag.

The volunteer took off his cap and again dusted it mechanically. He said. "I know that you are illiterate and ignorant. It is a pity that you cannot write your own names. If you had learnt to write your name, you would not have been reduced to this sorry state."

One of them stood up and said, "That old Gilmil Sahib wanted to teach us English. But he didn't like the sound of the *dheki.*[8] It was always that sound which disturbed him, dhuk, dhuk, dhuk!...."

Another joined in, "Then one day, Gilmil Sahib got so irritated that he uprooted all the *dhekis* and hung them up in the *rabab tenga*[9] tree in front of his house...."

Another voice spoke up, "We know what those white *sahibs* were up to, and their self-serving tricks! They went on feeding us opium to break our strength, to make our voice weak...."

Someone shouted, "Not only in our South Bank here! Those white monkeys messed up the whole country!"

One man admonished. "Be quiet! Silence! The *netaji* (leader) is going to speak again......Do you know that he is the secretary of four *maujas?*[10] He has got great power and he can arrest anyone without warrant!"

Everyone looked back to see who had spoken. He was a lean and thin man with a pair of dirty shorts on. He worked as a cleaner of a truck that transported timber.

One old opium-eater, leaning on a bamboo staff, shouted, "Shut up, you dogs!"

Another snubbed him, saying, "You lousy cholera-ridden corpse! Whom are you calling dogs?"

These two almost came to blows but another volunteer, with a cane in his hand, intervened and calmed them down.

The volunteer's voice could be heard again.

"Listen, brothers! I will tell you about the amendment quite soon. But I have heard that the opium-eaters on the bank of Jagalia river slaughtered a goat and laid out a grand feast for those opium smugglers from Garo hills! If this continues any longer, take care! You will find yourselves behind bars! The Government has spread out a net of spies. They will soon find out!"

The other volunteer interruped. "No witnesses will be necessary!..."

"The government has set up a camp for your welfare and medical treatment. You will get free food there..."

The truck cleaner with the shorts cried out. "Free food! Free medicines! Splendid! But what about those women who are also opium addicts? What will you do with them?"

"Those fat and lazy women! What will they do?"

"Good-for-nothing sluts who steal for themselves scraps of the opium they sell! Those *barabhateris*[11]! What will they do?"

The leader took off his cap rather nervously, started dusting it and said, "Thinking about the future of your wives and children, the government has set up a camp at Haramdo for treatment and rehabilitation. As for the women who have fallen into this evil habit, they will be taken to the camp forcibly, if necessary."

Silence spread over the crowd again.

"The government is acting for your own welfare. I am sure you know that we have formed our own government after independence. And this government doesn't believe in force or compulsion. It only wants your cooperation with love and understanding. We will arrange four medical officers for this camp. Two doctors will visit regularly from Gauhati and one from Palasbari. The doctor from Amranga here will also take a major share of this responsibility. You must save yourselves from this poison, you must save your motherland!"

The silence continued. One old opium-eater in shabby tattered clothes, shaking in every limb, stood up with the help of his stick. Indranath frowned. The old man pointing his finger at the leader with a trembling hand, said, "Is it true that little balls of opium will be fed to us during the treatment? And somebody told me just now that pigeon curry with *papaya* will be served to us. Is it...?"

Another opium-eater broke in, "And we will have curd made in big earthen pots, to eat as much as we like? Is it also true that four opium-eaters gave up opium after going to the camp and went straight to heaven?"

Indranath muttered to himself.

"Damn fools!"...and walked away disgustedly with heavy steps along the road.

From somebody's backyard, the sweet fragrance of sugarcane wafted to his nose. He saw a pair of foxes crossing the road in broad daylight, probably intoxicated by the honeyed odour of the sugarcane. He heard the sound of bullock-cart wheels...krr, krr, krr...A cart was approaching him. He could see that the hood was not made of palm leaves, but woven from thick, glistening *jangur*[12] leaves. Probably some ladies from a Gossain's house, on their way to spend some days with their relatives. The cart passed by. A colourful curtain at the rear met his gaze. No one peeped outside, there was no singing...perhaps they were going to a *shraddha* ceremony....A fragrance of tender coconuts and *jabakusum*[13] oil, blended together, reached his senses. The sun was sinking behind the *sal* trees. The glow of the dying sun's rays through the dried yellow leaves made a golden crown round the sun. The patches of yellow light were like golden fish swimming in the gloom of the forest. The sinking sun appeared to be gathering the golden fish in its net and dragging them down with it.

When Indranath reached Boloram's gambling den, it was already dark. Bolo was preparing for the night's game—arranging soft mattresses and round cushions on wide wooden cots. The petromax lamp was already primed. It was hanging from the branch of a *kamini*[14] tree nearby, throwing its white dazzling light all around. Bolo saw Indranath, pushing the bicycle alongside. The sight of the Gossain pleased him. He shouted excitedly.

"Saru Gossain! I was about to despatch a couple of my men to fetch you! We are having an all-night session of cards tonight. I have also arranged a Brahmin boy to prepare your tea and pudding."

Indranath heard peals of laughter from some women inside the house. He said, "I am sure they are playing *golokdham* inside. Your young wife will definitely disturb us many times, asking what move to make next!"

"No! She isn't there with those ladies. She will go tonight to Chikarhati to see the *palla*[15] of Surjathakur."

Indranath said, "Our *mohura* Purushottam, you know that man, with a big belly. He has a role there. He plays Bhisma. He has disappeared since early morning. Even went without his breakfast."

A decorated bullock-cart came and halted by the gate, near the *godhuli-gopala*[16] bush. Three ladies came out from the inner room, their chaddars pulled low over their faces. Seeing Indranath, they bowed to him. One of them, the youngest wife of Bolo, said, "Saru Gossain, please don't stay here too long. That naked ghost has appeared again. He swallowed all the curd from the curd-seller's pots."

Bolo laughed and exclaimed, "Milk! He drank up all

the milk in one gulp!"

The ladies entered the cart one by one. The cart driver flicked his whip and off went the bullocks, their bells jingling, and the wheels protesting—krr, krr, krr! A distinctive, tantalizing fragrance tickled Indranath's nose. It came from the women's skin who had just left. It reminded him of fresh sugarcane juice. Even the newly flooded Jagalia river gave off this rare odour. Indranath was lost in reverie. This fragrance always had a mysterious influence over him....

It carried him to a distant scene in the past...slim legs uncovered up to rounded knees...and the eyes—like the reflections of twin suns in the golden–brown waters of the river....

The game continued with great enthusiasm far into the night....Boloram was a prosperous trader of the village. A big, fat man with a bulging stomach. His bald head had a thin ring of brown hair, like a halo. The round, protruding stomach of Bolo reminded Indranath of the sand dunes of Jagalia where he hunted for tortoise's eggs in the cold month of December.

The forefathers of Bolo came from Marwar. He had grown rich during the war by supplying rations to the military base camp at Mirza near the *sattra*. During the freedom struggle, his family had donated two guns to the militants.

...Suddenly there were sounds of two cycles being flung against the *kamini* bush. The servant who was knitting a fishing net in the courtyard, called out, "Oh, look who has come! *Mahaldar*[17] Choudhury of Khanapara and Das! Now they will play the whole night long!"

Choudhury and Das bowed respectfully to Indranath and started playing. The game continued with a new vigour. Soon it was midnight....

After the game, Indranath told Bolo, "You will have to give me one *bandha*."

All the four players exclaimed. "*Bandha*! what?"

Indranath said further, "Not only a *bandha!* I will require two earthen pots like those used for carrying curd or lime. Let them be empty ones. He will carry them."

Bolo laughed out loudly and heartily.

"Now I understand! You want to catch that ghost on the bridge."

The card players also joined in his laughter.

Bolo said with amusement.

"You Gossains are as cunning as foxes. That's why it is said that—

Sudrar halowai bai hal

Bamunar halowar katha he sar

(Bullocks of Sudras plough the field, bullocks of Brahmins only talk, talk and talk!)"

Bolo looked at the two servants in the courtyard and instructed them. "You two there, both of you are to go with the Gossain."

One of them, Kaliman who was knitting the fishing net with wooden needles, put aside his things and turning his back towards the petromax lamp said, "Oh, *Prabhu*[18]! See these marks on my back? He attacked me once. I threw my mustard-oil bottle at him and somehow managed to escape....Somebody removed the skin of a dead cow and dumped it in the jungle. There are no scavengers here! It must be that naked ghost who stalks at night!"

The *bandha* named Phatik nodded in agreement.

"Yes *Prabhu!* He's right. There are no scavengers here. It is that ghost all right. But I'll carry the load for Gossain here all the same."

Bolo addressed Indranath.

"You take him with you, Saru Gossain! He is completely fearless. Do you known what he did once?"

Bolo came near Indranath and spoke in his ear.

"You must have heard that sensational story about Bamdeo *Maujadar.* His young and beautiful wife was drowned in a well. Later it was confirmed that she had committed suicide. Bamdeo didn't show the dead body to anybody and quietly buried it in his backyard! It created a sensation! He had some connection with a nurse of Khatiamari hospital...."

Phatik chimed in.

"Yes, yes, she was buried but before that her body was made ready for cremation. The body was almost half burnt. Then there was a lot of hue and cry from the people! The half-burnt corpse was pulled out of the fire and then buried by Bamdeo *Maujadar.* Then a strange thing happened. On getting the scent of the half-burnt body, some foxes dug it out!"

Mahaldar Choudhury now added.

"Our scriptures say that people who commit suicide should be buried:

Atmanan ghatyedyastha
Vnigra grayanshammby bhik
Tasya Tiratra mashauchan
dritmyetrathi sansayah
Tritiyetudakan kritva chatnuthe
shredhyamisyate.

Chaudhury recited slowly and hesitantly with many errors of pronunciation.

Indranath smiled and said, "*Mahaldar* Choudhury, your original house was in Bhagwatipara, wasn't it? All the *purohits*[19] of Gossains came from that place...."

"Yes, yes! They are all *purohits.*"

Choudhury gave a mysterious smile. Indranath could understand the meaning of this smile. The echo of that threat, that fear, reverberated in his mind....Yes, the threats, what those Communists said!...Gossains will be forced to till their own land one day!...

Bolo was speaking again.

"Saru Gossain, you take Phatik with you. He is very courageous. He was near that corpse for five hours, all the time admiring her dead limbs. They were as smooth and beautiful as tender bamboos, even in death and after destruction by fire...."

Bolo wanted to continue with the narration of his story but it was already quite late, past midnight. Indranath prepared to leave for home. His mother and Durga must be waiting for him, half drowsy. Now that Giribala was there, she too would sit up for him. The image of these three women, sitting and waiting for him on the verandah, irritated Indranath. It pierced the barriers of his mind and released a sigh of frustration and helplessness....He heard the foxes howling near the wooden bridge over Jagalia. He turned to Bolo and exclaimed, "I must go now! Give the pots to Phatik and let him follow me."

Indranath set out briskly on the road homewards.

* * *

Near the wooden bridge, Indranath looked up at the sky. It was clean and bright with moonlight. The moon was limpid, lustrous, starkly radiant like a beautiful woman who had thrown away her clothes and stood gloriously naked!

He went through the *sal* forest. He could see the sand dunes of Jagalia washed white by moonlight, like a flock of white sheep.

Phatik was following close behind him. The silence was deep, gloomy and fearful. Both walked fast and in silence. They could hear each other's footsteps and the sound of dry clods crushed under their feet....Suddenly on the right-hand side of the bridge, they saw an outline of a woman coming out on the road. Phatik's footsteps faltered....Who was she? The earthen pots in his hands shook and trembled and crashed to the ground! Turning round, he fled in the direction he had come from.

Indranath stood still. He peered in the moonlit night. Nothing! He could see nothing. Only the house of Bhagwati sitting squat like a ruminating elephant....Then he saw again the figure of the elusive woman at one corner of the bridge, near a large bush. She was coming towards him. Indranath felt as if blood had stopped circulating in his body; the sensation of a cold wave swept over him. He shouted.

"Who...who is there?"

The figure came nearer, quite close. He saw that it was an old woman with a stick in her hand, her face and body covered with torn, threadbare clothes. She spoke to him:

"Don't you recognise me? Don't you remember we met that day on the South Bank of Jagalia? And the daughter of the *purohit* who was with me?..."

Indranath exclaimed.

"Yes, yes! But why are you here at this time of the night?"

"There's no other time except this hour. We all know that you return at this time from Bolo's den. I have been waiting for quite a long while."

The veil slid down from her face. Her straggling hair like dry white jute strands, appeared ghostly to Indranath. She wiped her face with a corner of her *gatala* and said,

"Saru Gossain, please pardon me. I am in danger. That's why I have come at this ungodly hour."

"Danger? What sort of danger? Probably that opium-eater has fallen into the volunteer's net. Good! I want to see all opium-eaters wiped out from my *sattra.*"

The old woman objected.

"No, no! It is nothing like that. I have come to tell you about Eliman."

"Eliman?..."

An elusive, undefined sensation swept over him. He should not be here listening to this old woman. After all he was the future *adhikar* of the *sattra*. He had to be cautious, discreet. He must preserve his dignity. The fortunes of the *sattra* revolved round each step he took in this direction. But he was caught in a net of illusion. He could not stir himself and leave the place. The old woman sensed his uncertainty. She came a step nearer and said.

"That girl is in trouble...!"

"Trouble?"—Indranath uttered.

"Saru Gossain, I don't feel ashamed to talk to you. That's why I have come to you in the dead of the night."

Indranath was impatient. He cut her short.

"Tell me! What is it? Quick!"

Just at that moment, the *lantana* bush near the bridge quivered, its branches parted and a slim figure of another woman moved forward like a shadow....Was it the priest's daughter?...The old woman pointed a finger towards the girl.

"Don't be afraid, Saru Gossain! People know that we sometimes come out in the middle of the night for toilet. Listen! A time comes when fear disappears. Even a tiger or a mad elephant cannot scare you anymore. A man is something else altogether!"

Indranath said, irritated.

"Why is she standing there? Snakes crawl about near bushes. Ask her to come forward. What's all this between you two?"

The old woman covered her chin with her *gatala* and spoke hesitantly.

"She cannot come. She has blood on her *mekhala*."

Indranath exclaimed.

"Blood!"

"Listen, Saru Gossain! There are certain loathsome, malicious women who visit the backyards secretly at night, just to find out whether the young girl of the house has reached puberty. I am afraid the same thing has happened with this girl here. I have brought her here because I am afraid of them. They'll spread the news. Yes, they'll certainly do so, and this girl will not get married. Those old Brahmins will declare her and her father social outcastes. But I know! I know how many girls there are in South Bank who have already reached puberty. But it's all hushed up! They have some strong protection. This girl is like a frail creeper! Who will protect her?"

Indranath was stunned. He could not utter a single word. What a strange situation!

The lantana bush shook a little. In the moonlit night, the tender, flower-like body trembled and shrank into itself with shyness and shame.

In front of Indranath, behind that bush, stood a girl who had just stepped on the threshold of puberty. Did a Gossain ever find himself in such an odd situation? Did a Gossain's daughter ever have to face such circumstances?

In the middle of the night, near the wooden bridge over Jagalia river, the three of them stood, in silence, as if carved out of stone. After a while, Indranath said,

"Take her back to the house."

The old woman uttered.

"I have not yet told you about the danger that is now hanging over our heads!"

"Tell me! Quick!"

"Her father once said that the Brahmin from Cooch Behar, that wretched, opium-eating rascal, would take her even if she reaches puberty and thus save the family honour....."

Indranath murmured.

"A Brahmin from Cooch Behar?"

"He says so! He claims to have some land in Cooch Behar, but nobody has gone there and checked. For the last two years, he has been supplying opium to her father. God alone knows from where! Now this Brahmin will learn about her condition and will arrange for *telarbhar*[20]."

The *lantana* bush shook again, as if the girl hiding there had shivered....

"Saru Gossain, I can speak to you frankly without any reserve. From the day she met you on the river bank, she has lost her heart to you. She lost her mother when she was very young. She has grown up, sucking milk from my breasts...."

The old woman's voice choked with emotion. She dabbed her eyes with the soiled *gatala* round her shoulders and continued.

"She doesn't want to go back to Rajapukuri again. How can I allow her to marry that opium-eating bastard?"

The old woman now broke down completely and started crying loudly.

The *lantana* bush again quivered. The body of the girl behind the bush was trembling...like a bare *sewali* tree with its leaves and flowers shaken off by a violent storm....

The old woman took a few steps forward. Her feet stepped on the broken pieces of the earthen curd pots dropped by Phatik in panic. In a barely audible voice, she said, "Gossain! It is true that in your family nobody has married ordinary Brahmin girls but...I have heard...in the South Bank, among Damodariya Gossains, there are cases of marriages with North Bank Brahmin girls...Disciples have never raised their voices...Times are changing Gossain...Gossainees who had never stepped beyond the front halls...they go to Gauhati...fight for their land and go to court for justice..."

Strange! On this dark night...standing on the broken pieces of curd pots...what was this old woman babbling about?

"You'll never find a girl of her beauty in the entire South Bank....With these two eyes of mine, I have seen them all...I have opened the hairs of all those eligible Gossain girls...but believe me...you'll never find one like her anywhere. See! There she is! Like a piece of moon fallen from the heavens! Listen. Saru Gossain! Your *gotras*[21] are different. You are Chandilya *gotra,* she is from the Bhardwaj *gotra.* I have studied everything! That's why I have come to you. Your word will be enough."

The *lantana* bush shivered. Everything was now revealed, as if the girl was standing before this man naked!

The old woman resumed speaking in a very humble tone.

"Dakhala. Bamundi, Rajabaha—in all these places, Gossains have married Brahmin girls! We know this. Where are the disciples? Take a look at her face! Gossain, rescue her from this torment. Only you can do it."

Indranath stood motionless for some time. He must

give a reply...he spoke to the woman.

"The shadow of my father, the great *adhikar,* is over my head. I cannot say anything now. Give me some time."

...It is high time...past midnight! Cannot wait here any longer. He must go away from here!...

The old woman stepped forward, as if to obstruct his path.

"But there's very little time left! That Brahmin from Cooch Behar is hiding in the *dhekal* with his stock of opium. There's nobody else to help us!"

Her mouth almost touched Indranath's ear. She whispered, excitedly.

"Inform the police! Tell the police to go at once and check up! In the *dhekal*! They should look inside the stick. It is hanging from the roof, packed with opium! There's also opium hidden inside a bunch of bananas there! Hurry up, Saru Gossain!"

The old woman, exhausted, became breathless and gasped for air. Indranath's nose was assailed by a sour odour emanating from her body. Sometimes Durga gave off this peculiar odour...and those peasant women, breasts heavy with milk, leaving behind their suckling babies, to work in the rice fields....

"The *paltan*[22] is now idling in Haramdo. You go! Quick! Only you can inform them. I hope you understand! If that rascal is behind the bars, she is safe...till the time you make up your mind!"

The *lantana* bush trembled again. What will he say? This man—the saviour of her destiny?

Indranath remained silent. He felt as if a finely drawn silk thread of emotion and sentiment was winding around him, round and round, and helplessly bound, he was being thrown at the feet of the girl behind the bush!

He broke the silence.

"You go now! Both of you! I'll do what I have to do. Go now! While I am still standing here, go inside the house."

The old woman and the girl took the shorter way under the bridge and after a while, disappeared from sight.

Behind the lantana bushes, one could see jackals. Two small cubs, playing in the moonlight, rolled down the slope of the embankment like two mud balls. For sometime, Indranath stood there silently. Did anybody ever have to face such a situation? That girl who had just stepped into puberty, standing before him, her undergarment probably stained with menstrual flow...Is it possible?...He remembered...As a child, once he had embraced his mother when she was having her monthly period. What a crisis it was! His mother fasted for one day and the family priest had to come and purify him! Even now that Sanskrit *sloka* echoes in his ears.

What was he to do?...Should he hand over the opium smuggler from Cooch Behar to the Home Guard? Indranath remembered....Once he had run into an excise inspector passing by on a bicycle. The latter had jumped down from his bicycle, made obeisance to him and addressed him respectfully. "Saru Gossain, the opium habit has gripped your village. But you are only watching silently."

Indranath remembered he had replied. "Who says we are silent spectators? My father, the *adhikar,* nowadays never encourages those opium-eaters when they come to him for mortgaging their land in exchange for opium! Also during the yearly *sabha*, he invariably gives a lecture on the evils of opium eating. The opium addicts rehabilitation camp at Rajabaha was actually started by my father!"

"Then why don't you help us. Saru Gossain? In Tiniali, there are three shops selling opium. They are doing roaring business. Some years back, anybody could apply and get a licence for selling opium. Nowadays opium selling has spread all along the Jagalia bank right into the fields where you tie your elephants!"

"Yes, yes! I know! Once in the Assam Government's budget the revenue from opium held the second place. Am I correct?"

"Yes, I am happy that you remember everything! But let me come to the real point. Nowadays even the opium eaters must have a permit! Each opium-selling shop is advised to get a fixed monthly quota of opium for sale to public. But even then the *mahaldar* often takes out a quantity of opium from the treasury, showing various reasons. This is happening everywhere on South Bank. But do you know what's happening in your place?"

"What?"

"Shops here have almost stopped taking opium from the treasury! This is something very odd and curious! It should be investigated properly."

"In that case, the revenue from opium has also dropped?"

The inspector laughed and said, "The *mahaldar* said that the reason for the decrease in sale of opium is due to the fact that the opium-eaters have forsaken their habit. Can you believe it? Is it possible?"

Indranath was dumbfounded! He had seen things with his own eyes over the last few years! Once the creepers of *pan* were heavy with leaves, winding round the betel nut trees. But gradually these creepers dropped like dried-up intestines as all the *pan* leaves were consumed by the opium-eaters. So how is it possible that old opium addicts had abandoned their habits? The betel nut leaves are not available even for marriage ceremonies. They have to get them from other nearby villages. This is the real situation! And now this man says that according to the *mahaldar*, people are leaving their old opium-eating habits!

The inspector continued.

"Listen, Gossain! In you area, there are only about ten licence holders. But according to the excise police report, more than 80 per cent of the population is addicted! So why don't you help us? I personally feel that the opium smugglers have contacts in the Garo Hills or in the Cooch Behar. Do you know, Gossain, how much opium has been seized in the port of Calcutta? A forest route for opium smuggling leads towards Burma and Malaya. I think, in your village also, such a connection has been established! You have respect and authority here. People like you should protect the public from the vicious poison!"

Indranath had not forgotten the words of the excise inspector. He also remembered the talk he had heard about opium during the card sessions at Bolo's place. One or two men had spoken about poppy flower plantations in Garo Hills. The colour of the opium from the Garo Hills was different from that of the opium issued under *challans* from the treasury. In this connection, one man had told him about how one *mahaldar* had had a narrow escape from being caught! Indranath had never paid much attention to these stories as he had been so engrossed in the card game all the time. But now he recalled everything! He even remembered some horrifying tales about opium that he had heard long back. It was said that in the old days there was a connection between the custom of *sati* and opium. In Dhaka, most of the *sati* women were fed opium before they were burnt on the funeral pyre. Once a Brahmin from the bank of Jagalia who had *jajmans* in Dhaka, was horror-struck by the sight of a *sati* jumping out from the fire. Fire-blackened lumps of flesh were hanging from her breast, her arms and legs. It was a most sickening sight!

The historians, Wilson and Mill, had written somewhere... yes, he now remembered what it was. Between 1815 and 1828, within a thirteen-year time-span, 710 women in Dhaka and 5100 women in Calcutta were burnt in this inhuman manner as *sati!* Who would believe that the Garo Hills of Assam had a hand in the burning of these widows? Opium from the Garo Hills was well-known and was in great demand, even in those days!

Indranath stood motionless near the bridge, perplexed and indecisive. What should he do? Would it be really wise to go to the excise police at Haramdo. Suppose the priest, Eliman's father, was also caught in the same net? Then?

Indranath remembered Amendment 10 of the Opium prohibition Act of Assam, 1947. According to it a person sheltering an opium smuggler was an accomplice to the crime and liable for punishment! If her father was involved, then where will she go? The very thought of a Brahmin priest, who washed the family deity of Rajapukuri, going to prison made Indranath pause apprehensively. Those hypocrites, opium-addicted Brahmins! Fools! They were reluctant to go to the treatment camp at Haramdo, out of false prestige! But it was an open secret that the father of Eliman and the opium dealer from Cooch Behar had a working partnership in buying and selling opium. In what way could he save the old man? That foolish old woman who wanted the smuggler to be arrested, had no idea of the implications!...

...Yes, yes! Now everything was becoming clear! He had also read the fifth amendment of the Opium Act, "Provided that an accused who is found on evidence to be a smuggler of opium or seller of opium, shall not receive a sentence of less than two years' rigorous imprisonment as well as fine"...Two years is a long time and many things can happen in two years.

Indranath started walking. He crossed *hathi bandha bakari* and reached the old banyan tree where the outcast leper eked out his wretched existence. At this hour of midnight, he was not to be seen there. Where was he? Probably he had gone somewhere for a call of nature or perhaps he was crouching in the verandah of a house nearby in terror of the prowling wolves.

Indranath crossed the bamboo gate of Dibakar Bhagwati's fencing. He saw dim rays of light percolating through the chinks in the cane and mud wall, which was almost coming apart. Suddenly he heard the 'krr, krr' sound of bullock-cart wheels. He saw two carts overloaded with goods coming in his direction. A voice called out all of a sudden from one of the carts.

"Is that Saru Gossain? Is this the time to return home?"

Indranath understood immediately that it was the voice of their ancestral priest, Purshottam Bhagwati. He turned round and saw the bald pate of the priest shining in the moonlight. His shoulders were covered with a *chaddar* as white as a crane's feathers.

"Gossain, how long will you go on roaming like this? Your *mohura* is gradually eating up your lands. The other day Gossainee wept before me, she complained that you were not taking any interest in your landed property. Have you heard? The draconian land ceiling act will come soon. All your *Nispikheraj*[23] lands will be taken away! One should have a crane's perseverance and a fox's craftiness! These are the two qualities most essential today for survival!"

Indranath was hardly listening. Moreover the cart

wheel's noise made it difficult to hear the priest's words clearly. Now the priest jumped out from the cart and came near him.

"Saru Gossain! So late in the night! It appears you have been drinking. We know that you go there to play cards, but drinking? You never used to do that!"

Indranath did not reply. His eyes went to the loaded bullock carts. They were packed with bunches of tender jackfruit, big earthen pots of curd, baskets of paddy, wooden jars of jaggery, betel nuts and *pan* leaves. Two *bandhas* were holding on to the curd pots tightly to prevent them from spilling. Their bare backs glistened in the moonlight.

"Indranath, everyone knows that you are a man of few words. I was just joking about the drinking bit! In the ancient days, *soma rasa* was the wine of Gods, but they used it to gain strength of wisdom! It is said that Indra, who drank it for pleasure, didn't leave behind any scriptures of lasting human value...but the ascetic sages also imbibed *soma* and composed divine *mantras*, the *Upanishads* and the *Vedas*! The story of *soma* juice is very colourful."

The previous month's rain had made the road surface rough and full of pot holes. On this surface, the carts were creating more noise than usual. Indranath came nearer to the *purohit* and walked shoulder to shoulder with him.

"So you have come from the *jajmans*[24] have you?"

"Yes, I had gone to Bangara. You know, that *maujadar* is also one of my *jajmans.*"

"Yes, yes, I have heard about him. His wife fell in a well and died. People here on the banks of Jagalia are spreading all sorts of stories about it!" The priest came nearer.

"It is very serious, Indranath!"

"Why?"

"The story doing the rounds in Jagalia is not untrue. The *moujadar* had an affair with the nurse of the hospital of Khatiamari. She had come to his house also. This led to the quarrel between husband and wife."

The fat, bald-headed Brahmin whispered right into Indranath's ear.

"From my talk with the *moujadar* today it appears that the quarrel took place near the well. In the tussle that followed, the wife...er...fell into the well."

"So he has confessed at last. That's good! He should be ready for prison meals!"

The priest almost shouted.

"Confess? What confession? He hasn't admitted anything! He even managed to get a doctor's certificate before the funeral! But the most important thing about the whole affair is that the conscience of the *maujadar* is now tormenting him. He is seeking atonement."

The Brahmin then started uttering the Sanskrit *sloka* for atonement in his peculiar nasal voice and faulty pronunciation.

> *Atryee Brahmining hatva chareddada-shavara-sikan. Yadvasikan tatha kshetran Vaishya Srivasikan Bratah Sradhasamveta sorn shudramagyandala dhar eratu.*
>
> (A Brahmin who kills a Brahmin woman must atone for twelve years; if he kills a *Kshatriya* woman, then he has to undergo six years atonement.)

Indranath's mind again wandered and he barely listened to the priest's words. By then the bullock-carts had reached the sugarcane fields of the Gossain. The sweet fragrance of tender sugarcane tickled his nostrils.

The priest was saying.

"Listen, Indranath! Yagyavalkya has laid down a most terrible act of atonement for this crime! A sinner of this nature had to carry a human skull balanced on a stick right through a period of twelve years and beg for rice from house to house. He had to survive on this rice only. If all those terrible rules are strictly observed, then there won't be such evil deeds in this world. But nowadays everything has to be made simple! I, myself, with these two hands, have compromised on these ancient rules."

Indranath interrupted him abruptly.

"Bapu[25], when you knew everything about the *Maujadar's* guilt, you should have reported at once to the Palasbari Police Station."

"What are you saying, Saru Gossain? He didn't say he had pushed her into the well. He said she had lost her balance during their tussle and fell inside. Moreover, the doctor's post-mortem report mentions she had a heart attack and fell inside the well. The doctor gave his certificate immediately."

They walked together in silence. Indranath felt a twinge of pain somewhere inside his heart. Fresh fragrance of lime wafted up to his nose. An owlet flew over their way calling, *ulululu, ulululu*...They continued on their way without talking and reached the *batghar*. Indranath halted and said to the Brahmin priest.

"Bapu! I want to ask you something!"

"Go on! Go on! Ask your question! Today you seem quite absent-minded."

"Did any *adhikar* of our *sattra* ever marry a girl from an ordinary Brahmin family?"

The priest remained silent for some time as if he was

calculating something. Then he spoke.

"Well...er...listen, Saru Gossain! To answer that question, I must go back to the year 1400 *saka*[26]. I have to start from Santa Dev's Garaimari, which he founded before this *sattra*. I remember one Brahmin girl of Dakhala. A Gossain had presented her with a pair of gold earrings. The arrangements were almost complete. But the disciples objected most vehemently and the marriage didn't take place. I heard later that the Brahmin girl got married in Bamundi. There was a rumour that even after her marriage, the Gossain had an affair with the girl! There are so many girls in Dakhala and Samaria, of low caste, who were abandoned by these Gossains, after giving them gold and having had relationships with them. But I am still unable to recollect any instance of a Gossain marrying an ordinary Brahmin girl."

All of sudden, near the thorny bushes, some jackals started howling. Both of them were startled by the sound. The two overloaded carts went ahead along the road. The priest remained behind with Indranath. He asked, "But Sarubopa! Why are you putting this question to me?"

"No, no! Just like that! I think I should know these things."

"Listen, Saru Gossain! Bad times are looming ahead! On the other side of Jagalia, Damodaria Gossains have started marrying ordinary Brahmin girls. At Rangamati, the Communists with red banners are terrorising the people. And Gossain Brahmin girls are reaching puberty before their marriages! So much sin everywhere! Did you ever hear of such things? But you are asking about a Brahmin girl. Why? I fail to understand you...."

"No, no, Bapu! Forget it! Nothing to worry about...really!"

"I know you won't do anything which will stain your spotless family history. Do you know who *Dharamatma* Yudhishtir called a *purusha*?"

> *Divyanan shprishati bhumishan shavdeh*
> *panyana karamana yabat sa shavdo bhabhati*
> *tavat purusa uchyate.*
>
> (Echo of good deeds touches heaven and earth.
> As long as this sound exists, man will be known
> as *purusha.*)

* * * *

Indranath bade the priest farewell and crossed the *batghar* into the courtyard. The latter hurried after the receding bullock-carts. Indranath walked across the courtyard and climbed the verandah steps. From this vantage point, the Jagalia looked like a bleached bone dug up from the earth. As usual he saw his mother and Durga sitting and waiting, their heads resting on their knees. But he also saw a third figure, of Giribala, leaning against one of the wooden posts. Slightly irritated, Indranath wiped his forehead with his *chaddar,* went to the well in a huff and washed his face and limbs. Standing there, drying his wet face, he gazed beyond the bushes into the distance. A part of the Jagalia, bleached white bone, was visible.

Five

Durga was pouring water from the well on Giribala while she squatted on the plastered brick apron, cracked in places and peeling with age. The lever beam had become dark-grey like the colour of a crocodile's skin.

Giribala was wearing a chemise made of *markin* with pleated neck. On her waist, she wore a *mekhala* woven with fine thread. The wet clothes clung to her full body and accentuated the curves of her body.

Durga had only a cotton *mekhala* tied round her bosom. One could see from the well a part of the *kecha*[1] road coming to the *sattra.* Both the women were taking baths in a playful mood, pouring water over each other's bodies in turn. Suddenly they heard shouts of children. Durga and Giribala looked up towards the road and saw a man on a cycle, dressed entirely in white, with an old felt hat on his head, looking very much like a crane. The village children were running after the cycle shouting—"*Sanyasi* Sahib! *Sanyasi* Sahib! Where are our sweets? We want sweets!"

The two women stood on their toes and craned their necks to see better what was going on out there on the road. They could see that the cycle was loaded with a big odd-looking bundle. The man was smiling at everybody around. Giribala exclaimed. "Who is he? Who is this man?"

"That's Mark Sahib! He has come again. Probably he has brought a letter from the Commissioner along with other official papers."

Giribala asked curiously, "What are those papers? And why has he brought them?"

"He wants to write the history of our *sattra*. He collects ancient manuscripts. You know! Written on *sanchi* leaves. He goes to each and every house and gives away free medicines. He visits the opium-eaters and lectures them on the evils of opium. Last year, I read out to him the old Assamese manuscript *Vyasa Ashrama*[2] and he copied it down in English."

Giribala was astonished. "You read the manuscript?"

"Yes, he can read printed Assamese but he cannot make out hand-written ancient Assamese script. The way he read the manuscript, stumbling and groping like a blind man. I felt sorry for him! The way he laboured over writing down the text, sweating profusely, the drops even falling on the paper!"

The noise of the old bicycle, the shrill notes of its bell and the shouts of the children could now be heard from near the *batghar* and finally the courtyard, where Mark stood with his bicycle. Durga and Giribala ran from their bathing place, across the open space into their room through the rear door, clutching their wet clothes.

After a while, the two women, clad more decently, came out in the verandah. Gossainee, Indranath and Sombhu *Mohura* had also come out, greeted Mark Sahib and made him seated comfortably on a wooden chair...All of a sudden, there was an abrupt cry from Durga. She had found to her horror that Mark Sahib's shadow had fallen on her body! A *firingi's* shadow on a Goswami widow! She fled immediately to the well and prepared for a second bath!

Mark Sahib bowed with respect to the Gossainee and said in broken Assamese.

"It will take time, I think, I'll have to stay here longer. If you can allot a hut for me in the elephants' grazing ground, that will suffice."

He took out some coins from his pocket, put them down beside Gossainee's feet and again paid his obeisance. Gossainee said, covering her forehead with the *chaddar*, "Stay as long as you like! Our people are simple villagers and they will be happy to hear good words from you."

Indranath added, "This time, there is even somebody to help you. A girl."

"Who?"

Indranath pointed towards Giribala.

"That's the girl."

Giribala and Mark looked at each other. Mark's eyes fell on her dark hair, still damp after her bath, her freshly washed body singing like a pod of *leteku*[3] fruit. Mark lowered his eyes.

Indranath said, "I was thinking of putting her in school. But....my parents are not of the same view. Here girls from Gossain households still don't go out in public, let alone to school! And she lost her husband only a few months back. Now she has all the time in the world!"

Mark Sahib glanced again at the girl. Her eyes were dry and blank. Like the shell of a dried-up *phol*[4]. Just then Gossainee went inside to make tea for the guest. Indranath continued.

"Last time when you were here, you had told me that you would study the papers left behind by that German Sahib, Gilman."

"Yes, yes! I wanted to write his biography and that

desire is still strong in me. For this purpose, I'll have to stay for sometime in the tribal villages of *Rabhas*."

"That's fine! Do you know that Gilman Sahib, better known here as Gilmil Sahib, married for the second time here and it was a *Rabha* village girl? Poor girl! She took devoted care of him till his last days...."

"Yes, I have heard all this. I heard that he, in turn, had also done a lot for this backward tribe."

In a corner of the verandah, sat Sombhu *mohura*. A fat bald-headed man with a bulging stomach, he was wearing an old waist-coat over a clean dhoti reaching up to his knees. An old tattered umbrella lay by his side. He joined the conversation.

"I don't know whether the Sahib knows about it or not. Gilmil Sahib had the power to settle *foujidari*[5] cases. This power was given to him specially by the Commissioner! He could give up to six months' imprisonment for assault and battery cases....When the *Rabha* woman died, they found money hidden inside the mattress. She had saved this money for their bad days and emergencies, without Gilmil Sahib's knowledge..."

"Money inside the mattress?" All those present in the verandah exclaimed.

"Yes, yes! Most of it was in paper notes stitched inside the mattress. People said that she had saved this money for the Sahib's medical treatment. He had some chronic disease."

Everybody started laughing.

Even Mark Sahib smiled. Giribala was observing Mark. She found him very handsome. His eyes reminded her of those water hyacinth flowers which, in the monsoon, flourished everywhere. His head was covered with a profusion of honey-coloured curly hair. His complexion was not that of a common Britisher. Probably due to wandering from place to place in the open sun, it resembled the complexion of *jajmani* Brahmins.

A *bandha* came, carrying a wooden pestle with mortar (for crushing betelnuts), a *sarai*[6] loaded with betelnuts and *pan* leaves and a small brass container of lime paste. He put down all these things before the fat *mohura* who was fanning his face with a *gamucha* to drive away the hovering flies. Sambhu *mohura* filled the mortar with the right proportion of ingredients and started pounding the mixture with the pestle. With each stroke of the pestle, the hidden aroma of tender Garo Hills *pan* leaves permeated the air around those sitting there.

The *mohura* said.

"Sahib listen! Let me tell you an interesting story! There was one *Maujadar* Monjoi Choudhury, who was a fine hunter. He had a beautiful gun made of brass. Some say his forefathers had purchased it from the East India Company, while others say that his ancestors got it from some French merchants of Goalpara who were salt traders about a hundred years ago! One day, he entered the forest of Mirza riding an elephant and shot at a plump wild boar...."

The *mohura* scooped out the mixture from the mortar and popped it into his mouth. He chewed with relish for some time and then continued:

"By a strange coincidence, when Monjoi Choudhury fired at the boar, there was a loud report of another gun-shot from the opposite direction! One from the east and the other from the west! As if the target of the two gun shots was the same! The *Maujadar* went deeper into the forest and found the beast dead, its portruding teeth thrust into the earth, near a bamboo bush. Two streams of blood ran out from the dirty yellow (like that of an old thatched roof) head of the slain boar. Its body was plump with flesh. Manjoi Choudhury stood there thinking that he would take the carcass to the near-by village, Dolagaon, and distribute its flesh among the villagers there....Then his next impulse was to hide the dead boar with some grass and branches of leaves....At that moment, suddenly he heard a heavy stamping of boots coming down the forest path. A human figure emerged, to the utter surprise of the *Maujadar,* from the middle of the *german ban, tara, khagri* and thorny *kutuha* bushes. It was a short, peculiar looking man wearing an old army dress of *khaki* colour. His complexion was the colour of foaming milk. One eye was missing. Monjoi Choudhury was struck dumb with the realisation that the intruder was none other than Gilman, the old German from the nearby Bordowa Tea Estate! In broken Assamese, the German said, 'I have killed this boar!' Choudhury screamed. 'What do you mean you have killed the boar!' He waved his gun and screamed again. 'See this gun? It can shoot up to a distance of thirty feet, and this boar is lying exactly within thirty feet of the spot from where I shot it. I have killed this boar, do you understand?' The other man, who looked more like a white monkey, chuckled derisively and taking the gun off his shoulder, retorted. 'Do you see this gun? It's an Enfield 303! It belonged to my son Alexander who gave his life in the war. I was there, up in that tree, when I shot dead this wild boar!.....'

"Both of them went near the carcass and stanted examining the wound. They found to their great surprise that the two bullets had hit exactly at the same spot! They exclaimed together. 'The same spot! What a strange coincidence!' Now Gilman shouted triumphantly. 'I hit it first. It was my bullet that killed it!' The *Maujadar* reacted violently and almost screamed. 'What rot! My bullet struck it first! It was I who killed it!' They argued for some time. Ultimately it ended in an exchange of blows. Choudhury planted on Gilman Sahib's cheeks four mighty open-handed slaps!"

The audience of Sombhu *mohura* exclaimed in unison, "What! Four slaps! To a white sahib! *Baap-re baap*!"

"The Sahib was in a great rage. He ran to the road crossing, mounted his elephant and went straight to Gauhati to meet the District Magistrate. This magistrate had cordial relations with the German. He advised him: 'My friend, you already have the power of trying assault and battery cases and other minor criminal offences. You can pronounce your own decision in this matter. But take care! If you use a gun, you are allowed only one bullet. You should always remember that!'

"Gilmil Sahib mounted his elephant again and went posthaste to the Mirza road crossing. He hailed imperiously some of Monjoi Choudhury's men and declared, 'I have brought orders from Gauhati for your Choudhury. To pierce his bloody body with a bullet! I'll finish that bastard with one bullet only!'

"All the *Maujadar's* men fell at Gilmil Sahib's feet, terrified for their master. They knew very well about the *faujdari* powers of the German. They pleaded with him and prayed for Choudhury's life. Now one of these men of Manjoi Choudhury was quite smart and cunning. He was a dark fellow, lean and tall. He scratched his head for a moment and said, 'Sahib! You are a first class hunter of South Bank and Choudhury is also a damn good hunter who can shoot two tigers with one bullet! Now this is a fine chance for us to find out which one of you is the greatest.'

"Gilman asked, greatly puzzled, 'What the hell do you

mean? What chance?' The lanky young man replied. 'On the weekly market day at Barihat, in the evening dust, Choudhury, riding a white horse, will cross the length of the whole market in one jump. Exactly at that moment, Sahib, you'll have to shoot him with one bullet!'

"Gilmil Sahib and Choudhury both agreed to this proposal.

"...The appointed market day at Barihat came. The market place was chockful of people who had come to see this contest between the one-eyed German and the intrepid Monjoi Choudhury. They had gathered from different places like Taluapara, Rajabaha, Jharobari, Khatiamari and other places. All these people, along with the regular customers of the market, made it look like a carnival. The sun almost dipped into the west, the expected time approached...the setting sun looking as if it had fallen into the *hathi bandha bakari.* And from that direction, the hazy white figure of Choudhury on his white horse could be seen thundering down through the evening air, thick with smoke and dust!...Gilman Sahib was also at rigid attention, his gun cocked and ready, aimed at the right spot.

"...The throng pushed and pulled and shouted excitedly.

"'Look there! Look! That half-blind Sahib will now shoot Choudhury!'

"'There's the Sahib! Look!...Curse him! Let the heavens fall on the one-eyed Sahib!'

"'Look! There! Choudhury with a white turban on his head, a white *chaddar* on his shoulders, wearing a white *punjabi*......'

"'Look, there he goes, riding on his white horse!...See how fast he goes!...'

"'There, he's coming fast!.......He's come!.......There, he's gone......'

"'Went by very fast!.....He's escaped!'......But side by side, with the hue and cry, there was a loud report from Gilman Sahib's gun, it sounded like a big explosion! Nobody knew where, on that Bharihat road, Choudhury and his horse had disappeared...."

All those sitting around the *mohura* exclaimed.

"Oh! Poor Choudhury! He died, alas!"

The *mohura* looked at the excited faces, flicked at the flies on his face with his *gamucha*, and continued:

"Oh, ho! You haven't understood anything!"

They all shouted.

"Why? What happened then?"

"I'll tell you! That was a dry banana trunk, a bundle of straw, a mop of jute fibre...all put together cleverly with Choudhury's clothes on a horse that was trained to perfection...so that was the Monjoi Choudhury everybody saw that evening in the market...."

There was a loud burst of laughter all round.

"Is it really true, you cunning *mohura*?"

"Yes, it's very much true! That lanky youth, with his fox-like cunning, made a big fool out of the German Sahib. The dummy was tied so firmly on the horse that even the turban didn't shake or fall off! Gimil's bullet had passed through the dummy's stomach and lodged in the fig tree behind the market! Do you know what the people sang about the German? No? Then listen!....

Gilmil blind!
Gilmil blind!
Choudhury became
Police friend!"

Again there was a round of hearty laughter. Even Mark's face registered a gentle smile. He said, "All this happened before the time of the great earthquake, didn't it?"

Sombhu *mohura* nodded his head in assent.

"Yes, yes! It was the time when those French merchants had come to Goalpara with their sacks of salt and when our Santa Dev *Mahaprabhu*[7] had shifted the *sattra* from Garaimari to this place and installed the prevailing deity, Gopinath, with great pomp and glory. But the famous steps, cut from solid rock, at Garaimari were swallowed up in the great earthquake. And the Brahmins from Kanyakubja were attracted to the South Bank by the prospects of good farming and settled down on its fertile soil."

Indranath who was sitting silently enjoying the *mohura's* narration, now joined the conversation.

"As far as I know, Gilman died at Bordowa in 1925. I have heard this story before. But in the end, when Gilman heard the true story about the deception, he saw the humorous side of it and like the sportsman that he was, he went to Choudhury and shook his hand in friendship."

Meanwhile, Gossainee came out of the inner room—a fair-skinned, slender old lady, her lips stained a dark colour because of constant smoking. Durga followed her, carrying a tray with brass cups and tumblers of various shapes. She put down the tray on the floor. Carefully avoiding the shadow of Mark Sahib she placed a widemouthed glass near him. Observing her, Mark spoke to Gossainee jokingly, "I suppose you have kept the utensils from my previous visit separately in the *dhekal* room. We are after all *mlechas*[18], aren't we?"

Everybody laughed loudly. But Gossainee pretended not to hear and said, "I have got roasted rice, curd and newly-made jaggery syrup. Will you take some now? Gossain is reciting his prayers in the 'sandal room'. Will you wait for him?" Mark nodded his head in assent. After a while, everybody left the place, one by one. But Giribala remained standing there, leaning against the wooden pillar. Her hair was still wet. She wore a chemise of coarse cotton cloth, with a peculiar pattern of pleats round the neck. She had also put on a finely weaved *gatala,* which covered her shapely, swelling breasts. Mark raised his eyes and looked at her. Her fresh alluring beauty stirred his senses. He dropped his eyes immediately. He felt a mute pain in his heart, thinking about the tragedy of her youthful widowhood.

He said, "So, from tomorrow, I'll be your student. I've gathered so many manuscripts from South Bank. God alone knows when I'll be able to compile them for publication! I am sure you'll help me."

Giribala did not reply. From the fig tree, near the well, came the peculiar notes of an owlet bird...*ulu-lu-lu-lu*...Then they heard the foot-steps of the Gossain coming from the 'sandal room'...

Six

The widow Gossainee who lives all alone in this *sattra*, actually hails from a place called Pathaldia. She was married to the Gossain of this *sattra* who died young. Her disciples are scattered in various places like Goral, Bamundi, Majhkuchi and other villages.

This Gossainee is an exceptionally good-looking lady. She is so fair that even on the darkest night, her form can be discerned by alert eyes, looking like an ivory statue. Her complexion resembles that of the white-skinned soldiers who had camped nearby during World War II.

During the *daul*[1] festival, a group of *pandas*[2] had come from Jagannath Puri Temple in search of Brahmin widow devotees who wished to have a glimpse of Lord Jagannath. The Gossainee was the only widow from her *sattra* to have gone with these *pandas* and stayed at Jagannath Puri for a long period.

It is the month of December. The *bogori*[3] fruits have ripened and taken the colour of old *muga* silk. In the past so many years, at this time, the people of the *sattra* used to hear the sound of carts laden with sacks of paddy coming from Pathaldia. But over the last two or three years, their coming and going has become erratic. When her husband, the Gossain, was alive, the paddy sacks used to be stacked properly and measured out with meticulous care. Saru Gossainee was generally unaware of the passage of time. But when she heard the sound of bats in the *bogori* trees, she strained her ears and tried to catch the sound of the carts from Pathaldia. After the death of the Gossain, she had also noticed the irregularity in the arrival of carts with paddy sacks. Mahidhar *bapu,* the *jajmani* Brahmin from Haramdo, had warned the Gossainee that lately some strange men had been loitering around Pathaldia, carrying red flags in their hands. They went from one field to another and held meetings.

Saru Gossainee went to the *batghar* of her house and looked across at the *Adhikar's batghar.* It was the time of the day when Durga came to her for a chat or gossip but there was no sign of her. Had she again quarrelled with her sister-in-law? But when she fought with the Gossainee, her heated, loud words would be heard very clearly. But today only silence! Sometimes she would see her come rushing out with her clothes in disarray. Then she would stand just inside the *batghar* (she would never venture beyond it) and jabber away excitedly. In her stream of words, Gossainee would catch one word repeated often "brother-in-law"

"Will my in-laws leave me here in this hell? They'll surely send the youngest brother-in-law to take me back. Just you wait and see!"

...And so on! But till now Saru Gossainee had never seen anybody come from Chikarhati to fetch her....She wished Durga had come....She liked to talk and gossip with her. Saru Gossainee could understand Durga and sympathise with her. Now that Giribala had also joined the family, Durga's frustration and anger had increased.

She looked across again with hope, but no, there was

no sign of Durga or anyone else....Saru Gossainee's mind went back to Giribala. She had been such a pretty child! When she had her monthly period, she used to call Giribala. The child would run to the kitchen and bring out her afternoon meal....How small she was! And now she had come back a widow! What a terrible world it is! Tears welled up in her eyes. Suddenly a voice startled her.

"Mother! We have to get oil from Barihat."

Saru Gossainee adjusted the *mekhala* wrapped round her bosom and restored the *gatala* properly over her shoulders. Two or three veins in her soft, fair body trembled. The voice belonged to Mahidhar *bapu*.

She has observed for some time that this ripple of excitement would pass through her body whenever he came near her. She turned round and saw Mahidhar wearing the same *dhoti* that she had got for him when she had gone to Pathaldia to meet her disciples. He had a clean *chaddar* round his shoulders. Mahidhar was a handsome man with a thick mop of hair and straight nose. He had bright shining eyes. The glow came from within, like a luminous red partition illuminated by an oil lamp within. Only the other day, Durga had told her that people were gossiping about her and Mahidhar *bapu* even in Haramdo and Medhipara. They whispered that *Bapu* drew water from the well for her evening bath and that he even held a kerosene lamp for her when she went out in the night for her nature's call!

"You are really courageous, Saru Gossainee! No other Damodariya Gossainee has dared to stay alone like you after becoming a widow! Everyone knows that wild wolves come and sit on your verandah during the night," Durga had exclaimed.

Mahidhar was still there with an empty bottle in his hand. She said, "So, there's no oil?"

"No, how much oil do you think newly married couples bring when they come for your blessings? Only the other day, Mahajan's son and daughter-in-law had come. What a miserly quantity they offered!"

"Yes, you are right. The bottle didn't fill up even up to the neck! Now the round coins have almost disappeared. *Thagee*[4] is nowadays decorated with only flowery copper coins."

Saying so, Gossainee went inside the dark room where her bed lay. She went to the wooden post round which was tied a bamboo container with a jute rope and took out some money. Meanwhile Mahidhar went to the door and stood near the threshold. Without touching him, Saru Gossainee put the money on his palm. Like other days, today also, he looked at her wooden bed. It was covered with an old, tattered *endi chaddar*[5]. Gossainee wondered. Today too she could not fathom the meaning of his glance towards her bed.

It was almost a dark room, a dim light seeped through the gaps in the wall where the plaster had fallen off like decaying flesh. The reed partition, revealed beneath, looked like the carcass of a dead cow. Before the Gossain died, he had thought of selling some land and building a tin-roofed house. After his death, everything had changed. Life had become dark and gloomy. The ancestral Rangamati estate was infiltrated by Communists. The latter had influenced the tenant farmers to such an extent that when Mahidhar went there to collect the revenue, he had been chased away and had escaped being hurt by a hair's breadth.

Now, as Saru Gossainee stood there looking at the retreating back of Mahidhar, a kind of fear gripped her. Her throat felt dry and rigid like a wooden board. For some time now, this unknown fear had been haunting her and devouring her soul bit by bit. Who knows! What days are coming! If they refused to give her her share of paddy, what would she do?...If they resorted to violence and broke Mahidhar's bones, what would be her fate?...If they kill Mahidhar, what would she...? It was possible that a day might come when she, the Gossainee, the ruler of three *sattra* Gossain families, who once owned immensely vast lands would have to face hunger, starvation and death!...Saru Gossainee was the daughter of the Gossain of Dhakala. When the *teen sattra* Gossain of Amranga came to know about her, he was determined to have her as his daughter-in-law. Right from the time when she was five or six years old, the Amranga Gossain had wooed the Gossain of Dakhala with gifts of *endi* cloth, curd, paddy and jars of mustard oil, etc. The palanquin in which she finally came to her in-law's place, had magnificent handles of silver. She wore heavy gold *dugdugee*[6] and *galpata*[7] round her neck. But unfortunately she had to part with her gold *dugdugee* for the treatment of her sick husband by an unscrupulous doctor from Palasbari. This doctor overcharged her and always demanded payment in gold jewellery. At the same time he also insisted that he should be taken to and from Palasbari by the horse carriage of Didaruddin, the only carriage run by a Muslim in those days....

Saru Gossainee came out of the room and bolted the door. She looked up at the sky. It was covered with dark rain clouds. She must make her tea immediately. Otherwise, once the rain starts the half-collapsing kitchen shed will bring out the deadly cobra that has been lurking near about the kitchen for a long time now. One day its dry discarded moult was almost blown into her noon-time meal!

She went inside the kitchen and started blowing air

with a hollow bamboo tube into the heap of rice husks with its heart of smouldering ashes. Soon tongues of flame leapt out. She put a saucepan of water over the fire. This saucepan had been given her by one of her relatives from Manipur who had got it at Mirza from a Negro soldier. Saru Gossainee did not know that it had come from a military camp. Only recently when she had crossed the *batghar,* she had run into Kaltu, the mahout, carrying a similar saucepan! When she questioned him about it, she learned, to her horror, that these things belonged once upon a time to foreign soldiers! Kaltu then elaborated on how he had got hold of this saucepan. He used to take his elephants to the river for bathing and there he had struck up a friendship with a batman, who used to come with a bucket and collect leeches plucked off the elephant's body. These leeches were fried and eaten with great relish by the soldiers with their quota of rum! This batman presented Kaltu with a saucepan as a token of their friendship.

The Gossainee was startled out of her reveries by a loud knocking on the door. The water in the saucepan was boiling vigorously. She put down the pan and looked back. Durga was standing near the door: her hair was uncombed and wild. Even her *gatala* was not in its proper place. The upper portion of her bosom was visible. Saru Gossainee exclaimed, "What's happened to you? I was waiting for you in the afternoon... "

Durga said in a choked voice, "What! Haven't you heard? Giribala has been bitten by a snake! The Gossain has gone to visit his disciples. Indranath is not here either. He has gone to Rangamati, to take action against those communists." Saru Gosssainee cried out, "Bitten by snake! Oh, my God!"

"Why should it not bite her? That girl, to help that Christian, roams about all the villages in search of manuscripts. She has left out none! In the *dhekal* of Kallapara's *jajamani* Brahmin, she climbed into the attic in search of manuscripts. There, that nasty snake attacked her. Those people had pleaded with her not to go into the attic. But that girl! Would she listen?"

"What kind of snake? Is it poisonous?"

"How can anybody know? It disappeared...Gossainee has sent for you. Come with me"

Saru Gossainee sprinkled some water on the glowing embers of the cooking fire. She closed and bolted the door of the kitchen and with Durga by her side, walked out with quick, swift steps. They crossed the *batghar* and entered the other *batghar* of Gossain *Mahaprabhu* with its tin roof crenellated at the eaves.

In the courtyard, there was a commotion. A small crowd had gathered. Seeing Saru Gossainee, the Gossainee cried, gesticulating with her hands, "Do something! Save her life! Who can save her from death? Oh, quick! Do something."

The Gossainee could not contain herself and burst into tears. She sobbed her heart out. One of Giribala's legs was tied tightly with a jute string and the foot with the snake-bite wound was kept immersed in a pan of water. Giribala's eyes were wide open. Her face was blank and expressionless.

The Gossainee spoke in between sobs.

"The doctor of Barihat came and saw her...and then went back. Said he didn't have the proper instruments. Told us to take her to Palasbari hospital...Oh, my God! Who will take her? One elephant has gone mad! It has broken loose and is roaming about ferociously...They are all afraid to take her to Palasbari..."

"What! Has the elephant gone mad?"

"Yes, yes! That rogue *makhana*[8] has eaten its own liquid flow with grass."

Saru Gossainee exclaimed with dismay.

"Oh, no! Then it is very serious! Did the elephant eat mud?"

"It would have been far better if he had eaten mud. Then inserting cloves under his ears would have cured him!"

"Yes! Two cloves under each ear should have been enough."

One voice rose from the crowd.

"That young elephant from *Mahaprabhu's dohar.* He has fallen into a pit! Anything can happen!"

Gossainee cried out.

"Now there's none available for taking her to Palasbari hospital...please do something..."

Gossainee became almost hysterical and shouted again and again.

"Come and see! Oh, look at her! She has turned green! Oh, do something! For God's sake, help her!..."

Saru Gossainee went to the prostrate girl and touched her hand. She looked up quickly and said.

"No no! She hasn't turned green! She hasn't been bitten by a poisonous snake. Perhaps it was a *shalike dhutia*[9] snake."

Someone said, "Who knows what kind of snake it was? The other day, the fisherman's daughter had been alive for three days after a snake-bite. People say that the Gossain kept her alive by reading that book, *Dhatu Tamreshwari*[10]. Who will recite from that book now? God knows, where he has kept it!"

Another man shouted from the crowd, "Nobody here knows Sanskrit! To recite that book, one of the *jajmani*

Brahmins from Haramdo has to be called."

Now the Gossainee became more hysterical, almost frantic. She paced the verandah to and fro and wrung her hands repeatedly. He hair came undone. Dishevelled, distraught, she continued pacing the verandah. Meanwhile, some more curious onlookers were joining the crowd, jostling each other to have a closer look.

Just then, Mark Sahib thrust himself through the crowd and appeared before the Gossainee. The latter shrank back and stood some distance away from him. Even in this tense moment, she had not forgotten that he was a low-caste *mlecha,* a Christian! Mark said, "Please give me a sharp knife...Quick! And leave me alone with the girl...Please...."

For a moment the Gossainee looked perplexed and uncertain. She looked here and there, she was still shaken and her limbs trembled.

This is the most auspicious room in the Gossain's mansion. Here he keeps the wooden sandals of his ancestors. The Gossainee glanced around again. Nobody was objecting or protesting.

Even the disciples standing near her had kept quiet. They are not resisting this Christian's words. It is the most crucial moment...she must decide fast...time is ticking by...

One by one, all the people left the room. Even the opium-eater, who always followed Mark Sahib carrying his old manuscripts, was not allowed to stay. Sanyasi Sahib closed the door.

Most of the people stood outside and waited, with anxious eyes fixed on the closed door. The Gossainee could not stand still. She paced the verandah restlessly.

The sky was overcast. Black clouds were gathering fast. The clash of distant thunder came nearer and became louder. Suddenly the window of the closed room was flung open by the force of whipping wind! The Gossainee rushed to the open window. She peeped in. The mustard oil lamp near the wooden sandals was still burning. What was the Sanyasi Sahib doing? She was shocked! She saw him sucking blood from the wound, cut open with the knife, where the snake had struck. Then his head came up. He spat out the blood on one side and again bent down to suck some more blood. The *gamucha* round his neck had become red with blood.

But Giribala? She is still reclining there motionless...And her clothes! My goodness! Her *markin* cloth chemise is almost...The Gossainee looked away in shame and distress. But her sharp eyes had noticed that this Christian—engrossed in sucking out the poisoned blood—had no hand in the disarrayed condition of her clothes. She blocked the window, holding the bars with clenched fists. No other person should peep inside and see what she had seen! It was a scene so undignified, so sorrowful! Giribala! Even after all this pain of the wound being cut and blood sucked...Why is she lying there without stirring, motionless...like the dead? Oh, God, why? She is still unconscious? No, no! she is conscious! Her eyelids looking yellow like a hornet's body in the light of the mustard oil lamp. Yes, there! She saw them flickering!

The Gossainee stood there like a watch-dog. She will not allow anybody to come near the window and see the scene inside.

Giribala did not flinch with pain when the wound was cut open by Mark Sahib. Oh! My God! Is it possible? For a moment the light from the oil lamp flickered brightly. She was still lying there, absolutely still. Was she dead?...Gossainee strained her eyes in the dim light and watched tensely through the window. Was she still alive?...No, no! She is not dead! Her eyes are shining like glow-worms, but her lips...they are still like wood!

The Gossainee's mind was in a turmoil. Giribala, her own daughter, was lying stretched out, almost naked, as if she was sleeping in the arms of that *mlecha*......Oh, my God! What a loathsome sight she has witnessed! Oh, Lord! Forgive me!.....Only a few steps away, the sacred sandals of their dead elders are kept for worship!.....She turned her eyes away with revulsion....Oh! What fate! What a fate that a Damodariya Gossainee had to tolerate a Christian inside her house! Will she have to go through the rituals for atonement for this sin?....

The Gossainee came away from the window and sat down near the *tulsi* plant in the courtyard. She remembered that, in the past, she herself had given moral strictures to so many of her disciples. They came from various places like Haramdo, Rajabaha and Bamundi and so on. Her forefathers had left behind scores of these religious norms and strictures. If a low-caste man pulled the hair of a Brahmin, he must go through twelve *dhanu prayaschita*[11]; for touching the corpse of a Brahmin, he must observe *chandrayana prayaschita;* and if a carpenter or a washerman or a dancer broke the sacred thread of a Brahmin, he had to pay a fine of fifty-three *maunds*[12] of shells....Oh, she has preserved in her memory all these norms and strictures! How can she forget them? The book containing these rules is lying with the family priest. Only the other day she had given her ruling to a Gossain who had committed the sin of eating the flesh of a deer killed with a gun....What should she do now?....Her head started reeling and she felt as if a haze of smoke had covered her eyes.

After some time, she looked up and saw Guimeni standing near her. Guimeni, her companion of many years, who shared tobacco with her.

Guimeni said, "What are you brooding about? That *Sanyasi Sahib* has already come out of the room. It is raining now. Come inside, the rain is quite heavy and you'll get wet."

They ran to the verandah. Mark was standing there. He said, "It won't be necessary to take Giribala to the hospital at Palasbari. I have taken out all the poison. It wasn't much, luckily the snake wasn't very poisonous."

He showed them the *gamucha* covered with spots of poisonous blood he had sucked out from Giribala's leg. Then he took it to the end of the verandah, struck a match and set it on fire. He came back to the Gossainee and pointing to the crowd of spectators still standing there, said. "Tell them to go away. It's going to rain some more...and don't worry, she'll be alright now."

The Gossainee exclaimed, "What kind of a snake was it? Was it a cobra? A *machuagom,* or *hulungagum* or *mairgum?* These cobras are always lurking about in the *dhekal* of those Brahmins, where they store all kinds of things, sacks of rice husk, broomsticks and God knows what else...and this girl went to such places in search of manuscripts just for your sake."

Sanyasi sahib bowed his head and said. "Don't worry so much. She is now out of danger. Please go and take your bath."

The Gossainee was even then unconvinced and restless. She went to the *batghar* and stood there waiting for Indranath. There were claps of thunder, a storm was fast approaching....Now there will be more rain. Will it be possible to bring a doctor from Palasbari?....She was now drenched by the rain, but she did not leave the *batghar.* Meanwhile, after bidding farewell to the Gossainee and Durga, Saru Gossainee ran through the pouring rain to the *batghar* of her house and disappeared inside.

* * *

As soon as Saru Gossainee reached her bedroom, she removed the wet *gatala* and *mekhala* (she was not in the habit of wearing a blouse or a chemise), dried her body with a *gamucha* and put on a dry *mekhala*. Meanwhile the the rain had increased. Over the noise of the rain, she heard the loud trumpeting of the frenzied elephant, Jagannnath. Will he attack that cow elephant from the *dhar?* Yes, yes! She could hear the calls of two elephants from that direction. Saru Gossainee was now worried about Mahidhar *bapu*, as he had to take the way near the elephants' corral. Probably he did not know that the rogue elephant has entered the field....Oh, my Lord! Let him reach safe and sound!....The rain still poured down relentlessly. The roof was leaking in several places. Soon there was water everywhere on the floor.

The old *mahout* had once told her that if the elephant ate his own liquid flow with grass, madness would grip him very badly and he would uproot even big trees with great ease. In this state he could be very dangerous.

"Mahidhar *bapu*, Mahidhar *bapu*!" Saru Gossainee opened the door and came out on the verandah. She felt agitated and restless, almost frenzied. She stepped out in the courtyard, heedless of the rain, and began walking towards the *batghar.* She remembered the day when she had first met Mahidhar. That day she was having her period. She had remained inside the house, taking only unboiled milk at meal-time. All of a sudden she had heard someone calling from the courtyard. Who had dared to come straightaway into the courtyard and call out to her like that? She wondered...She came out and saw a well-built, muscular youth. She had never seen such a robust man before in the South Bank. She pulled up her *gatala*. Her long hair fell gracefully over her shoulders and bosom. He introduced himself saying that his name was Mahidhar Sharma Pathak, that he was at Datara before he came to Haramdo, that his wife had died at childbirth and he was now alone.

Gossainee asked him. "How long has your wife been dead?"

"It will be two months this full moon day."

"What are you doing now?"

"Why? Didn't you hear anything about those *jajmani* Brahmins?"

"What?"

"There were arguments and quarrels between us about who should serve the *jajmans*. They even tore off each other's sacred threads! We observed mourning for this terrible sin and repeated the *Gayatri* one hundred times. We were left without work in a wretched condition. That's why I have come to you, Saru Gossainee. On the way, while crossing the Jagalia, I met Saru Gossain Indranath. He said that you should keep a man to help you as the times are bad. These days, who has proper regard and respect for Gossains? Really the times are very bad. I have come to serve you, Saru Gossainee. The tenant farmers have turned into foxes. Only the other day...It happened before my own eyes. A potter's son beat up a Brahmin and injured him badly over some land deed. The people wanted to bring him for judgment before the *panchayat* but they were afraid to do it. They could not make him attend the meeting. He did not care for anyone and moved about with a Nepali dagger in his hand."

Saru Gossainee was stunned. In the meantime, the latter removed his canvas shoes, dusted and cleaned them and kept them aside. Then he sat down on a bamboo mat, which was lying there in the courtyard and waited for Saru Gossainee who had gone inside the house. When she came out, the fragrance of *jabakusum* oil in her hair permeated the air.

She said, "I am not afraid of anything, nor I am afraid of staying alone. But there is a need for a Brahmin who can go and collect taxes from my Marabhitha land and other lands, and who can also accompany me when I visit my disciples. But how much can I give you for your services? When the Gossain was alive, it was altogether a different matter. There was plenty to spare. Now I don't even get any paddy from Marabhitha. They don't come anymore with the revenue due to me. Same is the case with my Pathaldia lands. And my land at Garal.....for the last two years I haven't heard anything from the tenants there. My condition is so bad that I think the government men will come soon to auction my house and other properties for not paying taxes."

"Yes, I can understand. What can you expect from these opium-addicted peasants of South Bank? Don't worry, Saru Gossainee. I will sleep in the room near the *dhekal* that is kept aside for the rehearsals of *jatra* parties. As for clothes and other needs, it will be provided for when I go with you to visit your disciples." Mahidhar clucked in sympathy.

Saru Gossainee's eyes were drawn towards that room near the *dhekal*. It was in a very bad state. The mud plaster on the walls had fallen off in several places exposing the cane framework inside. The roof was probably leaking. She could see the drawings of Rama and Ravana made on the walls by the boys of the *jatra* parties....But it was quite close to her own bedroom....

* * * *

Now many years have passed and Mahidhar *bapu* has become her right-hand man. In good days or bad, at times of crises or otherwise, he has become a part of her life. Once he was taken to bed with cholera. Saru Gossainee nursed him day and night without sparing a thought for herself...But her conscience pricked her time and again...whatever is happening, is it proper and correct for a Gossain's widow? This feeling remained with her like a second skin. She could not cast it off.

It was still raining. She walked through the rain, completely drenched, to the *bokul* tree just near the courtyard fence bordering the road to the *sattra.* She could now hear the elephants quite clearly in spite of the din made by the rain....What if Mahidhar gets killed? Can she survive after his death? No, no! Never!....Her eyes filled with tears. She stood under the *bokul* tree, transfixed, as if a powerful force was holding her there!

Suddenly she heard footsteps. Some people were coming this way. Oh, my God! What will she do now? How can she run back to the house? And her *mekhala* soaked with water....it was sticking to her legs....how could she run now?

They are coming nearer, fast. She could hear Indranath's voice.

"It appears that the mad elephant has attacked and

killed that cow elephant from the *dohar*."

"With whom was she taken in the *dohar*?"

"With Chikarhathi's Gossain. Her leg is infested with *karhi*. We had to feed her milk with a bottle. Durga made boiled rice and gave it with banana trunk."

Suddenly Indranath exclaimed.

"Who is that standing there? Under the *bokul* tree?"

The other man shouted.

"Run! The mad elephant may come and trample you! Who's standing there?"

Indranath flashed his torch-light on the *bokul* tree. He was shocked to see the figure of a woman with long hair, completely drenched in the rain. He shouted.

"Who's standing there? In this storm and heavy rain?"

The woman had covered her face with her *gatala*. Indranath could not make out who she was. She said in a feeble voice, "Can't you see? I have come out for..."

Indranath and his companion resumed walking. He wondered...that fair complexion...and the long hair. That woman, somehow, appeared very familiar. But who was she? Was it some new arrival in the village? No, no! It couldn't be...that complexion...No other woman had a complextion like that in the whole of South Bank. It must be Saru Gossainee...Saru Gossainee!

Strange! Why has she come out here, near the road, when she has her own courtyard? Strange!...Strange indeed!....Indranath saw a group of people standing near the *baatghar* with lanterns in their hands. Some of them shouted.

"Has anybody given the report to the Forest Office?"

"A pair of men have gone to the ranger at Rani."

"We have heard that the Commissioner will send his

paltan tomorrow!"

An opium-eater who had come with Indranath said, "What! The Commissioner will come himself with a gun to shoot the mad elephant?"

"Keep quiet, you idiot!"

The opium-eater said loudly, "The *ojha* from Dakhala has taken away the liquid flow from the elephant's ear. He'll never be cured. After he's shot dead, I'll take his tusks."

"You bastard! Shut up! Who is that *ojha* from Dakhala?"

"Didn't you see him? He was loitering around the elephant's yard for many days....With a bald head like a dried-up gourd. He knew in advance that this would happen! Didn't you hear him sing?"

In the *batghar*, Indranath took off his wet shoes and removed the water inside. Then he squeezed the water out from the end of his *dhoti* and wiped his face dry.

The same thought tormented him like a deer trapped in a net. Who was that woman? Was it Saru Gossainee? But why was she standing there under the *bokul* tree on a rainy night? Perhaps he should have gone back and inquired. But...Why was she so elusive?

Lightning flashed and with a loud clap of thunder, it began raining even more heavily than ever. Suddenly Indranath saw the figure of a man, soaked, running towards the *batghar* of Saru Gossainee's house. Then a moment later he was shocked...the house...that woman was Saru Gossainee!

Seven

Just before dawn, when Durga went out for the open air toilet, she heard a bus coming to a halt on the road to Loharghat. It struck her that probably it was the *pandas* of Jagannath Puri and Prayag come to pick up the Brahmin widows from South Bank who desired to go on a pilgrimage to these holy places.

Time and again, Durga had beseeched the Gossainee, her sister-in-law, to give her the money for a trip to Jagannath Puri and Prayag. She had even assured her that her dead husband's brother would return this loan. On their part, there was no dearth of money as the Chikarhati Gossain had a profitable crop from his lands that year.

...Durga saw the *pandas* coming out of Saru Gossainee's *batghar.* They crossed the road and stood under the portico where the elephant's equipment was kept. Gossainee was also there on the verandah, with a tray of betel nuts and *pan* leaves in her hand. The *pandas* bowed to her respectfully. A *bandha* provided some *mats* for them to sit down.

The thin *panda* with a foxy face spoke in broken Assamese.

"Mother, last year we had taken seven widows from

South Bank for pilgrimage to the holy Prayag and Jagannath Puri. But this year only two Gossainees are ready to go with us...."

From his manner of speaking and accent, he appeared to be from Upper Assam.

The Gossainee said, "Yes, I know. But what can you expect? Almost the whole of South Bank is in the grip of the opium habit."

"We thought that Saru Gossainee would go with us this time. But she has some problem about collecting revenue from her lands. After the Gossain's death, even the flow of paddy has declined. Moreover she has already gone on the pilgrimage once."

At this moment, Durga came and stood before the *pandas*. They looked at her expectantly. Covering her head with her *gatala,* she said to the Gossainee.

"Give me the money for this holy journey. Don't worry, my brother-in-law will return it to you. I am feeling weak and feeble and my head reels sometimes. Before anything happens, I want to immerse my husband's ashes in the sacred Ganga."

The *pandas* interjected eagerly, "We'll take only one hundred and twenty rupees. Once we cross the Brahmaputra, our responsibility for the lady begins as soon as we reach Amingaon."

Like hunters closing in on their quarry, they persisted excitedly.

"Don't worry, Mother. This way or that way if anything falls short, we'll make it up.....and we'll take very good care of her! We had carried the old Gossainee of Autal on our backs all the way. She never took food from anybody's hand. For her, all the others were untouchables and unclean!....We'll handle everything. You won't have to worry at all! Praise be to Lord Jagannath!"

The Gossainee stood silent for a while. Then abruptly, muttering something to herself, she turned and went to the small room where she always smoked her *hookah.* Guimeni was waiting on the verandah, in anticipation of a puff and some gossip with the Gossainee.

The three *pandas* began talking amongst themselves.

"I think Gossainee has gone inside to think it over."

"Yes, yes! Certainly!"

Then they looked at Durga and added, "For the Gossainee, one hundred and twenty rupees is a very small sum of money—isn't it? When your *sattra* has a thousand acres of land? We have heard that the Gossain is visiting his disciples. When he comes back, he'll bring cartloads of gifts and revenue! Baba Vaishwanath will definitely fulfill your desires."

Durga kept silent.

"Last time also you had made plans to go with us. You said your brother-in-law would send you. And you had spoken to the Gossainee also, hadn't you?"

Again Durga did not utter a word in reply.

"We hear that your in-laws are very rich and possess vast lands. Don't they look after...."

But Durga did not heed their words and walked away, disgruntled, straight to the Gossainee's small smoking room. She halted outside the door. Her nostrils were quivering and her bosom heaved with suppressed sobs. Then striking at the door with her fists, she shouted, "My mother had given you a pair of gold earrings on her death-bed for my marriage. You never gave it to me! Where's it? I want that pair of earrings now! Right now!"

The Gossainee replied from behind the closed door in a bitter, spiteful tone.

"You slut! Who has given you those gold earrings? Did your wretched husband give you anything? Why did you leave your house and come here?"

Hearing the loud exchange of words, a small crowd gathered near the verandah. The old mother of Kaltu the *mahout,* who had come to draw water from the Gossain's well, tried to pacify Durga.

"Calm down! Compose yourself! Why do you want to pick up a quarrel with the Gossainee? As it is...nobody has come from your husband's place to take you back."

The other women added.

"Yes, yes! That's true! Nobody has come from her in-laws."

"And now you're living under the umbrella of the Gossainee."

"You should listen to her and try to live in peace."

Durga felt drained. A cold tremor passed through her body. She stood frozen like a statue. Her arrogance, her anger turned to ashes.

...Yes, why haven't they come? Three years have passed...and nobody has come to take her back to her husband's place...not even a word from them! Why, why? Once, long back, a cartload of jack fruits and two big clay pots of curds had arrived from Chikarhati, but since then they had not cared to find out whether she was alive or dead.

Durga heard another voice from the crowd.

"Your share of land from your in-laws rightfully belongs to you. It's high time you arranged for a lawyer and claimed it."

Durga flared up and shouted at the speaker.

"Don't poke your nose into my affairs! Can a daughter of this house go to the *kacheri* at Gauhati? You wait and see! They'll come one day and take me back to Chikarhati with honour and respect."

Overcome by emotion, her voice trembled. She ran to the far side of the verandah and crouched there covering her face with her *gatala*.

Silence fell over the crowd gathered there. Only the noise of the *hookah* could be heard from the smoking room of the Gossainee. She had remained inside with Guimeni, unperturbed, calmly puffing at the pipe of her *hookah.*

An old woman left the crowd and came near Durga. Her *mekhala* had become untied. She just held it loosely with her hands. Her two shrivelled breasts like dried-up bananas were visible but she was absolutely unconcerned about it. She spoke to Durga.

"*Maichana,* listen, to get your property you must go back and stay in your husband's village."

Another woman interrupted her.

"You're like one of the berries in a tray. With every movement of the tray, it rolls here and there. You should be very firm, like Saru Gossainee. Just look at her, how she is managing her lands herself with a firm grip on the rod of authority!"

Durga ignored her and marched towards the sacred sandal room. All the women stared at her dumbfounded and at the same time wondered what she would do next. Durga entered the room and in a fit of rage pulled out a wooden box from one of shelves lining the wall. She dragged the box to the threshold of the door. Some women rushed towards Durga and attempted to hold her hand. But they drew back suddenly, realising that they could not touch her—

after all she was a Gossainee. They cried out in unison.

"Oh you daughter-in-law of Chikarhati! What are you doing? Why are you dragging that box out?"

"Don't tell me anything! I am going to Saru Gossainee."

One woman from the crowd shouted.

"Wait for a moment, *maichana*! The box is too heavy for you.....Tell Birohu *bandha* to carry it."

Birohu was, all this while, watching with wide eyes. When he heard the woman's words, he looked sheepish and hesitant. He glanced timidly towards the Gossainee's smoking room. But the door was closed. He went up to the box with dragging, reluctant steps, lifted it up and balanced it over his head. Durga started walking with quick steps towards the *batghar*. Birohu followed with the box. The entire crowd now fell in line behind the *bandha,* excited and bursting with curiosity to find out what would happen next.

Meanwhile Saru Gossainee had been watching the scene from the window of her house. When she saw Durga, Birohu *bandha* and the big crowd of women following them, she came out immediately on the verandah. As soon as they came into the courtyard, Birohu dumped the box on the ground and fled from the place, as he was terribly afraid that the Gossainee might see him.

Durga ran up to Saru Gossainee, slumped down near her feet and burst into tears. Her long hair had come undone. At this moment, this forty-year-old woman looked like a small girl.

Meanwhile the women who had followed Durga, whispered among themselves.

"My, my! Nowadays even Gossainee ladies fight like cats and dogs!"

"It does happen. When one falls into the pit of

unhappiness, everyone behaves in the same manner."

"There was a time when the Gossainee of Pathaldia and Bamundi never raised their voices. Now one can hear them right up to the *batghar* of their houses."

Saru Gossainee came out swiftly and scolded the women.

"That's enough! All of you go home now! When I call you for pounding rice, you women are too busy, now you have all the time in the world to meddle in the Gossainee's life."

She then went quickly to the entrance of the courtyard and pushed aside the bamboo pole for the women to go out. One by one, they went out. Saru Gossainee got a whiff of bad odour, like that of a rotting jack-fruit from the bodies of the women as they passed by. She covered her nose immediately with her *gatala*.

Saru Gossainee replaced the bamboo pole and turned back into the courtyard. Now only the maid from Rajabaha remained. She was sweeping the backyard. Durga was still squatting near the wooden box, sobbing loudly. Saru Gossainee came up to her and said gently.

"Durga, it's our fate that we are born as women. We should learn to lead our lives with patience and tolerance. As it is, our lives have been shattered by the death of our husbands. Now tell me, why have you brought this box here and what does it contain?"

Durga stopped sobbing and remained silent for a while. Then she said.

"There's one gold *dugdugee*[1] weighing four *tolas.*[2] Then there's a *chandrahaar*[3] that the late Gossain got as a gift from his disciples...and a pair of gold *phutis*...The rest are my clothes."

Saru Gossainee queried, "So all your ornaments are made of gold?"

"Yes."

Saru Gossainee's voice showed a trace of reluctance mixed with irritation.

"Then why did you bring them here? It was much safer with the Gossainee in the manor house."

"What else could I do? These ornaments are the only things left which I can sell and raise money to go to the holy Ganga for immersing my husband's ashes. That's my only desire left now."

Saru Gossainee felt sad and also anxious for Durga. She said.

"Listen, Durga. My house is ramshackle and unsafe. The roof is leaking. How can I muster enough courage to keep your valuables here with me?"

Durga remained silent. Saru Gossainee continued.

"There's a large attic in the Gossain's manor house. I would rather advise you to take the box back to the Gossainee and keep it in the attic. It'll be safe there."

She held out her hands to Durga.

"Look at my hands! No gold bangles or rings. Nor do I have any. They were gone long back when the Gossain died in the fire-works with his brain clouded by the fumes of opium....Mahidhar will come any moment now. I'll send back the box with him."

Durga flared up and shouted.

"Don't you dare to send it back to that ogress, the scheming witch! I consider you as my own and trust you. You must keep my box in your house."

Saru Gossainee was shocked.

"*Chikau, chikau*! How can you call your own elder sister-in-law an ogress and a witch! Your mind is in the throes of a terrible misunderstanding. Come, drink some cold water, you'll feel much better."

She made Durga get up and walked her to the well. It was an unlined well. Saru Gossainee could not get it plastered from inside with cement, due to lack of money. It was surrounded by an old, broken bamboo fence. The bamboos had become green and black with moss.

She drew water from the well with the help of an old brass pot tied to a thick jute rope. Pouring the water into Durga's cupped hands, she said, "I still think the box shouldn't be kept here. Anyway let Mahidhar become....I am thinking of growing paddy myself on ten *bighas* of my land. Those tenant farmers on my Pathaldia land refuse to vacate it. It's so difficult to get things done. Mahidhar says he can drive them out by paying them some money. Alas! We are passing through such bad times!"

But her words were falling on deaf ears. Durga was still sobbing and wiping off tears constantly with her *gatala*. Saru Gossainee went to the backyard and called out to the maid from Rajabaha,—"Go and see whether Mahidhar *bapu* is out there on the road. He was talking to Indranath Gossain. Tell him to come here immediately." The maid replied. "But Mother, he was here, listening to both of you."

"What! He was here?"

"Yes, Mother."

"Then why didn't you call me?"

"Where was the time? He listened to your talk for some time, standing behind the wall. Then he left immediately afterwards."

Saru Gossainee laughed and said, "I am sure he has been successful in removing those tenants from my Pathaldia land."

Durga implored her, "I beg you! Keep the box with you, inside your room on the wooden *peerah*. If I lose the gold ornaments, there will be nothing left in my life. For me even bright days will be like dark and fearful nights."

Saru Gossainee remained silent for a while. Then she said grudgingly, "Alright, you keep the box under my cot. But take your meal with me today. Then you must go back to the Gossainee in the manor house. When you have already lost everything, what's the use of pride or propriety? Your greatest mistake was to come here with Indranath from Chikarhati, forsaking your husband's place. You don't have any children. Then why should your in-laws part with your share of the land and property? And for all that, you will have to go to the court at Gauhati. Is it possible for you? Can you do it?"

Durga replied, "Indranath will help me. He has great love and respect for me....Till now, none of the Damodariya Gossainees have stepped into the court at Gauhati. But I won't have to do it. I am sure they will come one day and take me back to Chikarhati."

Saru Gossainee wanted to say something more to Durga but she restrained herself. Just then she had seen the *pandas* of Jagannath Puri on the road, coming from the direction of Haramdo.

* * * *

The sun was dissolving behind the Matiapahar, in a yellow hue in the sky like the yellow flowers of a gourd creeper. The soft silken light that covered the trees and shrubs suddenly gave way to darkness.

Saru Gossainee and Durga were sitting on the verandah after their evening meal. Both were waiting anxiously for a call from the Gossain's manor house, hoping fervently that the old Gossainee would come herself or send somebody to take back Durga to the house. But there was no sign from across the road. Probably Giribala was engrossed with that Christian, Mark Sahib, in some old crumbling manuscript.

Durga wiped her face with her *gatala* and said, "Indranath has gone to Baghjap to meet his disciples. Had he been here, I would not have been left here till the late hours of the evening."

Her eyes filled with tears. But then suddenly, she saw a ray of hope. It was time for Indranath to return from Bolo's place. As soon as he found out about her from the Gossainee, he would come running to fetch her. Yes! He would certainly do so! He would not allow a daughter of the Gossain's house to stay outside even for one night.

It was past midnight. Saru Gossainee and Durga were squatting side by side on the verandah. Overcome by sleep, Saru Gossainee's head would sometimes rest on her drawn-up knees or sometimes incline against the wall behind. Durga, still awake, was assailed by anxiety and fear for Indranath.....He is the future *adhikar* of the *sattra*, and what does he do?—Plays card at Bolo's den all afternoon and late into the night! That mad elephant is roaming about. What if he comes out on the road in the dead of the night and attacks him? God forbid! Let him come soon, safe and sound!

Saru Gossainee was now sound asleep, resting her head on her knees. Out on the Matiapahar, jackals foraging behind bamboo groves suddenly started howling. An owl flew abruptly from the well and settled down on the roof of the rice husking shed. It stared at Durga with its big round eyes. What will she do now? She left the verandah and walked to the *batghar.* That inauspicious bird, the owl, also followed her and perched itself on the roof of the *batghar.* An elusive, strange fear turned her blood cold. Remorse gnawed at her mind. Why had she come away like a fool? Pride, honour, position—at this had no meaning in her life now....What should she do now? Go to the temple and sleep there? Durga stood inside the *batghar*, confused and undecided about the next step. Then suddenly her eyes caught the movement of a light, probably a lantern, in the Gossain's house.

In great excitement, Durga went running to Saru Gossainee and woke her up, crying out, "Look, who's coming! Didn't I tell you that Indranath would definitely come?"

Just then, Indranath entered the courtyard, carrying a lantern in his hand. Saru Gossainee stood up in a flutter, re-arranged her *gatala* and smoothed out her crumpled *mekhala*. Her fair complexion, like that of the British sahibs, glowed in the light of the lantern. She said, "It's good that you've come, Indranath. Take her away. She must stay with your mother, under her shelter. She was quite hysterical when she come here. Now she's all right."

Indranath walked out on the road. Covering her head with her *gatala*, Durga followed him. That persistent owl too took off from the *batghar* and flying over them, settled down in the portico where the elephant's equipment were stored.

Saru Gossainee closed the gate. Then picking up the clay mustard oil lamp, she went to the *dhekal* where a hanging oil lamp shed its dim light on the bed. She stood for a while watching Mahidhar, fast asleep on the bed. The hair on his bare chest shore in the pale glow of the clay lamp, as if someone had just washed them with the clean water of the Jagalia. Saru Gossainee stood still, watching. She had never before seen such a robust physique in the South Bank.

Why didn't he enquire whether she had taken her meal or not? Why didn't he ask, "Gossainee, what is worrying you so much? Tell me, I'll try to sort out your problem whatever it is?" She glanced again at Mahidhar's body. The colour of his skin now resembled the dazzling brown colour of the mud on the bank of the Jagalia river. She suddenly longed to touch him.....Ah! That was Shri Ramchandra himself, sleeping there after a day's exhausting march through the forest during his exile! There! The *pokhraj* ring in his sacred thread sparkled in the glow of the lamp!

Saru Gossainee stood there, watching. Should she step inside? Go a little nearer? A step or two closer?

All of a sudden an owl swooped over her head screeching loudly, and landed on the roof of the *dhekal*!

Saru Gossainee returned to the verandah. She felt like a wounded prey. Self-reproach mixed with sorrow overwhelmed her whole being, mentally and physically. It is a grave sin! It will plunge her into the fires of hell and burn her completely! Oh, God, forgive me! Forgive me!

She could hear the shrill cry of the inauspicious bird perched on the roof of the *dhekal*. She looked up at the sky. She uttered to herself. "That inauspicious owl! It has come inside! Oh, Lord, forgive me!"

She went inside her room. The big wooden box of Durga confronted her with its solid presence. She hastily got hold of an old tattered shawl and draped it over the box. She felt suddenly quite weak, as if drained of all her energy. She went slowly to the bed and lay down.

Eight

All the old Congress workers had become Home Guards or prohibition officers of the opium addiction eradication camp. They dressed always in khaki shirts and shorts and carried long staves in their hands. Some of them went round and probed every nook and corner of the *sattra* till they had, with great difficulty, compiled a list of all the men and women who were hopelessly addicted to opium. At times they even acted as spies to ferret out the opium smuggler's operations. The amendment of the Opium Act, 1949, had given wide powers to the Home Guards and the prohibition officers. They could enter any hut or house without warrant.

After the peculiar circumstances of his meeting with Eliman that night, Indranath had made a firm resolve to help the Home Guards in throwing a net over that opium smuggling Brahmin from Cooch Behar.

He must act fast! The old woman had, so far, managed to hide from Eliman's father the truth about his daughter's coming of age. If that rotten Brahmin from Cooch Behar happened to get hold of this information, he would immediately go to the father with *telar bhar*[1]. Indranath's memory was haunted by Eliman's beauty. His whole being was suffused with this lingering mision.

An opportunity suddenly presented itself! It was the month of July. Indranath had started for the den of Bolo's card players on his cycle. It was drizzling. All of a sudden Indranath heard a trumpet. It was the rogue elephant which had escaped from its chains! He could make out from its sound that it was the tusker and not the *makhana,* as the people thought. This elephant had been brought to the *sattra* from a *dohar.* Indranath had a soft corner for him. It looked so masculine and strong! It had been shaping up well in its training period. Ah! Such a powerful trumpet! As if a thousand conch shells had sung in unison! No, no! This full-throated angry roar cannot be compared with the sound of conch shells. This was the sound of not only anger but defiance and raging destruction! He could hear bamboos being trampled upon and crushed.

The Forest Department official from Rani had come to investigate. The Gauhati police has also visited and taken away their report. It was said that this rogue elephant had already destroyed two paddy fields but it had not, as yet, taken any life. But any moment, anything could happen and the Commissioner might even issue orders for shooting the elephant. Meanwhile expert noosemen from Bangara, Datara and Chapathuri had tried to catch him but had failed. In the elephant corral, one exorcist had even tried his mysterious spell to subdue the beast!

In the morning, his mother, the Gossainee, had warned him.

"That rogue elephant is roaming nearby. Don't go out to Bolo's den tonight. Please, son! Promise me!"

With affectionate amusement, Indranath had replied, "Ah! All the elephants know me well. They'll recognise me and leave me alone!"

"But, my son, an elephant in frenzy forgets even his master. He is not in his senses to recognise anybody."

He had told her sarcastically, "Do you remember, mother, his first tusk cutting ceremony? From that piece of tusk, I had made buttons for my *panjabi*[2]. I will wear that *panjabi* today! Do you recollect how well he used to behave? He learned the different commands so fast? Those words for sitting down—'*dhat*', '*chamavaith*', '*teravaith*'!"

The Gossainee retorted in anger, "Leave that nonsense! As if that animal will recognise your precious buttons!"

Indranath did not wait any longer. Before his mother could say anything more, he took his cycle and proceeded to the *batghar* as if possessed by an unknown compulsion....By a strong desire to see again the rays of light from the oil lamp burning behind the flimsy, dilapidated mud and reed wall......

The rain had just stopped. Droplets of water were falling from the leaves of the *bhatara* bushes and *katahi jamun* trees. Some drops fell on Indranath. The arum plants had grown vigorously in the rain, the broad wet leaves glistening. Small water snakes had come out and frogs were leaping here and there. Last year, in similar weather, he had stopped going to Bolo's place. But now there was this strange compulsion! Also, lately, some of the volunteers of the opium addiction eradication camp had started visiting Bolo's den. It was a good opportunity to meet them and talk to them.

The leper was there in his usual place. He was squatting, his knees clasped tightly to his chest. He was completely drenched and looked like a bedraggled vulture.

Indranath was now close to Bhagwati's house. He could see the earthen lamp behind that broken wall, sending out dim rays of light, making the room only partially visible.

This glow of light had a strange attraction for him....Behind the ramshackle wall, he could make out a circle of figures, probably opium addicts enjoying the smoke of smuggled opium, because he could also see wisps of smoke drifting out. The odour of roasted betelnut leaves mixed with that of elephant's dung from a nearby stable assailed Indranath's nose. He knew that this smell of roasting came from the room with the hanging oil lamp. That Brahmin from Cooch Behar must have certainly arrived! This is a good chance! He can be caught red-handed! This opium gang must not be allowed by any chance to shift to its original place, Rajapukhuri. It will be difficult to catch them there, as the opium prohibition volunteers of Rajapukhuri were not quite so active.

Yes! This was the moment! The golden chance! He must not miss it!

Indranath stepped out on the newly laid stone surface of the road. That German Sahib, Gilman, had got this path repaired. It used to be a very bad road some years ago. Gilman Sahib's small Ford car could come only up to Maniari Kiniari during its rare visits. Then it had to be pulled by elephants to this *sattra* and Bordawa Tea Estate...

Sometimes the white-skinned Sahibs from Gauhati and the tea estates beyond, took this road when they went. Their cars often got stuck in these bad patches. Then these sahibs would come running, out of breath, to the elephant's stable and beg. Some of the elephants had become quite adept in this task! Particularly this rogue elephant, he had pulled out so many Ford cars of these *firangi* sahibs...

When Indranath came to the wooden bridge, he was reminded of the meeting, that moonlight night...One full week has passed!...No, today there is nobody near the bridge. The stream under the bridge flowed fast and deep. The roaring sound of the rushing waters filled the air. The broken branches of uprooted *lantana* bushes and grass carried by the flood gave out a peculiar smell....

Indranath went ahead.....He removed the cross bar from Bolo's gate and entered the den. Tonight Bolo had made excellent arrangement! In the open air, a tarpaulin was stretched over bamboo poles and secured firmly. In two corners, two gas-lights, well primed, burned bright and lit up the place as if it was daytime. The old Congress veterans and some volunteers of opium prohibition committee had already joined the card party. They were sitting relaxed, smoking *bidis.* Choudhury and Das, regular members of Bolo's card parties and great card players sat cross-legged on the soft *gaddi*[3]. Here and there, lay scattered thick brass tumblers full of tea and a betelnut *sarai*[4] within easy reach of the players. Everybody stood up as lay soon as they saw the Saru Gossain, Indranath, in their midst. The two Home Guards, probably from lower castes, prostrated themselves before him respectfully and rubbed the dust from his feet on their foreheads...

* * * *

The card game went on till midnight. The Home Guards from the opium prohibition committee stood up and approaching Indranath, addressed him.

"Sir, tomorrow morning a meeting of the committee will be held. Our three secretaries from the South Bank will also attend it."

Indranath looked at them and said, "Our place here, it is rumoured, has become a centre of smuggled opium. I think you are aware of it and are on the alert!"

"Saru Gossain, so many persons are involved but unfortunately, we could catch only one culprit. That notorious woman from Maniari Kiniari, who kept aside small portions of opium for herself while cutting opium balls, was nearly caught redhanded. But when we searched her person, her opium had disappeared! We still don't understand in which part of her body she had concealed it! It was a very strange affair! We had arranged another woman to undress that witch and searched her naked body. But she found nothing, absolutely nothing? Very strange indeed!"

Everybody laughed uproariously. Bolo said, barely able to control his laughter, "Home Guard bapu, a woman's body is as mysterious as her mind. What to speak of a small opium pill! They can even hide a whole elephant in their body!"

Again all present roared with laughter. Indranath got up from his seat. But Bolo held his hand and tried to stop him.

"The rain has just stopped and the moon is shining brightly. Where do you want to go now?

Choudhury, who worked in *jatra* parties, said, "I think you are afraid of the rogue elephant and want to hurry home. I have heard that he had roamed as far as Jirang but now he has returned to Matia Pahar. Saru Gossain, that day you had gone away boasting that you would catch the ghost! Did you succeed?" and laughed sarcastically. Indranath replied, "I am not at all afraid of that elephant. Here, look at my *punjabi*! I am wearing buttons made out of his tusk! And that damned ghost! Just watch how I uproot that figment of imagination!"

* * * *

Indranath also came out with the two Home Guards, each pushing his old cycle along. They walked silently for some time. When they reached the wooden bridge, Indranath said, "Do you know why I left the card game suddenly and came along with you?"

"Why, Saru Gossain? Why?"

"I have discovered some clues!"

"Clues? What clues?"

"I have found out about an opium smuggler! He is here right now! Not very far from this spot!"

The two Home Guards were highly excited. One of them said, "Saru Gossain, please give us the details! We'll put it in the meeting tomorrow morning."

"Yes, Gossain, we'll even get a reward! You know how we are blamed for not taking any action. It makes us hang our heads in shame."

The other guard asked, "Who's he? Is he a spy roaming secretly in the South Bank?"

"No, no! Not a spy! He is a smuggler. A real smuggler!"

"Oh, my goodness! Smuggler? In this *sattra*?"

In their excitement, they fell at Indranath's feet.

"Please, Saru Gossain! Tell us his name. We'll be extremely grateful."

"I don't know his name but he comes to Bhagwati's house, specially when that priest from Rajapukhuri visits Bhagwati. This man also accompanies him....Do you want to know how to recognise him?"

Both of them exclaimed, "How, Gossain, how?"

"This man always brings a bunch of *malbhog*[5] bananas tied to the handle-bar of his old bicycle. That's how you will recognise him!"

"What! That's all? Come on then! Let's hurry!"

The two volunteers started walking fast, their staves making loud tapping sounds on the road.

For some time, Indranath stood still near the wooden bridge. A old *jamun* tree stood near one end of the bridge. Some drops of rain water fell on his *punjabi* and on his senses....that of decaying leaves littering the ground, mixed with slushy mud. Suddenly he looked back. What he saw made him freeze with fear and excitement! He stood rooted to the spot. About ten yards away stood the rogue elephant, a towering figure, his big flat ears flared out, wild creepers entangled in his tusks! His body was covered with slush that had dried up in patches. What an awesome sight it was! Indranath's whole body started trembling. There! There he stood! Nine feet tall! He stood there, silent and menacing, just behind the *jamun* tree! There! His tusks with blunt ends, slanting downwards and his thick trunk swinging and curving like a python!

Indranath seemed to hear frantic shouts, "Run! Go on! Fast! Run, run."

...No! The elephant would not charge! He stood still.

Here he was! *Mahaprabhu's*[6] most beloved elephant, Jagannath! So many times Indranath had sat on his back and gone to the Kulsi river to witness the pulling out of boats, loaded with timber logs, which had got stuck in the river-bed. There were so many scars on his head, made by the goad in the hand of the *mahout*....The sight of these marks used to make Indranath very sad....

The *mahout* Kaltu often told him, "This Jagannath! He is the most naughty elephant I have ever handled! He wants to attack anything that he doesn't like....And when he loves anyone....It's a bad sign! One day that greedy opium-eating thief, Baltu, came and told me, 'What a majestic elephant! Gossain rides on him like a king to visit his disciples.....can you not give me, this poor opium-eater, one chance of sitting on this fine elephant? Oh, please! Give me this one chance! I'll get some opium for you also.' Saru Gossain, what could I say? For this temptation, one day I unchained Jagannath and took that opium-eating thief, Baltu, on his back. We went for a ride to Barihat. When we were passing the *jamun* tree near the bridge, the elephant stooped suddenly and behaved as if his back was itching! He started rubbing his back against the tree trunk. Slowly his rubbing increased and it grew so hard that Baltu lost his balance and fell down with a thud! I had to restrain Jagannath with great difficulty. Otherwise that elephant would have trampled the opium-eater under his feet! Baltu fled somehow. Saru Gossain! I have spent half my life on the backs of so many elephants. Till this incident, I didn't believe, as other people used to say, that elephants are divine, heavenly creatures.....But now I believe it is so."

Jagannath! There he stood! The rogue elephant who had struck terror in the hearts of people for the last four days! He stood there, as if nothing had happened! As if he was eating rice from a tray held out by the Gossainee. Ah! That smell of decaying leaves and slush! And the odour from the wounds on his head like that of newly cut bamboo shoots!

Oh, God! Oh, God!

Indranath clutched the handle bars of his bicycle tightly with both hands and stood perfectly still. He stared steadily into the blood-shot eyes of the elephant. They stood staring at each other!....

...Ah! Aa!...Ut!...Aa! Aa!...Ut!...

Uttering these weird sounds, the frenzied elephant

turned his back on Indranath and disappeared like a flash of lightning into the *sal* forest!

Indranath stood rooted to the spot as if a bolt had struck him! Was it that Jagannath, this elephant in frenzy, had recognised him? It is said that nearby objects appear very large to an elephant.....of course he must have seen him and recognised him!

A sharp pain bit not only his flesh and blood, but also cut deep inside his bones. Poor Jagannath! A time would come when he would have to be shot....Indranath came to himself....Pushing the bicycle, he started walking.

When he came near the banyan tree, he saw that there was lot of movement and activity outside Bhagwati's house. A crowd had gathered outside. At last! The Home Guards had probably raided the house and caught that rascal, the opium smuggler from Cooch Behar! Indranath stood there watching for a while. All of a sudden, a voice startled him. He looked around. It was the leper,

"Master! you will be the future *adhikar* of this place. An opium smuggler has been caught in your *sattra.* What's there to see? Go home, it's quite late."

Indranath quietly walked away.

★ ★ ★ ★

That night, a meeting had been organised with the secretaries of South Bank—Sonapur, Barihat, Battarhat, Rajabaha and other places. Volunteers were also supposed to attend this meeting. But when the news about Jokram Bhagwati spread though the *sattra,* they all converged at his house.

One of the two Home Guards carried a shot-gun, normally used for killing birds. He fired two shots in the air. Then they started shaking and knocking on the door of the corner room. Suddenly, to their amazement, a man dashed out and ran towards the backyard. The two volunteers, bent upon catching him, gave a hot chase. The man turned towards Matiapahar hill. When he reached the top, he hauled himself up a teak tree as fast as possible. Probably his brain was still befuddled with opium fumes. Nearby, on a *machan* built on another tree, Jamaluddin *Garia*[7], *the mahout* of the elephant of Khan Sahib of Dakhala, was keeping a lookout for the rogue elephant. He called out suddenly, in great anger, "Hallo there! Who are you? Why are you disturbing me? I have been sitting here with a rope for the last two days...That rogue is still somewhere nearby. I can hear his ears flapping!"

...Silence!....But now there were other sounds, of running feet, of whistles being blown. The volunteers had arrived....

Again the voice from the *machan* rang out, with more fury.

"What the hell is going on? Who's making all that noise there? I have caught three rogue elephants in South Bank. The fourth one is still here nearby. You are spoiling my chance with all this noise. Who's climbing the tree? Don't you know that the elephant will charge you and finish you off? Can't you hear him trampling on bamboos? Are you all deaf?"

The opium-eater on the tree, terrified with this price of information after hearing about the elephant, lost his grip and fell down with a crash! The Home Guards surrounded him immediately. Meanwhile, some other volunteers also joined them. They tied their prisoner with a rope. It was dangerous to stay there any longer because of the rogue elephant. They left the place in great haste and proceeded towards the Gossain's *batghar.*

Even at this late hour of the night, the *batghar* was crowded with people. They were shocked to hear about the arrest of a Brahmin opium smuggler. This was the first time in this South Bank that a Brahmin had been caught smuggling opium!

The prisoner was leaning against one of the wooden posts of the *batghar*. One of the Home Guards brought a bunch of bananas and kept it on the ground before the smuggler. When the latter saw the bananas, he sank down slowly on to his haunches, clutching his head with both hands. The Home Guard started peeling the bananas one by one. From each banana, he took out six or seven pills of opium. Every time he squeezed out a few pills, there were exclamations from the crowd. It was amazing how cleverly and expertly the pellets of opium were concealed inside each banana!

Somebody from the crowd exclaimed, "Look! How neatly he has done the job! The banana peels look as if they have been glued together....."

....Dawn was approaching. Swirling flocks of parrots were coming from Matiapahar and winging towards Jagalia river. A long line of wild ducks flew majestically in the same direction. Fragrant wild berries added to the sweetness of the early morning air....

....At last the Home Guards and the prohibition officer wound up the enquiry. The prohibition officer said, "This is the first time we have caught a real smuggler on South Bank. Now the mystery about the smuggler's hideout in the Garo Hills will come to light. Even in the port of Calcutta, they say our opium is being seized everyday in large quantities!....."

One Home Guard shouted excitedly,

"Certainly this Brahmin from Cooch Behar had links

with the Calcutta port smugglers!...."

There were comments from the crowd,

"Ah, how he deceived everybody!"

"He used to come and go so freely!"

"Just like any one of us in this *sattra*!"

"Ah, we have never heard of such a Brahmin crook before!"

Meanwhile the Home Guards brought Jokram Bhagwati and his brother, the priest of Rajapukhuri, to the Gossain's *batghar*, their hands secured with handcuffs.

The hair on their head was half black and half grey. Even the eyebrows of one of them were half grey, half black. They had longish noses with flat cheeks falling away on both sides. Jokram had dull, lustreless eyes like pools of ditch-water reflecting the sun. Both were wearing soiled dhotis reaching up to their knees. Even the sacred threads they were wearing did not look so clean. They looked more like the dried-up entrails of an animal! Both wore old *endi punjabis*. They squatted on the ground and lamented.

"Please! Have mercy on us! Please don't take us to the police station at Palasbari!"

They pleaded with folded hands. Somebody from the crowd shouted, "Why Palasbari? You two will be taken to Gauhati Jail and you'll have to eat coarse rice cooked by low caste people!"

Many people shouted together.

"There's no religion left! it's finished! What bad times we are living in!"

Jokram Bhagwati suddenly remembered that, according to the amendment to Clause No. 10 of the Opium Act, even those who protected or helped opium smugglers were liable for severe punishment with three years rigorous imprisonment!

He begged the Home Guards, "Can't we talk to *Adhikar* Gossain for a few minutes? Please take us to him."

One powerful official from South Bank spoke up.

"The Gossain cannot take the law into his own hands in opium cases. Nobody will be allowed to go near him. We have to go to Maniari Kiniari now. The police from Palasbari station will do their duty, whatever is necessary."

The Brahmin priest from Rajapukhuri threw his dignity to the winds and started weeping hysterically. In a broken, agitated voice, he whined,

"You sinners! You'll all go to hell! Yes, sinners, to hell! For killing a Brahmin!....Do you know what is written in the holy scriptures?"—

> *Prithivyam Yani Tirthani*
> *tani tirthani sagare:*
> *Sagare yani tirthani*
> *Viprapadekam tani cha....*
>
> (In this world there are many holy places. These holy places exist in the oceans also...And the same holy places can be found on the lotus feet of Brahmins too!....)

Jokram Bhagwati also started quoting from the holy books, to escape from the arrest threatening them!

"It is also written that in the hand of a Brahmin exist heaven and Lord Hari....And in his limbs are found the most auspicious pilgrimages and *yagyas*[8]....in his arteries exists *trigunatmik prakriti*[9] and in his neck there is *gayatri mantra*....."

The prohibition officer interrupted Jokram impatiently—

"There is no time to listen to all this! We must start for

Maniari Kiniari at once!"

Suddenly the Brahmin from Cooch Behar, the main culprit, stood up and pointing to the other Brahmins, pleaded—

"These two are not guilty. Please, Sir, let them go! I came here again and again because I wanted to marry the daughter of this priest from Rajapukhuri. To keep them happy, I smuggled in opium for them. Please release them, Sir!"

But his plea was ignored. The Home Guard tightened his grip on the smuggler and tied him up with jute rope. Jokram and his brother were so weak and groggy that it was not found necessary to tie them up. They all went towards the main road....

Such a sensational event had not occurred in this *sattra* before! A Brahmin priest being taken as a prisoner for opium smuggling! The news spread like wild fire throughout the villages. People started gathering along the route or even following the prisoners and the Home Guards.

* * * *

Nearly all the women of the *sattra* congregated in Bhagwati's house to console and sympathise with Eliman, who had been left alone with the old woman after the arrest of the three Brahmins.

She was sitting on a mat laid out on the mud floor, completely dejected, her eyes glued to the ground. Her thick hair lay open, uncombed, on her back. A part of her beautiful hair was entwined round her upper arm. She was not wearing any blouse. Only a *gatala* and a *mekhala* covered her shapely body. The wife of the *Bhakat* said,

"Lord forbid! A beautiful girl like you! That scoundrel

from Cooch Behar. Was he a good match for you? What a shame! People say that he has already left one woman behind in Cooch Behar. Lord forbid! Lord forbid!"

"What's the harm if there's another woman at home? Dakhala's Gossain has kept two Gossainees and doesn't feel any shame! Isn't that so? I have heard that when one Gossainee is in the Gossain's bed, the other sits on the verandah before a fire to wait for her turn. Her hands and feet have become black due to sitting constantly before woodfire. Her whole body has dried up and become thorny like those *nagphana*[10] bushes....."

Guimeni now spoke up. This old woman was short and hunchbacked. It was she who usually sat with the Gossainee and smoked *tankhu*[11] with her.

"Don't cry, my child. Saru Gossainee will get your father released very soon. You mark my words! I heard it with my own ears. So now, that's a good girl! Come on, get up.....'

The old woman, who always remained with Eliman like her shadow, now got up and started clearing up the awful mess left behind by the opium-eaters. She collected the pots and pans, the clay pan for frying betelnut leaves, wooden needles (like spoons), *bhem*[12] made by breaking the top part of a clay pitcher, and clay pipes for smoking, and took them inside.

Guimeni, who was bent double by the hump on her back and always supported her waist with both hands, spoke up again, "Who's that black-faced monkey who dared to bring this proposal?"

The old woman replied, "What can I say? The priest's condition is very bad, almost hand-to-mouth. She's a grown-up girl. Some even demanded dowry! Must be from Bangala country[13]....I have heard that when the Gossain's daughter here got married, her in-laws from Chikarhati demanded – seven hundred rupees for their son's education at Calcutta. What bad times have come!"

Another woman exclaimed—

"Seven hundred rupees?"

"Yes, yes! Who will marry a wretched priest's daughter just like that? Her father has sense only to run after opium! She will become old in her father's house like a *daldahi tiri*[14]."

"What rot you are talking, you stupid old woman! You're blinded by the steam from the rice pot. Look! What beautiful hair! And the lovely colour of her skin! As if she has just now descended from the heavens! Come, come! All of you get up and search this room. There may be money left hidden in hollow bamboos! It'll be a sin if this Brahmin girl has to fast."

The old woman, Eliman's constant companion, started searching for bamboo posts with lime marks on them. When she found one such bamboo post, she cut it open with a betelnut knife. A cascade of silver coins flowed to the ground! All the village women sitting around were dumbfounded at this spectacle. Guimeni cried out,

"Certainly this money is left over from the days of those white-skinned soldiers! That good-for-nothing, wretched Bhagwati! Everybody knows he made money by selling leeches collected from elephants' bodies. He was a contractor of the foreign soldiers. He arranged for them whatever things they wanted. Because of him, all the ducks disappeared from the villages. He sold them and made huge profits. At that time this verandah was bigger and many people used to come and go."

Suddenly Guimeni burst into a song written about those *gora paltans*[15]—

"Oh my friends,
Pick up your sticks,
Gora paltan has come.
To the hills of Jalukbari
To burst their bombs!"

Eliman's companion, the old maid, did not pay any heed to Guimeni's words. She went on searching silently for more bamboo posts. Suddenly she found two more bamboo posts with lime markings. But she did not want to break them open before all these women. She looked at them for a while, and then shouted—

"Don't you have any other work to do in the morning hours? It's already time for rice planting. I saw the Gossain's *bandha* going out long back with his load of jackfruits, boiled rice and jaggery."

The old woman's admonition goaded all the women into activity. They got up hurriedly. Many of them had not even done their early morning chores. Their enormous curiosity to see the Brahmin opium smugglers had brought them here. One by one they started going back to their homes.

But Guimeni had no such compulsion.....All her daughters-in-law were terrified of her and did all the work, leaving her free to spend most of her time with the Gossainee for her tobacco smoking sessions. So she picked up an iron mortar and pestle from a corner of the room, sat near Eliman and started pounding betelnuts.

She said, "*Aichana*[16], you look quite mature already. Your bosom is like a pair of doves swelling with eggs. Have your menses started?"

The old woman retaliated—"Guimeni, I think you don't have any work at all nowadays. You used to sit in the weekly market with a heap of coins. Do you remember how you once fell down under the *bokul* tree while carrying a heavy bundle of coins?"

"Why shouldn't I remember? In those days, due to those white soldiers, there was a demand for coins. Now where's the need? Times have changed. I don't have to do that work any more. But I have stayed back to ask you something! Something very secret and very serious!...."

Eliman, who was till now sitting with bowed head, raised her head and looked at Guimeni. Her old maid came and sat down near her. But Guimeni would not utter anything in front of Eliman. She took the old woman to the *dhekal*. There she whispered.

"Big Gossainee has sent me here! Now you tell me the truth. If you tell lies, Gossainee will curse you and you with your seven generations will suffer from her curse!"

The old woman stood before her, stunned and dumbfounded.

"The Gossainee has heard that Eliman and Indranath Gossain met one night near the wooden bridge. Face to face...Can it be true? Is it really so?..."

The old woman stood petrified as if struck by lightning....

"Come now, tell the truth. Don't you remember what happened to me under the *bokul* tree? After I spoke about the old Gossain and that low-caste woman?"

"Yes, yes! Everybody knows about it! While you were returning from the weekly market with your bundle of coins in the dark of the night, the black spirit attacked you and beat you up. Your coins lay scattered on the ground. All the little boys had great fun collecting those coins! But we also know who was that black spirit!"

Guimeni leaned towards the old woman, holding her hump with both hands

"Who.....who was it?...."

"People say it was the old Gossain himself! He was waiting for you, hiding on the bokul tree."

Guimeni burst out angrily—

"You slut! Shut up! It is true I got a beating and in the darkness, I couldn't see who it was. You old hag! Am I a fool to believe at that hour. Would he leave his duties and hide on a *bokul* tree?"

"Yes, yes! The Gossain was there on the *bokul* tree. Everybody knew the Gossain used to present that low caste woman with *phuti* and *dugdugee.* He used to take her for joy rides in a covered bullock-cart to Gauhati. Oh, how angry he would be if somebody pointed it out."

Guimeni screamed—

"Oh, you witch! Die of cholera! You speak ill of *Mahaprabhu*? You'll rot in all the seven hells! Mark my words...you slut!..."

"I've told you what I heard from others. Don't you go and tell Gossainee about it! Everyone knows that the present Gossain is a saint! He has given land for schools, for hospitals. There's no end to his kindness. He has even donated land for an opium prohibition committee camp! What a godly man! May he live long!"

Guimeni removed one hand from her hump and pointed skywards—

"Don't try to reach for the full moon! A Brahmin priest is not a Gossain. Now you swear the truth! On that road, on the newly laid stones of Gilmil Sahib, what went on between Indranath Gossain and Eliman? Beware of hellfires and tell me! Speak you old woman!"

The old maid remained silent for a while. She recollected all of a sudden! The bullock-cart of the chief priest! It had passed along the same road that night.

Probably he had seen them together. Oh, God! Yes, everything is clear now! The priest had gone for the atonement ceremony of that man who had killed his wife. The bullock cart was loaded with jackfruits and big earthen pots of curd. The wretched Brahmin was always sharp and alert like a leopard. Certainly he had seen everything! Without any doubt, he had reported to the Gossainee. He would not leave such a good opportunity, the grabbing, corrupt Brahmin! Like a python, he could mesmerise his prey and grab it in his jaws. Just as a big elephant could pick up a small coin with great ease, this cunning Brahmin picked up small bits of information and blew them out of proportion! He was as devious as a hermit crab which wore a discarded snail's shell and deluded the world. The old maid exclaimed—"Terrible! Terrible!"

Guimeni screamed again, "Speak out! Quick! You wretched woman! Have you lost your tongue?"

Out of fear of a Gossain's curse, the old woman started trembling. She remained tongue-tied for quite a long time. Then she uttered in a low voice—

"Guimeni, I don't know how to tell you.....That night, Eliman went out to relieve herself. As that rogue elephant was roaming about, she was afraid to go to the usual place, which is quite a distance away. So she went near the wooden bridge which is much nearer. Indranath Gossain was coming from Bolo's den at the same time, and by chance, he saw Eliman there."

Just at that moment, the two old women heard sounds of sobbing. Eliman was crying, her sobs interspersed with broken irregular muttering. They could catch only a few words but it sounded as if she was saying something about Guimeni..."Are you human or a man-eating tigress!...We two...left all alone...Father and uncle arrested...and...you putting such nasty questions!"

Guimeni put both hands on her hump, leaned sideways and looked at the door. She stood still and thought to herself—she is the daughter of a Brahmin. She hasn't even eaten anything. No, this is not the time to ask such questions!

She did not remain long afterwards. It was time for her to go and join the Gossainee. She must be wearing her red *mekhala* and preparing to go to the small room where she smoked her clay pipe. Guimeni clutched her hump and limped to the compound gate. She turned to the old maid and said, "Listen! Times are bad, very bad! That handsome elephant who used to carry the Gossain's *howda* has become *must*[17]. In his mad mood, he can crush anyone, any moment. An unclean Christian is pacing the floor of the Gossain's sandal room. If the old Gossain had been here, he would have peeled off the skin of such men, just as a sacrificial goat is stripped of its skin."

She opened the gate and hobbled to the road-side where tall reed stalks had grown up thickly. She lifted her *mekhala* and relieved herself, quite unconcerned, without looking around....

✯ ✯ ✯ ✯

Somehow Eliman believed that her father and her uncle would return soon. And that obnoxious Brahmin from Cooch Behar! She was greatly relieved that he had been put behind bars. She had observed lately that this person wanted to talk to her in private. Whenever she went to the backyard to pick vegetables from the garden, he would follow her under the pretext of plucking a few *pan* leaves from the creepers snaking round the areca nut palms. And that look in his eyes! She had never imagined that a man's gaze could make her feel stark naked, as if he was tearing off her clothes! That a man's eyes could cut her flesh into small pieces. She had tolerated that man long enough!

The old maid, meanwhile, had collected all the coins from the hollow bamboos and tied them in her *gamcha.* She was thinking about Indranath. She somehow felt certain in her inner most heart that he would soon come himself or send someone to enquire about their welfare.

She went near Eliman, picked up the mortar and pestle and sat down on her haunches. She placed the mortar between her feet and started pounding betelnuts.

She said, "Don't open the fence gate and go out. Your monthly flow has started! The greatest sin is already hanging on our heads! So don't add to it! If you have done some good deeds in your past life, surely God will bless you. Indranath Gossain will come and take you away. He knows that we are left alone and helpless here. Mark my words he'll come!"

Then she added, emphasising her words, by pointing with the forefinger of her right hand—

"He won't bow down to the talk of other people! After all the blood of *Santa Dev Mahaprabhu* is flowing in his veins!"

Eliman touched the floor and then placed her hand over one ear. She said in an agitated voice, "Shut up, you foolish woman! If he is like *Santa Dev Mahaprabhu,* do you think he'll marry a Brahmin's daughter?"

The old woman threw down the pestle, lifted her hands heavenwards and paid obeisance to *Santa Dev Mahaprabhu.*

"He is truly a God! The tailor who stitched his clothes once saw four hands on him!....You recite his name in your heart. He'll come to your rescue and fulfill your desires. So many Gossain *adhikars* from South Bank have married ordinary Brahmin girls! Their disciples have not even opened their mouths. Come on! Recite the divine name of *Santa Dev Mahaprabhu*! That's a good girl!"

The old maid then scooped out the mashed betelnuts from the mortar and dumped the whole fistful into her mouth. She looked around in all four directions, leaned towards Eliman and whispered into her ear—

"There's no one here now! All those women have gone. Some to plant rice in the fields, others for pounding rice. When Indranath comes, don't let him just stand outside! Use your head! Bring him inside."

The old woman gave her a long and meaningful look. Then without saying another word, she stood up. Picking up a basket and a shopping bag, she went out of the house, heading towards the market-place of Barihat. Eliman could see her shadow crossing the wooden bridge. She brooded...When Indranath comes on his cycle. Can she do it? Will she have the courage to invite him inside?

Yesterday's incident! Certainly Indranath had a hand in them! That made it quite clear. He had a soft corner for her! Otherwise how could the cunning Brahmin from Cooch Behar have been caught red-handed?

Eliman got up. She went to the well in the backyard. The bamboo fencing round the well was falling apart. But the *kathana*[18] flowers were in bloom. They looked beautiful and alluring. The white flowers reminded her of the pure whiteness of a healthy cow's milk.

She could see, from where she stood, the verandah of the Gossain's *haveli*. The door through which Indranath came and went, was a little ajar....No, no! He would not come! But why not? He knew she was alone.

She stood under the *kathana* tree for a long time.

She craned her neck and looked again. No, nobody was there! A little depressed, she went back into the house. She glanced around. The old maid had cleared up the room where the opium-eaters used to assemble. She had removed the pots and pans, and all the other things used by opium eaters. Low *urium*[19] wood stools were kept in a line against one wall. Eliman lifted one of them. She placed it in the centre of the room and started dusting it with her *gatala*. When he came, she would bring him here. She would make him sit on this stool in the backyard. There were two *kathana* trees in this backyard also. Blooming with white flowers they curtained off the place and formed a nice cosy bower! Yes, he'll sit here and we'll talk. Nobody will see us!....

He is the future *adhikar* of this sprawling *sattra*. And he has the divine radiance, like a prince. Her mind was turning into a multi-hued butterfly. Someone was stretching out his hand to touch the brilliant wings...She was melting and dissolving, becoming one with the imperceptible!

Carried away by the high tide of her feelings, she ran to the well again. Her eyes scanned the verandah of the Gossain's house. There he was! Indranath stood there! What would she do now! Yes, yes, there! He was looking this way and she...she stood here, one with the *kathana* flowers! Certainly, the clusters of *kak*[20] bamboos have not hindered his sight. Yes! Now! He was looking at her! Her mind, her soul, her body are now one with the white *kathana* flowers. But...why was he not coming this way? Surely he could come here by the path leading towards the backyard? Why did not he come? How long would she wait here?

✯ ✯ ✯ ✯

The shadow cast by the sun now almost touched the

broken old fencing round the well. Gradually the shadow crept past the *kathana* flowers and beyond the backyard towards the wooden bridge.

Indranath did not come.

The old maid returned from Barihat. She put down the basket on the verandah and went to the well. She drew some water and splashed it on her face and limbs. She could somehow guess what had happened in her absence. She sighed......Lifting the *mekhala* up to her knees, she began washing her legs vigorously....

She entered the house and going near Eliman, said, "You are a silly girl! You haven't even cooked the rice. Go! Foolish girl! Take your bath first and then go to the kitchen." She took out the things from the basket and arranged them properly. All the while she murmured—

"What's right is right! After all he is the future *adhikar.* How can he enter a house of women staying alone? And then after what happened yesterday how can he come just like that? Like a thief for making love. Once he starts coming, so many eyes and ears will open wide? Tongues will start wagging! He'll come only at the right moment, and that too with betrothal gifts. You mark my words!"

Eliman burst out—

"Stop it! Will you stop this nonsense?"

"Ah! Why are you angry? For so many days, your father was living on that Cooch Behar Brahmin's money, wasn't he? Tainted money, wages of sin! Today he has fallen in the dragnet of police. Well, it had to happen that way, hadn't it? That's why there's a saying: One who talks too much is eaten by his own words! The expert doctor is often himself bitten by the snake. An astrologer is eaten up by the nine planets. And the Brahmin is devoured by his sins."

Eliman, by now exhausted, wailed,

"Oh! If both of them don't come back, what will happen to us?"

"So young and so much fear? *Are*, why are you frightened? Indranath Gossain is behind all this! He'll certainly find a way out."

The old maid then went near the cooking place and started splitting firewood into small pieces.

The evening shadow, playing in and out of the wooden bridge, at last plunged into the Jagalia river and vanished.

* * * *

Footsteps could be heard. Khaki-clad Home Guards escorting Jokram Bhagawati and the priest entered the gate. They had come back! Both had shrunken faces. They looked very thin. Skin and bones had come together, whatever flesh they had been left with had taken the colour of opium. They looked the very picture of down and out opium-eaters.

The guards left them and took off. The two men went to the well and washed their limbs and faces. When they entered the house, they were seething and howling with anger. Pointing his forefinger at the old maid, Jokram cried—

"Did Eliman go to any of the houses of this *sattra*?"

"The other day the Mahajan had invited her to the *haihal*[21] of his daughter-in-law. But I didn't send her. After all she is a Brahmin's daughter. If she just steps out of the compound gate, she'll have to take a bath after coming back inside."

Jokram Bhagawati roared—

"Shut up, you old bitch!"

The old woman started crying—"I came with her mother as her maid servant after her marriage. Now she is dead.....Will this girl suffocate inside a closed room? Why can't she go out? She'll certainly go to the Gossain's house for the *shradha* ceremony of old Gossain. I know very well where she should go and where she shouldn't. This hair has turned white and these bones have become old in this very duty. I am guarding her like a shadow....always....."

The Brahmin priest now shouted—

"Then who has made this wound in my bosom?"

"Why won't they make the wound? Even a tiger invites death after killing and eating a hundred cows! All these days you have living off the wealth of that good-for-nothing Brahmin from Cooch Behar. And your opium-eating comrades! Will they keep quiet? People rightly say—

> *Mayakar nam Tiliki bandi!*
> *Pitakar nam Sultan Gaji!*
>
> (His mother is as sharp as a dwarf maid and his father is as notorious as Sultan Gazi[22].)

The priest burst out—

"Eliman has grown up! We have to put the basket under the pounding horse[23]. Who will come seeking her hand in this ramshackle house? I had such high hopes of that Brahmin! Whatever he might have been, he had enough money. Her life would have been much better than this miserable existence. I am sure he'll somehow get out of the prison with the power of his wealth!"

The old maid howled—

"Shame on you! What kind of a father are you? Giving your daughter to a dirty rotten thief! Casting greedy eyes on his money! They are right when they say

> *Bamunar munak nubulibi saru*
> *Chaul dhare, charu dhare*
> *are dhare bhatara garu.*

(Don't say that the Brahmin's bag is
a small one! It holds rice for cooking
and a cooking pot too! And above all
It can also hold one big steer).

Eliman's father was now on the verge of tears. He cried out—

"What shall I do then? She'll become mature any day now. If I don't get her married off, we'll be made outcastes!"

Meanwhile Eliman was listening to the talk of her elders with increasing agitation and embarrassment. She shrank within herself and tried to hide her voluptuous form as much as possible. But her whole body was blooming like white kathana flowers. How long could she veil it from the eyes of the world? Even through the cracked mud walls of this ramshackle house, her growing body yielded tantalising glimpses to prying eyes, like the broken, scintillating image of the moon on the ripples on Jagalia.

Eliman's restlessness grew. Why could not that man come? Status, dignity, self-respect, are they so important? Could not he set them aside and come? No, no! Perhaps this type of situation had not arisen in this *sattra*! He was the future *adhikar.* How foolish of her to think like this! An inexplicable pain pierced her heart, somewhere deep inside. Her very soul shivered with an elusive apprehension......

Nine

The *shradha* ceremony of the old Gossain had ended. The disciples of Haramdo, Rajabaha, Tallapara, Maniari Kiniari, Boku and other places started preparing to leave the *sattra*. The old Gossain was the father of the ruling *adhikar.*

Indranath's father, the ruling *adhikar,* today wore the ceremonial dress. He had on a *pat* silk *dhoti* and on his shoulders, an *uttariya*[1] of blended *pat* and *muga* silk. On the verandah of the backyard were placed two big decorated *peerahs*[2] on which sat Indranath and his father. The former also wore the same ceremonial dress. In front of them were placed two big copper *thagis*[3]. These trays overflowed with coins—silver rupees and other big and small coins.

The disciples had big *urmals*[4] and small cloth bags tucked into their waists. One by one, they approached the *peerahs*, offered coins in the *thagis* from their bags and taking dust from the feet of the *adhikar,* departed. From time to time, when the heaps of coins in the trays became too high, young boys of *jajmani* Brahmins took away the trays and emptied the contents on a big bed in an inner room of the manor.

Giribala had counted the large clay pots of thick curd

and had undertaken other similar tasks connected with the ceremony. She now stood on the verandah, where there was the sacrificial pit for killing young goats during ceremonial functions. Near the verandah, there was a small room that now lay unused. In this room lay the old palanquin that had brought the old Gossainee from Urput to this house. This palanquin was made of *urium* wood, but over the years, even this hard *urium* wood had been gradually eaten by weevils. The *dhekarmari*[5] on both sides of the palanquin were made of some kind of metal that shone in spite of the long passage of time.

Giribala had kept all the manuscripts she had collected in this palanquin. She went inside, took out the manuscripts, one by one, and began counting them. They were on various subjects. There was even a manuscript of one chapter of Tulsi Das's *Ramcharit Manas* translated into Assamese by Shreekant Surya Vipra. Mark had been working on it for some time now. It was nearly one-hundred-and-fifty years old! Here were some *sanchi* leaves of *Purush Mohini Mantra*[6]. Giribala laughed and picking up one of the leaves, began reading it....

Phular pukhuri phular par
Phul phuli ase jatiskar
Eai phul amikir murat chare
Amukik on amukai japar
Kapor hen dekhe.

(There is a pond of flowers and its
banks are also made of flowers.
These flowers will decorate the head
of some lady; someone (a man) will
think of her as a precious, fondly
kept cloth in a basket.)

Certainly, Mark must have come for the ceremony. Probably he sat in the backyard with low-caste *kamars,*[7] holding a *dona*[8] in his hand. Should she go and see whether he was there? Today she was not wearing the short *gatala.* She had on a *chaddar* woven with fine silk threads. The *markin*[9] cloth chemise with pleated neck was covered by a blouse with "pistol cut"[10] sleeves. She had combed her hair with a comb made of bamboo, with neat, clean strokes and made two plaits. In these fresh, clean clothes she looked like an angel.

Crossing the threshold of the small palanquin room, Giribala headed towards the backyard to find out about Mark. It was packed with villagers but there was no sign of him! She went running to the huge open kitchen. The level of cooked rice in the rice pits (pits dug in the ground lined with plantain leaves and kept filled with cooked rice for serving) had gone down. Even the stock of mutton and black *dal*[11] stock, *labara*[12] and plain *rahar dal*[13], kept in large bowls, had diminished.

Giribala then went to the huge courtyard near the granary. The half-naked village children were sitting there with big plantain leaves and *donas* before them on the ground. They had thin limbs and bloated bellies.

She heard their voices—

"Bring more mutton, you Brahmin cook!"

"We have this feast only once a year. Why did not that old Gossain die more often!"

"Oi! Oi! Curse them! Curse them!...Let the Gossains die several times!"

"Shut up, shut up! The Gossains will hear you. They'll skin you alive!"

Giribala could see the pitiable state of the old Brahmin

servers. They had to dole out the food and at the same time, they were afraid that the waving, excited hands of the children might touch their bodies. No! Mark was not there with these little devils!

The aroma of black beans cooked with mutton tickled her nostrils! She went back to the open kitchen. The white, fragrant *kharika joha*[14] rice in the pit, which measured nearly ten feet long and six feet wide, looked like an ivory pond. Brahmin boys from Rajabaha and Bhagwatipara were busy attending to the guests, serving rice and curry. Ah! What a tempting fragrance wafted from the rice and black beans! They must have certainly used ginger and black pepper. Probably a layer of *ghee*[15], made from cow's milk, shimmered on the surface. And in the distance, she could see the skin of the slaughtered goat hanging on the honey fig tree. It fluttered in the strong breeze like a cloth. The pit where it was killed still remained unfilled. The excavated earth was lying outside. This time also, she had not been allowed to see the ritual of killing a goat. Even in her childhood, it was prohibited place for her!

Suddenly Giribala was startled by a loud voice. It was Sombhu *mohura*, shouting at some boys—

"Get up, get up! You devils! It's now the turn of Brahmins. Get up! Quick! You want to sit here forever, do you?"

The Brahmin servers were jolted into action. They wore *mukcha*[16] round their heads and waists. Streams of perspiration ran down their naked backs. The gold rings in their sacred threads danced to the fast movements of their bodies. Giribala watched them carting brass bowls of mutton curry in quick succession! What a delicious, tempting aroma! But all of a sudden, she got the aroma from some other place nearby! She was perplexed. Had some greedy

Brahmin hidden a pot of mutton curry with black beans in the palanquin room?

They do have this old habit. Definitely somebody had kept a bowl of mutton curry in the room!

She looked around and entered the small room stealthily. She was right! Discovered a clay bowl covered with a plantain leaf! It was hidden under a fodder sack.

Just then, from outside came the uproar of Brahmins who had started collecting their gifts. This fighting and clamour always took place at the time of *bhojan dakshina*[17] distribution. At the time of the first *shraddha* of the old Gossain, when land, *urium* wood cots, rice baskets, *endi chaddar* were being distributed, the Brahmins had started quarrelling among themselves. After some time, it ended in fisticuffs and complete chaos! An arm of a Brahmin was fractured and he had to be admitted to a hospital at Gauhati.

Now they were busy with the same *bhojan dakshina* ceremony. So definitely no Brahmin would come this side now! The *bandhas* and the field hands were also occupied in clearing away the dirty plantain leaves and *donas* left over from the feast. They too will not come this way. Near the garbage heap, dogs and crows were having their own feast! Who will come near the *dhekal* now! Even the *kurmas*[18] were engaged in watching the *bhojan dakshina* ceremony. Giribala peeped at the main verandah. The half-naked old man was playing on *kalia*, a kind of wind instrument made from buffalo horn, in front of the Gossain.

This was the chance! The right moment! She sprinted up to the earthen pot in the palanquin room and removed the banana leaf. She stretched out her hand, but in the next instant, she withdrew it. What was she doing? It was an unpardonable sin for a *Damodariya Gossain*[19] widow to eat flesh! It had never ever happened anywhere!

Giribala went back to the verandah, near the pit where the goat was killed. She saw Durga, some distance away, sprinking water on some rice, dropped accidentally by the *jajmani* Brahmins. She had a copper water jug in her hand. The way she bent forward and threw water here and there, searching for dropped rice, she resembled a ghostly witch with her skeletal body. Ah! Again that irresistible, tempting aroma! Certainly, along with ginger and pepper, they must have put *garam masala*[20] also! No doubt! The Brahmin who cooked this mutton with black beans must have come from Bangara. Those Bangara Brahmins knew the correct measurement of all the ingredients—ghee, pepper, ginger and spices.

Giribala had heard from other people that her late husband, Latu Gossain, liked this preparation by Bangara Brahmins very much. He generally roamed with *jatra* parties and almost everyday that notorious woman, the opium seller of Maniari Kiniari, used to feed him pigeon curry cooked with papaya. Once, out of a sense of guilt, he had done *prayaschit*[21] conducted by a Brahmin from Guimara. He had two elder brothers, so he had no fear of succeeding to the seat of *sattra adhikar*, a prison to him. His mental make-up was like that of a free bird. He was dead now, but his words still stung her mind like poison—

"Yes, daughter of three *sattras*...as those poets say, you have a body like a young date-palm! But since we are already married, you better know one thing. You'll have to tolerate some of my habits. People say they are bad habits but you will have to accept them!"

She had kept silent. He had shouted angrily—

"Tell me! Do you agree or not!"

Out of fear, she had blurted out—

"Yes, I accept...."

"I love women. I like their company. When I roamed with the *jatra* party through all those places—Bordowa, Samaria, Dakhala, I had taken tea from the hands of low-caste women. And that woman of Maniari Chowk, not only does she make pigeon curry with papaya for me, but she also cooks *ou* fruit with deer flesh. But listen! You daughter of Gossain! I have done *prayaschit* every time I ate those forbidden things. Sometimes by calling a Brahmin priest and other times by reciting the *gayatri mantra*....."

Bhenpoo! *Bhenpoo*! *Bhenpoo*! The loud notes of the *kalia*[22] shattered Giribala's ears. Probably that hunch-back was blowing the instruments with more enthusiasm as he approached the *jajmani* Brahmins for more gifts.

Had he only eaten *ou-tenga* prepared by her hands? Or had he clasped them also? Who didn't know that he had slept with that woman? He had gradually reached the lowest rung of debauchery possible for a dissolute son of a Gossain family.

Oh! God! Oh! God

Outenga and deer flesh! Probably it gave out the same aroma as that from the pot of mutton with black beans. It was said that smelling food was almost as good as eating it. And for a Gossain widow, it was a great sin even to smell the aroma of forbidden food, as written in the scriptures.

She stood still, perturbed. That noise from the *kalia* was making her almost sick and splitting her ear drums.

That delicious odour! Again that tempting aroma!

She suddenly remembered one incident from about eight years back. Indranath and his two friends from Calcutta had once gone to Matiapahar for hunting. They had killed a big fat iguana with an old double-barrelled gun. Indranath and his friends had then skinned it, cleaned it and cut it into small pieces. Outside the house, they had cooked it on a wood fire, mixing all varieties of spices ground on stone and big *vilayati alu*[23]. At that time, she was so small that she did not even wear a *gatala.* The aroma of that iguana curry was almost the same as what she was smelling now. Everybody had then sat down with banana leaf plates to eat the curry. The expert Brahmin who cooked it hailed from Patdai. That day he had cooked the rice of *prasad joha*[24] variety. That Brahmin used to say that this variety of rice went very well with iguana flesh. With them sat big fat Sombhu *mohura.* His words still echoed in her ears.

"We once killed an iguana at Mysanpur. The flesh of that iguana tasted like the flesh of young deer. The taste was sour and soft."

The Brahmin who was making rice paste for thickening the gravy, said—

"So the taste is quite sour, is it?"

"No, no! It is like *barali*[25] fish."

Somebody interrupted loudly, "No, not *barali.* It is like *sal*[26] fish. The colour of the iguana pieces looked like that of mushrooms."

Yes, yes! She remembered very clearly! Everybody had sat down in a circle with banana leaves in front of them. Even Indranath had taken a banana leaf, setting aside his decorated bronze plate. That was the first time they were eating iguana flesh. The curry had been brought in a big container. The gravy was thick with a layer of pure *ghee.* Its colour golden brown. The very sight of the curry was overwhelmingly tempting! Everybody started gulping it with relish. But Indranath just kept playing with the curry and rice, caught in two minds. His companions started laughing and shouting—

"Ha, Ha,......what are you doing?"

Indranath tried his best to put a morsel in his mouth but he could not. He tried, not once but twice, thrice, but he just could not eat it! Why Indranath! Even those Brahmins from Patdai who cooked it and the lanky son of the *mohura*, even they could not eat it! They left their banana leaves and went out to the *keccha nad*[27], where they gargled and cleaned their mouths thoroughly, making loud 'oke' 'oke' sounds.

But she? She had a strange surge of greed. She ate up that iguana curry with great relish! Not only the iguana curry! She had even finished off some *olchahara*[28] prepared by her mother for Indranath who could not take the luncheon dish. Her mother, wearing a red *mekhala*, was about to enter the kitchen when she saw Giribala and cried out—

"*Chiko! Chiko!* What are you doing? Such greed for flesh is very inauspicious for a girl!"

The women, who had come for pounding rice, also cried out—

"Look! Look! She's eating meat like an ogress!"

That day, only Indranath's friends could eat the iguana curry. Whatever was left was finished off with gusto by pot-bellied village urchins, like vultures falling on a dead goat!

Yes! Yes! Certainly her husband, Latu Gossain, must have held that woman's hand! He had greater greed than her.

That aroma! It has spread all over the place. Probably the Brahmins from distant places were eating in great haste. Fear of the rogue elephant was in the minds of all and they are eager to hurry back home before dark.

From the verandah, Giribala saw Durga's hair tied up in a big bun. She was so sharp and alert! She had keen ears and eyes and knew what was happening anywhere. Probably she would not come to this side now. Giribala darted into the palanquin room and picked up the pot of mutton cooked with black beans. She forgot everything....religion and rituals, wisdom or restraint....she started gulping it down in great haste.....

After her widowhood, she had taken only rice and pulses boiled with some vegetables, adding a pinch of salt and a little *ghee* made from cow's milk. Her tongue had become dull and dry. She was fed up with this diet.

What a delicious taste! She swallowed one morsel after another!

That woman of Maniari Kiniari must have certainly cooked in the same way for her husband! The curry must have been so delicious that he must have sucked her fingers greedily when she fed him with her hand. Giribala took one more large helping of the curry. Her mind was all awhirl with strange mysterious thoughts. But she did not stop eating. She almost emptied the pot. For the first time, a Gossain's daughter, in the manor of a *sattra*, had committed this heinous act!

* * * *

A loud screech startled Giribala. She jerked her head around. In a flash, she saw that Durga had almost fallen down in a faint near the palanquin. Near the door, two *jajamani* Brahmins stood rooted to the ground, trembling with fear and horror. Somebody shouted, "So that was the pot of mutton curry! Grab her hand! Grab it! Drag her out of the room!"

Hearing the shouts, those attending the ceremony started gathering outside the palanquin room. In no time at all, there was a big crowd there.

When the Gossainee heard about it, she left the kitchen and rushed to the spot. In a fit of rage, she caught hold of Giribala's braids and started kicking her. She was like a tigress in rage. She pulled her hair, punched her and clawed at her—as if she would tear off her flesh!

All the onlookers stood with their mouths open, stupefied and transfixed! Meanwhile everybody had forgotten about Durga. She still lay on the ground near the palanquin in a dead faint.

All of a sudden, a male voice exploded in the air. Indranath, pushing his way through the crowd, rushed to his mother and seizing her hand, shouted, "Do you want to kill her? Come to your senses! There are ways to purify her! Rituals for atonement! Why beat her so much?"

The *jajmani* Brahmin shouted—

"Yes! Yes! Let her atone! According to rituals in our books! Let her atone!"

The crowd had doubled within a short time. In the midst of the uproar and the excitement of the people, suddenly, a Brahmin boy darted into the palanquin room and kicked hard at the earthen pot. The contents, whatever was left, splashed out and flew in all directions! Brahmin women, standing nearby, screamed in horror and fled, helter-skelter, to avoid having even a tiny drop of the curry on themselves! Or they would have to take a bath again!

Meanwhile Brahmin women from Haramdo lifted the unconscious Durga, took her to the sandal room and sprinkled water on her face. Giribala lay in the palanquin room, surrounded by the crowd.

Jajmani Brahmins from Haramdo and Bangara were now divided in two warring groups, quarreling and arguing noisily....Who would take charge of this atonement ritual? The Brahmin who would perform the purification ceremony, would get a *mukcha* and a *sidha*[29] with a basket of rice, some potatoes, turmeric, salt and pure *ghee* in sufficient quantity to last for a few days, and also a pair of sacred threads. But when the chief *purohit* decided that he himself would undertake the ceremony, the fight between the Brahmins died down. This chief has already acquired several *bighas of miyadi kheraj*[30] land by performing such ceremonies for the Gossain.

He shouted—

"Bring water from the well and make her half drenched! Rest of you, now get out from here! Quick! Bring some rice, one copper coin, and some shells! Ah! And some flowers, *tulsi leaves* and a few *donas* please!"

Some Brahmin women from Haramdo pulled Giribala towards the well.

The Gossainee returned to the verandah near the sacrificing pit and sat down on the floor, her knees hugging her breasts, her head resting on her knees. She was not one of those women who break down easily and weep copiously in public. Her companion, Guimeni, stood on one side, quietly observing her.

The priest dipped *dubori* grass, in water and sprinkled it on Giribala at intervals, uttering a Sanskrit *mantra* at the same time in his peculiar faulty Sanskrit accent and getting it all garbled.

Bidhava Brahmachari cha
Kamenaiva yadaskrita
Matsya mansan Samashiliyat
Eaindvatsu Samacharet
Matsan mansan mansuransa tambulan
Bhustrinatha
Eatnan Yagdhatu bidhava kuyaccha
nan-drayan brata.

> (If a widow or a *brahmachari*[31] partakes knowingly of fish and meat, they will have to go through eight *dhanu prayaschit*[32]. If they eat *masoor dal*[33], betelnut, white pumpkin, they will have to practice three *dhanu prayaschit* etc.)

Three Brahmins, who had only recently started wearing sacred threads, stood near the well and talked among themselves—

"The *vidhan*[34] of the South Bank should be changed."

The other Brahmin exclaimed—

"Yes, Yes! It should be changed! In this old wretched *vidhan*, even if you eat without wearing a sacred thread, you have to utter the *gayatri mantra* a thousand times!"

"Yes, nowadays which Brahmin does thirty *dhenu prayaschit* after taking food prepared by a washerman or a fisherman!"

"Yes, yes! Nowadays nobody does four *dhanu prayaschit* after eating the flesh of deer killed by a gun. Have you ever seen our Indranath Gossain doing *prayaschit* after eating a dove or a deer killed by a bullet? And those thieves caught redhanded in the Gossain's house. Will they do twelve years' fasting according to rituals?"

Somebody shouted from the crowd—

"Look! Giribala is trembling! She'll collapse. Oh! She's falling down! Catch hold of her!...Somebody...Catch her!"

* * * *

This drama of purification and ritualistic atonement went on for quite a long time. Then there were admonitions and stern warnings and moral lectures from the family members, so that Giribala would not repeat such detestable sins. At last the tumult and the excitement died down and peace descended on the Gossain's manor.

* * * *

Giribala could not recollect afterwards who brought her to the small room adjacent to the sandal room. The room was so tiny that just one cot and a wooden box filled up all the space. The lid of the *urium*-wood box was flung open…inside she could see her *mekhalas* and *gatalas* and other things necessary for a Brahmin widow, dumped anyhow by the maid-servant…

She was still trembling and shivering. Her dress was wet with perspiration and the water sprinkled on her for purification. She changed immediately. Her arms, legs, neck and face, were covered with bluish bruises and scratches. Tiny beads of dark red blood had oozed out on her skin. She looked around the room. All the doors and windows are tightly shut. From the wooden ceiling above her head, came soft sounds of weevils boring into the wood. These sounds of inexorable destruction struck further terror in her heart.

The Gossain and Saru Gossain got up. All the disciples had paid their respects and departed. The trays of coins were overflowing. They went inside the sandal room.

From the *batghar* came the sound of argument between two *jajmani* Brahmin boys. Probably they were exchanging or selling the gifts they had received. It might have been a *urium*-wood stool or a brass *ghati*[35], exchanged or sold for something else unwanted by one of them.

Sounds of conversation between the Gossain of Bamundi and one of the *jajmani* Brahmins also floated on the air…

"Manu, the law maker, has rightly said..."

"What did he say?"

"Manu said that in the *shraddha* of the gods, it is sufficient to feed only two Brahmins. If it is the *shraddha* of your father or grandfather or great grandfather, then three Brahmins are required. If it is the *shraddha* of both a god and your father or grandfather, then only one Brahmin will suffice....Now look at all this chaos inside the manor! What was the necessity of such a big crowd of Brahmins?"

Suddenly the voice of *Adhikar Mahaprabhu* came from the sandal room—

"Didn't the same Manu also say that the soul of the dead person, may it be father or grandfather, becomes enshrined in the bodies of Brahmins who are invited and fed in the *shraddha*? So the invited Brahmins should speak about these matters with restraint and respect!"

For a long time now, calm had prevailed. Giribala, locked up inside the small room, thought after hearing this exchange, now the topic of my transgression will come up and the whole atmosphere will again be vitiated. She opened her eyes and stared at the closed door. Her ears picked up some words again. No, they were not talking about her. The conversation now was about the rogue elephant who had escaped.

"The rogue has gone towards Jirang."

"And a widow has eaten what she shouldn't have eaten! These are evil omens."

"Yes, yes! It isn't the *makhana* as the rumours indicated. It is the tusker, the most favourite elephant of the Gossain! *Mahaprabhu* travelled astride it, not only to visit disciples but also to attend the marriage ceremonies of the Mahajans of South Bank. Ah, what a sight it used be! The elephant, most magnificently decorated!"

"The Gossain is very unhappy though it doesn't show on his face. He is so restrained. He and his father and his grandfather spent their lives riding in *howda* on their elephants. And now this tusker has thrown away the *howda* and become frenzied. Bad times have come!"

Another voice whispered—

"Did you notice that the Gossain didn't even glance at the overflowing trays of coins at his feet? And when he got up from his seat to go inside the sandal room, the wooden stool gave out a 'krr, krr' sound? Mind you! It's not a good sign!"

Shadows were lengthening. It would be dark soon. Suddenly they all became conscious and remembered that they must hurry home before the night set in. Who knows? The rogue may cross their path!

✯ ✯ ✯ ✯

Somebody brought a small kerosene oil lamp to the dark coffin-like room.

Nothing seems all right! What will I do now? What can I do? Suicide? Ah, that Christian! Why doesn't he say anything? Leaving aside all other work, I collected all those manuscripts....brought them for him to the *dhekal* room!....

Night deepened. Giribala sat on the wooden cot, hunched, her knees hugging her chest in a tight squeeze, her arms clasped round her legs, staring vacantly at the dimly glowing lamp.

Suddenly a sound of knocking on the door! She stood up with a start, went to the window and opened it hesitantly. Bright moonlight jumped into the room through the open window and bathed the interior with a silver glow. Outside stood Mark Sahib, outlined against the heavenly light of the moon! She could see his eyes reflecting the colour of the red-tinted silt of the Jagalia river. He said through the window—

"I can't imagine how to express my pain at what happened today. Please try to understand and forgive my helplessness!"

She did not reply. Mark remained silent for some time, then spoke again—

"The desire that has no end or that which cannot be fulfilled. Why worry about it? Leave it to God!"

Again silence! Giribala did not say anything.

"To some extent, we are all sinners. In the temple of God, the vessel on the altar is pure, but we have made it impure by drinking wine in it. Each one of us has an invisible banner hanging over one's head, on which are written our judgments and punishments! When weighed against God's commandments, we always come out much less in weight...And we..."

Giribala spat out passionately, "Shut up! Shut up, you white man! Now listen! The manuscripts you want are lying on the wooden plank overhead in the *dhekal.* Go and take them."

Then she came very near the window and gripped the grill bars with her two hands. She stared at Mark for a moment. All of a sudden, she thrust her right hand through the bars and caught hold of the collar of his *punjabi.* Mark Sahib gently prised open her fingers from the collar and pushed her hand inside. He uttered softly—

"Do you know what our Saviour has said? You, who want to follow me! Come after me, each one of you carrying his cross."

Giribala's body became slack, her shoulders drooped.

She went back listlessly, without a word, to the bed and fell down on it like a broken piece of wood. Mark stood outside the window for a long time. Suddenly he became conscious of some persons peering at him curiously. He turned away from the window and headed towards the *dhekal* to collect the manuscripts.

After some time, Giribala opened her eyes. Her gaze went to a corner of the room. A big umbrella with red, green and pink-coloured fine satin cloth, was lying there. It was a ceremonial umbrella used by the Gossain for offering sacrificial meals to his dead ancestors in the waters of Jagalia.

She could see the fine satin silk shining in the dark like the skin of a snake...

A flash of memory passed through her mind...It was the day when her husband had come to this house for the first time after the marriage for the *niyata*[36]. From the *batghar* to the house, Indranath and Sambhu *mohura* had escorted him by holding over his head this same red, green and pink umbrella. But this memory did not evoke any sensation of love or respect for her husband. The man who had tied himself in a disgusting relationship with that notorious woman, the opium seller. How could it?

What has happened to her?

The satin seemed to undulate, shining and shimmering, dazzling her eyes. She got up slowly from the bed and walked softly towards it. She began caressing the cloth. It was soft and smooth like Mark Sahib's skin...so soft, so smooth...She rubbed the silk on her cheeks, her neck, her breasts...all over her body in a soft, languid movement of her hand...as if she desired to pull all the silk on to her, wrap herself in its softness...

This silk, this umbrella that had brought her husband into the untainted precincts of a Gossain's house with due respect and religious formalities....This silk was now the skin of a *gora mlecha,* a Christian!...was it possible?....Did anybody, in this place, ever have such experiences? Giribala's eyes filled up with tears.

A whisper escaped from her innermost being—

"Oh! Please! Take me out of this wooden coffin! Please! I beg you!"

Ten

Till now the rogue elephant had not taken any human life. Hence the question of shooting it had not yet arisen, even though considerable panic gripped the people in the area. Almost everyone had sympathy for the elephant, he was such a fine animal. He could roam wherever he liked, provided he did not harm anybody. The elephants of the Gossains of Urputh and Pathaldia had also turned rogues and escaped, but after some time, they had disappeared into the thick forests of Jirang. Let this elephant also follow the same path and disappear! He was such a majestic beast. He had eighteen nails on his feet, an auspicious mark. His curving tusks were like the graceful swords of Sikh soldiers. The hair at the end of his tail spread out like a peacock feather. An elephant's tail which is long and touches the ground is considered inauspicious. But this elephant's tail was not so.

For the last four months, there has been repeated attempts to capture Jagannath. The famous *phandi*[1] of South Bank, Jamaluddin Garia, was keeping vigil on a *machan* in Matiapahar, with a firm resolve to catch him at any cost. He boasted a lot of his exploits, of how he had caught rogue elephants of other Gossains. But now, after facing dismal failure, his pride and arrogance had mellowed to some extent. However, he remained glued to his *machan* with obstinate foolhardiness!

One day, the *bhagat*[2] of the *sattra* stood before the stable of the elephant corral and said—

"Why should the rogue elephant go anywhere near Jamaluddin? That fool had killed his mother when Jagannath was still a baby. That was a long time ago. Jamaluddin knew that the *kunki*[3] he was riding was very headstrong and unpredictable. Finally he had to kill the mother to capture the baby."

Other *phandis* were curious. They asked him—

"How did he kill the mother elephant?"

"Oh! That was a horrible scene! The *kunki* gored the mother with his sharp tusks and had trampled her. All the while, the mother stood steadfast, protecting her baby under her bely! Oh! I'll never forget that scene! At last she fell under his savage attack. There was thick blood all around. With great difficulty, they pulled out the baby, still alive, from under the dead mother."

"But isn't it against the law?"

"That part of the forest is so thick that not even a bird can fly through it. Who would care to go inside and get the actual facts? But still...I remember, the permits of the *phandi* and the *kunki* were impounded."

"Yes, nowadays who cares for the forest laws and rules, regulations! Only the other day, our old Gossain along with the Gossain of Urput had gone hunting in Matiapahar forest. There they suddenly confronted a rogue elephant! They killed him and with their own hands...in the silence of the night, they cut the carcass into pieces and threw the pieces into the river!" The old *bhagat*, with a drooping beard, dressed in tattered clothes, now spoke—

"Did you see what this frenzied elephant did in broad daylight?"

"What did he do, the great Jagannath?"

The old men said:

"Within three months of bringing Jagannath from *dohar,* he was fully trained. He was clever and learned fast. He even picked up the trick of playing on one of those flutes made by children from the trunk of plantain tree! On the command *agate,* he would go forward, much farther than the line marked out for him! On hearing *chei,* the command for the elephant to lie down flat on his right or left side, he would instead start romping around amidst the children gathered there...purposely...And when the word *biri* was uttered..."

The other men become impatient and one of them interrupted him and said—

"Yes! Yes! That's all very interesting but what happened that afternoon in broad daylight! Come on! Tell us quickly!"

"Oh, yeah, yeah,......It happened near the *batghar* of the old manor. After the great earthquake of 1818, the Gossains had left Geraimari and settled down in this *sattra.* They had decorated the *batghar* with tin sheets cut on all sides in attractive designs. Now they are rusted all over and look like a camel's skin. In fact it is now sagging and slanting in such a way that it does look like a camel! Just before the Gossain went to visit his old disciples, and to meet new ones, Muslim artisans were called from Bholagaon to clean the elephant's *howda.* They came, in a group of three or four, clad only in *gamuchas* wrapped round their hips. They first took bath in a well nearby, before sitting down in the *batghar* to do their work. They dusted and polished all the different parts, cleaned the finely carved designs and repainted the woodwork. When that afternoon, the incident occurred, these Muslim artisans were doing the same job..."

All of them exclaimed together, "Yes, Yes, go on! Tell us what Jagannath did in the *batghar* of the old manor!"

The old man, thoughtful, his head bowed, continued—

"You know, elephants are almost divine creatures. They are all-knowing...."

"Yes, yes! But what happened!"

"At dawn, he came down from Matiapahar and tramping along the bank of Jagalia river, reached the *batghar* and stood near the *howda*. The Muslim artisans, who were at that time cleaning and repairing the *howda*, were at first stupefied at seeing this huge animal at their elbow, but then they panicked and ran for their lives! Then what do you think happened? It was an amazing sight! Jagannath wrapped his trunk round the *howda*, lifted it and just walked away with the damn thing! Right through the *sattra*! Some of those who saw him were speechless with amazement and terror."

Cries of 'Terrible! Terrible!' escaped from the mouths of some of the people present."

"Then?"

"Jagannath took the *howda* to the river side, laid it down on the sand of Jagalia....and then, with great fury, he trampled on it and broke it into a thousand pieces. Then he flung the broken parts all around on the sand, playfully throwing them into the air and kicking them as if possessed by the joyful spirit of *holi*."

The men listening to the old *bhagat* exclaimed—

"But why? Why was he furious with the *howda?* It's most puzzling!"

"Who can say why? God alone knows! But I can tell you one thing. When the old Gossain died, at that moment, three *puhkars* (the evil unauspicious planets) were in ascendance; it indicates the downfall of the dynasty! Did you not hear now the Communists in Rangamati are clamouring for the Gossains to till their own land or quit? Have you ever heard of such a thing? Can a Gossain go to the field and plough the land with his own hands? Can he soil his hands with mud and slush?"

The *kaamla* of the Gossain's elephant, a short, stocky man clad in only khaki shorts, now spoke—

"That *howda* had come down from the time of the old Gossain's grandfather. His old copper sandals are still lying in the Gopinath temple. I can tell you many scandalous stories about this grandfather of the old Gossain."

The men around him cried out—

"Scandalous stories? Do tell us!"

"That old Gossain had a terrible temper! Once, in great rage, he thrashed and kicked his wife to death...."

The men exclaimed—

"What? Really to death? Is it possible?"

"When King Siva Singha heard of it, he immediately sent his sentries to arrest Gossain. When the news reached Gossain's ears, he mounted his tiger in a flash and fled into the jungles of Jirang. There, he locked himself into a stone house with iron doors."

The others cried out in disbelief—

"What did you say? His tiger!"

"That's how the story goes. Perhaps it was a tame tiger or his horse named Tiger. Siva Singha's sentries couldn't catch him after all....And this *howda*, which Jagannath destroyed, actually belonged to this old, old Gossain whose copper sandals can be seen in Gopinath temple even today."

A Home Guard of the Opium Prohibition Committee

was listening to all this great interest. He had a square face with thick eyebrows meeting over his nose. Under his eyebrows, his small eyes darted here and there suspiciously. He said—

"The elephant won't destroy the *howda* without any rhyme or reason! There is definitely something behind it....."

From the corral came the sounds of elephants flapping their ears. A female elephant of Monpur Gossain, brought from the *dohar,* had been injured rather badly and she was now lying in an enclosure. Her cries of agony came through the air, mingled with the sounds of flapping ears. They were all apprehensive that the rogue elephant Jagannath would smell out this cow elephant and come charging to this place to attack her.

The Home Guard spoke again, emphasising his words by thumping his staff on the ground—

"*Bapu*, in your long life, you have seen many elephants in frenzy and heard many stories about them. Tell me, what are the symptoms shown by this elephant? Do you think he can be caught? Or will it be necessary to kill him?"

The old *bhagat* looked at the ground and pondered for a while. His face was covered with a network of wrinkles like a flimsy worn-out cloth. Some of the lines around his eyes now stood out deep and distinct with thought.

Finally he uttered, as if he had not heard the question—

"During the time of Vrikodar Gossain, one rogue elephant had killed a man and disappeared into the forest of Jirang. He was never seen again. People say that he was as large as a mountain and his tusks were curved like the sword used for sacrificing buffaloes in Kamakhya temple! A wooden stool would be slung by two ropes from his tusks for the Gossain to sit on and he would travel to Gauhati like that! Ah! Those were the days!"

The Home Guard cried out excitedly—

"Vrikodar Gossain! Who was killed by his own disciples! Is it really true? How awful! Such a thing was never heard of before.....by his own disciples?"

Saying so, he picked up some loose earth from the ground and touched his forehead with it.

A whiff of the alkaline odour of elephant dung, carried by the wind from the corral, assailed the nostrils of the men gathered there. The old man covered his nose with a corner of his *gamucha* and continued—

"Some say that he was stoned to death, some say that the *tantric* sorcery of the Mayangs killed him. It happened near Beltalla."

He wiped his face with the *gamucha* and sat for some time, staring absently before him.

Meanwhile some children, who spent most of their time wading through pond water in search of small fish hiding beneath arum plants, had joined the Home Guard, the *kaamla* in *khaki* shorts and others, sitting around the old *bhagat*. When the latter suddenly stopped speaking, some of them burst out impatiently—

"Why do you stop in the middle from time to time? Go on, tell us the whole story!"

"Once Vrikodar Gossain punished a man in a very cruel manner. He was made to lie down on the ground on his back and a big heavy stone was hoisted on his chest. He was forced to lie like that for a long time, poor soul....He died in extreme agony. This incident incensed the other disciples and kindled their wrath! So they killed him!"

Suddenly a *Kaamla,* the one in shorts, shouted in great astonishment—

"Oh God! Look at these twisted nails!"

He picked up a wooden beam from the ground that

was once the bottom part of a *howda* and showed to all those gathered around, two twisted nails sticking out from its bottom.

Everybody exclaimed—

"How terrible! Those two nails must have rubbed against the elephant's back and made very painful wounds without anybody knowing about it."

The air was filled with sighs. Someone remarked—

"Everybody saw the gorgeous *howda* and the fine ceremonial clothes of the Gossain. They were dazzled by the grand spectacle and forgot about the poor elephant's back!"

Another man exclaimed at the top of his voice—

"I remember now! The shoulders of the Gossain's palanquin bearer got infested with worms. The same thing must have happened to the elephant's back also....."

The Home Guard uttered forcefully—

"Stupid palanquin bearer! He should have exhibited his anger like that rogue elephant! Why did he not kick and smash the palanquin into bits and pieces?"

"Alas! That poor fellow died of tetanus! His body arched like a bow and became as rigid as teakwood!"

* * * *

Indranath had taken out his teakwood pipe after a long interval. He filled it with tobacco, struck a match and started puffing at it. He was pacing the mud floor of the verandah from one end to the other. He was unhappy and restless. There was serious trouble again over the land at Marabhitha. It had become a symbol of status and prestige for the Gossain family. And for Indranath, it had taken the shape of a malignant wound. This patch of land had been immersed in water since long and it was useless. Even then, the Gossain continued to pay taxes on it at Lohar Ghat! Then gradually the water receded, and after three years, due to siltage, a stretch of fine fertile land came up. Without the knowledge of the Gossain, many villagers began to farm there. The land produced rich, luxuriant crops, season after season as if the river had deposited gold in it. Then, by chance, Sombhu *mohura,* who had never cared to oversee this piece of land all these years, visited the site, and what he saw dazzled his eyes...fields of waving golden heads of paddy in a lush green carpet! He summoned all those working on the fields. When they gathered in a group near him, he began shouting at them in a cold, harsh voice—

"You fools! You are cultivating this land without the permission of the Gossain. Just because he's a gentle, pious man, do you think you can do whatever you want without his knowledge? This cannot go on, do you hear me? It cannot continue! The Gossain has been paying taxes for this land. Something has to be done now...you all must agree to pay either *adhi*[4] or *chukani*[5]."

Nearby on a triangular-shaped field, a red-coloured pennant was fluttering on a bamboo pole. Under it sat an old man with overflowing hair and a long beard. He now stood up, and staring hard at the *mohura,* said in a cunning, sarcastic tone—

"*Mohura*—you bastard! Who doesn't know you around here? Are you telling us to pay *adhi*? Are you? We now know what to demand! We know our rights! We no longer pay bribes and make out false land deeds...do you hear me? No longer! No more of turning temporary land lease into a periodic one!"

Some people, intending to join the crowd, turned away after hearing the old man and left the place. But one old peasant, probably still loyal to the Gossain, approached the *mohura* and said in a whisper—

"Tell the Gossain to come here on his elephant, in that old *howda.* His very presence will cast a divine spell! All these people...", and he moved his arm in a semi-circle, "...all these people will fall at his feet. And that red flag will be torn into shreds and thrown into the river!"

The old peasant wanted to say something more but just at that moment, two big clods of earth, probably hurled by people at the fringe of the crowd, fell on Sombhu *mohura* and the old man. This was followed by a veritable shower of clods. The old peasant fell down and the *mohura* fled for his life. Later, news reached the *sattra* that the poor old peasant had died from the wounds he had received that fateful day of Sombhu *mohura's* visit. As for the latter, he dared not go again to Marabhitha!

Indranath continued pacing the verandah, drawing on his teakwood pipe from time to time. Thoughts of that ill-fated piece of land still troubled his mind. The progress of his thoughts, their different turns and twists were reflected in the way he smoked his pipe. As if the pipe itself had become the embodiment of his thoughts.....

The Gossainee was also there on the verandah, sitting on a wooden stool, a red *mekhala* tied round her bosom. Guimeni, the old hunchbacked village woman, was squatting beside her on the floor hugging her thin legs, greedily awaiting a share of the tobacco, feeding her with the latest village gossip. It was almost time for the Gossainee to enter the cooking-shed as she always prepared her own food. Before that, it was her habit to take a few puffs of tobacco pipe in the quiet solitude of the small wooden room. But today, her mind was preoccupied. The issue of the Marabhitha land had come up. Whenever this vexing question raised its head, it numbed and silenced. Even the presence of Guimeni could not make her utter a single word.

Suddenly, a bullock-cart came to a halt in the court yard, with a lot of racket and in a cloud of dust. The Home Guard of the opium prohibition committee, the *Kaamla* and some *bandhas* jumped out and began unloading and dumping broken pieces of a *howda* in one corner of the courtyard. Everybody came out and stood around the ruined *howda* in ghostly silence. The Home Guard broke the long spell of silence—

"You shouldn't feel so dejected. Something can still be done. Those Muslim carpenters can perhaps repair the broken parts and join them again."

Encouraged by these words, the *Kaamla* felt bold enough to say—"Ah! It was such a wonderful showpiece! Such a fine *howda* cannot be found in the whole of Hindustan!"

The Home Guard retorted—

"It's all very well for you to say how wonderful, how valuable it was! But what about those twisted nails sticking out underneath the *howda*? You could have noticed them earlier, couldn't you?"

Indranath removed the pipe from his mouth and exclaimed—

"What! What's this about twisted nails? What twisted nails?"

The Home Guard explained—

"From the square frame at the bottom of the *howda,* four hook-like nails were seen sticking out, when the broken pieces were gathered. God alone knows whether they are the handiwork of the carpenters who made the *howda* and for what mysterious purpose, or whether the nails came out later on. But it is true that the twisted nails must have dug into the elephant's back and made painful wounds."

The Gossainee, who was sitting hunched on the verandah with Guimeni, now interrupted, in an incredulous tone—

"What's so mysterious about it! All elephants carry this type of *howda*. Even that old Cowriah, who makes small clay toys, fashions same type of *howda* from clay and puts it on the toy elephants. So what's the mystery behind those protruding nails? I don't understand...."

She got up and came down from the verandah. She went to the heap of broken pieces and started examining them. Guimeni followed her.

The Home Guard suddenly remembered something. Once in Ukkiam in the Garo Hills, hidden under the canopy of thick cane and bamboo trees to catch an opium-smuggling merchant, a youth with Communist leanings had joined him. Just at that moment, two elephants had passed by carrying people on their backs. The youth had remarked—

"Look! There go some merchants from Cooch Behar! Sitting so comfortably in those decorated *howdas*! Those elephants carry the heavy load of people all their life till they are half-dead...almost. They are like you and me...people like us. They are *gajamurkha*[6] and we are also *gajamurkha* like them!"

The Home Guard was almost on the point of uttering loudly—"Do you know what is the symbol of the decorated *howda*?" but he stopped abruptly when he saw the angry face of the Gossainee...

Looking at the *bandhas*, Indranath shouted commands—

"Hurry up! Pick up those broken pieces and stack them

in a corner of the *dhekal*! Be careful! Don't allow anybody to touch them!"

Gradually everyone dispersed. That evening, the Gossainee did not re-enter the small tobacco room for a smoke, but instead went straight to the kitchen. Guimeni waited in vain. Finally, in great disappointment, she left.

Indranath went to the backward, still puffing at his pipe. He stood there silently. For a long time, a kind of depression settled over him. He felt totally frustrated. Suddenly his eyes fell on Bhagwati's house in the horizon. His mind was diverted. A cool breeze seemed to caress forehead. That *kathana* tree opposite wound with white flowers! A wild creeper bloomed round and round the trunk of the tree occasionally hanging down like honeycombs. He was annoyed. This thick creeper would obstruct his view. He would not be able to see her when she come out and stood near the well! What kind of a creeper was it? How much of it would grow and how much would die and fall down? Indranath looked up. The sky was clear and clean...like her fair face. On the day she had surrendered herself, he had felt he had attained something, achieved something rare and invaluable in life!

He resumed pacing the length of the backyard. After some time, his pipe went cold. The tobacco had burnt out. It was almost time for the Gossain to come out after his prayers. Today he had to go to the North Bank for his annual ceremonial visit to his disciples. Bhagwati the priest had consulted the astrological charts and calculated that the best time to start would be in the second half of the day. It would be the most auspicious time for a journey in the northernly direction.

The *bandhas* were busy taking out from the attic the paraphernalia that would be taken with the Gossain—

the *chandrataap*[7], a huge satin umbrella, brass containers and copper dishes, brass and copper chalices in the shape of wine glass for drinking, brass and silver tumblers, brass and silver quarter plates with decorative designs, mosquito nets, handwoven shawls, brass and copper spoons and ladles of different shapes, kerosene lanterns, clay and copper mustard oil lamps and cane mats of assorted sizes. All these items would be taken in bullock carts.

Indranath stood before the door of the sandal room. He could see the Gossain inside. He was wrapping religious manuscripts very carefully in clean white *gamuchas*. Indranath waited to tell him about the wrecking of the *howda* by the rogue elephant.

* * * *

Durga was neatly folding clothes for the Gossain's journey in a skilfully crafted wooden box. There were fine *Shantipuri dhotis, telach* and *barkapurs*[8], towels of various designs, silk *chaddars* and sacred threads. After completing her task, she went to the well outside for a wash and a drink of water. Suddenly she saw, coming along the road, a group of *pandas*[9] from the Jagannath temple of Puri. Some were short, some tall, some thin and others fat. But all of them wore saffron coloured *dhoti and chaddar.* Each one of them had a red *ghantakarna*[10] flower hanging from the stump of hair at the back of an otherwise clean shaven head.

A lightning wave of excitement passed through Durga's body. At last her chance had come to go to Jagannath Puri with these *pandas*! Who knows when such a chance will come again? For a long time, a dull, dry cough had racked her chest, a sharp pain she had hidden away. Who knows, probably it was that dreaded disease T.B.? She glanced at her arms and legs. There was no trace of any flesh. Just skin and bones! The village women often made fun of her, saying that when she went out in her *mekhala* and *gatala*, she looked like one of the witch dolls made by Kawria for the festival held on the bank of Jagalia. No! No! She would never let go of this chance. One desire preying constantly on her mind. Who knows, she may go further on to Prayag and immerse the sacred bones of her dead husband in the divine Ganga water! She had resolved even to offer her hair to the deities....

"Oh! You'll offer your hair?"—Saru Gossainee had exclaimed, one day. Her *mekhala* and *ghatala* were clean and her hair gave off a smell of fragrant oil. People said that she brought this hair oil from the *marwari*[11] merchants settled on the Brahmaputra bank at Palasbari.....

* * * *

Incredible! The *pandas* were going in the other direction, bypassing the manor! Ah! Probably they had come to know that Damodaria Gossainee would not go for pilgrimage this year. What's the difference between these *pandas* and notorious spies! They knew the pecuniary conditions of women from Gossain families and Brahmin families, as far away as Chikarhati. They knew everything—Certainly they knew everything about the house! The frenzied elephant who was creating havoc all round. Giribala's wayward behaviour with that Christian missionary. And the Communist threats on Marabhitha land! Indranath's attraction towards that Brahmin girl.

No! No! Today none of the *pandas* had entered the *batghar*! They were heading towards Talukdarpara and Haramdo. Those two tall *pandas* and the three short ones were lagging behind! Would it be all right if she called out

Actress Trisha Saikia in the Assamese film *Adaja* based on Indira Goswami's novel *Datal Haatir Une Khowa Howdah*. The film has won several national and international awards

Actress Trisha Saikia in *Adaja* based on Indira Goswami's novel *Datal Haatir Une Khowa Howdah*. The novel has been listed as a classic by the Sahitya Akademi and listed in *Masterpieces in Indian Literature* published by the National Book Trust

Actress Nandita Das and American actor Nathan Scott in the Hindi television serial *Kamrup Ki Kahani,* based on Jnanpith recipient Indira Goswami's novel *Datal Haatir Une Khowa Howdah*

Nandita Das as Goribala and Nathan Scott as Mark Sahib in the Hindi television serial *Kamrup Ki Kahani*

Actresses Trisha Saikia (Best Actress at the State Film Festival, 1998) and Tribeni Borah (Best Supporting Actress at the State Film Festival, 1998) in the national and international award-winning Assamese film *Adaja*

Actress Nandita Das and American actor Nathan Scott in the Hindi television serial *Kamrup Ki Kahani*

A scene from the Hindi television serial *Kamrup Ki Kahani*

Assamese actress Trisha Saikia and Hindi film and TV actor Tom Alter in a scene from the Assamese film *Adaja*

to them? She became restless. She had to do something! She went quickly towards the *batghar.* Yes! Yes! If that killer disease had possessed her body, she must do something now! Immediately!

If the end does come soon, she has no fears about her own cremation. That good soul, Indranath, would do every thing required for the last rites. Yes, if she died, even the Chikarhati Gossains would. Wasn't she also a daughter-in-law of the same Damodariya Gossains! And had disciples who respectfully gathered dust from her feet and marked their brows with it.

She left all her work undone and waited for the *pandas.*

* * * *

With the devotees crowding around, cheering and successful journey, the Gossain took his seat in the decorated palanquin and started on the first leg of the journey towards Maniari Kiniari. This time, the usual team of elephants did not accompany him. Only one old elephant trailed behind carrying a heavy load of luggage.

Of course, before starting on this auspicious journey, the Gossain had called Jamaluddin Geria and blessing him, had told him—

"Be sure to maintain the excellent reputation of your ancestors who were expert *phandis,* and showed great intelligence in catching rogue elephants! If you are successful, I will grant you seven *bighas* of *miyadi kheraj*[12] land in Ukiam!"

Then the Gossain looked at Sombhu *mohura* who appeared even more fat in an old *endi punjabi*—

"If you fail to settle the matter of the Marabhitha land, then you must go immediately to Gauhati. That lawyer from

Upper Assam, Jagdish, has taken such cases of South Bank Gossains, and he has managed to settle their land disputes with dignity and honour."

At the mention of Marabhitha land, a shadow of apprehension passed over the faces of those standing nearby and they immediately looked down.....

The Gossain now turned towards Indranath, his face registering serious concern. He guided the latter to the palanquin and spoke to him in a low voice—

"A couple of men have told me that you had a hand in the release of that Brahmin priest of Rajapukhauri. It is true that we don't like Brahmins to go to jail....but then many of them have been found guilty in the past. After all, a crime is a crime, and it's a serious matter. Why should you think in terms of caste differences in such a situation? Even our religious scriptures have said that, in crime, all are equal, and there are no caste barriers! But...."

The *adhikar* glanced swiftly at Indranath's face to see if one or two lines of remorse appeared on his face? No, nothing! The Gossain stood silent for some time, stunned.

The Gossain turned away and began scanning the backyard, towards the pounding shed. Everybody in the crowd could guess who he was searching for. Their eyes also turned in the direction of the pounding shed in the backyard. Where was Giribala? Generally she would be there, right in the front ranks of the crowd, to see the Gossain off! The Gossainee, standing near the threshold, said—

"Two men were here. They took her to Machkuchi. She had come to know about some old manuscripts found in the *dhekal* of Machkuchi Gossain and...that Christian missionary has also gone there! I don't think she'll be back before evening."

The *chaddar* with a floral border in *muga*[13] slipped from his shoulders and fell on the ground. He bent down and picked it up himself. Then without looking at any one, he silently turned round and entered the palanquin. The palanquin bearers, of *shuri*[14] caste, lifted the palanquin and their chests swelling with pride, took off in a rhythmic trot. Old Kowria, clad only in a *gamucha* tied firmly round his loins, blowing vigorously on his *kaalia,* followed the palanquin bearers. Behind him, joined the entire retinue—Brahmin cooks from Haramdo, *bandhas* for making plantain *donas, ojhas* with their group of chorus singers, drum beaters with their musical instruments (who also perform acrobatic feats), and others. From Maniari Kiniari, they would go ahead by different modes of transport—some by bullock-carts, some on elephants and others by bus from Palasbari. Only the Gossain would travel in the old Ford car, sent specially for him by the disciples of Upper Assam.

One old *makhana*[15] elephant from the elephant corral followed slowly behind the retinue. The road between Maniarai Kiniali and Palasbari was very bad. It was a routine practice to take an elephant along to pull out the car from the potholes on the road. This old *makhana* had not done this type of work before. Now, after independence, the Gossain had only two elephants left in the corral. It was the other elephant, now in frenzy, who always accompanied the Gossain and pulled out the car if it got stuck. The old *makhana* was not at all good looking. His trunk was too thick. His tusks had been missing for a long time. His dull hide looked like a tortoise shell.

A tremor passed though the Gossainee's body. She felt very uneasy. This time the Gossain had left the mansion in a disturbed mood. He also looked annoyed. He had not taken his usual affectionate farewell from her. Certainly the

Gossain was not pleased with Giribala, the way she had gone away without telling anybody! But poor Giribala, when did she get the time? In the morning, one young couple had come for *haihal*[16]. The Gossain was busy with them for quite a long time. Giribala had not had the opportunity to talk to him. But then why should the Gossain frown upon the Christian missionary? He himself had approved of Mark Sahib and said that this missionary had special qualities. He would be the right person to search for and compile a list of all those precious writings of *Santa Mahaprabhu*, whose manuscripts lay buried, here and there, in old manors.

The piercing sound of Kowria's *kaalia* slowly died down in the distance as the Gossain's party crossed the Jagalia bridge. The Gossainee looked on as Indranath moved from his place, took his bicycle and started pedalling towards Barihat....

* * * *

Normally, at this time of the day, Durga would be sitting by the loom, on which the Gossainee would be weaving cloth and she would be spinning thread on her spindle. The whole atmosphere would be serene and peaceful. But this had changed ever since Durga had taken away her box of jewellery and kept it in Saru Gossainee's custody. A wall had arisen between her and the Gossainee.

After the Gossain's departure, Durga went to the *batghar* and stood here. She saw Guimeni coming out of the courtyard. The latter had just taken a puff of tobacco and she had nothing to do. She was thinking of going with the small children of the *sattra* to the bank of Jagalia and catching some small fish swimming in between arum plants. When she saw Durga, she stopped abruptly, perplexed. Why was she here? Guimeni put her hands on her hips, straightened her hunchback, and addressed her—

"Ah, *maichana!* Your *gatala* is looking like an old, torn rag! Your bones stand out like thorns! What has happened to you? And for whom are you standing here at this hour?"

Durga knew that this old hunchbacked woman was a cunning spy. She carried tales to the Gossainee about whatever was going on in the *sattra*. In return, Gossainee poured out her innermost thoughts to Guimeni. When the Gossainee was in trouble or agony, Guimeni wept for her.

Durga did not utter a word in reply. Guimeni's sixth sense warned her that something unusual was afoot! She sat down on the ground, resting her crooked back against a wooden pillar of the *batghar.*

"Perhaps you are waiting for your relatives from Chikarhati, are you?"

Again Durga did not say a word.

"Eh! *Maichana*! So many days have passed and they haven't come. Will they come now? You had better abandon all thoughts of shame or dignity and go back to your in-law's place. It is better to breathe your last in your own husbands house."

Again Durga did not reply!

"Why don't you wear a chemise? Your chest bones are sticking out. You are looking like a scarecrow. How long can you live with this body and this face?"

Durga's mind, which had started simmering, suddenly cooled down when she saw the *pandas* returning from the opposite direction. Three short and two tall men with bald pates and saffron coloured clothes. She felt as if the ruling deity of the *sattra*, Gopeshwar, was holding out a bouquet of flowers! Forgetting about Guimeni's presence, Durga cried out—

"There! There! They are back!"

She stood up and looked towards the road—

"Oh, those *pandas*! They came long ago. They found a woman in Haramdo. Now they are on their way back."

But Durga's mind was in a turmoil. Guimeni's words fell on deaf ears. She rushed towards the *pandas*.

"*Are,* what are you doing, *maichana*! Now you are standing in the middle of the road!"

The *pandas* bowed to Durga.

She returned the obeisance and said—

"This time, I'll also join your auspicious pilgrimage!"

A tall, lanky *panda* with a parrot nose looked at her critically and said—

"What about expenses?"

"I have some old ornaments. I am thinking of selling them."

Guimeni screamed with horror—

"What! Sell your gold ornaments?"

The *pandas* were struck dumb and stared at Durga stupefied. After a while the two short *pandas* spoke together—

"Ah! That's an excellent idea! Who else is there to wear them? You are an issueless, unfortunate person.

Guimeni with one hand on her back and the other pointing at Durga, now spoke in a commanding tone—

"*Maichana*! How can you talk in this way? Without first taking proper advice from those who have given you shelter, who have cared for your welfare?"

Again Durga ignored Guimeni's words. One of the *pandas* quoted a saying about widows:

Bari Gahanir dhan
Lokoko nidie, apunio nekhai
Chai thakibar man.

(Those old greedy Gossain widows
and their wealth. Neither do they
enjoy it, nor do they give it away. But
they keep on counting and watching over it!)

Durga did not pay any heed to these words and headed for Saru Gossainee's *batghar,* with the *pandas* trailing behind her. Guimeni also followed her.

Saru Gossainee was known for her cleanliness, and the appearance of her courtyard showed it. It was kept meticulously clean with a coating of white clay from the banks of Jagalia. It looked as white as the wings of a crane. All of them came to a halt in the middle of this courtyard.

Saru Gossainee was at that time in the open air toilet in the rear courtyard. It was overgrown with *khaira*, *paba* and *hissal* trees and *lantana* bushes. When she heard Durga's voice, she finished her toilet hastily, poured some water over her body and came to the front courtyard. But she stood a little distance away from the group of visitors and said:

"The mats are lying in the *dhekal*. Please fetch them and take your seats."

The *pandas* were quick to exclaim:

"No, no! There's no need of mats! We are in a great haste. We must cross the Jagalia and reach Khatiamari soon. We had heard that two Gossainees wanted to join us for the pilgrimage so...."

Saru Gossainee did not come forward. Standing under the wild berry tree, she said.

"Is there anything important, Durga? What is it?"

"I have come to take back my box."

"That's good! It is under the cot inside. Call that lad, Birohu! He'll pull it out for you."

Durga stood up suddenly and went forward. Some doves perching on the *tenga* trees in a corner of the courtyard were scared by the sound and took flight. Just then, a loud ear-shattering trumpeting call of an elephant was heard from the direction of Matiapahar. Everyone stood still, shocked. The same thought struck their minds! Jamaluddin had at last managed to catch the rogue elephant! And why not? He knew all kinds of elephant *mantras*. With a certain *mantra* he could even drag out an elephant from the thickest of jungles. Why not, indeed! He was the most skilled *phandi* of the South Bank!

Saru Gossainee's bedroom was small and dark like a well. It held the sandals of her late husband in one corner, lit up with a clay lamp of sweet mustard oil.

Durga entered the room gingerly, went upto the cot, bent down low and dragged out her box. Suddenly two small rats, the size of jack-fruit buds, jumped at her face almost grazing her cheeks...a lizard also fell on the floor and disappeared in the darkness...Durga sprang back in fright!

She brought the box out in the courtyard. It was tied securely with a jute rope generally used for cows and bullocks. With the help of the *pandas*, she started untying the rope. One *panda* exclaimed-

"How is it that you have tied it with only a rope? You have not locked it!"

She replied —

"I begged and whined for a lock, but who cares for me in that house!"

Durga opened the lid with some effort and taking out her old *gatala, mekhala, barkapur*, placed them in a neat pile on the ground. These old clothes had now taken the colour of *ghee* kept in hollow bamboo containers. Some petals of *ketaki*[17] flower fell out from the clothes, dry and withered, like wings of cockroaches. With great delight and inquisitiveness, all the *pandas* watched the movements of her hands. Suddenly Durga sat up, stunned and horrified...A long silent moment passed by...Then...with a frightening cry rushing out of her throat, she fell down, in a swoon!

✯ ✯ ✯ ✯

"Water! Water! Somebody please bring water!"

"Hold her! Hold her !!"

Her hair came loose. Her short tattered *gatala* came off and lay on the mud floor. Suddenly Durga stood up and screamed, "I am ruined! I am eaten up! Eaten up!...Oi! Those beasts have sucked my blood! Oi! I am eaten up!..."

The *pandas*, in their excitement, tried to hold her arms and console her. But in vain!

"Be patient, Gossainee! Be patient! Why don't you tell us what has happened?"

Tearing her hair and beating her breasts in anguish, Durga wept loudly and bitterly. Within a moment, there was chaos in the courtyard and quite a big crowd built up. Saru Gossainee was having a bath at the well. She came running and tried to take Durga, who was rolling on the mud floor and crying loudly, in her arms...But Durga pushed her away with inhuman strength and she lost her balance and fell down a few feet away against the old *rabab tenga* tree! A group of boys were returning, covered all over with mud, after collecting fish from the holes they had dug in Jagalia bank during winter and which had got filled up with water and small fish during the monsoon floods. When they heard the hue and cry from the courtyard, they too joined the crowd encircling Durga.

The *pandas* could not understand what had actually happened. They tried their best to pacify everybody,

"Gold ornaments of the Gossainee have been stolen. Their value cannot be counted in rupees."

The young lads cried out,

"Who comes to the Gossainee's house? How's it possible?"

Someone from the crowd shouted,

"No, only one man comes here! Comes and goes from this house! He's Mahidhar *bapu* of Haramdo!"

"And one maid servant from Rajabaha comes daily to sweep and clean."

"It's definitely some known person who has done it. There's no visible hole anywhere in the walls."

One hot-blooded youth roared angrily,

"Bring that Brahmin thief from Haramdo! Drag him by his hair here!"

Oh! God! Saru Gossainee felt as if somebody was peeling off her skin. Her wet clothes clung to her body. Her face had become red like fire. She uttered in a broken voice,

"I haven't even seen what was in the box. Ask her whether she showed me the contents before she kept it here. Somebody must have taken out the ornaments before she brought the box to my house."

There was complete silence for a while. The logic of Saru Gossainee carried weight. The assorted *pandas*, young and old, tall and short, fat and thin, now pointed their fingers at Durga and admonished her, "Now, now! Didn't you show the contents of the box to her? That was a serious mistake!"

Durga roared like a wounded tigress, "That's not true! Look! How her blood's burning to save the skin of that son of a Brahmin bitch! Only two days back I opened the box. Everything was intact. Only two days back! Oh! I am eaten up. *Hai re*! I am eaten up."

Pausing for breath, she screamed again,

"That *dugdugee,* the drum-shaped pendant studded with rubies from the Cooch Behar disciples! And the pair of gold earrings studded with rubies in the design of pomegranate flowers. They were all there inside that box. Saw them with my own eyes!"

". . . Die! Die! . . ."

". . . May your seven generations go to hell! . . ."

Guimeni who was running excitedly back and forth, between the two groups, now shouted loudly, "*Hai*! *Hai*! Who is the witch who has eaten up her wealth?"

Saru Gossainee felt isolated and helpless. She went to the verandah, sat down on the floor, with knees drawn up. In utter despair, she started crying. The *pandas* now went up to her and spoke to console her,

"Mother! You are are in great trouble now. Better call Indranath Gossain! Moreover you will not allow the police or the Home Guards to enter your private room. Indranath Gossain will help you."

Saru Gossainee murmured, "Police . . . police . . ."

"Those excise officers are going from village to village in search of opium thieves. The police are also with them. You are a lady of the Gossain family, ignorant of worldly matters! How will you catch the thief? You must seek the help of the police."

Saru Gossainee shuddered from head to foot. Again she felt as if some body was peeling off her skin from top to bottom…

The *pandas* had no time to watch till the end of the drama. One of them said, "We have very little time. We have to cross the Jagalia and you know about the mad elephant roaming about. We must go now. Gossainee, please don't mind!"

The *pandas* had left the place, but the crowd did not disperse. As if they were keeping vigil over two corpses—one of Durga and the other of Saru Gossainee.

Saru Gossainee was waiting for Indranath impatiently, with a great hope in her heart that his presence would bring her back to life and clear her name.

The bright sun now became gradually pale and took the colour of a tender camel's skin.

* * * *

After some time, Indranath returned from Barihat. With great excitement, Saru Gossainee heard the tinkling of the bell of Indranath's cycle. Someone had already informed him about the day's episode when he was crossing the bridge over Jagalia. He came running through the *batghar* and pushed his way through the crowd around the two women. The entire crowd, the lads who had come back from fishing, the working women from the fields, and even Guimeni became silent, in the presence of Indranath.

Durga was still sitting before her big, black box. Pointing his finger at her, Indranath cried out, "Why did you bring this box here?"

Then pointing his outstretched hand to the wall of the ramshackle house, he roared again, "Can't you see the broken-down walls? WE have a sturdy attic made of urium wood! Instead of keeping the box there, why did you keep it here?

Guimeni now screamed, "Her eyes were dimmed by the steam from boiling rice!"

Saru Gossainee got up slowly and walking up to Indranath, clutched his arm. She pleaded in a broken voice, tears running down her checks.

"Believe me, *bapa*! When she brought the box here, I didn't see what was inside. It's the truth! Believe me!"

Indranath said.

"Ever since opium has eaten up this sattra, robbery has increased everywhere. Even from our attic, elephant's tusks have been stolen."

Saying so, he went up to Durga, who had almost collapsed near the box. He caught hold of her arm, raised her to her feet, and supporting her, took her slowly towards the *batghar*.

But before being led away, Durga showered a few barbs of poison and a terrible curse,

"Gods above are my witness! I am a widow of Chikarhati's Gossain who will now die from the sorrow of not offering her husband's funeral bones to the holy river. Let my curse fall upon those who have done this harm to me!"

But before she could finish, Indranath dragged her by force towards the *batghar*. Guimeni could not remain silent, she screamed in lamentation,

"Hai! Hai! When her husband was alive...she lived on the thick cream at the top of the curd pot. Who has made this deep wound in her heart?"

The village boys said grimly, "Let that Brahmin rascal from Haramdo come here! We'll give him a taste of *bijuli* bamboo pincers!"

One by one, they began leaving the courtyard.

Saru Gossainee again felt as if someone was peeling

the skin off her! She closed her eyes. Guimeni, who had got up to go, now stood before her in her typical pose. Her hands on her hunchback and leaning a little forward, peering at her, she said, "Gossainee, how can you trust this race of rotten men? These bastards! They live double lives. They sometimes look like heavenly saints . . . but they are actually devils from the darkest hell! How could you believe them? But, Gossainee, tell me! In case the police come, will you allow them to enter your sacred sandal room?"

Saru Gossainee remained silent. After a while she said, "I know! My sixth sense tells me that they themselves won't enter the room. Let them come!"

★ ★ ★ ★

The crowd had by now dispersed. The big black box was still lying there, its lid flung, wide open. Saru Gossainee felt that it was like a pit dug out in a graveyard for buying a coffin.

What has really happened? And why? Who has done this black deed? Is it really possible that those things were stolen from her room? No, no! Never! It couldn't be possible! Mahidhar *bapu* was the only one who was permitted to come near the sandal room. Then is it possible that he... No, no! That cannot be...

Saru Gossainee again had that agonizing sensation, as if somebody was peeling off her skin!

...That Brahmin never even glanced at her cot. Her thoughts...this way...No, no! It's a sin! It's a sure and certain way to hell!...

...Only that day, he had brought the revenue of Pathaldia land. He had accounted for each and every *pie* of the money and had placed the entire amount in her hands. And that Pathaldia land! It was like a pain in her neck. So difficult to manage! But as soon as Mahidhar *bapu* took charge...he dealt with everything.

...And that *miyadi kheraj* land of Mirza, Nargaon and Rani. The account of paddy was all tangled up. He sorted out everything, made it all straight and simple. No, no! He cannot do such a thing!

...Or is it that maid of Rajabaha? But she is her disciple! She had even taken the *haihal mantra* from her. How can she do it?

...Then?

* * * *

The large disc of the sun disappeared behind the thick cluster of leaves of the *rabab tenga* tree. Nobody had come as yet to take away the box. The maid from Rajabaha had already left after completing her work. Before leaving she had said, "Gossainee, go and boil your rice now! You haven't even offered flowers and *tulsi* leaves to your husband's wooden sandals today. The Lord above looks after everything. Go to the kitchen, Gossainee!" But Saru Gossainee did not get up. Her wet clothes had dried on her body. In between, probably she had dozed off for a short while. In that half-conscious state, she had seen a dream...There! He is lying in front of her, naked...blood is oozing from his mouth... Somebody has stabbed him with a sharp weapon all over his body... Those boys who would not heed their Guru or Gossain or anybody else! They are standing there with fishing spears in their hands!

...She woke with a start. Dazed, she looked around fearfully. Her whole body started shivering. Even then, she did not leave the verandah. The big black box was still there, its lid flung back, like a big black hole!

She had a foreboding. Surely something inauspicious

will happen. If Mahidhar was removed from her life, could she survive? Was it possible? Was it possible? No! No! She could not allow her imagination to go that far! But then! What had Durga hinted at maliciously! Perhaps, in a dark corner of her mind, some immoral thoughts had crept in and had taken root? Was it possible? Had she fallen so low? This Gossainee, who gave *mantras* to her disciples, who proudly wore the crown of religious rectitude on her head, had she become such a sinner? Was it possible? And today...this book of sin was wide open for all to read! Oh! Lord forbid! Lord forbid!

...It could not be true! She tried to convince herself. What wrong had she done? For the last two years, she had slept alone in this ramshackle room. And about ten yards away, that Brahmin...No, no, she had not behaved wickedly! Did she even go near his bed? He, who felt unhappy when she suffered, and was delighted when she was happy. Did she ever go to his bedside in the dead of the night, with a clay lamp in her hand?

...This question lay buried in her heart. Sometimes it should like the bright sunshine of truth, at other times, it was a falsehood as dark as night! For many days, this conflict has been raging in her mind. It went on and on, like a wounded horse running away from the battlefield, never stopping!

Several instances of Mahidhar's attachment to her came flashing to her mind. Once, returning from Pathaldiya, he had said, "At Ukium you have some *ejamali* land—but without your consent, the two Gossains from Bangara and Chapathuri have started ploughing it. Nobody has even cared to inform you about it! But this time, we must take action and till this land ourselves. Of course, only if you agree!"

Then he took out some coins from a small string purse and placing them at her feet, uttered, "For the last four years, those two families at Ukium hadn't paid your half-share. I spent three days and three nights in that lonely, mosquito-ridden place. I managed to collect the rent in cash. Here it is!.... Once you told me that you had no ready cash in your hands. Do you remember? It pricked my heart!"

She had picked up the money and gone inside. When she came out later, it was a bright moonlit night. She could see, through the chinks in the derelict mud wall of *dhekal* room, Mahidhar reading a manuscript in the flickering light of a clay lamp. After some time, he had put out the flame and gone to sleep on a cot in one corner of the room.

Saru Gossainee began pacing the verandah from one end to the other. A pleasant fragrance floated in the air from the nearby lime bushes. There was a path, from the house, going up to Matiapahar. If the rogue elephant had not been roaming about freely in that region, she would have enjoyed taking a stroll up the path to the mountain. From up there, the moonlit view of the countryside would have been wonderful. She had often enjoyed it in the past...

She looked heavenwards. There were white clouds in the sky, thinly spread out, almost transparent. The moon, it seemed, had got entangled in a heap of silken cloth... Her eyes went to the *dhekal* again... Yes, he was sleeping. Sleeping soundly as if he had no worries at all. Gossainee walked softly towards the *rabab tenga* tree. From there she watched him stealthily...this well-built man with a straight nose and manly muscular charm!...

...Shame! Shame on her! What has come over her! Watching this sleeping man, lying there almost half-naked, behind the broken down mud wall? Should such thoughts flicker through the mind of a thirty-year-old widow?

Saru Gossainee's white skin, like that of the Australian soldiers who had come to Assam during the Second World War, blushed. The nipples of her breasts became hard and rigid, just as in the old days when the Gossain used to touch her. Can this happen to a thirty-year-old widow?

She forgot all about the sweet fragrance of lime and the peaceful moonlit night! The silvery moon, caught in the heap of silken cloth, cracked into several pieces. They were like sharp pieces of glass which lacerated her bosom.

She went running to her room and collapsed near her dead husband's wooden sandals.

Wickedness had never tainted her thoughts or her actions. Even when Mahidhar was not present in the house, she had never touched his cot or sat on it. She had bound her life tightly with her daily routine and she had never tried to break this chain. Then why did Durga utter that terrible accusation . . . those malicious words? . . . And nobody had even tried to stop her?

What then should be her next step? Tell him to go away? Yes, tell him to go to Pathaldia or Chakrad and look after her lands there. But immediately a shadow of fear flitted across her mind. Her entire body trembled. Never, never! She cannot leave this man! Her entire existence was linked with him. It would be like cutting off an invisible part of her body. No, no! She cannot do it! . . . And that persistent fear? Those tenants from Chakrad, Garal, Ukium. They always threaten to convert the *riyati patta* into *miyadi*!

...As if someone always whispered in her ear—You don't have the wealth or the status now to bribe the vulture-like, old village surveyors who measure the land, inch by inch, so meticulously! As if the entire measurement and calculation lies in their palm.... Now the palanquin won't come to your door-step to take you to the houses of your disciples... Their sons have gone to Gauhati to study in schools and colleges. They have now become inspectors and policemen! Now you'll have to wear tattered *gatalas*...

The government will fix a limit on the possession of land. Land ceiling is coming soon... And whatever land is allotted to you under the ceiling... Suppose you cannot save it from the clutches of the village surveyor?... What will happen then?... No, no! Let Mahidhar stay!... He must not go away!....

A deep sigh was forced out of her chest as if her heart was torn into two halves.

She was still sitting in a corner of the verandah. Her wet *gatala* and *mekhala* had dried up on her body long back and had become stiff like starched cloth. There lay Durga's box with its yawning mouth and scattered on the ground were Durga's *gatala, mekhala, telach* and other garments, like so many pieces of dried-up goat's skin!

She stood up, collected the clothes one by one and put them back in the box. Then she dragged the box slowly to one side of the verandah. At that dark hour, she felt like a witch, on a diabolic mission!

She went inside the house and bolted the door with its wooden cross-piece.

★ ★ ★ ★

Eleven

A covered bullock cart carrying Giribala was winding its way slowly over a hilly road. Giribala was wearing a *gatala* and a *mekhala* of white silk over a chemise made of *markin*. Her uncovered arms and legs gave out a beautiful luminous glow.

A young *bandha*, a boy with a thick-set body was sitting beside the cart driver. Her friend of Majhkuchi, where Giribala had gone, was afraid to send her back alone. So she had sent along this boy to look after her. Throughout the countryside, the rogue elephant had struck terror in the hearts of the people. It was also reported that in that particular stretch of the road, he had attacked many a traveller.

Now the cart entered a thick forest of *dudhkhadi*, *gahara* and *pama* trees with an undergrowth of thick bushes and creepers.

Mark Sahib was following the cart on a strange, old bicycle loaded with bags and what not. He knew why Giribala had gone to Majhkuchi. He knew that she had gone there to collect old moth-eaten manuscripts from village to village. Now he was cycling parallel to the cart. Giribala could see, over the shoulder of the cart driver, Mark's golden hair.

When their eyes met, he cycled near the wheel of the cart. She could not take her eyes off him. As he traveled constantly in the open air, in heat and dust, his complexion had taken a red burnished look, like the skin of those Brahmin boys from Haramdo who sit near sacrificial fire for long hours.

He said, "Giribala, I am very happy to see you moving about like this, instead of stagnating in that damp wooden room. One day, I'll take you to the opium-eaters' reform camp of Haramdo where both men and women are kept for curing their addiction."

Suddenly Giribala thrust aside the flowery curtain at the back and exclaimed, "Look! This is the place where once a prosperous *mahajan* had his household! See those ruins scattered all over. This *mahajan* and his family were alive during the time of Gilmil Sahib."

Mark looked at the mysterious place and its ruins. There were bushes and creepers everywhere. A thick growth of *hadganasha*[1] had completely swallowed up the big wooden pillars of a ruined canopy. Termites had eaten up the wooden railing of the verandah which hung down at several places at awkward angles. Creepers were climbing up or hanging down all over the broken walls. In one place, they were entwined in the shape of a cross. Mark Sahib gazed at the spot fascinated. *Mohlata* creepers covered another spot shaped like a crocodile, with a fine network of small leaves like a fishing net. He shouted to Giribala with great excitement, "Why don't you stop the cart and get down? Let's see this place properly!"

Giribala appeared to be waiting for this invitation. She told the cart driver to stop immediately. The latter said with fear and astonishment "Why do you want to stop here?

You know everybody there closed their doors and windows for fear of the mad elephant! Why get down in this God-forsaken place? I cannot advise you to roam about here. Any moment that crazed animal may turn up!"

The *bandha* boy exclaimed,

"*Ojhas*[2] says that the ghosts of *mahajan's* dead family haunt this terrible place. Please don't go there!"

But Giribala and Mark ignored his words. Mark had left the cycle leaning against a *silikha* tree. Both entered the deep dark place.

The cart driver was stunned and could not believe his eyes! A highly respected Gossain family's widow venturing out alone with an unclean low-caste Christian, into such a thick forest ! He was a potter himself and he still remembered how once Giribala's mother had dragged her away when he had picked up Giribala, then a little girl, in his lap to play with her. Her mother had forced the child to take a bath to purify her of the touch of a low-caste man!

Approaching the ruins, Giribala and Mark saw an old dried-up pond of the rich *mahajan*. Once this pond overflowed with water and shoals of fish, big and small, swam here and there. Now all that had disappeared and only a dry bed like a crocodile's skin met their eyes.

Mark sat down on a rock bleached white by sun and rain and folded up his trousers a little above this ankles. The sweet fragrance of some wild flowers touched his nose. Giribala said, "This was once the *dhekal* of Bhogi *mahajan*. It was here, in this very place that two merchants from Cooch Behar and Darbhanga, were killed by his *bandhas*, under his orders...."

Dusting his honey-coloured hair, Mark enquired, "Were they beaten to death by bamboo staves?"

"Yes. My grandmother told me that those merchants used to come clandestinely with Victoria silver coins, concealed in fine jute bags, to buy young robust elephants. That year Bhogi was not a happy man. Two elephants he had caught in the jungle had died of septic wounds. He had to pay heavy fines of two hundred rupees for each elephant. That year he had only three elephants. One of them was Ganesha, the auspicious one, with one tusk only. The two merchants had set their greedy eyes on Ganesha. They had come all the way, by mysterious paths and trails, from Cooch Behar and Darbhanga, to buy this elephant with their Victoria coins..."

Mark pointed to another rock nearby and asked Giribala to sit down. Above their heads, a *dhakar* bird with its peculiar cry, 'chi, chi, chi', flew away. Mark said,

"These *dhakar* birds usually stay near water. Probably it sensed some water in this place. After all there was a pond here once upon a time."

".... Tempted by those bags of Victoria coins, Bhogi lured the two merchants to this *dhekal* by some cunning trick. They were tied up with ropes used for cows and then beaten to death by his *bandhas.*"

Mark asked with wide open eyes.

"Is it a fact? Is it true?

"Yes, yes! It's true! Their dead bodies were kept in the cow-shed during the night. At the crack of dawn, they were buried beneath bamboo clusters in the deep jungle. Next morning when people saw blood marks in the cow-shed, they were told that one of the cows had given birth to a calf during the night."

Mark looked up and said, "Who knows? It might have been under the same cluster of that *dal* bamboos there."

Both of them stared at the *dal* bamboos. It was the only one growing near the spot where they were sitting.

"Look carefully! Perhaps you might find the bones of the murdered men!"

Giribala glanced hesitantly at Mark and moved closer to him. Both sensed the odour of each other's body, the physical proximity they had not experienced before. She mumbled, just to restrain herself, "Bhogi *mahajan* killed them out of greed for their Victoria coins. Then they became ghosts and destroyed his family and this place. Two or three members who survived left this place in fear and horror and settled down east of Jagalia at Nahira."

Mark said, "I heard somewhere that they all died of black fever and malaria. In Kamrup and Goalpara districts, one fourth of the population had died, at that time, from this same epidemic of black fever and malaria. Don't you remember the horror of sand flies? Clouds of these flies had burst over these places! They swarmed over people's bodies noiselessly and sucked their blood without their knowledge. Then the flies used to rest on the leaves of the surrounding trees. Like devilish snakes, they did all their work silently!"

Mark leaned closer towards Giribala and continued, "There's one interesting sidelight to the story of the murdered merchants. Rumours were floated that the two dead merchants had gold chains round their necks. People started digging here and there for the remains. Come, I'll show you the pits they dug up!"

They moved forward. Now they stood under a *neem* tree. A pattern of sunlight filtered through the *neem* leaves and fell on them. Mark suddenly said, "Do you know how beautiful you are? In this open space, surrounded by nature, you look even more ethereal!"

Giribala looked at the ground under her feet. Her complexion, at this moment, glowed like bright sunshine. Perhaps when a woman is with her beloved, her body takes on such a glow! She lifted her beautiful eyes to him and said.

"How long will you be staying here?"

Mark became thoughtful for while. Then he said, "I want to work for some time in the opium-eaters reformation camps. Then I want to complete the biography of the German Sahib, Gilman. Moreover your father desires that I should write a life history of *Santa Dev Mahaprabhu* in English. For that I'll have to go to Khamar and Dhubijani to collect some material."

"People say that two or three priests, staying with you, have converted many men and women into Christians in the Garo Hills and Tura. Have you ever done this? Tell me!"

Mark looked straight at Giribala's face. His clear penetrating stare went deep into her heart.

"With whatever little power I have, I try to relieve the pain and suffering of humanity. Religious conversion is not my sole aim. Those who make it their life's ambition are not really doing great work."

"My grandfather used to say that the missionaries were annoyed with the *adhikars* as they could convert only one thousand men and women of Mikir tribe. These Mikirs now come down for trading in old timber logs. Not a single caste Hindu could be converted by the missionaries; the *adhikars* had kept them tightly under control in their iron fists."

She paused for some time, and in a broken voice, she continued, "I cannot reach the depth of your heart! And religion! I don't know what it actually is. But if ...if I can stay always with you by becoming a Chris..."

Mark exclaimed loudly, "What!"

But immediately he brought his emotions under control and said softly, "I, myself, am not a member of the North-east Baptist Church. But of course, I have moved about with them, learnt Assamese from them. They have their head quarters in Ukium and Damarah. I really have some aim and purpose for coming to this *sattra*... Believe me! I really have some purpose!"

Suddenly his glance fell on Giribala's face. He was shocked to see tears rolling down her cheeks, "Dear! Dear! You are weeping! What's come over you?

Her eyes became like two pieces of glass smeared with oil. She could not answer immediately. She clutched a corner of her *chaddar* with her teeth and tried to restrain her tears, "I am afraid you'll go away from this sattra soon."

Mark remained silent. Giribala continued,"You know, Sahib! A strange feeling has crept inside me....very mysterious and elusive! I have a feeling that it's all connected with that rogue elephant. If Jamaluddin is successful in catching him with his special *mantra*, then...then all these inauspicious things happening around the *sattra* will stop...Last night I dreamt a dream! That magnificient elephant is standing in the corral with the glorious *howda* on its back! And that dream whispered in my ears that you have remained behind in the *sattra*, and not proceeded towards Gauhati and Upper Assam. And the red flag has disappeared from Marabhitha. Instead golden paddy is waving in the cool breeze. And Indranath is strolling in those paddy fields. That beautiful *howda* has grown two golden wings . . ."

Mark exclaimed, "Golden wings?"

Giribala did not pay attention but continued, "Listen, Sahib! Then I saw . . . I felt that the sign of the cross was deeply embedded in my bosom! The same cross you always carry with you."

Mark's gaze again fell on her face.

"Just you wait and see! Jamaluddin will catch that elephant! Everything will become smooth and easy again!"

"Yes, everything will become simple and I'll take even more interest in collecting manuscripts for you. I'll go to Bangara, Chikarhati, Ukium and other places in search of manuscripts. *Sanyasi* Sahib! Believe me!"

Mark was again silent for some time. She continued.

"I feel that the *Bhagwan* Cross that you wear round your neck, has shown you the path to the *sattra*. It is also embedded in my heart here!"

Mark was taken aback. But at the same time, her simple conviction struck a chord in his heart. He said, "You have been reading all those old manuscripts out to me. Probably it has put these thoughts in your head. Indranath wanted you to gain some knowledge from these old manuscripts along with me. Listen, Giri! Whatever you might think, I am still a foreigner, an outsider! If this continues, it will be more and more difficult for me to show you the right path. Do you understand, Giri?..."

Suddenly there was a rustle of dry leaves. They were shocked to see a *shalike dhutia*[3] snake flash over their feet like a streak of lightning! At the same time. Mark's eyes fell on a bundle of old papers lying on a broken foundation stone. He ran to the spot like a curious child and picked it up. They were very old papers, brown in colour, almost crumbling, tied neatly with a jute string knotted in two places—documents connected with transactions in the *hathi mahal* (elephant market) by Bhogi *Mahajan*. Mark discovered that some of the papers were related to *mela shikar*[4] of elephants and the Government rules and regulations connected with it, up to the year 1920.

He read out from the old documents:

License for catching wild elephants by *Mela Shikar:*

Under the Elephant Preservation Act, 1879 (VI of 1879), I hereby grant you this license for one seat to capture wild elephants in the district of Garo hills under the following conditions:

1. That this license is subject to the provisions of the Elephant Preservation Act, 1879 (VI of 1879) and the rules made thereunder.
2. That this license is limited to the area described viz. all over the Garo Hills District.
3. That this is valid for the period from I October 1933 to 15 March 1934.
4. That you shall capture elephants by *Mela Shikar*.
5. That you shall bring to the depot as fixed for the time being by the D.C. all elephants caught as soon as possible after capture.
6. That you shall have the training of the elephants commenced within 24 hours of their arrival at the depot and shall see that adequate supplies of fodder and water are given to them during training, and shall ensure that the training is mercifully conducted.
7. That you shall report to the D.C. and the Forest Depot Officer each case of elephant dying or being killed during capture or after or during or after training.
8. That you shall pay royalty for every elephant captured, whether dead or alive at the rate of Rs. 200/- for each elephant except for that which is released or taken over by the Government under Clause II, to the Treasury at Dhubri, Tura

or the Forest Office within 14 days of their death or arrival at depot.

. . . .

10. That you shall not remove or allow the removal of any elephant from the depot till you have obtained a transit pass, which will be issued by the Divisional Forest Officer on production by you of the Treasury receipt showing the amount of royalty paid...
11. That should the Government decide to take over...any elephant captured by you, such elephant shall be chosen by an officer deputed...and you shall thereafter be responsible for up-keep and training, you shall hand it over to Government...trained sufficiently to carry a man without being tied to a *kunki* and to fetch its own fodder...you shall be paid the price as mutually agreed upon with the D.C....etc. etc."

Mark exclaimed,

"This is a treasure! We are indeed lucky to find it!"

Giribala and Mark read the old papers with great interest.

How transient is life, they thought! Within a short span of time, this vast property—the house, the land, countless elephants, etc.—had crumbled, fallen to pieces, and become a ruin, run over by bushes, creepers and trees, infested with snakes and reptiles!

The fragrance of *ketaki* flowers came from Giribala's *mekhala* and *gatala*. Probably she had kept *ketaki* petals in the folds of her clothes while storing them in her box.

They became suddenly aware that the dappled sunshine, like a leopard's skin spread over the forest ground, was cloaked by deep shadows of *gahara*, *dudh khadi* and *bokul* trees. Giribala came closer to Mark Sahib and said,

"Oh, Sahib! I am fed up! Durga *pehi* says that I am neglecting my late husband's wooden sandals; that I don't offer flowers and *tulsi* leaves like a pious widow! And on top of that, I tasted goat's meat on the day of my grandfather's *shraddha* ceremony! She says that I am a sinner. She doesn't even take water from my hands and she cannot tolerate my presence while she is praying in the sandal room..."

The blue eyes of Mark, the American youth, filled with sympathy for this beautiful unhappy girl.

"But, Sahib, what a strange thing! I don't feel guilty of any sin at all. Even after taking goat's meat that day! It didn't shake me even a little bit..."

She paused for a moment...Mark moved away from the broken pillar and madeas if to touch her arm in consolation. But Giribala, a little hesitantly, avoided his touch. She looked into his blue eyes. It would be so peaceful to live under the blue and serene sky of those eyes! She spoke again,

"Oh, Sahib, can you understand me? I cannot just exist, just for the sake of remaining alive, like Durga and Saru Gossainee. My father, the *adhikar,* said: Your future and Durga's future are now linked together. Durga has found her path, and you must follow her! You must observe all the rituals. You must offer flowers, *tulsi* and water daily to your dead husband's wooden sandals. You know that her husband is like life's blood for a Hindu woman."

She stopped abruptly and tried to laugh. She resumed after some time, "Do you know? That husband of mine touched and played with that notorious woman who sold opium. He even slept with that woman! Do you know what he said to me on our first night? Pushing aside my *gatala*, he said—'There cannot be any enjoyment in bed with the woman one brings in marriage! Absolutely none!'. Still I try to put flowers and *tulsi* leaves on his wooden sandals. But if it continues like this, I am afraid I'll turn into a ghost . . ."

Mark exclaimed loudly,

"No, no! Don't be so disheartened! Human life is the greatest gift of God and he exists even in our bodies. He was crucified because of our sins. His blood purified us. His wound marks have given us strength."

Giribala got up. Moving a little distance away from him, she sat on a tree stump. She had absolutely no desire to hear the gospel from this Christian youth.

She said, "You go and give your sermon to Durga! Nowadays she likes to hear this kind of talk, and of late, she is completely broken down and confined to bed. But once upon a time, do you know what she used to do?"

She again came upto Mark. He got the elusive fragrance again from her clothes! Was it the fragrance of *ketaki* flowers?...or crushed sugarcane?...

"After my widowhood my father had ordered that my bed should be next to hers. He wanted me to be her shadow. In the dead of night, I often saw her get up from her bed, pick up her dead husband's wooden sandals and then go back to bed again, to sleep with those sandals clutched to her bare bosom. She had, for sixteen years, a happy and sound conjugal life. Both were like shadows of each other. But, Mark Sahib, to me she used to look like a ghost during those moments in the night! But now, after she has lost her ornaments, her face looks terrible. In the dead of the night, when she wakes up . . . Now all her feelings are like dead wood because she cannot immerse the ashes of her husband in a holy river. I watched her constantly, and then one day I told her, 'Take my ornaments that are lying with my mother. I have no use for them now. I have no desire to put the ashes of my husband into sacred waters.'

"Durga looked at me with her haunted, terrible eyes which bored into me. I was frightened. Suddenly she spat on the ground and said scornfully: It would be a sin to take anything from a person whose tongue utters such words....!"

Giribala stopped abruptly and, hiding her face between her knees, started sobbing. Mark came very close to her. He held out his hand to touch her hair, but he did not have the courage to do so. The cart and its driver were just twenty yards away, waiting for them. Probably the driver was even watching them or hearing their conversation. He knelt down beside her and said softly, "Calm down, Giri! Have patience! I am sorry I couldn't console you properly. I am grateful that you have disclosed your feelings to me. I feel kind of responsible for you now, you know....!"

The *dhakar* birds suddenly became very noisy...

* * * *

All of a sudden they heard a great uproar, shouts and screams, a discord of chaotic sounds, coming through the jungle, nearer towards them. Giribala and Mark stood up, uncertain, wondering what it was. The cart driver waved his hands and shouted frantically,

"Come! Quick! Hurry up, you two! The mad elephant has killed a man. It's coming this way, fast! Run! Run for your lives!

The roaring sound was coming nearer and nearer . . . In panic, the cart driver quickly untied the bullocks and pushed them off. The two bullocks sped away into the fields. Running after them, the driver shouted again—

"*Maichana,* come this way! Run fast! Bring sahib also! Run!...The elephant has killed a man! Elephant...killed man... Run!..."

A sound like that of a thunderstorm drew nearer and nearer...

...Crack! Crash! Boom! Bhoom!... Dham!...

...There! There! The trunk of that terrible elephant was partly visible! There! You could see those twin blunt instruments of terror, his blood covered tusks, entangled with creepers and wild grass! Now the huge mad elephant was fully visible. He gave a mighty kick to the abandoned cart and sent it crashing in twisted pieces. The flower-patterned curtain fell down near Giribala and Mark.

Giribala, terrified and hysterical, clung to Mark. There! Real death stood only five yards away! Death, with red blood-shot eyes! There! There he was!.

A tense, tortured whisper forced its way out from Giribala's throat.

"Kill me! Kill me now! When I am holding this Sahib in my arms! Kill me now! At once! I'll be most happy! Don't you remember? Me, riding on your back to the river side! Pulling out leeches from your back. Don't you remember? You, spraying my naked body with mud and water! Then I used to soothe the pain of your wounds, made by the mahout's goad, with the soft caress of my palm. Don't you remember? Kill me! Now! That girl who sat in the auspicious *howda* of the *adhikar mahaprabhu*, now lies in the arms of an unclean, low-caste man. Kill her! Kill her!"

Giribala went limp and fainted in the arms of Mark Sahib.

* * * *

Boom! Boom! Dham! Dham! Sounds of drums beating came nearer and nearer! A group of about twenty men with burning brands in their hands was approaching. The flickering light from the torches played on their glistening, sweating naked backs.

There were two men of *shuri* caste with an old palanquin between them. The rest of the group was made up of men trained in the art of controlling wild or rogue elephants. As they marched forward, they sang a song to sway the elephant,

Aste Aste ya mere Sunder-Rana
Aget ya mere Sunder-Rana
Aa! Ee! Dhat!
Aa! Ee!! Dhat!!
(Oh! My handsome Rana[5]
Walk softly, go slowly forward
Oh! My handsome Rana
Walk softly. Go forward.
Aa! Ee! Dhat!
Aa! Eee!! Dhat!!)

The search party came to a halt near the bullock-cart, smashed by the frenzied elephant, lying there like a skeleton.

Someone exclaimed, "*Maichana* has managed to escape. I am sure! The mad elephant must have gone towards the mountain of Jirang . . ."

Suddenly Mark Sahib appeared from the ruins of Bhogiram *mahajan's* estate. Seeing him, there were jubilant shouts and exclamations from the party.

"There! There! The white sahib! His cycle is still in one piece!"

"What will he say now?"

"Perhaps he can tell us about *maichana*."

Mark came near them. He seemed still dazed by the terrible experience, only a few hours back. He said, haltingly, "Are you...looking for...Giribala? There! There she is, sleeping... Lift her gently...into the palanquin...and take her to the manor..."

* * * *

They carried her to the palanquin. She had not opened her eyes. She was still unconscious.

The *shuris* lifted the palanquin and the whole party marched back along the same route they had come, but at a faster pace. They were singing,

Chei dhat yuk
Dhir!
Aste aste aget
Yare mera Sunder-Rana
Chei Dhat yuk dhir
Aste aste aget

* * * *

Jamaluddin was dead. His body was lying under a *machan* in the branches of a *jamun* tree, on Matia Pahar. One by one, people came from the *sattra* and crowded round the body. It was dark. They held burning torches in their hands. They were impatient, and fear constricted their hearts, but at the same time their ears were pricked up. Where was that "killer", the frenzied elephant?

Indranath arrived. He was visibly shattered by the sight of Jamaluddin's mutilated body. He took out his handkerchief and dabbed his face repeatedly. He composed himself with an effort and said, "His body shouldn't remain here like this. Come on! Be ready! Lift the dead body and bring it to the *batghar.*"

A Brahmin youth of Haramdo exclaimed, "We won't touch a Muslim! It's better to call some Muslims from Bholagoan."

Others shouted, "Who'll go to Bholagoan at this hour! With that mad elephant spreading terror everywhere?"

The Brahmin cautioned Indranath, "Saru Gossain, keep yourself seven hands away from that body! Otherwise you'll have to go through *chandrayan prayaschita*[6]! Do take care!!"

Another Brahmin shouted, "That opium-eater Kaltu's sons are here. If they carry this Muslim's body, they'll escape with only one *dhanu prayaschit.*"

Other youths gathered there whispered among themselves, "What does he expect from us? Can we touch a Muslim corpse?"

Indranath exploded in anger, "Shut up! Shut up! If nobody comes forward, I'll myself take away the corpse! We cannot let it remain here all night!"

A tremor of shocked disbelief passed through the crowd. There were subdued comments,

"What's he saying?"

"What does he mean?"

"Is our Saru Gossain in his senses?"

In the flickering light of the burning torches, the mutilated body of Jamaluddin, in black clothes, looked like a bat lying spread-eagled. The forehead, nose and cheek bones were crushed. Teeth had fallen out. The chest was gored and the stomach was cut open. The intestines and other organs lay on one side in a blood-splattered mess.

A broken voice was heard.

"Poor Jamaluddin! He tried his best to catch the rogue

elephant! He never moved from that *machan* for so many days and nights!"

Another voice uttered, "On the South Bank, now, there's no other *phandi* who can ride a *kunki* like Jamaluddin. None to equal him!"

Another man joined in, "In Rani's elephant corral, the *phandi* who displayed such courage got an award of Rs. 1600 from the British *Sarkar*. Jamaluddin knew all the *dandis*[7] of wild elephants like the palm of his hand. He knew where the patches of salty earth lay because wild elephants are fond of this delicacy. He had a kind of mystic, almost supernatural, relationship with wild elephants."

Someone else said,

"All the *kunkis* of the Gossain of Dakhala, Chakrad and Ukium knew him well. Which *kunki* would kneel down in its own peculiar style, on the order of *chambaith*[8]. Which *kunki* would behave in what manner, on the order of *khol buk*[9]. All this was stamped on Jamaluddin's mind like the pages of a book."

Suddenly there was a loud wailing cry. It was Kaltu the mahout:

"Oh, my brother! Where have you gone? Don't you remember how you saved my life when I first caught Jagannath? Don't you remember? In your hand, there was the noose of half maund jute that you had made on Saturday. In the action that followed, the *galsi jari*[10] and *mit dao*[11] slipped from my hands and fell near the foot of the wild elephant. Oh, shame on me! I had taken too much opium! My hands were shaking. Oh, why did I go for an elephant hunt in such an intoxicated state?

"My *kunki* had raised its trunk, pointing towards the wild elephant, and had attacked. And there was I, defenceless! But you moved fast and skillfully on your *kunki!*

You saved my life! Ah! My *kunki*! He was a big rogue, from Dattya's Bhikaru Gossain. With his sharp tusks, he gored Jagannath's mother again and again till she fell down. Poor thing! She was only protecting her baby! Oh! shame on me! I should have cut my *kunki's* tusks. In my opium daze, I forgot this basic rule of elephant hunt! Fie.... Oh! I had to pay so many fines! Two hundred rupees for killing a wild elephant on hunt. Besides, other fines for not cutting the *kunki's* tusks. Woe on me! I lost my *kunki phandi* licence also! But I bow to you most respectfully ... you saved my life that day!"

A Brahmin lad from Haramdo uttered,

"Elephants know everything! They have long memories! That baby elephant, Jagannath, never forgot his mother's slaughter. Now he has taken his revenge! He came like a thief, silently, toppled Jamaluddin from the *machan* and killed him!"

A second Brahmin boy joined in.

"It's strange that he failed. Very strange! Even white sahibs like Humphrey, Bore and Milroyd took his advice on how to ride *kunkis* and wrote down what he said in great detail. Revenge! It's pure revenge! He was carrying all these years, in his mind, the picture of how his mother was killed by Jamaluddin's *kunki* when he was a baby!..."

Many others shouted together,

"Yes! Yes! We have seen with our own eyes! Far into the night, besides a rice husk fire, Humphrey Sahib sitting before Jamaluddin and noting down everything about elephant's diseases about *jaharbat*, *mit khara, churangi, Karih*[12] and many things! He also told those white sahibs everything about the herbal medicines for curing these diseases. And what's even more objectionable, he revealed to them all those *mantras* for curing these diseases!"

Another chimed in,

"Those white sahibs presented him with a *coat pataloon* suit, and with great pride, he used to wear it to the festivals! Everyone know that he was originally a Hindu. But his parents were involved in some sexual offence and were banished to Gorokhiya-gaon[13] where they became Muslims..."

Meanwhile Indranath stood motionless, like a statue, near the dead man's body. Sorrow and fear surged through his mind and tortured his soul. A bamboo frame was improvised and some scheduled caste men and boys from Heerapara and Dompara, the flsherman's villages, lifted the blood-soaked body on the frame.

The frame was hoisted on the shoulders of four men and behind it, forming a close procession, the crowd started going down the mountain side. Fear of the mad elephant bound them all in a tight group, and to keep up their spirits, some men followed in the rear, beating drums. Indranath was leading the procession. As he walked downhill with slow, measured steps, the throbbing of his heart fell in rhythm with the drum-beats.

... So it has happened! It's as if an era has passed away. Now only one *makhana* has remained in the elephant yard. He's not fit to be a *kunki*. He cannot even pull boats or lift timber logs at Jirang! His trunk is unnaturally thick and out of proportion. The *howda* would look very awkward on his back... Ah, the *howda*! It had been smashed to bits by that mad Jagannath!

Can the Gossain make a new *howda* to suit this *makhana*?

Dhuk! Dhuk! Dhuk! His heart throbbed in unison with the drums. He'll have to go to Rani and report to the Forest Officer. After all the Gossain's elephant, Jagannath, has killed a man ... That hunter from Chakrad, who has collected tusks by killing wild elephants and rogue elephants and has obtained the Elephants Control Licence, is waiting for this chance of hunting down Jagannath and collecting his magnificent tusks. Now the District Commissioner will soon issue a warrant from Gauhati, to shoot Jagannath down. He has after all killed a man.

... Where?... He was always tied to the *bokuḷ* trėe in front of the *batghar* ... Oh, if he is shot dead near that tree?... How will Indranath and his family suffer that agony? How will they bear it? And the terrible sight, when his tusks will be carved out of the lifeless body! How will he tolerate that horrible spectacle? Jagannath was like a part of his body, like a member of his family. How can he stand that cruel scene? And look at the heartless play of destiny! He, the master and friend, himself will have to sign and receive the proclamation order for his death!

... Indranath's eyes filled with tears... *Dhuk-dhuk! Dhuk-dhuk*! His heart beats sent rays of pain shooting through his chest! He walked downhill with the procession...

Twelve

Saru Gossainee had taken her bath. Wearing a clean pair of *gatala* and *mekhala*, she stepped out into the courtyard for her daily morning prayer and obeisance to the Sun God. The courtyard surface had only recently been scrubbed with mud and cow-dung mixture. It was shining like the coat of a young and sprightly deer. She was wearing her *mekhala* a little short and her dainty ankles and feet shone in the morning sunlight.

After offering prayers to the Sun God, Saru Gossainee walked slowly towards the horizontal bamboo pole that served as the entrance gate to the courtyard. She stood there for a while. It was the month of November. The bamboo clusters on Matia Pahar were thick and lushly green. The early morning fog covered the bamboos. Each bamboo cluster appeared as if it was enclosed in a fishing net. The fog was spread out unevenly. Some patches were dark, some transparently thin and light, like the tattered *gatala* worn by the poor but beautiful dark girls of Hirapara. Saru Gossainee observed that the straw heaps, which once looked like skeletons, were now tall and fat. Small children climbed to the top and slid down gleefully, again and again. The early morning air was filled with their shouts and laughter.

Ah! The sweet fragrance of autumn paddy! Saru Gossainee inhaled deeply this heady fragrance and wondered which variety of rice it was! Yes! Yes! it was *bateshwari shali*[1] rice. Once, long back, she had seen a swarm of locusts swoop down on this paddy, like sparks of fire. From that experience, she had learnt that whenever *bateshwari shali* grew healthy and strong, it attracted this pestilence. This paddy also got afflicted by *bhur* and *gundhi* insects and for protection against these pests, *bandhas* from Gossainee's house had cut down and taken away branches of *pachatiya*[2] trees. Everything appeared all right. There was a bumper crop. Sounds of threshing and winnowing floated in the air.

The pounding horse was being pressed vigorously. Yes, everything was well! But her own granary was still empty. For the last one week, she had stood near the bamboo gate, waiting to hear the sounds of bullock-cart wheels, but those carts laden with paddy never came from her fields. Strange! For some time, after her husband's death, things went on well but gradually they deteriorated and now everything was almost on the brink! And what had happened to the disciples of Pathaldiya, Garhal, Dharpur? They had not yet sent their baskets full of rice! What was wrong? They had not even come with gifts of floral *mukchas*[3] and ripe jack-fruits, to invite her to visit their places! For quite a long time after her husband's death, parties of disciples used to come with drums and trumpets, to take her to their villages. They would make their camp in the prayer hall for days together. When they reached their village with Saru Gossainee in the palanquin, they would put down the palanquin in front of the village prayer-hall and stretch a long cloth, from the palanquin to the entrance of the hall. Saru Gossainee would then step down and walk over the cloth to enter the prayer hall.

A long time has passed. Epidemics of cholera and black fever struck the villages of Garhal and Pathaldiya. Many devoted old disciples surrendered their lives to these dreaded diseases. Now it appeared that this generation of devotees, who regarded her with high respect and moved about with the dust of her feet smeared on their foreheads, had disappeared forever.

The country has gained independence. But for Saru Gossainee, the old order was no more! Before his death, the Gossain had told her, "My dear, don't be afraid! With the independence of our country, all our people, old or young, will become responsible citizens. Even here, in this remote corner of the country, our people will learn quite a lot of things. After my death, even if you are alone, our disciples will be more concerned about you and give you the same respect and devotion..."

But now, what was happening? What was going on? All these problems with her lands! Harrassment, disputes! It looked as if the disciples would drag her to the courts of Gauhati. She, the Gossainee, who had not even looked at the open sky above her head!...

From the bamboo gate, where she stood, Saru Gossainee saw Kowria near the *batghar*, holding his *kalia*, the musical instrument made from buffalo horn. Even from that distance, she could see the huge hump on his back that made his neck appear as if it was drooping. Probably there was a ceremony in the Gossain's manor.

She also saw a few boys with shaven heads making *donas* from plantain bark, just beyond the *batghar*. Perhaps somebody had come to the Gossain for performing the act of mortification for some sins committed by him. Nowadays the Gossain had started changing the traditional rules of the scriptures, according to circumstances and convenience, which Saru Gossainee found quite astonishing. But why only the Gossain! She had heard that even Purshottam Bhagwati, the Gossain's own tenant priest, was manipulating the holy scriptures for his own selfish ends. Of course she herself was not averse to a slight change that served some beneficial human purpose. Once the *mahout* of Bhikharu Gosain had come to her. He had a wife and one child, but another woman wanted to enter his house with his full consent. This *mahout* was a Kachari who was considered a low caste, but she had initiated him to a higher social status by performing hard and arduous initiation rites. He had sent a man to her to take her advice as to how he could take a second woman, under the rules laid down in the scriptures. But at the same time, the *mahout*'s wife, with the child at her breast, had come and fallen at Saru Gossainee's feet. That day, she did not even consult the religious books. She knew what to do and she gave a fitting reply to the man sent by the *mahout*,

"A women who deliberately destroys the happiness of another man's wife, deserves contempt and I will give her a curse that will destroy her lineage ..."

After hearing these words, the *mahout* dared not take the other woman into his house and all ended well, though in the scriptures, having more than one wife was allowed and many men in the villages had more than one wife. So many unpleasant things were going on all around the *sattra!* While one woman was being received by the man of the house at the front door with open arms, the other woman, the spouse, was kicked out by the rear door! And that poor woman! What happened to her, where she went, nobody cared to know!... And those *diyas*[4] have become common in the North and the South Bank even among the high castes.

There was an unused old well near Matia Pahar that was considered haunted. When the volunteers of the opium prohibition committee cleaned the well and removed the age-old muck inside, they hauled out many skeletons of women. Only the other day, a famished woman, almost like a skeleton, had come. Saru Gossainee had made her sit in the courtyard and had given her some puffed rice and liquid jaggery to eat. The poor woman gulped it down gratefully. She narrated her story between sobs.

"It's all due to that evil thing, opium! Soon after it entered the *sattra*, sticks have rained blows on the back of us unfortunate women. The days are so bad now! Is it wise to stay all alone like this? You should also keep somebody with you."

The shaven-headed youths had finished their work of making *donas*. They had disappeared into the backyard where there was the space for killing goats. Saru Gossainee could now understand. These people were from the Kachari tribes of Jirang or Hathimara Ghuli. They must have come for religious lessons or *prayaschit* for some sin committed by them. Yes, the religious rites are very clearly stated. The *sudras* who stay within their religious bounds, invite four *dhanu prayaschit*[5] if they drink wine made by their own hands, and if they take wine made by the *shuri* caste, they must do six *dhanu prayaschit*[6]... Who knows what they have done? Perhaps they have killed a cow or brought into their house a woman of an unknown caste.

The *kacharis* were simple, straightforward folk. Even when they walked along a path, their eyes would be glued to the ground. They always bring for the Gossain the best vegetables grown in their gardens.

Suddenly she heard the "krr krr" sound of bullock cart wheels. She stood there with attentive ears... No, no. It was going towards the Gossain's house. A mute pain shot through her bosom. If the tenants from Ukium and Pathaldia do not come soon, there will be a terrible crisis. For the first time in this Damodariya Gossain's *sattra*, a Gossainee would have to wear old torn clothes and almost starve without proper food. As far as memory goes, this has never happened. The level of mustard oil in the drum had almost touched the bottom. Only that day, the disciples of Rajabaha had brought their offerings. She was stunned to see the scanty gift of mustard oil in their baskets.

In every house, there was an opium den and fortunes were sinking. When the Gossain was alive, the gifts for conducting marriages, or at the ritual celebration of a young girl attaining puberty or at the time of a young bride's entry into the kitchen would contain a sizeable quantity of oil—so much so that she would have to distribute some of it. Yes, those were the days! The Gossain would sit in the warm courtyard, bathed in sunlight, and he would rub the mustard oil all over his body, languidly. His skin was so beautiful like that of *gora paltan*[7]. His hair looked so much like Indranath's—dark and curly. He was also lean and tall like Indranath. He used to coax her.

"Come, Saru, rub some oil on my back, with your soft and tender hands! Come on, Saru! Don't feel shy, nobody will see us here."

Her eyes filled with tears. She stood still near the gate. Ah! How wonderful those days were! He did not have even a single spot of blemish in him. He never seduced young low-caste girls with gifts of gold earrings, like many other Gossains of South Bank. She was his world and he passed all his free hours with her and no one else. Saru Gosainee wiped her brimming eyes with the end of her *gatala*.

Khaki-clad Home Guards of the Opium Prohibition Squad marched up to the *batghar* of the Gossain's mansion and collected into an orderly group there. They looked like those constables who came to collect revenue.

It is said that in Haramdo, the camp for the rehabilitation of opium addicts had already started. The Gossain had supplied free all the bamboos and the timber required for its construction. It is also said that the beds for the inmates were made of flat bamboo strips. There were separate arrangements for women addicts at the camp. Saru Gossainee remembered seeing three or four women passing by on the road and lamenting loudly.

"Oh! Brothers! Sirs! Have pity on us! We took opium only to relieve the pain in our backs, otherwise how could we work the tread-mill for husking rice or plant seedlings in the fields? May a curse light on those who informed the police about us! We beg you to save us...!"

She had recognized the voices of these women. They often came to her courtyard for pounding rice and other tasks. In between their work, they would take rest for a while near the well, eating jaggery with crushed wild berries. And during the mango season, when the whole *sattra* turned green, they would savour crushed raw mangoes with hot green chillies!

The fragrance of *bateshwari shali* rice again wafted towards Gossaineee. A wave of sadness and discontent passed through her body. There is no sound of wheels, only the noise of pounding rice in other people's houses. It echoes the throbbing beats of her heart!

Whom to send now to Dharpur, Pathaldia, Garal? Mahidhar was away with *ojhas*, cooking meals for them, He would not come back before three days. This time those *ojhas* would visit almost all the places of South Bank.

Mahidhar is so poor! At least he will get free food, *gamuchas* and money from the *ojhas.* That was something! She herself had encouraged him to go. And she admired the smart *ojhas* with their magnetic personalities, and their dashing ways. She herself had a passion for them.

When she had first come to this *sattra* from Pathaldia, after her marriage, a *jatra* party had come. Their perfomance had started... Men and women sat separately with a cloth stretched between them serving as a partition. She was made to sit down with the other ladies. She had witnessed for the first time the acting and dancing skills of Vishnu *Ojha* from Haramdo. A bright pertromax lamp nearby spluttered and hissed loudly. The old lady who sat next to her was one of the women who had come to her village to look over the prospective bride. She had opened her hair, measured the length and felt its texture. She had made her walk to and fro and tested her grace. This lady now took her hand, made her get up and took her to a place nearer the stage, away from the noisy lantern.

She had watched Vishnu *Ojha,* her eyes fixed on him, bewitched by the graceful, sensuous movements of his arms and body. She had felt something stirring inside her; a wave of sexual excitement passed through her body! The drum beaters, their torsos bare, wearing flower garlands, were dancing and beating their drums with abandon.The *Ojha* wore a long wide skirt with gold embroidery, which swirled and waved around his body. There was a white turban on his head and gold earrings shone in his ears. He danced and weaved between the drum beaters, never stopping even for one moment, and sang.

Mukhe geet hate mudra
Pawe dhare tal

Garuda sadrisha bhrame
Sehi ojha bhal.

(Song on the lips,
Gestures in the hands,
Rhythm in the feet,
In motion like an eagle,
Such an *ojha* is the best!)

...Yes, yes! Vishnu *Ojha* is the best! A warm sensation passed through her breasts. Her nipples hardened. The *Ojha's* words became flowers and fell on her body. His eyes became swords and pierced her. This play of flowers and swords lasted for a long time...

The people on the banks of Jagalia used to say that in *madan sawan*[8], *bogula sawan*[9], *newl sawan*[10] and other poses, the *Ojha* could not be surpassed by the other *ojhas* of the South Bank. The people of South Kamrup said that a copy of the book of *ojhas, Taujattikasaar*[11] that had almost disappeared from Assam, had fallen into the hands of Vishnu *Ojha* and he had learnt the magic of his art from this book! Magha *Ojha* of Pathaldia and Krishna *Ojha* of Jambuori had tried their best to get this book from Vishnu *Ojha* by bribing his assistants and even through black magic but they had failed in their nefarious efforts.

His rhythm and grace, his poignant rendition of Behula's suffering and agony. She had wiped tears from her eyes with a corner of her handkerchief. Giribala, then a child, had asked with a puzzled frown, "My lovely aunty, why are you crying?"

Giribala used to get up early in the morning and collect the scattered beads, flowers and ribbons left behind on the stage after the previous night's performance.

Dham, dham, dham! Saru Gossainee returned with a

start from her reverie. A band party was approaching for the other end of the road ... Whose marriage is it? Perhaps a daughter of some rich contractor of the military camp at Mirza or someone from a well-to-do family of Haramdo. It appears to be quite a big band party!

Saru Gossaineee went behind a *gulanch* tree near the gate and watched through its creepers. When the marriage party came near the *batghar* of the Gossain's manor, the band stopped playing and the bride stepped down from the palanquin and walked with the others, according to the age-old custom of paying respects to the Gossain. Gossainee smiled. She felt happy to see that some people still followed the old rituals and customs of the *sattra*. She remembered that the old Gossain had once beaten up a low-caste fellow with his palm leaf fan only because he sat down thoughtlessly on a wooden stool in the Gossain's house! Until that day, even the family priest and others could sit only on hand-woven mats spread out on the floor.

Now the times have changed. Indranath, who will be an *adhikar* one day, goes to Bolo's gambling den and drinks tea and takes betelnut and leaf from Bolo's hands. Bolo, a person of lower status! She had never heard of such goings-ons before!

The blare of the wedding band could now be heard only faintly. The marriage party had passed by the Gossain's house quickly and gone ahead towards Lohar Ghat.

The sun's rays were mildly warm. The Gossainee saw that the *dudhkhadi*[12] tree had grown up quite fast and was now resplendent with green leaves and the sun danced over it. She looked around... The sun is a skillful fisherman, she thought. He has cast his net wide and gathered a golden harvest. The berry leaves, the winding creepers of betelnut leaves, the heaps of straw, even the scattered chunks of elephant's dung,.. everything in the *sattra* was caught in his golden net!...

Suddenly Saru Gossainee became conscious of somebody shouting. It was the maid servant from the backyard.

"Oh, Gossainee! Look! A dog has entered the kitchen! Come, come! Quickly!"

She ran to the kitchen, and breathlessly, through the wide open door, she threw whatever that came to her hand, at the dog inside, crying,

"Shoo, shoo, shoo! Get out, you devil! Shoo! . . ."

A dirty, mangy dog, ribs sticking out, its tail between its hind legs, ran out by her side. Saru Gossainee could step back just in time, to avoid its touch. The maid rebuked her, "Mother! Why did you leave the door open? The sun god's already up over your head! Now you'll have to take out all the utensils, put them in fire and wash them! What a load of extra work you have put on your head, Gossainee!"

Saru Gossainee tucked up her *mekhala* and entered the kitchen. She had put some left-over rice, soaked in water in a vessel, for the maid. It was all gone, eaten up by the dog. She sat down, exasperated, and mopped her sweating forehead with the end of her *chaddar*. Meanwhile the maid had piled firewood outside and lit a fire for the purification of the tainted utensils. Saru Gossainee got up and busied herself with the inevitable task. She brought out the rice pot, the frying pan, spoons and other cooking vessels, old and black with age, and dumped them into the fire. The maid, who was standing a little distance away, remarked, "Mother, you were waiting at the gate for Mahidhar *bapu*, weren't you?"

"Yes. Even now the paddy carts haven't arrived! Can't

you smell the fragrance of *bateshwari shali*, coming from the houses, and hear the threshing of paddy? If Mahidhar had come, I could have sent him to Ukium and Pathaldia, to find out!"

The maid remarked, "By this time, last year, the Brahmin girls from Haramdo had come for pounding roasted rice."

Saru Gossainee did not reply and set about cleaning the utensils. She took them out, one by one, from the fire and scrubbed them with straw and ash. The maid from Rajabaha watched silently and felt sad for the Gossainee. Here she was, a high-born lady, cleaning vessels in the hot afternoon sun, her noble blood running out in streams of sweat! The maid knew very well how constrained her condition would be if the paddy carts did not arrive in time. She also knew about her weakness for Mahidhar. If somehow he was late in coming back, the Gossainee's mind would flutter like a parrot in its cage. She knew all this and felt sad. She spoke a little apprehensively,

"Mother, he has gone with Vishnu *Ojha*, and the *Ojha* is performing in North Bank only as he is afraid of the mad elephant here."

Gossainee interrupted impatiently,

"That elephant has entered Jirang forest after killing Jamaluddin. Doesn't Mahidhar know that?"

"Who knows whether the elephant has really gone into Jirang? He may be loitering in the forests of Mirza!"

"He has gone there! Gone there! I know! Indranath went with the dead body of Jamaluddin right up to Bholagaon. Nothing happened on the way!"

"Yes, yes, I remember everything! Indranath Gossain has done something very bold! And daring! He was not at all afraid of the elephant and didn't hesitate to go with the corpse to a Muslim village. Who had ever heard of a Gossain doing such a thing!"

Saru Gossainee's long hair came undone and fell down in a cascade. Her fair skin, coated with perspiration, shone in the sun. She took the utensils to the well. It was an ordinary well without a trestle. She let down a rusted bucket, and drew out a bucketful of water. She washed out the grease and dirt from each utensil and put it in a cane tray. When all the utensils were done, she took some cow-dung and clay paste inside the kitchen and started coating the walls and the floor with the paste. After this task was over, she went to the well again with fresh clothes and prepared herself for a bath. She drew water from the well languidly and took her own time over the bath, thinking that if she prepared food later in the evening, Mahidhar may turn up by that time and get a hot meal to eat. Today, at Barihat, is the day for *pala*. He will certainly come with the *ojha* party, which always precedes the *pala*. The mere thought of his return gives her intense pleasure. His memory is like a golden ray of the sun...

Saru Gossainee finished her bath. Her clothes still drenched with water, she entered the small, murky room where she kept her late husband's wooden sandals. Under the citrus tree in the corner of her courtyard, the sunlight had a dull tint. The maid was sitting there, chewing some tamarind. When she saw the Gossainee going towards the kitchen, she said,

"Oh, Mother! What about roasted rice powder for *Bihu*[13]? Other houses have already started pounding it."

"Yes, yes. I'll call Nani Champa and Bhumi Champa. Their father is still teaching in that school at Haramdo. But they are married to *jajmani* Brahmins. When they come for pounding roasted rice, this house echoes with their merry laughter. I like to have them here. Otherwise it's like a haunted house after the Gossain's death."

She came out of the kitchen with a bamboo tray and some white pumpkin and potatoes. She sat down and began cutting the vegetables into pieces. The maid continued.

"Do you know, mother? Those white soldiers from Mirza had set their sights on these two sisters! This gossip was whispered all over the South Bank!"

"Yes, it is true. It was the day of their brother's first visit to his in-law's place. They had gone with him to Palasbari. Both had attained puberty. They had robust, healthy faces, red and rosy. They were going in a bullock-cart, covered at the back with a curtain. It was a cloudy, rainy day. When they were passing by the military base camp, unfortunately it started raining heavily. Even in day time, it was like night. Suddenly the cartman stopped the bullocks and shouted,

"'*Maichanahat*[14]! A clump of bamboo is blocking the road! Don't know how it came to be there. Too heavy for us to push it aside! Oh, God! What to do now?'

"Both the sisters cried out, 'It's the *bira*[15], the evil spirit! It always blocks the roads like this. Quick! Piss on some lumps of earth and pelt them on the *bira*! It's the only way to drive it out!... Come on!...'

"The cartman jumped down from the cart. Suddenly, in the dim light, he saw three white-skinned soldiers rushing out with guns from the bamboo obstruction. The girls also noticed them. Terrified, they shouted, 'Oh, Holy Mother! Save us! Save us from the soldiers!...'

"The cartman, who had got down to drive away the *bira*, was so frightened that he pissed into his own *dhoti*!"

(At this point, both Gossainee and the Rajabaha maid

burst out into laughter.)

"The white soldiers went to the back of the cart and shouted in a threatening manner, 'Who's there? You there, come out! Haven't you heard the siren? Come out! Soon the planes will come! Bombs will fall! Bombs! Bombs!'

"The two girls jumped out of the cart in terror and landed straight into the arms of the soldiers! They clung to them in extreme fear. The planes came and disappeared into the sky. But the girls were still hugging them for dear life!"

The Rajabaha maid cried out,

"How disgusting! How shameful! Were they deflowered?"

"No, no! I don't know really! It will be a sin to tell a lie, but this much I know that two white soldiers were often seen going towards Haramdo by the short cut over Matia Pahar. We heard that they gave several things to the husbands of Nani Champa and Bhumi Champa like *markin* cloth, saucepans for boiling water, and a tin box with a picture of a frog on the top..."

"Gossainee, what was that tin of frog?"

Saru Gossainee replied,

"The two soldiers told the husbands that it contained nectar prepared by no less than the cooks of Empress Victoria herself! The *jajmani* Brahmins asked the soldiers whether the cooks were Brahmins because they touched things prepared by Brahmins only. They assured them that the cooks were Brahmins. Nani Champa and Bhumi Champa then sat down with their husbands with banana leaves spread out before them for a banquet of the gods. They cut open the tin with a knife and a grinding stone as hammer. Then with great expectations, they spooned out the contents on the banana leaves..."

The Gossainee started laughing. She could not speak for some time. Then she continued,

"Do you know what came out? A big frog! Ha, ha, ha! Boiled in some kind of soup! Ha, ha, ha! All of them jumped like grasshoppers and fled from there!"

The maid commented, "I don't know where the cooks of Queen Victoria got such big frogs! Only by eating these frogs can the queen rule our *Bharatdesh!* No wonder!"

Saru Gossainee smiled and said, "Really you are an ignorant simpleton! The Empress ruled and died many years back when you and I weren't even born. Now our country is free and our own people are the rulers. Nowadays do you ever see the Queen's face on coins? It has disappeared long back. Don't you remember Gandhi *Maharaj?* And those volunteers who used to come for collecting donations? After Queen Victoria, three, four kings lived and died. Then came Gandhi *Maharaj* and made our *Bharatdesh* free!"

The Rajabaha maid stood up. She undid her *mekhala* and wrapped it again tightly around her bosom. The Gossainee caught a glimpse of her sagging flesh. Her *mekhala* had a three inch wide design of flowers and creepers embroidered on it. The cloth was so dirty that it had taken on the colour of dry sheepskin. and she did not wear any *gatala* over it. The maid said,

"Yes, Gossainee, I remember those volunteers. They used to collect money, sing songs, and shout *Inquilab Bindabun.*[16] Even now some of these volunteers can be seen in opium camps."

Saru Gossainee gathered the pieces of white pumpkin in the bamboo tray and took them inside the kitchen. But her eyes were still on the road. Mahidhar should be coming now. He will be tired and hungry. A hot meal will make him cheerful! Whenever she sees this man, fresh energy seems to run through her body and mind. Let him always remain as her shadow! Poor man! Only the other day he had advised her to put the plough to the *ejamali* land owned by her and other Gossainees. And now when he hears that the paddy carts have not arrived from Pathaldia and Garal, he will leave his meal uneaten and rush out to find what had happened! It is great help to have Mahidhar with her. As long as he has the power, nobody would dare to grab her lands, even for a short time. Nobody can make her *rayati patta* into *miyadi*. And that foxy *mandal*[17] would behave like a wet cat before him. But those communists! They have already come upto Marabhitha.What will happen if they come to her lands?...

That day, before setting out on tour with Vishnu *Ojha* party as a cook, he had stood in the shadow of the citrus tree and said,

"I will come back within three or four days. Near a place on South Bank, where I am going, good quality *urium* wood is found in plenty. I'll bring four *urium* posts for repairing your house!"

Then he had raised his head and looked at Saru Gossainee. She was like a beautiful vision! She had just come out from her bath. She was wearing only a short *gatala* over her bosom. Her whole body, her complexion was radiated a kind of mysterious light! Mahidhar shifted his gaze immediately. She will never know why he cannot look straight into her eyes! Does he also have the same conflict of mind which she is experiencing every day and every night?

The rice pot was boiling over. She took it off from the fire. She kept the straining vessel over another pot and drained off the hot steaming rice broth. The steam from the cooked rice enveloped her soft, beautiful face. She thrust some more pieces of firewood into the clay oven and hoisted a big, black, soot-covered pan over it. Then she took off the mustard oil bottle from its hook on the post nearby and tilted the bottle over the frying pan. To her dismay, she discovered that very little oil was left in the bottle.... If the paddy carts do not arrive in time, where will she get the money to buy mustard oil? She had never faced such a situation in her life before!

Mahidhar has to come back! She will not allow herself to become like Durga and other Gossain widows! Never! Never!... Mahidhar will certainly bring four posts of *urium* wood. Certainly he too has dreams like her, of staying under those four permanent posts of *urium* wood. Yes, Mahidhar, whose life was shattered in the prime of youth by the death of his wife. Surely he too struggles with himself, like her!

She put the vegetables in the little oil she could pour out from the bottle. Transferring the pepper, cumin seeds, ginger and red chillies to the grinding stone, she started making a fine paste... Fie on her! What is she thinking! Her mind is always haunted by the dream of those solid posts of *urium* wood, and that man! But she can save herself from the pull of the flesh. She has the will power and enough faith in herself. Faith in the moral force inherited from her ancestors! A sense of restraint that will transform, in a moment, the beautiful curtain of gold and silver threads, into an impregnable iron shield. Did anybody ever, in Damodariya Gossain families, face such a situation anytime, anywhere? Ah! Let Mahidhar come! Nothing can be more delightful!

Her attention was drawn to the frying pan. She turned over the half-cooked vegetables and scraped the sides of the pan where they had got stuck. She sat there a moment, thinking. What else should she cook now? Her eyes fell on the tomatoes in the bamboo basket. Some were quite ripe, others half-ripe. She'll make a sour dish of tomatoes, cooked with rice powder. It'll be an ideal dish for someone coming home tired from a journey!

All the while she was cooking, her ears were alert for any sound coming from outside. Once she heard the bamboo gate being pushed aside and she cried out,

"Oh! Rajabahini! See who has come?"

The maid replied.

"Mother! It's a *bhagat* from Pathaldia and from the opium camp, one Home Guard!"

Saru Gossainee felt a bit disappointed. She pulled out some burning sticks from the oven to damp the fire, and looked out through a peculiarly shaped hole in the mud wall of the kitchen. Quickly she washed her hands in a big container. She took off the *gatala* from the clothesline and covered her bosom. She came out and stood on the verandah. Meanwhile the *bhagat* from Pathaldia had already entered the courtyard. His hair was long like that of the disciples of *Purusha Samhati Sattra* and it was gathered into a top-knot on his head. He was wearing a clean white *dhoti* and a *muga* coloured vest. He had thin lips in a flat face. Though his feet were bare, they were quite neat and clean. He came up to Saru Gossainee, bowed down and touched her feet. Meanwhile the Home Guard had closed the gate and joined the *bhagat*. His head and face was covered with pepper-and-salt hair. He had on a loose pair of *khaki* shorts and a striped shirt. He wore mud-covered thick leather boots. He removed his boots and kept them in a corner with his stick. Then he came and bowed down respectfully to the Gossainee.

Saru Gossainee called out to the maid to spread out two mats for the visitors and then quickly entered the kitchen. She put down the frying pan from the oven and sprinkled some water on the fire.Covering the pan with green banana leaves, she came to the verandah. She sat down on a decorated wooden stool and said, "It's lunch time and you must be hungry. Go to the well and wash your feet. I won't give you *jakkra bhat*[18] but hot rice that I have just prepared."

Everyone in the *sattra* knew that Saru Gossainee would not allow any person visiting her at lunch time, to go away without sharing a meal with her.

The *bhagat* replied, "Even your stale rice is like nectar for us. But please don't trouble yourself, mother. We had our rice when we started from Pathaldia."

She asked, "What brings you here?"

"We have to admit some opium addicts in the rehabilitation center here. We have come to see about the arrangements. There's also another thing. Some of your tenant disciples want some information. We have come to you to get this information, mother."

Saru Gossainee wiped her face with the *gatala*. Her beautiful eyes wide open, she asked hesitantly,

"What...what information do you want?..."

"Dear mother, you are alone and you have only one stomach to feed. But those on your land...condition is very bad. On top of that, *kalazar* has struck down their grown-up sons. Mother, you already know about those mosquitoes that come silently from the Garo Hills and create havoc..."

"Yes, yes, I have heard....But what exactly do they want to know?"

"Mother, your most trusted man, Mahidhar *bapu*, the Brahmin who lives under your shelter, moves about in Pathaldia, among your tenant disciples. He has spread the news that you are planning to take *baina*[19] against your land..."

Saru Gossainee felt as if the sky had fallen on her head. She cried out.

"Do you say *baina*? Why should I take *baina*? Why should I sell my land?..."

"Your tenants' condition is wretched. The evil opium has gripped them. Even after selling away all they have, they still dream of owning a piece of land one day. But some unknown vultures may swoop on the land and grab everything!..."

Saru Gossainee cried out again.

"*Bhagat*! We don't have inherited land! The old Gossain had divided the lands and most of it went to the share of the ruling Gossain, Indranath's father. Amranga's forty-three *bighas*[20] of *kherajee* (on which tax is paid) land of the villages and thirty *bighas* of *rupeet*[21] land...not a single small piece had been given to our Gossain. All my disciples know very well that two hundred years back, King Siva Singha had donated to the Gossain immense *nispi-kheraj* land in Amranga, Doobjuni, Khidhirpukhuri, Tamuldi, Baku, Khamar and Chaigaon, for building *sattras*. During the time of that white sahib, Jenkins, Doobjuni, Bajrapara and Tamuldi were made *kherajee* (taxable). When our Gossain's father was alive, on the appeal of many disciples, each of them was allowed to make his own *patta*[22] of the land. And I have heard that since that time, Tamuldi, Kajalikura, Khidhirpukhuri have slipped out from the inheritance..."

Saru Gossainee wiped the sweat with her *gatala* from her shapely nose that looked like a beautiful *teel* flower.

"During the time of the great earthquake, the king of Rani had donated to the Gossain four villages including Satdhariya and Sarania, by copper plate grant. But those white-faced monkeys of the government denied the grant, saying that complete villages cannot be gifted away just like that! All these lands were made taxable. When the old Gossain made his will, our Gossain did not get even a small piece of that land."

The sun, looking like a big dried up ripe pumpkin, was visible behind the *bijulee* bamboo clusters on Matiapahar, as if it would just fall down from one of the bamboo branches. Saru Gossainee did not feel the pangs of hunger even though it was quite late, past her normal meal-time. The strong feeling of expectation of Mahidhar's arrival any moment, sustained her. The maid from Rajabaha brought some *pan* leaves and raw betelnuts to the Gossainee and said,

"Mother, I heard the drums of the *gossain ghar* long back and the *gopal bhog*[23] has been already distributed. When will you take your meal?"

The two visitors also cried out,

"Yes, yes, mother, you must go and take your food now!"

But Saru Gossainee did not heed them. She cut the betelnuts into small pieces, put some lime paste on *pan* leaves and offered them to the two men, taking care not to touch them. Only now the Home Guard observed the Gossainee carefully. He was wearing a crochet cap. He had small, cunning eyes that had the habit of winking now and then. The hair on his legs had become white with the dust from the road. He appeared to be a shrewd man. He addressed her respectfully,

"Mother, we want to put one question..."

Saru Gossainee again had the feeling...as if her skin was being peeled off slowly...

"Yes, yes, what is it?"

"That Brahmin from Haramdo has been staying with

you for quite a long time, hasn't he?"

"Yes, Mahidhar *bapu* has been with me for a long time. Why do you ask?"

Wiping his face, the Home Guard continued,

"Then after such a long time, he must have become almost like a faithful and trustworthy kinsman."

Suddenly the *bhagat* stood up and turning aside, spat out bright red *pan* juice on the ground. Then he said,

"He moves about and works like a sturdy buffalo. I don't think he has brought a *pachuwa*[34] as yet?"

The Home Guard also spoke with him,

"Ah! He behaves like the proud sons of those *adhikar* Gossains!"

Then he recited a short couplet in a sarcastic vein.

> *Dhutihe len chen dahihe nai*
> *Jotaihe phatar phatar dehanhe nai.*
>
> (He wears a long dhoti, but it doesn't
> have a gold border! His shoes make
> squeaking noise when he walks but
> there's no money in his pocket!)

Saru Gossainee grew impatient and at the same time, apprehensive. She cried out,

"It's just his way of talking! He comes from a family of high class Brahmins. They had migrated from Cooch Behar, and had received land along Jagalia in donation from the old Gossain. They have worked as *jajmani* Brahmins for the Gossain's family for a long time. Mahidhar has been treated like their own son, so why shouldn't he behave like that? Haven't you heard about his forefathers? Those *kanyakubjee*[25] Brahmins were adored by the Koch kings, Prana Narain and Bir Narain. They translated the *Drona Parva* and the *Kirat Parva* of the Mahabharata during their time. Do you know how much *miyadi kheraj* land those Koch kings donated to them before it was eaten away by floods?..."

The Home Guard interrupted her impatiently,

"So you trust him completely?"

"Why not? He has helped me in so many ways! On Chikarhati *ejmali* land that I own with some other partners, some outsiders had started cultivation without my knowledge. He went there, drove out the intruders, and now I get paddy from those lands. It was impossible for me, singlehanded, to collect the taxes from the tenants of Pathaldia land. Mahidhar collected each and every pie and placed the money at my feet regularly. For four years, I couldn't pay the tax on the land from which revenue is collected by the government. The constable of the revenue department used to come and go away with a sour face. But with his help, I have cleared all the tax arrears. When the constable came last time, he actually bowed low to me for the first time!"

Both the Home Guard and the *bhagat* began to fret. They got up and went a little distance away on the pretence of spitting out *pan* and betelnut juice. They stood there for some time, whispering in each other's ear. Then they came back. The *bhagat* now said,

"Mother, we have heard that Mahidhar has written on a piece of paper all the details and statistics about your land. Is it a fact? We have also heard that several *bighas* of *miyadi kheraj* land, about which you didn't even know anything, has been discovered by him and he has kept a note about this also."

Again that feeling of somebody peeling her fair skin with sharp pointed nails...

She replied,

"Yes, it's true. He has made a note of the reference numbers marked on the land survey map, of all my *miyadi kherajee, ejmali,* and *ekchania patta* lands."

The Home Guard now spoke up,

"But it is said that there's not much land in your name. The condition of your relatives in Pathaldia has been very bad from the beginning and you have to sustain them by sending rice from your stock. It is even rumoured that there was some mysterious quarrel between your Gossain and the old Gossain..."

"Yes, yes! There was something between them. But everybody knows about it."

"We are in darkness. Can you throw some light on it, Mother?"

"*Bhagat*, it's better if you don't hear about it from my mouth. Our Gossain was cut off from inheriting certain lands and immovable properties. By this time everybody should know about it!"

Bhagat said,

"We have heard that the old Gossain had given permission to a woman from Dakhala to take as much rice from his granary as she required. It is even said that he allowed this woman to sit in the inner chamber of his mansion. And on one occasion, when the old Gossain was to start for Gauhati on some work, Durga was very keen to go with him. She was sitting in the cart with a packet of jaggery sweets in her hand. But the old Gossain made her get down and took that woman from Dakhala with him to Gauhati. Durga threw herself on the dusty road and made a scene, crying her little heart out, and the jaggery sweets lay scattered in the dust. The whole village turned out to watch the scene. But that heartless, arrogant woman didn't even look back from the cart. She was wearing gold earrings given by the old Gossain. He, on his elephant, and that woman in the cart, both went side by side all the way to Gauhati. When they returned, your husband and Durga were standing in the *batghar*, like two cobras with flaring hoods. As soon as that Dakhala woman got down from the cart, Durga jumped at her with an old shoe in one hand and started beating her on her big protruding bosom. Your Gossain jumped up and down with excitement and encouraged Durga, shouting,

'Thrash the bitch! Once more! Beat her again!...The bitch!...'

"From the portico, the old Gossainee also joined in, 'Beat that *barabhateri*!...Thrash her!...'

"From that day onwards, your Gossain's father criticised the old Gossain's immoral behaviour openly in public and they became bitter enemies. Mother, what I have said is correct, isn't it?'

Saru Gossainee remained silent for a moment. Then suddenly her eyes filled with tears. The Home Guard said, "Mother, we are always thinking about your welfare. We are trying to assess the area of land owned by the big landlords of South Bank...That's why we are making these enquiries and you shouldn't feel bad about it. Mother, did you go through the paper prepared by Mahidhar *bapu* with all the details of reference numbers, etc.? Do you have a copy of this paper?"

She replied,

"I have little land left. If you don't believe me, then I can show you the old Gossain's will which is lying in my wooden box. I will bring the will and you can see with your own eyes how the old Gossain treated his youngest son and daughter-in-law..."

Saru Gossainee went inside the small, dark sandal room. Just then, the temple drums started beating, anticipating the closing of the gates of Gopinath's inner sanctuary. She closed her eyes and joining the palms of her hands, bowed her head in prayer. Then she went up to the wooden bed and dragged out from underneath a large wooden box. Opening the box, she took out the copy of the will. She came out and gave the document, which had the colour of very old *muga* silk, to the Home Guard. The latter took out an old pair of spectacles from his pocket. He started reading the will aloud, pronouncing the English words in a peculiar accent.

"Admissible under the Act XVI of 1903, exempted from stamp duty, under the Government of India notification No. 707 dated 24 January 1870. This is written by Harakanta Dev Goswami, *Adhikar*, whose father is late Madhav Kanta Dev Goswami, *Adhikar*; caste, Brahmin; profession, religious head; Distt. Kamrup, police thana Palasbari; *Mauja* Chayani; has executed this will . . . I have two sons living; the elder one, Krishna Kanta Dev Goswami and the younger, Rama Kanta Dev Goswami. My younger son is obstinate and disobedient, even with his father. He is also ruthless and vindictive. He acts against my wishes and keeps contacts with my enemies. He is a source of great torment and harrassment for me. In future, he cannot be depended upon to treat his mother well or look after her properly."

A deep sigh escaped from Saru Gossainee's breast. She cried out in anguish, "Just because he spoke out against the immoral behaviour of his own father, he became a thorn in his flesh!"

The hook-nosed Home Guard resumed reading out the will,

"Now that I am old, I wish to leave my lands in safe hands after my death.

1. For my son, Rama Kanta, there is the Appendix attached to my will, of some immovable properties. The *patta* (land deeds) is registered with the Revenue Court in his name. Besides the above properties, Rama Kanta has already acquired some land himself in Chayani *mauja* (subdivision), so I do not wish to leave any more land in his name. According to the Appendix attached to my will, all the *kheraj* (taxable) and *nispikheraj* (non-taxable) land is left to my elder son Krishna Kanta and my thatched house and tin-roofed house are also left in his name, in my absence.

2. Rama Kanta's capital of cash money was invested in loans and business and it has increased considerably. Whatever cash money I have at present, is left to my son, Krishna Kanta, and my wife, Omvati Devee. The details of my possessions like elephants, horses, cows, buffaloes, stored rice in granary, utensils, etc., are mentioned in the Appendix (G) attached to my will. In my absence, I leave all my moveable properties to my elder son, Krishna Kanta. My family deity's ornaments of gold and silver, flowers made of gold, canopy, altar, drums and sacred vessels, are listed in the same Appendix above. In my absence, the owner of the same will be my elder son, Krishna Kanta. In my absence, the title of adhikar will be given to my elder son, Krishna Kanta. All the appurtenances of the Adhikar's power like the ceremonial staff and umbrella, elephant's bells, palanquin and *sharadhi thagee* (ceremonial trays) are left to my elder son, Krishna Kanta, and my younger son Rama Kanta will not get any part of it. In my absence, all my disciples of Brahmin, Gossain and Sudra caste will take

my elder son Krishna Kanta as their Guru. This is the order of their present Guru.

3. In Bordowa *mauja, patta* No. 112/94, the value of whatever land situated therein is Rupees three hundred and twenty five and *kheraj* land of..."

The Home Guard stopped reading. He looked tired. He took out his handkerchief and started cleaning his glasses. Then he said,

"Below this Appendix, there is an account of *kherajee* land in your Rani *mauja* villages of Pathaldia, Nagaon etc. and there is also an account of the inheritance left to the old Gossain's elder son Krishna Kanta and all that which your husband was deprived of. Mother, shall I read it out?"

Once again, Saru Gossainee wiped off tears from her eyes with the edge of her *gatala* and said,

"People think that his daughter of Pathaldia has only one belly to feed and she has so much *kheraj* and *nispi-kheraj* land. I am the daughter-in-law of the old Gossain, the same Gossain who was so powerful and had vast lands and ten elephants! Has anybody cared to come and find out about the wretched condition of this daughter-in-law at present?...Has anybody seen that her *gatala* is tattered? In such dark moments, Mahidhar has come with a lamp in his hand and stood by my side. Only with his help, could I pay the revenue taxes and meet the daily expenses of my house."

The *bhagat* tied his long hair into a knot, muttering something to himself. Saru Gossainee continued,

"Home Guard, take a look that Appendix (B). You'll find in it a huge list of movable properties in the name of Krishna Kanta."

The Home Guard took out the wood-coloured old papers and started reading out loudly,

(1)	Rajendra, Airavat and Manik – three tusker elephants	Rs. 500/-
(2)	Two brown and one white horses	Rs. 160/-
(3)	Eight buffaloes (male) and four buffaloes (females) (All the calves born in future will also belong to Krishna Kanta only)	Rs. 150/-
(4)	Bullocks for plough – 20 and milch cows – 60 (All the calves born in future will also belong to Krishna Kanta only)	Rs. 80/-
(5)	Silver handles from palanquin – 2 nos.	Rs. 200/-

(At this point, a deep sigh escaped from Saru Gossainee's bosom. She remembered the day when the Gossain had sent a palanquin for her. It had handles made of mere iron. Ah! He was deprived of so many things!)

(6)	Copper door – 1 pair	Rs. 20/-
(7)	Brass pitchers – 17 nos.	Rs. 40/-
(8)	Brass trays – 3 nos.	Rs. 10/-
(9)	Stands for supporting big plates — 8 nos.	Rs. 8/-
(10)	Brass containers – 80 nos.	Rs. 40/-
(11)	Two big guns in my name	Rs. 50/-
(12)	Big bells for elephants – 8 nos.	Rs. 8/-

(Here the Home Guard stopped for some time. Neither he nor the *bhagat* had any further inclination to read the list up to the end.)

"Mother, the second list contains the items of two-roomed houses and four-roomed houses with tin roofs and tin shed for keeping accessories of ceremonial meetings and theatrical performances, Gopinath's gold necklace and gold coins, copper drums, etc. What's the use of reading all this? Nothing is mentioned about the land for your Gossain."

The *bhagat* now added,

"Ah-h-h! Old Gossain did not leave you even one maid servant to sweep the courtyard, to take over the duty of pounding rice, or to boil soiled clothes?"

The Home Guard and looked through the various appendices. Then he cried out,

"Here, in this appendix, there's a clear account of *bandhis* (maid-servants). Here are the names and their values:

Janaki, Mahima, Birehi, Ghentapi
and Ujha . . . . Rs. 150/-

Saru Gossainee said,

"Yes, yes, I know. Each one of them cost 30 rupees. Out of them, Ghentapi died only the other day. She was fond of opium and it took her life. I saw her in her last days. She used to lie in the portico all the time. She would get a drink of water if anybody passed by. Otherwise she just lay there, without water or food. Flies used to surround her face and add to her agony . . ."

The Home Guard straightened his back and looked at the Gossainee,

"Mother, where's that list of your lands? Surely you must have kept it with Mahidhar *bapu*."

Again that feeling crept over her, as if somebody was peeling off her skin with sharp, pointed nails! . . .

"Yes. Like you, Mahidhar also wanted to see the details of my lands. I gave the list to him."

The Home Guard exclaimed in some excitement, —

"Mother, did you sign a blank paper and give it to him?"

Ah! What's he saying? What's he saying? Does he want to cut me piece by piece and probe the innermost privacy of my mind? Will he leave me all naked? But what will they get? Mahidhar's existence is a part of her blood-stream. Even if they cut her into many pieces, they will not understand anything! This blood of hers has remained pure. It is not mixed with the dust of any land!...

"Yes, Home Guard. One day he asked me to sign a blank paper. He told me that he would put down all the reference numbers on this paper with my signature and then he would track down each tenant who had not paid my share..."

"Did you write the reference numbers of the land deed numbers with your own hand?"

"Where was the time? That Brahmin sat through the whole night before a kerosene lamp in his ramshackle *dhekal* room, writing on that paper, writing away the whole night! When I got up in the morning, I saw him still there, in the same position. Poor man! I told him, why did you torture your body like that! *Bapu* said, 'The account of your taxable land at Ukium. It was in a mess. I have cleared it. Now I want your signature on a paper!' When I came back from my morning chores and bath, I saw on the verandah my disciples from Pathaldia, a newly married couple. They had come for the *haihal* ceremony. So then where was the time? . . . Bring flowers and *tulsi* leaves, scrub the floor of the sandals room with cowdung and clay paste. Do this, do that! It kept me busy the whole day! Mahidhar stood on the threshold and said, 'You won't have any time to go through all these papers. Just sign on this blank paper and I'll do the rest.' He is faithful to the core. He came to me when I was going through a very bad phase. As if God had sent a messenger for me. Even now I am waiting for him. Paddy carts from Pathaldia haven't come as yet."

The Home Guard and the *bhagat* did not say anything. They got up and took their leave of her. Then they opened the bamboo gate and went out on the road.

For some time, Saru Gossainee stood on the verandah, watching them go, lost in thought. She was perplexed and at the same time, struck dumb by their visit. She was startled back to her senses by the voice of the Rajabaha maid, "Gossainee, when will you take your meal? It's already quite late. I tell you that Brahmin from Haramdo won't turn up now. You take your meal and allow me to go."

Some lines of worry on Saru Gossainee's forehead. So he will not come even today. What will happen now? Should she go to Indranath? The late Gossain had told her on his death bed, "They have deprived me of my share of land. Don't go running to them and make yourself small in their eyes. Keep your dignity!"

So far she had tried to manage the affairs of her lands all alone. She had never gone with bowed head to anybody for help. Again that fragrance of *bateshwari shali* rice being pounded in neighbouring houses! She went inside the kitchen.

Saru Gossainee took her meal, sent away the maid and came out on the verandah with a tray of betelnuts and *pan* leaves.

The *batghar* had become a breeding ground and home for bats. Now as the evening set in, their screeching filled the air. The setting sun and the rising moon, like big citrus fruits, were both riding the sky. The blended light of the sun and the moon cast a mysterious glow over the house and the surrounding landscape, as if a vast cloth of *pat* and *muga* silk threads had covered everything in sight. There was no movement or noise on the road. Ever since the elephant in frenzy had killed Jamaluddin, people were afraid of going out in the evening, in spite of knowing that the tormented elephant had fled into the forest of Jirang.

From the Gossain's manor came the sound of bells tied to the dancing feet of young boys who would take the part of *chakaris*[26]. Perhaps they were rehearsing their part under the guidance of the Gossain of Manpur who was distantly related to the old Gossainee. He was the master and the manager of this theatrical group. Nowadays boys from Gossain families joined these roving theatre groups and toured the countryside, from South Bank to North Bank. They even became masters of the art and trained other boys. Saru Gossainee could not believe it but it was happening before her own eyes.

As usual she was sitting alone on the verandah. On Matiapahar, a jackal howled. Her ears were alert for the sound of Mahidhar's footsteps. Will he not come after all?

That mysterious light covered everything in sight. It was so soft, so soothing. The sound of harmonium and the bells on dancing feet, this sound and the mysterious light blended into one harmonious entity.

She glanced at the betelnut tray. The maid had kept only a bunch of raw betelnuts. Probably she was in a hurry to go as it was quite late and she had no time to dig out the fermented betelnuts from the earth in the backyard. She took some pieces of raw betelnuts and started chewing. The reaction was almost instantaneous. She felt a burning sensation in her body. Her skin turned red. It was like being intoxicated. She felt hot and giddy! Should she go to the well and pour some water on her head? No, no, let it be! It will be all right after some time. She sat still, pressing her head with the palms of her hands. Even in these moments of discomfort, she remembered Mahidhar. As soon as he came, she would go quickly into the kitchen, warm some food for him and then tell him,

"Aren't you worried? Don't you care for me? For this lonely woman? The wall of devotion and respect is slowly crumbling. The opium-eaters have snatched away the moon-shaped pendant of Gopinath. Elephant tusks were stolen from the attic of *Adhikar* Gossain in broad daylight. The ornaments of the Gossain's widowed sister, Durga, were also stolen under my own roof. Aren't you worried at all about me? Don't you feel anxious?"...Yes, yes, let him come! She will tell him in no uncertain terms! Let him come!

Jackals howled under the citrus frit tree near the *dhekal* shed. The mysterious sun disappeared from view. In the gathering darkness, the moon shone bright like a silver disc. It was so pleasant! A small cloud hovered over the moon and it looked as if the moon is wearing a white turban. Ah! It is so enchanting! Ah! Now the moon resembled *Adhikar* Gossain's round face and the cloud was a ceremonial umbrella over his head! It appeared as if the Gossain was progressing towards the Jagalia bank for the *shradha* ceremony of the old Gossains of this *sattra*. Saru Gossainee smiled at this fantasy with amusement. But all the while her ears were alert for the sound of his footsteps. A kind of sensuous languor gripped her body. She had these spells from time to time. In such moments, she brings out the holy book and recites in her low, melodious voice.

She entered the sacred sandal room. It was quite dark inside. She searched for the matchbox. She found it, at last, under the bed and lit the mustard oil lamp on its wooden stand. Then she took out the Guru Leela[27], and opened it at the page where she had put a dry leaf as a marker. She started reciting from the chapter that described how Guru Damodar Deva had gone to Cooch Behar and propagated the new religion...

...No, no! Her mind was wandering from its path of concentration, again and again. That *bhagat* and the Home Guard! What secret did they find out from her? What mystery did they unravel? She had spoken frankly about her relationship with Mahidhar. She had not hidden anything. Now there will be rumours. People will gossip about her on the banks of Jagalia. All this would not have happened if the Gossain had been alive. Even now when she offers flowers to the late Gossain's wooden sandals, her eyes fill up with tears. But then what is the strange attraction for that man which she cannot overcome? She did not have any physical relationship with him, though she could have had if she wanted to! In spite of it there was scandalous talk about her! All the Brahmins on the banks of Jagalia were talking about it. Who can escape from this type of gossip? Even great people like Guru Damodar Deva had to face this situation! Who did not know that incident about Damodar Dev? Once when King Parikshit was away on a hunt, the ladies of his harem had gone to Damodar Dev and paid their respect to him. But all sorts of rumours were spread about this harmless meeting of the ladies and Guru Damodar. The latter became so unhappy at such unfounded gossips, that he left the place and went away to Cooch Behar. King Parikshit believed these rumours and was highly annoyed with the Vaishnava saint. The late Gossain once told Saru Gossainee that the king met with divine justice for suspecting a saintly Guru when the *Dilli Badshah* attacked his kingdom and destroyed it completely.

What a delicate heart this saint had! Once he had said

to the royal messenger of Vijayanagar that he hated bloodshed and sacrifices before Goddess Durga.

> *Balir laqat yadi kataya amak.*
> *Mor gala opar balir gala tal.*
> (If I am taken along with the victim
> for sacrifice, then my head will be
> the first on the sacrificial altar.)

But who obeyed his teachings now? In case of a serious illness or evil planets casting an ominous eye on them, the descendants of Damodariya Gossain families go running to Kamakhya temple and offer a black goat to the Goddess!

Krr! Krr! Krr!... Ah! Somebody had opened the bamboo gate! She came out running, but was soon disappointed. It was only a dog, chasing a rat, who had pushed aside the bamboo pole and entered the courtyard! Saru Gossainee went back and sat on the wooden stool. In the light of the earthen lamp, her body glowed like the lustre on a old *pat* silk cloth.

She closed the book of scriptures. The sound of the bells on the ankles of dancing boys had ceased. Perhaps their rehearsal had ended. As night progressed, there were more and more sporadic sounds of coughing from old opium addicts. The odour of frying *pan* leaves also became more intense at this time of the night. It was now time for Saru Gossainee to go to bed. She stood up and went to the corner of the verandah where she always kept a pitcher of water. She washed her feet. Then, walking on tiptoe, she entered the bedroom and closed the door from inside with its cross-bar. While still on tiptoe, she went to the bed, sat down and took out a *gamucha* from under her pillow. She dried her wet feet. She then put her hand to her bosom and murmured her prayers to Gods of the four quarters of the earth, the same prayers that she had uttered all her life from childhood. With a deep sigh, she lay on her back and closed her eyes to sleep. She had not blown out the oil lamp burning at the head of her bed. In its dim light, she looked like a painting by a master painter, with her hair scattered on the white pillow.

She could not sleep. Again and again, her ears strained to hear the sound of the bamboo gate being pushed open. She thought of Mahidhar. Suppose he managed to collect the taxes! With this money in hand, they could go together to Bhela Bhanga *Sattra* on the bank of the turbulent Tarma river. One of her nieces was married into a family there. Last time when she had come for the *shwari*[28] festival on the bank of Jagalia, she had said,

"Why don't you come to Bhela Bhanga? You'll see the *Bhagavat* written by the divine hands of Sri Sankar Dev himself, and the *Chaturbhuj* image of Lord Krishna."

A *jajmani* Brahmin from Rajabaha had gone to Cooch Behar to earn more money. When he returned, he was declared an outcaste by his community as he had become a *vileti*[29]. So he had come to the Gossain for expiation. He had to use the sacred Ganga water and drink cow's urine. This Brahmin had also urged Saru Gossainee to see the *Chaturbhuj* image of Lord Krishna on the bank of Tarma river.

Now she had a keen desire to go with this Mahidhar to the banks of Tarsa and set her eyes on the *chaturbhuj* image of Lord Krishna.

The late Gossain used to tell her that some of their relatives were also there. He also spoke sometimes about Purushottam Bhatacharya who had written *Ratnamala Vyakaran*[30] under the patronage of the king of Cooch Behar and was closely related to them. Bhattacharya also stayed there and they had a keen desire to meet him. Now it would not be so difficult to go to Bhela Bhanga. Those *shuris* were ever ready to take her in a palanquin up to Palasbari, while Mahidhar could walk the distance. And from Palasbari, the rest of the way was quite easy.

Saru Gossainee felt drowsy and soon fell asleep. She had a dream...She is walking with Mahidhar along the bank of Tarsa river. On both sides, *gahara*[31] flowers are blooming profusely and along the path, there are thorny bushes. Mahidhar says to her,

"Eighteen days after Lord Krishna left his mortal body, his half-cremated body merged with the ocean and turned into a stone. From this stone was born *Neel Madhava*[32] of Neelgiri. I'll take you to Neelgiri one day. You'll see *Neel Madhava* with your own eyes. He is the deity of a *shavar* who discovered him. This *shavar* was afraid that some-body might steal the *Neel Madhava*. So he never showed the path of Neelgiri to anybody. But the priest of King Inderduma was as cunning as a fox. He was not an easy one to deal with. So the *shavar* blindfolded him with a piece of cloth. The priest however played a trick. He took with him a bundle of cloth filled with mustard seeds. The cloth had a small hole through which the seeds fell down on the path to Neelgiri. After some time, the mustard seeds germinated and grew into tall plants with yellow flowers. Come, come! Saru Gossainee! We'll walk along that yellow path!"

With great joy, she and Mahidhar walk along that path bright with yellow mustard flowers. He cries with excitement,

"See! This is the path that will take us to *Chaturbhuj* as well as to *Neel Madhava*!"

Suddenly she sees a flock of *pandas*. Their heads are clean shaven and they are all wearing saffron robes. They are from the lineage of Madan Mohan Mahapatra Lalmohariya of the Jagannath temple. They come every year from Orissa to take Brahmin widows on pilgrimage. When these widows come back from the holy tour, their long curly black hair is gone and their heads are as clean shaven as the *pandas*. The instant she sees the *pandas*, the yellow flowers blooming on the path turn into thorny cactus plants! She can now see many other faces among the *pandas*—all known faces! There! Mark and Giribala! Indranath, smoking a pipe! The Gossainee and Durga! The *mahout* Kaltu! And all her disciples of Pathaldia and Ukium! They are all staring at her and at Mahidhar by her side.

Ah! It is as if somebody has set all the thorny cactus plants on fire. Where will they turn now? Where? A clanking of iron chains reaches her ears. It is coming towards her. Is it the frenzied elephant Jagannath?

Suddenly she hears the deep voice of Mahidhar,

"Come, Mother! Take my hand! I can overpower the elephant. I can even put together the smashed *howda* and saddle the elephant. I have the strength! How long will you carry on your shoulders the dead body of your past? Come! Come with me! Take my hand. If you go any further along this path, the flesh of your body will be cut into pieces by the thorns of *kataha* bushes! Come! Hold my hand!"

The bush fire flings out its tongues of flame and catches her *gatala*! Slowly her clothes and body get engulfed in fire. She screams in terror! A strange nightmarish cry bursts out from her throat and she wakes up with a jerk. Somebody is knocking heavily and persistently on the door!

"Wake up! Gossainee! Wake up! Something terrible has happened! Wake up! Gossainee, open the door!"

Saru Gossainee pushed aside the cloth covering her body and got up in a flurry. She ran to the door, lifted the cross-bar and pushed it open. Out on the verandah, she stopped, her body trembling uncontrollably. In the courtyard, a group of people had gathered, holding flaming torches in their hands. They looked like witches in the darkness outside. In the dim, flickering light of the torches, she saw the *bhagat* who had visited her in the morning. His hands and legs were covered with slush and his hair knot had come undone. Oh! That Home Guard! As if he had also come out from a battle! My God! What's that? Blood on his hands? Is it blood? Ah! Those are policemen! Yes! Police! Suddenly her eyes fell on something lying on the ground,

"Who? What is that? Who is lying there? My lord, who is he? Oh! My! Who's lying there?"

In the light of the burning torches, she could now see clearly a man, lying on the ground, his body tied in a fishing net. She came down from the verandah and slowly walked towards the body lying within the circle of men. She bent down and peered at the face. Then suddenly she jerked back with a cry. She somehow dragged herself to the verandah. Clutching tightly at one of the posts, she managed to prevent herself from falling down. The Home Guard, holding a flaming torch in hand, now came near her. He took out a crumpled piece of paper and said,

"Gossainee, look at this paper. Is it the one that you signed?"

In the light of the torch, Saru Gossainee recognised her signature on the paper. The Home Guard continued, "When we came here in the afternoon, you told us that you had signed a blank paper. Surely this is that paper?"

Saru Gossainee took the paper and held it in her fist. She muttered, —

"Yes, this is the same paper. I had signed two or three other papers also. Mahidhar told me they would be used to make appeals on my behalf."

There were cries from the crowd —

"Papers for appeal? What appeal?"

"About the wretched condition of the daughter-in-law of the Gossain of three *sattras*. About how she is not getting taxes from her tenant farmers. About how she is not getting her share of paddy. The tax collector has already threatened that he will take away her clothes, utensils and other things, if she did not pay the taxes in time."

With a trembling, broken voice, she continued,

"I have given my signature only for these appeals and nothing else..."

The Home Guard cried out,

"Gossainee, he has sucked your blood dry!"

A strangled voice escaped from her throat,

"Who...Who has sucked my blood?"

The Home Guard pointed to the man lying on the ground, soaked in blood and slush. Saru Gossainee came near the body again, bent forward and peered at the face. She shrieked,

"Mahidhar! Oh, Mahidhar! Who has caused this spear wound on your body? Who has tied you up in this fishing net? Oh, Mahidhar!"

She started shivering like someone seized by illness. She could not stand and clung to the post for support. The Home Guard took out a paper from his pocket and started reading out loudly in the light of a *mashaal*[33].

"Here is the *patta* number thirty-one of the *miyadi kherajee* land of Pathaldia and *patta* number twenty of the *miyadi kherajee* land of East Samaria...You have given authority to Mahidhar to take the *baina* of all these lands."

Saru Gossainee cried out,

"Oh God! Oh God! . . ."

The Home Guard continued,

"He was caught when he was trying to cross the river and run away with the money he had collected from *baina*. Everybody knew that you trusted him completely. That you had a soft corner for him in your heart. But we were suspicious and our boys followed him like wolves."

A policemen threw a bag at the feet of Saru Gossainee. Coins fell in a scattered heap out of the bag. A shining *phuti* also fell out and landed near her feet. She cried out again, —

"Goodness gracious! Whose *phuti* is this?"

The Home Guard replied,

"This is a part of Durga's ornaments."

There was a general cry from the crowd,

"So he is the thief! He had stolen the ornaments! . . ."

The world was a blur to Saru Gossainee. That man lying on the ground now looked like a python caught in a net. Ah me! Wretched me! Only a short time ago, she was walking with him along the path bordered with yellow mustard flowers, to the temple of *Neel Madhava*. He had held out his hand to her and said,

"Come, hold my hand! If you remain here like this, your flesh will be left behind in shreds on the thorns of *kataha* bushes. Come, come!"

The man with whom she had dreamt of spending her whole life was stripping her of everything and leaving her naked! Ah! There lay her love, entangled in the net like a snake! It had all ended! Love, religion, sacrifice . . .! The world that was before her eyes has vanished!

That man on the ground, the *bhagat*, the Home Guard and those people in the crowd, whirled round and round! Saru Gossainee collapsed in a swoon on the verandah.

Thirteen

Indranath stood, agitated before the cart with its colourful canopy and floral curtain. The teacher from Khatiamari, who happened to pass by on his cycle, had told him that some Rabha people, selling their wares, had seen the rogue elephant in a locality nearby.

Indranath had always thought to himself with great hope that the rogue elephant had vanished into the forest forever and would not return, like many other frenzied elephants of South Bank. He had not imagined that he would have to face the grim prospect of shooting him down if he returned to the *sattra*.

Puffing at his briar pipe, Indranath paced the verandah and at the same time, kept an eye on the cart being prepared for the journey. Durga was going to Chikarhati later that day. He was supervising the preparation personally because he wanted Durga to travel in as much comfort as possible in this long journey. His mind was already heavy with the thought of sending away Durga and now on top of that, this news about the return of the rogue elephant was all the more distracting.

For a long time, Indranath paced the verandah from one end to the other.

The cart was ready at last and it was brought inside the courtyard. Indranath stopped pacing and stood near the cart. Meanwhile a crowd had gathered in the courtyard. On seeing Indranath, the women pulled their *gatalas* over their heads. He could hear their conversation:

"She is on the verge of death. Haven't you seen her face looking like an old vulture?"

"She couldn't immerse the ashes and bones of her dead husband in the holy river. That's why she has become so thin, like a skeleton, due to her intense grief!"

"We heard that she is suffering from that dreaded *khenh*[1]..."

"Indranath Gossain tried so hard to get her admitted to the hospital at Gauhati. She didn't listen and lay on the verandah like a living corpse. She wouldn't eat properly nor would she go anywhere."

Durga came out of the sacred sandal room after taking the blessings of *Adhikar Mahaprabhu*. Her feet were bare and she was wearing only a *mekhala* tied round her bosom. She had covered her head with a big white cotton shawl. She walked unsteadily and appeared to be shivering.

Durga stopped and looked around. She saw the Gossainee standing near a post on the verandah. A red *mekhala* was tied round her bosom without any *gatala*. She looked at her for some time. Her eyes had filled up with tears. She went near the Gossainee, bowed down and touched her feet. A warm teardrop fell on the Gossainee's foot. She could not restrain herself and pulling Durga to her bosom, held her tightly in her arms. This scene tugged the heartstrings of the women gathered there and some of them started weeping. The Gossainee said,

"You have seen all the dark days with your own eyes. So don't put all the blame on me. You are a pious, God-fearing woman, you can open your heart and sense everything."

Durga did not say anything. She caught a glimpse of Giribala, hiding her face behind another post. She was trying to avoid meeting her eyes. With faltering steps, Durga went near her. Giribala began sobbing loudly. Durga said,

"We may not meet again."

At this, Giribala broke down completely.

Other women gathered there exclaimed,—

"Ah! Both of them stayed together, ate the same foot. Even cooking pots and utensils kept together make noise sometimes! Ah! A pity! Nobody came from Chikarhati to take her. All this misery has turned her into a skeleton."

Guimeni was watching everybody and their reaction with sharp, probing eyes. She was standing with a group of women who had come for pounding rice. She muttered to them.

"Indranath tried his best to take her to the hospital at Gauhati but he failed. She refused to go. Instead she would sit before a burning heap of rice husks and cough . . . and cough! If she had to die, everybody thought she had better die in her dead husband's house. It is a woman's religious duty."

The other woman nodded agreement.

"Yes, yes! It's written in the holy books. This way her soul would gain much merit."

Guimeni now said, "She has very few days to live. Look at her! Her stomach and backbone have become one! Old Gossain had also dried up like that and died coughing his life out. Poor soul! To top it all, her ornaments were stolen by the wretched Brahmin! A curse on him! The devil!"

Durga was now sitting in the cart. Looking at her, the Gossainee wanted to tell her, "Go, Durga, go to Saru

Gossainee and bid her farewell too. It was all written on your forehead. Why blame her?"

But these words remained stuck in her throat. She could not utter them.

The bullock cart began moving out. Sombhu *mohura* followed it on his cycle.

A crowd had gathered in the *batghar* to see her off. Probably this would be their last glimpse of Durga. She may not come back to this *sattra*. Mark Sahib was also there with an opium addict, who under his guidance had reformed. He wanted to say a few words to Durga, but he did not get the chance. She had already pulled down the rear curtain of the cart.

As if everything has ended! As if all the honour and pride have become one with the dust! But this dust also spoke to Durga sometimes. It seemed to say,

"We'll come and take you back. We have kept all lands and properties for you. Take them and cherish them! When the time comes, distribute them among the needy."

No, nobody came, nothing happened! And time was also running out! She had no grievance and she had no hatred for anyone....

The cart was now moving faster. The ringing of the bells round the bullock's necks filled the air with its music. Naked children, their mothers and other women came out to their compound gates, to watch the cart going by. They cried out,

"Look, there goes Durga *maichana*! She is alone, nobody came to take her away!"

"Poor lady! She'll surely die, she is suffering from *khenh*."

"She has lost everything, her gold, her land. She's now going to Chikarhati to rest her dried-up bones."

"Everyone says, 'ceiling' is coming, 'ceiling' is coming! Gossains are selling off their land in a great hurry. The Chikarhati Gossain also sold away Durga's land in this way."

Ding-dong, tink-tonk, ding-dong! The cart raced ahead along the road. The children and the women ran after it for some distance. Durga lifted the curtain and looked out. It was green everywhere. Green coconut palms waved in the breeze. Creepers of betelnut leaves twined around betelnut palms in green profusion. The green hue of *hijal* trees looked dark and dense. When will she see all this again? Perhaps never! Everything is turning vague and hazy. Yes, she will not see this again.

The road ahead was now a gentle slope. The bullock-cart raced forward, its bells making a merry tink-tonk-tink-tonk sound. After the slope, the cart came to a crossing where three roads met. On the crossing itself, under a banyan tree, sat the ragged, miserable figure of the outcast leper. His condition had now become worse but still he raised his voice and shouted,

"So you are going away! Go, go! Some go on horses, others on elephants, but everyone has to go!"

Durga's eyes filled with tears. Her body felt weak. The cart now ran along a large field bordering the Jagalia river. Here is her childhood, she used to come with the *mahout* to watch the *suari* festival where all the gods of various *sattras* on South Bank were brought in palanquins. It was here again that she watched the ritual of two elephants playing tug-of-war with bamboos. The bamboo snapped by the winning elephant was considered auspicious. A fishing trap made out of it was supposed to bring in a rich harvest of fish. Durga, as a child, when she used to move about without a *gatala*, had greedily consumed the fish caught by such traps.

The cart picked up speed and rolled on along the road. Suddenly Durga heard a heart-rending sound of crying. She raised the curtain and looked out. Giribala, weeping and running along the road, was trying to catch up with the cart. Indranath was also there, grabbing her hand and struggling to take her back to the manor. Durga could see a swarm of children surrounding Giribala and adding to the confusion with their hue and cry. Really, she was making such a scene! Was Mark Sahib also there? Yes, he was. Ah! She is really crying her heart out! Now Durga could not hold back the tears.

She dabbed her eyes with her *gatala*. She thought—in the innermost recesses of one's heart lies buried affection or love for certain people and one is not even aware of it. It comes out suddenly at unexpected moments! The cart moved on, its wheels making that characteristic sound — krr, krr, krr. Again her head began reeling. She felt as if a fire was raging in her heart. Ah! She will not return by this path again! She will die soon, very soon! She started coughing. She pressed her *gatala* to the mouth and tried to suppress the sound of coughing. The cartman asked,

"Shall I stop the cart?"

Durga spoke through the *gatala* in a choking voice,

'No...no...Go on..."

The ringing of bells now became clearer. Gradually the people following the cart turned back one by one. Durga peeped through a fold in the curtain. Indranath and Sombhu *mohura* were still following on their bicycles. She pushed aside the curtain and cried out to them.

"Go back, Indranath, go back! My blessings will always be with you! You'll be able to reclaim that Marabhitha land. I feel certain! It'll not remain a festering sore any longer. You'll bring back the old prestige of the family. Remember!

If I die, you must come and perform my last rites."

Indranath came nearer and said, "You'll be all right. I tried my best to take you to the hospital at Gauhati, but I failed."

Durga uttered again, "You must go back now!"

"When you are well again, I'll come and bring you back for Grandfather's *shraddha*. I promise!"

"Go, go!"

The bullock cart now took the path through the thick *sal* forest, its wheels making the "krr, krr" sound. Indranath stopped the cycle and stood there for some time. Then he turned and mounting the cycle, took a lane going towards the bank of Jagalia. Reaching the river bank, he sat down on a rock under a big *sal* tree. The "krr, krr" creaking sound of the cart wheels gradually faded away into the distant horizon. An arrow of pain shot through him. He rested his forehead on the palm of his left hand. He was unaware how long he sat there when the touch of a cool hand made him start. He looked up and saw Mark Sahib standing beside him.

"Get up, Indranath. Fate is inexorable. We can only fight against it. Those who cannot rise above the level of emotion, ultimately get washed away in the ocean of sorrow!"

Without turning his head, Indranath uttered,

"My dear Mark, did you notice her face?"

"Yes, Indranath."

"Do you think she really wanted to go away?"

"Why do you brood over it now?"

"I don't know! A kind of remorse is slowly corroding my soul. I feel as if everything inside me has become numb."

A silent cry rent Mark Sahib's heart, but he did not say anything. They stood silently for some time. In the stillness of the air, they could hear the gurgling sound of the Jagalia's current. Indranath took out his pipe, set a match to the tobacco in the bowl and began puffing at it. He looked at Mark Sahib and said,

"Have you completed your work?"

"I have yet to collect some material on that German Sahib. Then I'll go to Bholagaon and stay with the Muslims there. I'll stay for some time in the opium addicts rehabilitation camp. But Indranath..."

"What do you want to say? Tell me."

"If Giribala works with me...you know...on some three or four manuscripts we haven't worked on yet, will there be any objection? Will your father agree?"

Indranath took some time, pulling at his pipe, brooding over this question.

"What do you say, Indranath?"

"Her in-laws are coming to take her away. They are not very happy with her conduct here. The Gossain of Bangara. You know, Mark, they are very conservative. Then there's the question of respect and honour. We want her to die, when the time comes, with dignity."

Mark Sahib was speechless for a moment. He stood there, numbed and silent.

Indranath said,

"I know your feelings are hurt. But please try to understand me."

"Isn't it possible to arrange something for her? To occupy her mind? Such as reading, writing. Something that can help her to have a firm hold on her life? She is so young!"

Indranath remained silent. He could not reply. His teeth clamped tight on the pipe, almost biting into it.

Gripping his *Khadi* shoulder bag firmly, Mark continued,

"Indranath...."

Indranath cut him short,

"I know what you are going to say! In your language, we are digging her grave! Isn't this what you want to tell me?"

Mark Sahib did not say anything.

"Mark, you are a wandering scholar. A nomad in search of knowledge. On the banks of Jagalia, you will have many such experiences. Giribala is one of them. You should keep it that way."

Mark shot him a penetrating look. It made Indranath feel very small indeed.

There were many things which Indranath did not like. They were beyond the limit of his tolerance, beyond his ability to act. This too was such a pain, which he had to suffer silently, which he could not open out to others. Some small silvery fish jumped out of the water in a flashing arc and vanished into the water again. A few frogs hiding in the eroded parts of the river bank, leaped into the water, making plopping sounds.

Mark got up. His old canvas shoes, covered with dust, were in bad shape. His trousers were also old and worn out and he had hitched up the trouser legs up to his knees. Bidding farewell to Indranath, he made his way towards the *sattra*.

A deep depression gripped Indranath's mind. He lit the pipe again and started pufing at it. The long, black shadows of the tall *sal* trees now fell on the waters of Jagalia. It appeared as if the trees themselves had fallen across the water. The river looked dark, deep and mysterious. There was not a single soul around. Every-thing was enveloped in silence. Women and young girls with *mekhala* tied round their bosom, who caught fish with bare hands in the eroded portions of the river banks, were also absent.

Suddenly the silence was broken by the sound of a lorry. Perhaps it was going towards Loharghat. The rain and floods had not yet made the road muddy and slushy. The vehicles could proceed without the help of an elephant. The roar of the engine became louder and clearer as it approached Indranath. Now he realised his mistake. It was not the sound of a lorry, it was a jeep that was coming towards him. His heart missed a beat. An unidentified fear gripped him. What if this jeep was bringing the authorised hunters with the notice of proclamation for shooting down Jagannath? He could feel the painful throbbing of his own heart. The roaring sound of the jeep engine became even more loud and deafening. He stood up on the rock on which, only a moment ago, he had been sitting surrounded by complete silence. Now this silence was shattered by this roaring, sputtering sound as if battle horses were galloping towards him, their hooves thundering on the ground. Indranath saw hovering before his eyes the dry impersonal wording of the proclamation notice:– "Proclamation for destruction of a rogue tusker in the areas of...Whereas one Tusker of the following description has become dangerous to human life in the...has already caused death of...and said Elephant is hereby proclaimed to be a 'Rogue' and permitted to be hunted down under the Section...of the Wild Life (Protection) Act...No royalty will be payable to Government for killing the above proclaimed Elephant...Only gun licence holders and retainees of Rifle of 400 bore and above... Description of the proclaimed 'Rogue' Elephant: Sex, Nail, Tail, Height...circumference of the foot..."

Indranath felt a wave of dizziness sweep over him. He knew that the destruction of the rogue elephant was inevitable. He was even prepared for it. But now when the moment had almost come, why had he lost his self-restraint?

The jeep halted at the junction of three roads. A fat man with big moustaches, wearing rather loose-fitting khaki shorts and thick-soled boots, came out of the vehicle. He took out a handkerchief from his pocket, wiped clean the dust from his face and limbs and only then noticed Indranath standing there. For some time, the fat man stood still, a little taken aback and stared at him. Then he enquired softly.

"Is it Saru Gossain? Why are you here in this lonely spot? Are you fishing in the river? I am Warden *babu*. We have met at the elephant depot several times."

Indranath stood there mute and motionless. The fat man continued,

"We are going to the manor. We heard at Maniari Kiniali that the Gossain had gone away to meet his disciples. So we thought that the proclamation notice should be handed over to you. You can sign on behalf of the Gossain. Moreover there are some more papers. In the Gossain's absence, you can deal with these papers also."

Striking a little pose, the man said again, "I have heard it said that...you had...er...a strange relationship with that elephant in your childhood. Is it true?"

Indranath remained silent.

"We hear strange tales. Even after it became frenzied, you met this elephant face to face. Is it really true?"

This time too, Indranath did not say anything. The fat man was a bit perplexed by this silent confrontation.

"All right, Saru Gossain, all right! We will now come to the real matter in hand. The rogue elephant's right foot, — the measurement of its circumference. Please take a look at this paper. Could the measurement be possibly correct? We are a bit confused regarding this figure."

Indranath maintained his silence. Warden *babu* now became self-conscious. He took out his handkerchief and started mopping his brow.

"I can see that you are very much worried and we understand your anxiety. The same thing happened to Bhikaru Gossain. His elephant, Eravat, had become a rogue. He too didn't want his beloved elephant to be shot down. Meanwhile that rogue killed three people. All the villagers were up in arms and forced him to sign the papers."

Indranath finally burst out, "Yes, yes, I have heard all about it!"

"Indeed! you must have heard all about it! On the bank of Jagalia. It is on everyone's lips. It is also known that soon after Eravat was destroyed, the Gossain became a mental wreck. He didn't speak to anybody for nearly six months!"

Indranath brushed his words aside impatiently and said, "All right, all right! That's enough! Show me where to sign."

"We are really very unhappy about this. When we heard that the mad elephant had entered the thick forest of Jirang, we felt relieved, thinking that it won't return. And we were struck with admiration when the news reached our ears that you had accompanied the dead body of Jamaluddin to his village, Bholagaon, in the dead of the night, without caring a bit for the rogue elephant. You have really become a legend on the bank of the Jagalia!"

Indranath became even more impatient and said abruptly, "Come on! Show me where to sign!"

The warden waddled as fast as he could to the jeep and took out a file. Standing on the rock, near the edge of the Jagalia, Indranath signed all the papers without glancing at them. He had no heart even to go through the documents.

The Warden said,

"At first we thought that the old *makhana* had become frenzied but later on we were informed that it was your favourite elephant, Jagannath. Saru Gossain, we understand your pain. You can keep the tusks after the elephant is destroyed, though generally it is the hunter who is supposed to have them. We have already arranged a hunter. He also managed to collect a 400 bore rifle. There he is! Sitting in the jeep. The same man who killed Bhikaru Gossain's rogue elephant, Eravat! Would you like to talk to him?"

This time too, Indranath kept silent.

"Bhikaru Gossain had given us some valuable suggestions about how to kill his elephant. I think you know that he has plenty of experience and knowledge about elephants. Things like where to shoot the animal so that it dies with minimum pain and so on. Well, Saru Gossain, if you have any suggestions...though, of course, we have our own rules and regulations. But I assure you! We will try our best to accommodate your wishes."

Indranath raised his head and looked at the warden. But not a word came out of his mouth. The latter, after a little hesitation, shrugged his shoulders and clamping the file under his arm-pit, jumped into the jeep. Before the jeep started moving, he addressed Indranath,

"The Assam Gazette, the Commissioner, the Secretary,...all of them have received a copy of the proclamation. We have heard that on your field where you used to tie your elephant, the elephants of other Gossains used to take rest while going to Jirang to pull timber logs. For this reason, there was always a hustle and bustle on your field. There's still some doubt about the measurement of the right foot. It is clearly mentioned in the proclamation that no other elephant under this description is killed. So I think you understand, it will be better if you are there at the tirne of shooting your elephant. Well, Saru Gossain, I hope you are listening carefully. We'll inform you as soon as everything is ready. The rogue elephant is moving mostly between Matiapahar and the fields. He has stopped going to the *sattra* for the last two or three days. But once he steps again on the field on his next visit, it will all be over within a short time. Saru Gossain, you are a wise man, everybody knows it on this bank. Tie a stone round your emotions, please!"

Indranath maintained his stubborn silence. As the jeep started moving, the hunter, a man with a sharp pointed face, shouted,

"Wait! wait! Saru Gossain, before we go, we had better talk about the ivory tusks. If you don't mind, I should get one of the tusks. If it had been a wild rogue elephant, I would have taken away both the tusks. This is allowed under the Government rules and regulations."

This time too, Indranath did not utter a word.

The Warden *babu* now said, "Please forgive us if we have done anything wrong! We have only carried out our duty. Please be ready. When the jeep comes back, you'll know..."

The Warden *babu* then engaged the gear, stepped on the accelerator and roared out to the road. The jeep disappeared from view.

Like a wounded man, Indranath sat motionless on the rock. Ah! Everything has to end! Nothing remains, only void. The knots of love and pain in our mind get undone within a split second, and then everything is over! Nothing remains!

In Indranath's mind, those familiar faces tied to his heart-strings, appeared one by one and faded away...Durga, Giribala, his mother the Gossainee, his father the *adhikar*, and those who loved and trusted him, the people of the *sattra,*...and this elephant, Jagannath, his childhood companion! All of them were like invisible limbs of his body. Ah! This pain! Indranath clutched the front of his shirt in a tight fist and pressed it over his heart...

He stood up on the rock and looked around. There was stillness everywhere. He saw the thatched roof top of Bhagawati's house. Eliman lived in that house. Perhaps one day she would be a part of his life. But what has gone wrong now? Nothing inspires him. Only a few days back, that house, that courtyard, was a source of life for him, her shadow was everywhere! He knew pure love was a great foun of inspiration, but at this moment, it had all dried up, everything seemed lost, beyond his reach. His mind had become like the parched and cracked earth, visited by famine.

Indranath took out his pipe. Suddenly he saw the canopy of a bullock-cart, fording the river Jagalia and coming towards the road. As it came nearer, he saw that it was loaded with earthen pots filled with curd, some jackfruits and sheaves of sugarcane. Some *bandhas* sat inside, holding on to the pots of curd. Their bodies were bare except for the dirty *dhotis* round their loins and *gamuchas* tied round their heads.

The cart came to a halt in front of Indranath, and Bhagawati the priest came running out towards him. He was quite fat, clad in a *dhoti* coming down up to his knees and a clean *chaddar* hanging casually from his shoulder. Wiping the dust from his bald pate with the *chaddar*, Bhagawati said breathlessly,

"I have come as fast as possible. Because of that rogue elephant! Indranath, the *sattra* is under the shadow of some evil omen. Perhaps some evil stars are in ascendance. I'll have to check up in the manuscripts. You may have to perform a few auspicious ceremonies. Your elephant was like the crown of the *sattra*. See what has happened to him!"

Indranath remained silent.

"That day, in the dead of the night, you went to Bholagaon with the dead body of that Muslim, Jamaluddin. Perhaps you didn't carry the corpse yourself, but still you must do four-fold atonement to make yourself clean again. I am waiting for the Gossain to come back from his tour. That night you did something very extraordinary! Some have even praised you for it, but two or three Gossains have said bad, abusive things about you. After all it was the corpse of a Muslim, Indranath!"

Indranath turned his face towards the river. The cart started moving but Bhagawati clapped his hands and made signs to the cartman to stop. The *bandhas* shouted from inside the cart—

"Please hurry up! Hurry up! The rogue elephant may appear!...Any moment!..."

The gusty wind blowing from the river dragged at the *chaddar* covering Bhagawati's fat body and sometimes laid bare his chest and shoulders. The gold rings tied to the sacred thread, sparkled in the sun's rays.

"Indranath, tonight is *Kojagar Kumudi Lakshmi Purnima*. On this auspicious day, if you worship Indra and his divine elephant, Airawat, Goddess Lakshmi will always reside in your house. But alas! Your own Airawat has gone mad, he will be shot dead! Alas, this very night perhaps! What a misfortune! What a calamity!"

The cartmen and the *bandhas* again made a commotion inside the cart,

"God save us! God save us! Hurry up! The mad

elephant is coming! Bring the Gossain also! Oh! Please don't be late!"

Bhagawati waved his hand and indicated that they should wait. He turned to Indranath but the latter did not show any sign of moving.

"Indranath, your state of mind has also become like that of Bhikharu Gossain. He resisted that shooting of his elephant too. He relented only when the people threatened to beat him up. Milroy and Bore, the two English forest officers, consoled him. You know, Bhikharu Gossain held them in high respect. They had released him from paying the grazing tax on his elephants. Indranath, your condition will be like that of Bhikharu Gossain. The people will turn against you. And those squatting on your land with red flags. They are shouting—Gossain, come and plough your own land! I curse them! May their race perish!"

Indranath broke his long silence and said,

"I have given my consent. Any moment the elephant will come down from Matiapahar, and he'll be shot dead . . ."

The priest cried out, "He is a mad elephant. He may also come this way! Come, come! Let's go home!"

Indranath shook his head and said,

"They'll come and take me in their jeep. Because they want me to be present at the time of shooting the elephant. Moreover they have some doubts about the circumference of the footprint of the right foreleg."

For a moment, Indranath stood, lost in thought. The description of the elephant in the proclamation notice floated through his mind:

Sex	Datal
Tail	Full

Nails	16 nos.
Height	9 ft. 6 in.
Circumference of the footprint of the right foreleg	4 ft. 9 in.

The priest observed him keenly and said,

"Oh, Indranath! Wear an auspicious stone around your neck! You must be very particular this year about worshipping the worship of the planets. Your family is well known for its charity to Brahmins. You must give me one of the tusks of the elephant when it is dead. Donation of land is also absolutely essential. I had to sell the land that was gifted to me at the time of your grandfather's memorial service."

Indranath knew very well that with the proceeds of this land, the priest had purchased an excellent plot near Bangara. He also remembered that the priest had haggled and bargained most vociferously while trying to sell or barter his various gifts among the rest of the Brahmins. The memory of the violent quarrel that had broken out, was etched in his mind. In the struggle that followed, the priest had been injured on his forehead. The mark of that injury still existed!

Indranath's face became grim. But Bhagawati, the priest, was not a man to be easily cowed down. He said coolly and convincingly,

"It's an universal truth that rituals and religious ceremonies keep off evil stars and malignant spirits. Don't you remember the Gossain of Ukium? He entered the forest of Jirang and disappeared. Some said he was killed by a wild boar or perhaps eaten up by a tiger. His body couldn't be traced. For this reason his last rites could not be performed. The Gossainee all but went mad. She then sent her rickety horse for me. I went through *Vyavahar Darpan*[2] and then gave her the following instructions: Make a straw effigy, resembling a man. Then stick forty leaves of the *palash* tree on the head, and ten leaves on the neck; twenty more leaves in the stomach of the effigy. In the arms, one hundred leaves; in the intestines, six leaves; in the thighs; one hundred thirty leaves; in the knees, ten leaves; and in the genitals, three leaves; one hundred leaves in the toes of the feet...then the sixty *palash* leaves with a thread round the body of the effigy and plaster it with rice power completely all over...After doing all these things, the last rites of the Gossain were finally performed. The Gossainee collected the ashes of the cremated effigy in an auspicious pitcher. She donated six *bighas* of land to me. From that day onwards, her dark days were over and she became normal again."

The priest looked at Indranath. He had not uttered a single word. The priest continued,

"Indranath, you must also satisfy the planets. I hope the elephant is shot dead today. Tomorrow, just before sunrise, there is an auspicious period of time when the world is still dark, and whether it is a lake, pond or a river, the water is pure and sacred. The *Janti sanyasis*[3] take bath during this auspicious time. During this time tomorrow, give me one of the tusks of the elephant. I am sure the cutting and carving of the carcass will be over during the night itself. Ah! To give donation to a Brahmin at that moment!"

Indranath cried out,

"*Bapu,* please leave me alone for some time!..."

The cartman shouted from the bullock cart in exasperation,

"Our bellies are grumbling! We had only stale rice in the morning before we left. Don't delay any more! The mad elephant may turn up any moment. Oh! *Bapu*! Come, come!"

Bhagawati shot a curious glance at Indranath. But soon this glance was transformed into an expression of deep disgust. Abruptly he turned round and hastened to the cart. The cartman flicked his whip, the cart lurched forward, and with a 'krr, krr' sound went towards the *sattra*.

The face of Durga again rose up before Indranath's eyes. When the question of taking her to the hospital at Gauhati had come up, she had cried out in protest, "No, no! No hospital for me! I want to go to my husband's place and die there. Take me to Chikarhati!" This elephant was very dear to Durga. She used to feed rice to him from a bamboo tray with her own hands affectionately. This scene, along many other images and memories, swam in Indranath's head.

Probably she had already reached Chikarhati. Out of fear of the rogue elephant, the cartman must have driven the cart very fast.

On many auspicious occasions, round this very rock where he sat, Giribala along with other Brahmin women had passed by, on their way to Jagalia for fetching water. This procession of Brahmin women was always protected from prying eyes by a cloth held up all around them, carried by five *bandhas*. Giribala was a tall woman, her head was always visible above the top of the cloth. In the crook of her arm, she used to carry the special pitcher covered with mango leaves and smeared with vermilion and turmeric powder. At that time her husband was alive and she would decorate her forehead with a big round vermilion mark. Ah! Who knows? Indranath may not see her again! His nostrils began quivering. He took out his handkerchief and wiped his brow.

Indranath began to feel restless. His eyes went again and again to the road. Any moment that jeep would come for him! That jeep with its jangling sound of iron chains! Why hasn't it come as yet? Is there still a glimmer of hope?

A little distance away, there were a few water-holes. These were stagnant and almost empty, as the villagers from the *sattra* had already caught and carried away whatever fish they could catch. Now the surface of the water was covered with a mesh of dry thorny sticks and withered grass stalks as if yellowing ribs of a cow's skeleton, dumped there by someone! Indranath looked up at the big *hizal* tree nearby. It stood stark and bare without any leaves. All around it was dry and dull as if the place had been visited by famine.

Suddenly Indranath thought of his mother. She must be in panic, wild with anxiety over him. He must hurry home. But his legs would not move. He was rooted to the spot like the leper squatting beneath the banyan tree near the cross-roads. Yes, this leper who was once a mahout's helper, had told him only the other day that the rogue elephant had come to the *banyan* tree and rubbed his head against its trunk. But it did not attack him! The leper had remarked,

"The same thing happened to you also, didn't it? The elephant just curled up its trunk and didn't do anything to you! After all you are the Gossain! Once long back I had gone with you on its back to Cooch Behar. At that time I was a helper. My body was not eaten by this wretched disease. Ah! Don't you remember? Once he had gripped your waist with its trunk and wouldn't let you go? Yes, even after becoming a rogue, in spite of his deranged head, he couldn't forget you!"

Dham! Dham! Dham! The drums of the Gopinath temple started beating rhythmically. The sound resonated through the stillness of the air. Indranath listened. He was the future *adhikar* of this *sattra*! But his condition now was like that of a deserter from the battlefield, being dragged away after a courtmartial! There! He could see the jeep coming towards him, its wheels swirling up a cloud of dust. He could see its dreadful snout, like that of some terrible dragon! It's coming...it's coming!...

Now he could see clearly the shining barrel of a gun sticking out from the jeep. His hand went to the pocket of his *panjabi*. As he jerked out his handkerchief, his tobacco pipe fell at a distance away on the ground. His clenched fist gripped the handkerchief into a tight ball. A vein on his forehead started throbbing. From the eyes of the future *adhikar*, streams of tears welled out...

Fourteen

The lower primary school building had been converted into a centre for the treatment of opium addicts. The place was humming with activity. The kitchen of the camp was manned by two lanky Brahmins from Rajabaha. Their bare backs were glistening with sweat. The sacred threads across their chests had taken on the colour of dried-up intestines. In backyards of the opium-eaters'-houses, the creepers of *pan* leaf plants had taken on a similar colour and shape.

Three women addicts had been brought forcibly to the camp. Two of them were now sitting on a bamboo mat. All the three wore *mekhalas* over their breasts. One also had a *gatala* wrapped round her shoulders. She was sleeping on a raised platform of bamboos. These bamboo platforms served as beds for the inmates of the centre. The managing committee had some men from the local board as its members and medicines were supplied from the sub-divisional store.

The woman who was sleeping was pregnant. She was tossing and turning, groaning with pain and craving for opium that had been stopped completely after she had been brought to this camp. She had started taking opium when she was a girl to relieve the pain that usually accompanies the onset of puberty. Gradually the habit had taken hold of her and she had become a compulsive opium-eater.

All the three women were extremely quarrelsome. Their *mekhalas* were made of the *markin* cloth supplied by the camp officials. Their *gatalas* had become dirty and tattered. Just outside the room where these women were kept, a group of people was sitting and talking among themselves. They were mostly from Choudhurypara, Kharapara, Rajabaha and Haramdo.

The chief priest of the Gossain, Purshottam Bhagawati was also there, his forehead marked with sandalwood paste. He was smoking a *hookah*. Every time he sucked at the pipe, the water inside the bowl made a bubbling sound. The secretary of four *maujas*[1], Bhagat Das, sat on a low wooden stool, watching four Home Guards sitting near an old rickety table. They were making a list of opium-eaters who were reluctant to come to the camp and those who had fled out of fear.

The Home Guards were arguing loudly and blaming each other about the opium-eaters. There was confusion among them as to who had fled away and who was reluctant to come. The new compounder was busy counting and labelling the fresh stock of medicines and making entries in the register. There was no end to his furious activity as there was a rumour that a political leader was soon intending to visit and inspect the camp.

But above the noisy hubbub of this group, the cries of the three women addicts could be heard clearly.

"You have come with a swollen belly like a big basket of rice. What'll you do if the baby pops out here?"

There was a sound like a kick on the wall.

"Why are you bothering others? Call the damned thing Campu!"

"Shut your trap! You whoring slut!"

The other woman retorted,

"You bitch! Whom are you calling a slut? Everybody knows about your husband! Bloody pimp! He ran away with a girl. There was a police case! Now he roams about like a castrated bull!"

"Pooh! Is it only my husband? I know very well who is carrying on with whom!"

Then some of the most vulgar, unprintable abusive words followed. One of the volunteers thumped his staff on the ground and shouted, "You vile women brought up on opium! Stop it! If the secretary hears you, he'll tear off your skin strip by strip!"

Just then two prohibition officers entered the camp. They had gone to some neighbouring villages to make a survey of opium eaters. Both of them were veteran Congress Party workers, middle-aged, lean and thin. They wore *khadi punjabis* and *Shantipuri dhotis* in the style of Calcutta *babus*. They parked their bicycles under the *jamun* tree near the school building, walked up to where Purshottam Bhagawati was puffing at his *hookah*, and stood before him. One Home Guard went inside and brought out two wooden chairs for the officers. Just then Bolo also joined them. He was supplying rice and other rations for the camp.

Tea was served in earthen cups. The steam rising from the hot tea gave off an odour like the fresh smell of rain-washed soil parched for a long time. For Bhagawati the priest, it was served by the Brahmin cook from Rajabaha, in a brass tumbler. The old Congress worker, the prohibition officer, said,

"On the latest count, we find that almost seventy per cent of the people on the South Bank are opium-eaters, and here, in this *sattra*, it is nearly one hundred per cent. We must be very strict. If necessary, even very cruel! Otherwise this *sattra* will sink so deep in this evil habit that it will be impossible to save it from destruction!"

Bolo remarked,

"Do you know how this calamity came to the *sattra*?"

The tall probihition officer took out his handkerchief and said, as he cleaned his spectacles,

"During the time of Mohammed Ghori, Bengal's ruler, Bakhtiar Khillji mounted an attack on Kamrup but he and his men were defeated and driven out like a pack of monkeys. Some of his men were taken prisoners by King Niladhwaj. As they hailed from Gaur, they were called *gorias*. Actually these Muslims and Rajputs spread the disease of opium-eating."

The other prohibition officer joined in,

"Ah! There were so many invasions afterwards! Ghiasuddin, Jazbeg, Turbak, Hussain Khan, Mirjumallah, Mansur Khan and others!"

Another officer, in a bid to show off his knowledge, said, "No, no! I am sure it was the Burmese who first brought opium to this bank of Jagalia! In 1821, December, three hundred Burmese soldiers attacked King Chandra Kanta's Cantonment. Everybody knows this. But they were driven back up to Khananmukh. Then after 1824, the white British General, George Macmarain, came with twenty elephants mounted with guns and gun powder, and routed these cursed Burmese soldiers. Who doesn't know this historical fact? At that time, some of these fleeing soldiers took cover in villages here and there. Who knows? Probably some of them came here also? Number Twenty-three, Native Infantry with five companies of British soldiers! Naturally the Burmese couldn't confront them".

"I have heard from scholars that the place, Khamranga, mentioned in *Baharishtan-e-Ghaibi,* is actually our Amranga. These scholars also say that when Mirzanathan invaded this place, our soldiers of Bardowa fought them with heavy swords weighing nearly sixteen seers each! The king and the queen of Khamranga were both drunkards."

They all exclaimed,

"What! The king and queen, both drunkards!"

"Yes, yes, drunkards! Sankar Guru and Madhav Guru came here for establishing a *sattra*, but when they saw a layer of liquor floating on the waters of Jagalia, they gave up the idea and went back."

A lean and thin schoolmaster, clad in an old dhoti and blue shirt, who was listening to this conversation silently, now added in a mild voice,

"There are so many things to tell about the South Bank of those days. Most of the people here were merchants. They were so rich that they drank water stored in gold pitchers. Their trade extended far and wide, up to the Pacific and the Indian Ocean and the Arabian Sea. It is said that they even traded in silk with China! But now all the roots are scattered. The descendants of those merchants are nowhere now. In the religious strife for Brahmanic supremacy, they were reduced to the status of low-caste members of society. Now only a shadow remains of those glorious traditions of commerce and trade. Now like vultures attracted to dead bodies, Marwari and Bihari businessmen have grabbed everything and become fat on the loot!"

There was silence for some time. Then Bhagawati, the priest, removed the pipe from his mouth and asked a Brahmin cook standing beside him in a low voice –

"Who's this teacher? What's his caste?"

The lanky Brahmin boy whispered in his ear,

"*Dom*[2] from Dakhala. He's a teacher there in the primary school."

At once Bhagwati shifted his chair away from the shadow of the 'low-caste teacher' sitting nearby. Meanwhile a flock of naked, rickety children with bloated bellies rushed into the camp and started shouting,

"Ho, ho! Look, look! Look at those *kaanias*![3] They are vomiting after eating dove flesh!"

Then they started singing,

> *Kaniyani bole bap bap*!
> *Gadakhawayat mallo jap*!
> *Kaniya rai Gadakhyat padi*,
> *Ghaniyakak lage kani tin tala kari*.
> (The opium-eater says, O father! O father!
> I have jumped into a deep pit!
> He remained in the pit,
> Now his wife cries and
> demands three *tola*[4] of opium.)

Then there was a hue and cry from the children as the Home Guards drove them out with their staves.

The prohibition officer wiped his face and said, "Sir, there is no word in our Sanskrit literature for opium. The word, *ahphen,* that we use, is of Arabic origin. Those *barakandas*[5] brought poppy seeds to Assam in 1795 during the time of King Lakhsmi Singha and cultivated it first in Beltala."

Removing the *hookah* from his mouth, the priest asked, "What was the process of opium making?"

"Juice from poppy seeds was collected in a cloth and boiled in water. The thick residue is what we call *kaani* in our country."

Another prohibition officer with hollow cheeks now chipped in, "In the ancient medical treatises of Charak, Bhagabhatta and Susruta, there is no mention of opium. However we do find a reference to opium in the treatises of Shangadhar and Bhavamishra of fifteenth and sixteenth century respectively."

Bhagawati put down the pipe and said,

"Which disease did they use this opium for?"

"For loose motions and also indigestion."

The prohibition officer continued.

"The British government tried to make a law in 1928 for the prohibition of opium. They had planned to abolish the opium permit system gradually in ten years' time, by cutting down a certain percentage of quota every year for persons below fifty years' of age. But those damned opium-eaters, blinded by opium smoke, were so afraid after hearing this that they stopped registering their names. Then came black marketing! The government sealed all the opium markets in Dibrugarh and Sibsagar districts.

Why, only recently during the war, the tribals from the hills smuggled opium right up to Jirang. They used to come at night, along roads cut through the jungles by the Allied Army. In earlier times, there were fights all over Assam between the opium-eaters and the white sahibs. That Singer Sahib of Nagaon tried to implement this prohibition and he was beaten up so badly by the crowd that he collapsed and died! This happened in 1860."

Bhagawati exclaimed,

"Goodness! Did they really kill a white sahib? Only the other day, in *bhagat seva*[6], one *bhagat* flatly refused to give his blessings till he was given an offering of opium. Lord forbid! We are passing through an era of absolute degeneration!"

Suddenly a brown smoke billowed around them and floated through the camp. Bhagawati, the prohibition officers, Home Guards, the inmates — all of them began coughing and sneezing. The two old schoolmasters, clutching their umbrellas tightly against their chests, were unable to control their coughing and became exhausted and breathless. Bhagawati shouted, "Who's making all this smoke? What's he burning?"

One prohibition officer cried out,

"It's Mark Sahib, I think. I saw him come through the rear door. He must have made a bonfire out of the opium addict's paraphernalia. He has been threatening to do so for a long time!"

"Why don't you go and see what those things are?"

The prohibition officer with protruding teeth, replied— "About a hundred cracked and blackened clay bowls for frying *pan* leaves, same number of *bhem*, a large quantity of bamboo strips, many clay pipes, heaps of old, tattered clothes — Mark Sahib had vowed to pour kerosene over these things and set them on fire".

Just then Mark appeared in their midst. There was complete silence as they became conscious of his presence. Everybody stared at his eyes, brown like old *muga* silk, as if the sun was setting over the muddy waters of Jagalia. These eyes looked tired today. A Home Guard brought a wooden chair for him. As the chair was placed too near the priest, the latter shifted immediately a little away to avoid contact with this Christian. He addressed Mark Sahib,

"So you have done something worthwhile to prevent opium-eating. Everybody is praising you for it. But what about your work on Gilman Sahib who breathed his last in this spot? Have you collected enough material?"

"I did collect something and it's still going on."

"Gilman had helped some students in Gauhati. Could you get their names?"

Mark nodded his head in affirmation. The prohibition officer with protruding teeth looked at him curiously and said, "I know something about Gilman's quarrel with Nanda Ram Doloi. The Sahib used to visit the weekly market of Bardowa Tea Garden frequently. He used to roam about like a wild buffalo. Doloi was the contractor for this market. One day he shifted it to Loharghat. Sahib was very fond of going to the weekly market at Bardowa. He called Doloi immediately and had him slapped hard on his cheeks by one of his relatives. All the people of Bardowa and Loharghat set out for his bungalow to protest. But Sahib got wind of it and the same day he fled away on his elephant, taking the relative with him. The latter never returned. Gilman Sahib was protected by Bentink and the Conservator of Forests, Milroy."

Mark was restless. He did not pay attention. He looked sad, tired and crestfallen, as if entangled in a black net of fine silken thread of frustration.

Removing the *hookah* from his mouth, Bhagawati said, "I can understand the agony of your mind, Mark Sahib. You look so pale and restless."

The prohibition officers, the Home Guards, the cooks, even Bolo from Barihat, looked at the white Sahib and uttered sympathetic sounds. One of them remarked,

"Sahib looks so thin and pulled down, like a bamboo pole!"

Another said, "Why not! He makes trips to Datguchi, Kulchi, Kendukuchi, Hatpokholi and, crossing the Jagalia, he goes to Gargara, Haropara, Chanapara, Jhalimabari and other places. His shoes are worn out and his clothes are soiled and torn. Always in search of old, crumbling and moth-eaten manuscripts!"

Bhagawati's fingers played with the gold ring in his sacred thread, draped over his ample stomach, as he said. "Oh you elephant-headed idiots! It's not Chanapara or Jhalimabari. I know what's ailing his mind, it's something different!"

Many exclaimed, "What, *bapu*, what is it? What's wrong with him?"

The priest puffed briskly on his hookah two or three times. Then he looked at Mark through half-closed eyes and saw that his attention was elsewhere. With downcast eyes he was staring at the ground, as if his mind was concentrated on digging up the soil under his feet. He was lost in his own world.

Some of the people circled round the two men. They were rather fond of Mark Sahib and felt instinctively that the priest was on the point of saying something derogatory about him. They had the same respect for Mark and Gilman Sahib as they had for Brown, Bronson and Cutter, who had fought for the Assamese language when it was threatened by the partisan policy of the British Government. Moreover they knew very well that Mark Sahib had given away all his belongings to poor people, except for what he was wearing on his emaciated body. He had even taken off his *endi* shawl and given it to the wretched leper, residing beneath the banyan tree.

The cunning look in the priest's eyes could be clearly seen by all those present there. He said, "A couple of men have come from Bangara to take away the *maichana* of the Gossain, Giribala ..."

Bolo from Barihat remarked, "It is good that she will go back to her in-laws. Otherwise her fate would have been the same as Durga's, who was cast off unceremoniously from the Gossain's manor."

Everybody now looked at Mark. Most of the villagers knew that there was a tender relationship between him and the Gossain's *maichana*. Mark stood up. He looked at the faces around him in silence and then with bowed head, walked away with slow, measured steps. There was a gloomy silence all around. The people were not happy with Purshottam Bhagawati's barbed reference to Giribala. They knew that he had done this to hurt Mark Sahib.

The priest picked up the *hookah* and puffed at it for a long time. Then his hand went to the red flower in the sacred tuft of hair on the back of his head, to check whether it was still in place. A large, fat patch of his stomach became visible when he lifted his hand. He said, "Long back, when I saw her horoscope, I knew what was destined for her. The planets were not favourable for her marriage to the Gossain of Bangara. Alas! Who can hold back fate! Her puberty was drawing near and the sin of puberty had to be averted by marrying her off quickly...On the other side of the Jagalia, three or four girls from the Gossain families were married off secretly after the onset of puberty...but what of it? They are sunk deep in the dark pool of sin. But here, our Gossainees were brought to the *sattra* in palanquins by the time they were eight-years-old. The Gossain was extremely agitated and worried about this sin of puberty. The Gossainee almost lost her wits. I knew about the horoscope of the Gossain of Bangara. It was horrible! The marriage was fixed within one night. On the day of putting on jewellery, vermilion and oil on Giribala to confirm the marriage, it rained very heavily. In the storm, a tin roof of the *batghar* was blown off! That lecherous rascal! Everybody knew about his goings-on! With that slut of Maniari crossing who sold opium! The Gossain also knew, but alas, what could be done! He was in a hurry to get rid of her. Or else the sin of puberty would have disgraced the family."

The buck-toothed prohibition officer now interrupted the priest, "But about that *firingi* Christain and his frequent meetings with Giribala? What does the Gossain think about that?"

"Nowadays the Gossain is lost in his own spiritual world with the disciples. What does he know about what's going on? All this happened because of Indranath. He says, what will this girl do all her life? Let her remain immersed in books and scriptures! When Giribala was a child, Jhalimabari's Hansdev Pundit had taught her. She had learnt by heart Vishnu Bharati's *Dhruva Charit*[7]. But what's the use of such intelligence in a girl? It will bring nothing but blemish on the family's name. Women's education is of no use."

The prohibition officer interrupted, "What are you saying! How can she tarnish the family name?..."

The priest cut him short by speaking loudly, "Yes, yes! My sixth sense tells me so! You'll see! She will bring a bad name to the family."

All those present were struck dumb by his roar. They did not dare argue with him!

A *bandha* with curly hair, bare torso and only a *gamucha* tied round his waist now spoke up,

"Those two men from Bangara are now loitering in the *sattra*. They have brought a covered cart. When the Gossain of Bangara heard that daughter-in-law was preparing to run away with a Christian, he was mad with rage. He told them not to come back without her and if she didn't come readily, to drag her by her hair right up to Bangara!"

The old prohibition officer, fed up with this kind of talk, said impatiently, "Shut up, you rascal! Enough's enough! Keep quiet!" A Home Guard said, "Why do you all speak ill of the Gossain, you sinners? Don't you remember that incident of old Guimeni? She used to carry on trade of old coins in the market. You know what happened to her! She started spreading nasty rumours about the old Gossain, that he had presented a pair of gold earrings to a low-caste woman of Datkuchi . . . Everybody knows how she was thrashed by that ghost from the *bokul* tree! . . ."

The curly-haired *bandha* said again, "No, no! It wasn't the ghost! The old Gossain himself hid in the *bokul* tree and gave a thrashing to that evil-tongued Guimeni that she won't ever forget!"

A Home Guard shouted.

"Hold your tongue! If Indranath hears you, he'll tear off your hide!"

Bhagawati said, "The Gossain will have to go through wretched days. That Marabhitha land. The Communists are sitting on it. The Gossain wants to send his men to till this land. The tenant subjects there say, let the Gossain dare to come and plough this land! We'll see! We'll see!"

The prohibition officer with the crooked teeth said,

"But that land was water-logged, wasn't it?"

"Yes, yes! It was! But the Gossain continued to pay tax on it. Then one day it came out of the water and it wasn't merely a land—it turned out to be a mine of gold! People started cultivating the land without paying the Gossain the half paddy rent. When the *mohura* went to collect the rent, they rebuffed him, shouting — If the

Gossain comes here himself with the plough on his shoulder and tills the land, only then will we pay the half paddy rent. The *Adhikar* is in a fit of rage. Indranath is very upset and angry. He says that they'll fight this case out till the finish, they'll even go to the court at Gauhati!"

All those present said in one vocie,

"Yes, yes, the Gossain must go to Gauhati. It's a question of prestige. It's hard to believe how badly the tenants have started behaving. In the North Bank, it's said that one or two Gossains, unable to control the tenants, have even set up betelnut and *pan* shops!"

The priest lamented in a loud voice, "Alas! Alas! We have fallen on evil days! The Gossains with so many disciples setting up betelnut shops! May those people burn in seven hells! Only till the other day they used to bring *kachcha patta*[8] and dump them at the Gossain's feet!"

Again the loud screams of the three women addicts rose and fell. There appeared to be a terrible scuffle, as if they were breaking the bamboo platforms and hitting each other. The most vile, abusive language rent the air and offended the ears. Some of the people outside placed their hands over their ears, but nobody left the place. The hollow-cheeked prohibition office looked at around and said,

"It's rumoured that Indranath has become an ascetic. He is seen roaming about with bowed head."

The *bandha* with curly hair, cried out, — "Eli, that Rajpukhuri priest's daughter. She sent her old woman to him one day. That woman stood on the road waiting for him to return from Bolo's place, till late at night. She told him something but it seems he ignored her."

The priest said, "That opium addict Brahmin who wanted to marry her. Probably it's time for him to be released from the prison."

The *bandha* interjected, "Saru Gossain isn't thinking about betrothal gifts! On the other hand, that Brahmin will come out any day now...it's a peculiar situation!..."

The priest roared, "What rot! It's not so easy for Indranath! Have you ever heard of a Gossain sending betrothal gifts to an ordinary Brahmin girl? In this *sattra*, no Gossain has ever married an ordinary Brahmin girl."

The priest stopped speaking abruptly when he saw the district doctor, his compounder, along with several old Congress workers, coming towards them. The doctor was walking ahead of the other men. All those present, who were sitting on either chairs or mats, stood up. Bhagawati, the priest, put aside the *hookah* pipe and re-arranged the *chaddar* over his shoulders. The *bandhas* who were sitting there neglecting their duties, got up in a flash and fled away from the place.

✯ ✯ ✯ ✯

From the opium de-addiction camp, Mark went straight to his hut in the elephant corral. Previously this hut was used by *Kaamlas*, *phandis* and *mahouts*. Mark had filled every inch of the old dwelling with his manuscripts. It was usually kept in order by former opium addicts who owed their rehabilitation to Mark Sahib and followed him like a shadow everywhere. On one of the walls of the hut hung a wooden cross from a nail. One chair and a table, of *urium* wood, sent by Indranath, occupied the hut. Even the table top was cluttered with several manuscripts. In a corner, in a neat pile, were some crockery and a saucepan similar to those used by the soldiers in the base camp. Casting a shadow over the window, was a *gulmohor* tree. Its branches bore clusters of red flowers. Near the window, on a wooden stool was placed a newly discovered *sanchi* bark manuscript tied loosely with a garland of *gutimali* flowers. This had been discovered by Giribala in the house of a Brahmin in a remote corner of Rajabaha. There was a stench of elephant dung all around but even then, the sweet fragrance of *gutimali* flowers distinctly pervaded.

Mark's shirt was soaked with perspiration. The bottoms of his trousers were torn and frayed like the ears of an old elephant. He was perturbed and restless. Usually he opened the *sanchi* bark manuscript as soon as he returned home. But this time he did not do so.

What kind of frustration was this? Especially for a man who had discarded worldly life? Mark looked intently at the wooden cross on the wall for sometime. Then his eyes shifted to the words below — "The King of Confessions" written in Roman letters. Yes, this King of Confessions knows everything, hears everything! Like the setting sun, submerging in the muddy water of the Jagalia, Mark's eyes were pale and subdued. Whenever he encountered a damned soul in agony and torture, his heart would be wrenched by anguish and pain. Can the King of Confessions penetrate his heart and touch it? Will he not do anything?...

He went to the bed and lay on his back.

Next day, from early morning, the sky was plastered with clouds. Then rain drops started falling. The rain increased. The sound of falling water was like the hoof beats of horsemen thundering through the desert. The wind became more violent as if it would blow off the roof of the hut. Mark began murmuring a hymn that he had been taught in his childhood... The rain splattered down with greater intensity. Normally Mark would be greatly worried when it rained heavily, lest it damaged his manuscripts, notes and other valuable papers. He would rush about the room and cover them up with whatever clothes he had. But this time, he lay listless on the bed.

It was a terrible downpour. From the roaring sound of the falling water, it appeared as if it would carry away everything in its torrential current.

Suddenly he heard somebody knocking on the door, but he did not pay much heed to it, as he knew that generally the outcast leper took shelter in his hut whenever it rained. Sometimes he crouched under his bed. Mark, by now, knew many things about this poor fellow. The ghost, who figured in many anecdotes going round the *sattra* and who robbed way-farers in the dead of the night, was none but this leper himself. But Mark had kept this fact to himself as he did not wish to create any more trouble for this unfortunate outcast.

Suddenly the window crashed open bringing in a gust of wind that blew off some papers lying with the *sanchi* bark manuscript. These were all old letters, collected by Mark, written by the British Forest Officers to Bhuvaneshwar Goswami, the *adhikar* of Shrihati *sattra*. Among them, surprisingly, there was a letter in Assamese written by somebody called Milroy to this Gossain. The land of Shrihati was donated by a *Muslim Badshah*.

Mark got up, closed the window and tied the shutters together with a jute rope. Those old letters had also been brought by Giribala. If it had been any other day, he would have sat by the lantern and jotted down notes from the letters. In the light cast by the lantern, his face resembled that of Brahmin lads staying near the bank of Jagalia. Today he did not go near the lantern.

Ah, it appeared as if the roof would blow off! The odour of wet earth mingled with that of elephant dung penetrated the room...

Harr, harr, harr!
Harr, harr, harr!

As if somebody was throwing pebbles into an empty earthenware pitcher!

Should he go away from this place, today, tonight itself? Let all this remain here, the notes on Gilman, the letters of Milroy, Humphrey and Bore Sahibs to the *adhikars* of South Bank and the *mahaldars*[9]. Oh, those ancient papers that have taken on the colour of ant-hills. In the lantern light, those papers looked like the wings of honeybees. There lies, near the lamp, an appeal to Francis Jenkins from the Gossain of Shrihati. The writing on the paper shone in the glow of the lantern.

Karrak, boom, karrak! Thaarr!

There was a blinding flash of lightning. Mark realised immediately that this terrible lightning had fallen on the ancient jackfruit tree. Again that sound of pebbles being thrown into an empty clay vessel. Big drops of rainwater were now crashing down from the sky. He squatted, hunched, on the bed, his knees drawn tight against his chest. He was disinclined to do anything. Why this numb coldness of the mind? He looked at the wooden cross again. His eyes, pale like the colour of the muddy Jagalia water in the setting sun. Was it all due to that daughter of the Gossain, the fair Giribala?

He has roamed far and wide. North Bank and South Bank of Brahmaputra. Through villages and towns. He has come across so many faces — young, old, not-so-old. Then why has he become rooted here, in this place, after setting his eyes on that lovely face?

Strange! Strange! Strange indeed!!

Mark remembered his grandfather, the idol he always

wished to emulate. He used to help William Carey in household work. He loved to hold religious dialogue with the Indian visitors coming to Fort Williams College. His grandfather was the very embodiment of kindness and compassion towards the poor and the down-trodden. He was loved and respected by all. And till the end, he had remained the same saintly soul...But he, himself — why had he stumbled in the middle of the way like this? Was it a kind of fatal perversion? All the hard work, his research, his pursuit of the knowledge of life, was it all futile now?...What a disgrace!

But a voice echoed inside his being, — if this is perversion, then all the work he had done with his lifeblood — that is all futile!

He will go away! Forever! From this place. He will walk, unnoticed, up to Maniari crossing and take a bus to Palasbari. Wherever he may decide to stay, he will keep in touch with Indranath by letters. He is the future *adhikar.* If he wants to, he has the power to make drastic changes. God has placed in his hand the heavenly light. With it, he can banish the darkness. But . . .

He could see through the gap between the window shutters, flashes of lightning outside as if shining swords were clashing on a battlefield. Again someone was knocking on the door! Mark strained his ears. Yes, it was indeed a distinct knocking on the door. He got up to open the door, but before he could do so, it crashed open and a human figure, completely drenched, water raining from its clothes all over the floor, entered the room. At the sight, Mark's body turned ice cold and his soul cried out in a thousand tongues.

In this dark night of roaring rain and thunder and lightning, *Adhikar Mahaprabhu's* daughter stood before him! The sweet fragrance of her body pervaded the room. His mind became numb and he could not utter a single word...

The girl went to the wooden stool, removed the *sanchi* bark manuscript and other papers, and sat down.

She was soaked through and through. The wet, soggy *markin* chemise was stuck to the contours of her bosom. Her *mekhala* was drawn up to the knees. Her exposed legs, fair and slender, looked like a pair of deer's legs. With her bare legs, she looked like a very young girl. In the dim light of the lantern, her drenched body gave off a mystical glow.

Mark remained rooted where he was, wonder struck. Not a word came out of his throat. Giribala cried out, "Why don't you close the door, Sahib? Water is coming inside."

"Giribala, you are breaking the traditional code of Gossain families. Go back! Right now! Go back!"

Giribala got up and without heeding Mark's words, closed and bolted the door. Then she returned to the stool and sat down. She started squeezing out water from her *gatala*. She then held the edge of the *mekhala* with her teeth, to cover her breasts, and tried to open the wet, soggy chemise that had stuck to her torso like a second skin . . .

What is she doing? This Gossain's daughter! Mark turned his eyes away. Then suddenly he said, "Come! That's enough! I'll go with you and take you back to your house. Listen, Giribala! I know very well the condition of your mind. I understand everything and it's absolutely crystal clear to me . . ."

But no, she is not at all perturbed. She has by now removed her chemise, squeezed out the water and kept it aside on the floor. Now she has opened her hair and with rapid of strokes of her hand, she is trying to remove water from the soaking tresses. No, she is not at all agitated or concerned about anything! As if she has come here with a deliberate and pre-planned purpose, with a firm intention of not going back! She is quite calm and composed.

Mark knelt down beside her and reiterated his request. She looked into his eyes and said, "My father-in-law has sent two men. But I am not going!"

"Giribala!"

"I will not go back to that graveyard! I don't want to be buried alive. I'd rather die!"

Scores of images of Gossain widows passed before Mark's eyes. Widows who have stretched out their existence within four walls, who have never seen the road outside. Widows racked by deprivation and unknown diseases, brought on by harsh and cruel rituals. Widows who had died without fulfilling their craving to learn the rudiments of reading and writing, without drinking in the nectar of written words, out of fear of social censure. Oh! There are hundred, thousands of such women on the banks of rivers like Jagalia!...

And there before him, among all those images is Giribala, like the reflection of a lotus flower in the water of a lake, locked on all sides by high mountains.

What does she want to say now? Oh, Lord of Confessions?

She spoke again.

"After I came of age, all those Gossainees on the river bank used to tell me: you are an angel, you are a sweet angel! But do you know? That husband of mine, who often visited that notorious woman, the opium thief, he used to say, 'What's so great about your beautiful body? That lady of Kiniari! Even though she is a low-caste opium seller, her body glows with exciting sexuality... You are nothing in comparison ... They say, she always goes about sniffing at men, like a bitch in heat, but where's that lustful current of blood flowing in the veins of Gossainee girls like you?'

Giribala could not continue. Her eyes filled with tears. She crouched with her head on the knees and started crying bitterly, loud sobs racking her body. Her hair lay scattered on her back. Her soft arms and shoulders were bare and vulnerable. An inner voice whispered: Mark, why don't you lift her in your arms and console her! Lift her up in a tight embrace. You have seen her reflection in the water of Jagalia, in the muddy slopes of Matia Pahar. You have seen her reflection everywhere! Why don't you ask yourself? Was it not in your mind? You saw her in the wind and in the rain, didn't you? Why don't you look into your heart?...

Giribala looked up with red, tear-washed eyes. She said. "I couldn't bind him to me with either my body or my mind. But the flesh of that woman! Was it so powerful that before it, virtue and decency, all things worthwhile in life, became futile, like mere dust on the roadside? All the treasures of mind become as meaningless as dust only because of that flesh!... Can one believe it? Oh, my love, touch me and realise just for once....just once!..."

Mark took a step back. Mark's God, ruling over his heart, always so restrained, thirsty for knowledge, cried out with a thousand tongues. The half-naked figure of the girl glowed in the lantern light like mystical lamp burning in a dark cave. For the first time, his eyes had witnessed such a sight! He was stunned!

How deep must be this well of unhappiness, which forces a woman to self-destruction, when barriers of modesty collapsed. What a terrible test this is!.... How can he, a person who has never come close to a woman, know abut the mystery of a woman's mind? Though he stood rooted at the threshold of the door, his mind, his very soul was forcing his feet towards the girl. And there! He is lifting her up tenderly. But how can she read his mind? Just one touch and both will burn to ashes!...

This Christian youth had come here after crossing seven oceans and thirteen rivers. But never had he to cross this fire of ordeal!

For the first time, Mark broke down. He could not stop the tears pouring out of his eyes. In the dim light of the lantern, Giribala's fig-coloured flesh appeared to break into pieces just as the image of the moon broke into many pieces in the flowing water of Jagalia. No, Mark could not go towards her, nor could he lift her up in his arms. The lantern light grew dimmer. In this dark stormy night, his arms, as if paralysed, refused to lift up this unfortunate daughter of *adhikar mahaprabhu*. The wooden cross on the wall became a black shadow in the dim light.

Mark stood there, as if metamorphosed into an iron contraption which could move neither forward nor backward....

✯ ✯ ✯ ✯

The door burst open as if somebody had struck it with a mighty kick. Three or four well-built, muscular men rushed into the room. Behind them loomed the figure of Purshottam Bhagawati like Yama, God of Death. Sparks flew from the eyes of the priest. In the semi-darkness, they glowed like the eyes of a wild beast of prey as if it would leap on the white Christian, the destroyer of the religious sanctity of a Gossain's daugter. As if he would tear apart his bosom!

Lord forbid! Lord forbid!...

Such a dark deed was never perpetrated in the Gossain's house before. The priest roared,.

"Pull out that girl from his den! Pull her out! This *mlecha*[10] has taken advantage of her innocence!... Bind him! Bind him tight with a rope! Don't let him escape! Be quick! Go and bind him! Drag her out! Look at her *gatala*, her *mekhala*. She's ruined! Utterly ruined!..."

✯ ✯ ✯ ✯

The heat of the noon soared. A big crowd of men, women and children had gathered on the elephant's field. Under the old jackfruit tree crouched Giribala. She wore the wet chemise that she had removed earlier and kept on the wooden stool. Her *gatala* was also decently draped over the shoulders. Drops of water fell down on her body from the leaves above. Only some moments back, the darkest scandal in her life had been revealed and exposed to a shocked public. But it had left no trace on her. She sat under the tree, detached and motionles.

There! People stood, their feet stained red with the rain-soaked mud. Some held a big thatched roof made of bamboo and straw. They had come to make a hut for *masa daha*[11]. But they had abandoned the task, drawn by the scandalous drama enacted before their eyes. All the time, the girl beneath the old jackfruit tree stared vacantly at them with wide open eyes..... The *masa daha* festival is never held on the bank of Jagalia in the autumn month of November. But the boys of the new generation have changed the custom with the following words:

"By the king's command, if the spring festival is held in summer, then by the people's voice, if they so desire, the May festival can be celebrated in the month of November!...."

It is said that in the Rajapukhuri *sattra*, which is connected through marital ties with this *sattra* on the bank of Jagalia, the popular spring festival is observed in a grand manner in the month of April. This is because once King Siva Singha had come to see the sattra *adhikar* of Rajapukhuri and had expressed a desire to see the great spring festival, even though it was the month of April. In those days, a thatched hut was made with bamboos and dry plantain leaves. A live sheep was kept inside and after chanting sacred hymns from the scriptures, the hut was set on fire. But with the passage of time, the sheep was replaced by goat and a small opening was kept in the wall of the hut, as an escape route. The goat sometimes fled through the opening but more often it got burnt inside.

Purshottam Bhagawati could now be heard thundering.

"The Gossain hasn't returned from Upper Assam as yet, Indranath has gone to that ghost-ridden land, Marabhitha.."

A voice came from the crowd,

"That *mlecha* sahib has made her impure. The Gossainee won't let her enter the manor!"

Another man shouted,

"Who knew that this white ascetic could turn out to be a woman-chaser?"

"Ah-h-h! It's a case of *phulchuri*[12]."

The priest cried out, "Don't just stand there! Bring bamboos and logs! Come on, quick! Fix the thatch roof!... You have come for *masa daha*, We will now do two things in one stroke!.... Giribala will be purified before we burn the sacrificial goat ... Heavens! What's going on these days! Once upon a time, a Gossain's beloved daughter didn't look even at the moon and the stars in the sky!"

Nodody dared to say anything, and there underneath

the old tree, sat Giribala, motionless and unperturbed. The circumstances were growing more grave every moment. A serious outrage had taken place, but the onlookers were astonished to find the girl so calm and detached! Strange! Strange! A deep silence spread over those gathered there—young boys, Brahmins from Haramdo and Rajabaha, and all the disciples from the *sattra*.

Suddenly a ripe jackfruit fell down with a thud from the tree and splashed on the ground, the yellow seed pouches scattered all around. Normally there would have been a scramble for the juicy soft buds and within a few seconds nothng would have remained except the pieces of thorny skin like the intestines left over from a slaughtered goat! But now there was no movement from the shocked spectators. Even the little children ignored it!

Again the priest roared,

"You, there! You, bumble-bees and black louts! On your toes, hurry up! We must get over soon with the purification ceremony before this girl goes to the manor! After all she is the Gossain's daughter!"

Everybody remained silent as if united by a bond of mute sympathy for the girl, sitting under the tree.

Meanwhile the work on the thatched hut was progressing with speed. Whatever material was left behind by the *kaamlas* and *mahouts*, such as dry straw, firewood, thorns and sticks, were now dumped on the top of thatched roof. These were all very dry and highly inflammable. *Tulsi* and *dubori* leaves, flowers and copper coins were brought for the expiation ceremony. The priest then bade Giribala to enter the hut, and without a word, quietly, she went inside, as if she had been waiting for the permission.

The priest started reciting in a distinct and loud voice, those incantations which that marked in the scriptures for the nineteen *dhanu prayaschita,* for the sin of a Brahmin woman having illicit relations with a low-caste man.

During the recitation, at some places the priest's voice became shaky and indistinct due to his congested throat, but he carried on till the end and completed the ritual. Then waving his hand, he indicated to Giribala that she should come out of the hut. At the same time, he turned to a youth nearby, and said, "Go and set fire to this hut that is now impure! We'll build another one for *masa daha*."

Again turning to Giribala, he cried out,

"Come! Come out of that hut! It's now most impure! Hurry up!"

Time stood still. People waited. The priest again spoke to Giribala, "You are purified now and you can go back to your house. The rest we'll do after Gossain comes back. Look! Those men from Bangara are watching you! They have heard about you and that Christian..."

In a firm voice, Giribala uttered,

"Start the fire! I'll come out..."

The alert young man standing nearby swiftly put a match to the dry, instantly inflammable straw, sticks, *urium* wood dumped on the roof of the hut... Deep lines appeared on Purshottam Bhagawati's forehead. This daughter of the Gossain was behaving in the most bizarre manner. He could not even believe his eyes! He had never performed purification rituals for any other daughter of a Gossain. He had of course resolved other delicate issues, by going through the scriptures. Once the Gossainee of Choudhuripara had her menstrual flow while laying the ritual offering for her dead husband. The priest consulted the manual and saved the widow from her predicament. Another seriously sick Gossainee widow of Pathaldia could not perform the *shraddha* of her departed husband. He had found a solution for this also from the scriptures. But this queer misdeed of Giribala! Strange! Strange! Now she says she will come out only after the fire is lit! .... There! There! The flames are leaping, high in the air! But what's she doing? Why she isn't coming out? Oh! My God! What's she doing?

The priest shouted frantically,

"She's still there! She's still there! Inside! Quick! Do something! The roof is burning! Save her!"

The tremendous hue and cry of the people rent the sky... With a huge crash and crackling sound, the roof caved in and engulfed the motionless girl, Giribala. She disappeared into the raging flames!...

* * * *

Nothing remained to be done.... In the air and in the sky, there was only the stench of burning flesh. Only the stench of burning flesh... Human flesh!...

Fifteen

After taking his afternon meal, Indranath was getting ready to go to Bolo's den. This time he was going there at the bidding of his mother, the Gossainee. A group of disciples from Gangara and Sualkuchi was coming to the *sattra*, and pigeons and papayas had to be procured immediately for their meals. She knew that Bolo was the best person to select the right kind of pigeons and papayas.

Indranath's hair was not properly oiled or combed. His *dhoti* was crumpled and not very clean. His long, lanky face was lined with grooves of anxiety and anguish. After the shock of the recent tragic event, black shadows had appeared under his eyes. He had almost stopped going to Bolo's gambling den. After Giribala's death, even the Gosainee was not to be seen often. She now remained shut in the small room where she smoked tobacco, hour after hour. She did not weep much over the death of her daughter. But now this! Only tobacco, tobacco and tobacco!... Those around her were distressed by this addiction. Sometimes even her close associate, Guimeni, went away from her in disgust. She was left alone in that room like a ghostly shadow, holding the pipe of the *hookah* in her hand...

At the elephant's yard, Indranath did not take the road to Barihat, but went straight to the thatched huts of *Kaamlas* and *mahouts*, where Mark had stayed. He could still see, a little distance away, the half-burnt bamboos and the heap of black ashes. One or two crows were hopping over the debris.

Indranath took out a key from his pocket and opened the door of Mark's hut. Inside, it was as dark as a cave. He opened the window and a beam of light splashed in. All of Mark's possessions became visible. Inkpots and pens made from bird's feathers, scattered manuscripts that had taken on the colour of moth's wings. His eyes fell on the narrow mud wall where Mark had stuck slips of papers with different sayings from the Lord's prayers written on them. He had written the lines with great care. Each letter was clear and sharp. He used a quill pen only to improve his handwriting in the Assamese script and the result of his perseverance and hard work was visible on those slips of papers.

A kind of acute pain shot through Indranath's heart. He took out his pipe, filled the bowl with *bidis* and put a match to them. Then puffing at the pipe, he read the slips of papers on the wall, one by one.

As he read the lines, he remembered the poor students of *Sanskrit tols*[1]! They used to come out in the month of February and go begging from house to house. The *bhagats* and other people sometimes made them sit and write for them in their beautiful hand the sayings from *Namghosa*[2] and other religious scriptures. They decorated the slips of paper with drawings in the folk-art style.

Indranath saw the resemblance in the slips of paper pasted on the wall. They were the sayings of Christ, the son of God.

"Build the royal road for the Lord and make all his roads simple and straight-forward!"

"Enter through a narrow door because a wide door leads to destruction!"

"The road which leads to life is narrow and straight. Only a few can find and understand this path!"

All the letters of the Gossain of Shrihathi from the white Sahibs, Bore, Milroy and Humprey lay neatly bound in one corner of the room, so that the Gossain would have no difficulty in finding them. The *sanchi* manuscript was also there on the wooden stool, properly covered and tied with a garland of flowers. Giribala had collected the old manuscripts, from the attics and *dhekal* rooms of houses at Borharamdo, Saruharamdo, Rajabaha, Machkuchi and other places. She had not left untouchd even the sacred sandal rooms and other dark and dank interiors of the various manors.

Certainly Mark had wanted to stay on in this *sattra* His work was left undone. He could not even complete the biography of Gilman Sahib, nor could he write about the proverbial friendship of Bore, Milroy and Humphrey, the British officers, with the Gossains of South Bank. It was all over and done with. Mark would never be able to come back now. Would he ever meet him somewhere, sometime?

Indranath came out of the room. Over his head, the September sky was absolutely clear. It had rained earlier, but now there was bright sunshine. All the trees and bushes sparkled in the brilliant sunlight. The golden yellow flowers of the *sonaru* trees challenged the yellow luminosity of the sun. Suddenly his eyes were drawn towards the old jackfruit tree. Underneath sat a fisher-woman with a basket full of paddy that she had obtained in exchange for the fish she had sold. She was now measuring out the paddy to gauge its quantity.

Only some time back, these fisher-women used to give all their fish to the Gossain, just for a single basket of paddy. But now they gave a wide berth to the same Gossain, and took their catch to the *mahajans* as they got in bargain more paddy from them.

A heart-rending cry pierced the serene atmosphere. Indranath turned round with a jerk. The old poverty-sticken Kowria, who made his living by selling clay toys and playing on *kalia*, had lost his son. After the cremation, probably he had made the obligatory offering to the villagers. The red cloth on the *bijulee* bamboo, erected according to ritual, flutlered in the air. The people who had attended the funeral, were taking a mud and water bath in the Jagalia. The anguished cry was from the mother of the dead boy. Two woman helped her walk to the old jackfruit tree. The mother was crying and singing in grief stricken delirium.

> *Chari angulidi jukhi jukhi*
> *Chitakhan patila ai.*
> *Ai Ram thakak thake diya khari,*
> *hate dhara dhari,*
> *Sat mera ghuri,*
> *Ai Ram mukhe jalaila agani*
> (The pyre is measured, out with four
> fingers at a time. Oh! Rama! Fire
> wood is piled layer upon layer.
> Round and round the pyre seven
> times and then a touch of flaming
> torch to the mouth!)

This heart-rending delirious song touched everybody's heart. The boy had died after only two days of fever. The village doctor of Palasbari had advised them to bring a doctor from Gauhati. But how could this penniless poor father bring a doctor from Gauhati to treat his sick son?

Khat, khat, khat!
Khat, khat, khat!

Indranath glanced towards the road from Palasbari. He saw a white horse and a man astride it. Indranath walked to the wooden bridge over Jagalia and stood there leaning on the railing. As the rider came nearer, he could see that it was the son of Bhikaru Gossain, Devdutt. Both had studied together at Gauhati. But as he was the future *adhikar*, Bhikaru Gossain had called him back from Gauhati, just as Indranath too had to return to his *sattra*. The latter remembered how Bhikaru Gossain, after visiting his disciples, would hasten to the students' mess with a load of deer flesh! Indranath had never seen such huge portions of deer flesh. The Gossain also had a big elephant like his Jagannath....

Khat, khat, khat!
Khat, khat, khat!

The horse was on the bridge now. When he saw Indranath, Devdutt jumped down from the horse. After his sojourn in Gauhati, there was now an upper Assam accent in his speech.

"I have heard about Giribala and that bastard *mlecha*! Damn it! Why did you allow that fellow to enter the sacred sandal room?"

Indranath held up his hand.

"Oh, never mind! Tell me, where are you heading for?"

"Haven'it you heard? The government is going to skin us alive! Dear chap, land ceilling is coming! Land ceiling is coming soon!"

Indranath said,

"Oh! You are speaking of the fixation of ceiling on the land-holding act!"

Devdutt had learned English from Milroy, a British forest officer. But in spite of trying very hard, he could not speak the language in a proper accent. He said.

"Why don't you do something instead of just waiting lethargically? Cook up a cunning scheme to avoid this ceiling. Do you know, by 1956, it will become an all-India act? It goes something like this."

Then in his peculiar accent, he quoted in English:

"Nothwithstanding anything to the contrary in any law, customs or agreements, no person shall be entitled to hold as owner or tenant, land that exceeds the limit of fifty *bighas* in the aggregate, and this limit of fifty *bighas* shall be applicable to the aggregate of the land held individually by the members of a family or jointly by some or all the members of such family..."

Indranath was astonished. An act of the government that was not even passed and put into force—how could Devdutt quote it word for word? During one of the sessions at Bolo's den, someone had murmured into his ears about the land ceiling act. But he had not paid much attention to it...

Devdutt spoke again, "So take my words seriously! Better be prepared and believe me, do something about it!"

Devdutt paused and continued, "I have already sold some of my land just by taking hand-written notes. This work brings me here too. Many of my relatives are scattered around Chikarhati. After the great earthquake, followed the terrible famine there. There was an acute scarcity of rice. Some of my relatives became very rich and prosperous by smuggling rice from Rangoon and selling it here clandestinely. Indranath, take my advice seriously and do something before it's too late. Keep it a secret whatever you do! Sell all your lands at Jhalimabari and Gargara by hand notes. I'll send you the buyers. Transfer some of your land from your name to your relatives and friends and as far as possible, eliminate the tenant farmers. All the Gossains of South Bank have now learnt about the insults inflicted on you at Marabhitha. And the *Maujadars* of twenty-three *maujas*.... Do you know what they say?"

All of a sudden their eyes were drawn to a cart with a colourful canopy approaching them. Devdutt watched it approaching with a feeling of excited curiosity. Soon the sweet fragrance of *jabakusum* oil permeated the air. It reminded Indranath of crushed sugarcane juice. Probably the ladies inside the cart were daughters of Machkuchi Gossain, who had friends at Chikarhati. They often traversed this road, to and fro.

Devdutt keenly watched the gaily decorated cart to catch a glimpse of a pretty hand or a graceful leg. He had a soft corner for women. He said, "Indranath, I have heard that you were very keen on marrying the daughter of that priest from Rajapukuri. But lately I've learnt that you've given up all that and you have no interest in the fate of your land."

Devdutt paused for a while and continued, "In our family nobody has ever brought home a Brahmin girl. But if you are thinking on those lines, it's good! I am all for it!"

Then with a mischievous smile, he added, "It has also reached my ears that this girl has already attained puberty. And, aha, you know! ... Those prominent parts of her body, they are as large as baskets of rice!"

A sly smile appeared round the corners of his lips. Indranath felt a wave of resentment and nausea rising in his chest, but with a great effort, he restrained himself and suppressed it. He was well-acquainted with Devdutt's character, and therefore it was pointless to express his ire.

Devdutt resumed speaking.

"So, Indranath, everything's clear, I hope! Your father and my father, between them, have the largest holding of *nispikheraj* lands in their names. You come to me any time. I'll keep the customers and the *hundis*[3] ready for you!"

He took out a handkerchief from the pocket of his *punjabi* and started cleaning his muddy shoes.

"Listen! If there's any figure work or accounting to be done, you send your *mohura* to me... and another thing! If you've to give up land under the ceiling, let it be Gargara and Rangamati lands. They are under litigation and you'll be saved from a lot of trouble! But take care! Don't forget the insults showered on you and your father by those impudent bastards at Marabhitha! Damned riff-raff communists! Those pigs with red flags! They dared to shout slogans against the Gossain! Telling the Gossain to plough the land himself! With his own hand! What a great insult! Don't ever let them go unpunished! It's a question of our prestige, the Gossains of South Bank."

Indranath did not respond to this violent outburst. He kept silent. He wanted to get rid of Devdutt as fast as possible. The latter now went near the jackfruit tree where he had tied his horse, and turning round to Indranath, said:

"Listen, Indranath, all over South Bank, the Gossains are panicking. There's a scramble for hand notes and distribution of land among relatives and friends! To keep your lands intact, you'll have to be as patient as a crane and cunning like a fox!"

Devdutt took off his spectacles with round lenses and started polishing them with his handkerchief. He was not as fair-skinned as the other Gossain youths of South Bank.

He had a straight long nose that indicated a fair share of intelligence and astuteness. But his eyes often had a fickle and greedy look, which put people off. He had dark thick hair, parted in the middle and curled on the sides.

Indranath said, "I have met you after quite a long time. My mother would have been happy to see you. After Giribala's death, she hardly comes out in the sun."

Devdutt said in a low voice.

"Not today, Indranath. This land ceiling crisis has brought me here. I'll try to meet your parents after two or three days. You look pulled down, my friend. Why brood so much over Giribala's suicide? It's better it ended this way! Otherwise that beef-eating white bastard would have dragged your family's name through mud!"

Indranath exclaimed.

"No, no! Don't say that! Please!... Speaking for myself, I would't have minded if Giribala and Mark had united. Perhaps you won't believe it, but Mark was the most truthful man I had ever met. I respected him a lot."

Devdutt cried out.

"Strange! strange! Blasphemy from a would-be *adhikar*'s mouth? I've never come across such a heretical son of a *adhikar*! Don't be offended, Indranath. An incident has come to my mind. When we were studying together at Gauhati, do you remember, we Gossains of South Bank used to prepare our own food. One day, in the month of December, after having an early morning dip in the river, we were all sitting, covered with our *chaddar*, on the verandah, reciting the *gayatri mantra*. Just then, a *sambhu dom* boy of fisherman's caste, hardly four or five years old, appeared with a *khale*[4] full of *kaoi mach*[5]. He had thin, stick-like limbs and a bloated stomach. I told him to overturn the basket, just to see whether the fish were fresh and alive. The boy poured out the contents on the floor of the verandah. The *kaoi*, very much alive, started jumping, twisting and turning all over the place. Suddenly, one of them plunged into the poor boy's open mouth and got stuck in his throat! It was a horrible sight! The boy started thrashing about on the floor, in acute pain. Soon he was vomiting blood! But we, Gossain's sons, dared not touch him and help him because he was a low caste and we would've had to take a second bath in cold water. You were then down with malaria and were taking rest. But, on hearing the commotion, you came out like a hurricane! When you saw what had happened, do you remember the words you uttered? You shouted, 'No religion left in this world! No righteousness or humanity left!' You went like a bullet to the child. We shouted, 'Don't go near him! You've fever, you'll have to take bath. Don't touch him!' But you didn't care. You thrust your fingers in the boy's mouth and pulled out the wretched fish! Then we forced you to go to the Brahmaputra and take bath in the chilling cold water. Do you remember, Indranath? You couldn't perform the purification ceremony as you were burning with high fever."

Indranath did not reply.

"At that time, we discussed your strange lack of any feeling for customs and traditions as required by our religion and high caste. We wondered then in what direction your life will lead you! What'll happen to you in the years to come! We were very anxious for you.... Now Indranath! Tell me! You would have allowed that beef-eater to take away your sister?"

Though Indranath did not affirm or deny it, Devdutt realised with some misgiving that he would have certainly done something unconventional. He did not wait for Indranath's response, but mounted his horse and prepared to leave. His parting words were:

"Remember, Indranath, the land ceiling! All the Gossains are already in a frenzy about it. Those *miyadi kherajee* lands at Allibari and Dakhin Rani. If you decide to sell them, then come to me. I'll buy the lot! Now you promise me!"

Indranath maintained his stubborn silence, and did not even look up. Then he heard the galloping hooves of Devdutt's horse. When he raised his head, the latter had already crossed the elephant's field and was heading for the main road beyond the old jackfruit tree. On the stony surface of the road, he could now hear only the "khat, khat, khat" sound of the fast moving horse. Yes, probably there's some truth in Devdutt's words. "Ceiling's coming! Ceiling's coming!" But he had no inclination to sit up and do something about it. His heart was heavy! He felt listless—why this emptiness, this lack of feeling?

A cool breeze caressed his back, damp with perspiration.

The mourners, who had attended the cremation of the unfortunate Kowria's son, had finished their ritual bath in the Jagalia. Their thin, emaciated figures, like animated skeletons, now filed past Indranath, their wet dhotis still dripping with water. Some of them bowed low before him and walked on. One of the mourners prostrated, touching his forehead to the ground, and said.

"Saru Gossain, the epidemic of black fever is now raging through places like Baoharamdo, Saruharamdo, Tallapara and other villages. So many people have already died! Many more are affected. Even the red water of the government compounder couldn't save them! They vomit and they die! They vomit and they die.... Like flies!"

The tired, disheartened man walked on without waiting

for Indranath's reply. These men looked like a host of skeletons. They were all in the relentles grip of opium addiction....

Indranath took the road to Barihat. It was already late. The sun overhead was scorching hot. He took out his pipe and lit up another *bidi* in the bowl of his pipe. Yes, Devdutt is right! Land ceiling will destroy the Gossains. The strong bond they had with the soil over the last four hundred years will be snapped forever. He knew that, in the next four or five days, his father would say—"Do something, Indranath, do something! Don't you remember, our ancestor, Gaurikanta Gossain, made over all the land of Bajapara, by *pattas*, to his tenants as requested by them? And you know how that Garo *Maujadar*, swallowed up the entire Khamar by his bastardly tricks! But, my son, lately your mind has became elusive. I don't know what to make of it. Perhaps you don't realise how much sweat of our forefathers has gone into consolidating all these lands. After the Burmese invasions, we have seen better days only under the guidance of Lord Gopinath. Everyone knows that you're wise, but this detachment. Why? Indranath, why?"

Yes, his father's words echoed in his ears. It is true he does not have any interest in land, never had any! He still cannot make head or tail of the account of *nispikheraj* lands donated by the copper-plate edict of King Siva Singha, nor does he know anything about the Khajelikura and Khamar lands having been made *kheraj* by Captain Jenkin's orders.

Why has he come to think like this? Will it reach the stage when *Mahaprabhu* Gossain will be compelled to select a *dattak*[6] in his place? In South Bank, is there any other Gossain *adhikar* who had to take a *dattak* while his son was still living? Had it ever happened? If he remembered correctly, this type of *dattak* ceremony had never taken place on the South Bank of the Brahmaputra.

Why this state of mind? Why? But this kind of detachment was always a part of his mental attitude, which led him into mysterious pathways sometimes. Nowadays it haunts him even when he is playing cards at Bolo's den. Even the alluring beauty of Eliman is not exempt from it. Somehow this detachment drills a hole in the golden net of allurement holding him in its fold....

When he was studying at Gauhati, this mysterious depression would grip him sometimes. In those moments, he would walk up and down on the sands of the Brahmaputra. (It is said that Indranath was once caught and confined to prison mistakenly by the British authorities along with other Bihari and Marwari boys for the offence of defecating in public on the sands of the Brahmaputra! All this happened because he was loitering aimlessly, that time, in his black mood!)

A big *jamun* tree stood at one end of the wooden bridge on the road to Barihat. Under its shade, this place always remained cool and pleasant. From here both the banks of Jagalia are visible clearly. The banks are lush green and the blue sky is trapped in the flowing waters of the river, in between. The river became a blue snake squeezing its way through the green silken cloth of the earth! This is one of favourite spots where he can light his pipe and smoke in brooding silence for a while.

This part of the bridge, the shady *jamun* tree, the view of the green banks and the winding river, had a mystical association for him. It was here that he had suddenly encountered the rogue elephant, his own Jagannath, where he had left him unharmed; it was the same place from where he had bid farewell to Durga, straining to catch a glimpse of her till she disappeared from view; and it was here, at this very spot, on a moonlit night, that he had that unbelievable meeting with the lovely Eliman, chaperoned by the old woman...

No, no! He does not feel like lingering here any longer... The disciples from Gargara and Sualkuchi... his mother had informed him that they were very influential people. When he was at Gauhati in school, they had visited the *sattra* with many gifts of *endi* shawls, rice from old paddy, earthen pots of jaggery, ivory combs, *muga* silk *mekhala* and *reha* for the ladies of the house, and the like. Drum beaters, buffalo horn players and a couple of *ojhas* had also come with them. In the portico, where cushions and other trappings of elephants hung over a crossbar, a *Bhagavati*[7] from the South Bank had recited verses from the holy book, the *Bhagavat*. Indranath knew this Brahmin very well. He would sit on a big wooden *peerah* with an old copy of the *Bhagavat*, almost falling apart at its binding. People from all over, Borharamdo, Saruharamdo, Tallapara, Choudhuripara, would gather round him in a circle and listen to him with rapt attention. This *Bhagawati* always wore round reading glasses held in place over his nose with strings looping round his ears. They laughed and made fun of his odd pair of spectacles, but he was an excellent reciter of the *Bhagavat*. Indranath remembered even now how meticulously he had described some *Gauriya Vaisnavites*[8] of Biznee, and Damodar Dev, founder of this *sattra*, and his *Vaisnavism*, and how he followed the Vaishnavite scripture, and improvised to suit the audience or the situation. Yes, Indranath remembered everything. Changes can be brought about according to the man, or the situation. Even rigidity can be made pliable to suit a particular condition or circumstance. Everything lies in the hands of human beings! Yes, the hands of men and women! As if God is void, only the truth and faith are God! If there is any religion, then this is it! Indranath reassured himself.

Are all the windows of his mind closed now? No, no! Certainly not! From one window, he can still admire the beauty of Jagalia flowing through its green silken cloth banks. It reminded him of the long undulating hair of his beloved Eliman. He can still admire the full moon of *ekadasi* and imagine that its light is like a fishermen's net spread out on the surface of Jagalia's water. Yes, this is the bridge where he had met her!

Love is divine!

This love does not demand! All the roads meet and terminate here. So it seems to him!

Giribala, Mark, Saru Gossainee... Are their loves also assimilated in this divine path?

An undefined ache, in a corner of his heart, still pinches him. Guilt and remorse besiege him, how selfish he is!

And his heartstrings resonate with vibrations of Girbala's soul. Her voice echoes in his mind. "I know you, I understand you. I'll be happy when, at last, peace and tranquility descend on your turbulent mind."

It was he who had paved the way for their intimacy, thinking at the time that the task of gathering old manuscripts for Mark would help him in his noble venture, and at the same time, enrich Giribala's mind. He had seen how the women in the *sattra* lived out their days. Certainly they do not deserve to be buried alive in coffins of *urium* and teak wood walls and posts.

The scriptures of Mark Sahib, his friend, say:

"I have created buffaloes to live side by side with

wolves. Go thou into the world. But be intelligent and wise as a snake, meek and modest as a dove! But beware of humankind! They will strip you and exhibit you in their religious assemblies!"

Ah, what a mistake on his part! He had seen them together, standing face to face, among *nagarbera* and *bhatera* bushes; often he had watched them gazing into each other's eyes under the wooden lamp-post, but he had not said or done anything about it!

The same scriptures of Mark Sahib say: "We were hungry but you didn't satisfy our hunger; we lamented, but you didn't share our sorrow; and we played a tune on the flute, but you didn't hear it!"

Indranath started walking along the road again. The gate of Bolo's house was in sight. He halted before the bamboo cross-bar, pushed it aside to enter, but then he changed his mind, pulled back the bamboo in place and stood motionless for a while. A gaily decorated, covered cart stood in the courtyard under the shade of an *au tree*, Probably some ladies from nearby villages had come on a visit. There were sounds of merry laughter and gay banter from inside. Most likely a game of *golokdham* was in progress. It suddenly occured to Indranath that it would have been better for his mother if she had taken to games like *golokdham* instead of staining her lips black with tobacco smoke!

He was in two minds whether to go inside or not, when Bolo himself came out on the verandah to spit betelnut juice from his mouth. Seeing him standing outside the gate, Bolo called out immediately.

"Saru Gossain! Why are you standing there? Come inside!"

Indranath entered the courtyard. As he was

approaching the house, he noticed an old man seated on a wooden chair at one end of the verandah. His face was covered with a long beard and long hair fell down over his ears. Bolo introduced his guest.

"He is Jiva Ballabh Goswami of North Bank. He studied with your father at Gauhati in 1912. *Prabhu*, it was 1912, wasn't it?"

The old man nodded hs head in assent.

Indranath now recalled something his father had told him about this Gossain. He was so poor that he could not gather the obligatory *kanyapan*[9] for his marriage, with the result that he had remained a bachelor all his life. His forefathers had come from Shantipur in Nadia District of Bengal. They did not have any relationship with the Kanuaj Gossains of Amranga *sattra*. This Goswami had fought a battle against *kanyapan* and won. This was what his father had told him...

Indranath looked at the old man more closely. His hair was completely white, and he wore an old, soiled *punjabi* made of *endi* cloth that had taken on the colour of a loofah. He had thick-soled leather shoes on, and over the shoulders a clean cotton *chaddar* as white as those worn by young Gossain boys.

The old man's face brightened when he recognised Indranath. He exclaimed.

"I've heard about you in Bheladanga *sattra* of Cooch Behar. People speak about it everywhere! How you helped in carrying the dead body of Jamaluddin to Bholagaon without caring for the fierce rogue elephant, even in the dead of the night! Bravo! What you did was indeed excellent!"

Bolo now urged the old man. "Master, give your

blessings to Saru Gossain. Soon he'll go to that communist-infested land of Marabihta where those vermins are raising hell! Wish him good luck and success, Master!"

Indranath broke in.

"No, no! I am not at all greedy about land! It's only for the sake of my father. He feels very strongly about it and takes it as a prestige issue for the family. I feel very helpless, really!"

Bolo said, "Yes, we know! But they are threatening the Gossain. Telling him to plough his own lands! Those bastards! Damned dogs! That *mohura*—we also know how he collected 10 *lathi* blows on his back instead of paddy for the Gossain, when he went there!"

Meanwhile, a *bandha* brought a wooden stool for Indranath. Bolo brushed the seat with his *chaddar* and said, "Come, Saru Gossain, be seated."

The old Gossain said, "The power and glory of *adhikars* are on a decline. The land ceiling has turned everything upside down. Oh, the grand days of thirty, forty years back! Will they ever return, do you think? I used to play with your father. We had also studied together. We used to play the games of *mughal pathan*[10], in those days! Every week your elephant used to come from the village. Ah, those were the days! Curd in earthen bowls, as thick as butter, sugarcane stalks as thick as bamboos, and sweet sun-dried jackfruit buds. Ah, what a feast I had! I'll never forget those old days! Once I had come this side on your father's elephant. At that time, you had a headstrong elephant.... Now what was its name? If more than four people sat on its back, it would get annoyed and fidgety. And then everybody had to get down four or five times, to tighten up its seat again and again. Once, when the *mahout* was tying the rope round its belly, it hit out with its tusk and broke his head! We were in a great hurry that day because elephants were not allowed on Gauhati's Strand Road after certain hours."

Tea was served in brass tumblers, polished bright like gold. They sipped the tea in silence for some time. Then the Gossain from North Bank began speaking again.

"Your father was exceptionally brilliant. In those days, we read Macaulay's *Days of Ancient Rome*, even Shakespeare, the *Arabian Nights* and *Youth's Golden Path*. But your father liked to read Bankim's *Devi Chaudharani, Life of Nelson*—books like that! The magazine, *Bangabasi*, was always by his bedside. Once I had attended your annual *sabha* to see the theatrical performance. Your grandfather himself used to make the fire crackers. He filled the hollow branches of *banhka*[11] with gunpowder to make those crackers. He made the explosives by mixing sulphur and saltpetre with charcoal. The enclosure where the visitors were given *sandah*[12] was very large. Men from Talukdarpara had come to build the *shamiana* and drummers had come from Gargara, *ojhas* from Jayapur...."

Just then, betelnuts and chewing tobacco were served on a brass *bota*[13]. A *bandha* came with a *hookah* for the old Gossain of North Bank.

"Listen, Indranath! Once when I was here I heard that a Gossain of Nahira had been murdered. He had relationships with two widows and a married woman!"

Indranath, in his preoccupied state of mind was not at all inclined towards any conversation with this old man. He had just come to meet Bolo about a particular matter and would have been only too happy to get away from there as soon as possible. But the garrulous old Gossain was not a man to be easily shaken off. He attributed

Indranath's tense and anxious behaviour to the land ceiling act hanging over his head. He had seen similar distracted and woebegone young Gossains of North and South Banks, running here and there. But how could he know the actual cause of Indranath's turmoil?

The old Gossain now said,

"Back there in Cooch Behar, I had heard that you didn't have any particular attachment for land. But now, looking at you, I realise that it's not true, and it should be so! Who would like to forgo one's valuable inherited property or fortune? Not the young men of the new generation, I'm sure!"

Bolo interrupted vehemently.

"No, no, it's not like that! Indranath hasn't any lust for land! Why, he doesn't even know how much land was made *kheraj* during the time of Jenkin Sahib!"

The old Gossain broke in.

"The tax on *nispi-kheraj* land, which was levied at the time of Raja Chandrakanta Singha, remained in force even up to the days of the Burmese invasions. During the rule of the white sahibs, both *nispi-kheraj* and *kheraj* lands were taxed at the rate of eight annas per pura[14]."

Bolo questioned: "Oh, a white sahib? Was he David Scott?"

"Yes, yes! In Scott Sahib's days, the tax was eight annas. From 1834 onwards, during Jenkin Sahib's time, estimation and assessment of *brahmottor*[15] and *dharmottor*[16] lands was started, and there was no end to chaos at that time. Those lands that were found to be other than the lands donated by Ahom Kings were taxed at the rate of one rupee per *pura*. On both the banks of Jagalia, there were many such disputed lands. Do you know, Indranath, where these lands exist and what's their area?"

Indranath remained silent for a while, and then said, "All the land accounts are kept by our *mohura*."

He returned to his silent abstraction. Just then, there was a burst of laughter mixed with loud chattering from the ladies playing *golokdham* inside the house. Saru Gossain took out the handkerchief from the pocket of his *punjabi* and wiped dry his sweating face. Then he looked at Bolo's face and said, "Actually I've come to you on an urgent business."

Bolo prompted him rather excitedly, "Yes, yes, go on! Tell me! What is it?"

The North Bank Gossain said at once, "I'll leave you two alone if you wish to speak privately." Indranath reassured him.

"No, no, it's nothing personal. Please remain seated, Gossain."

Then turning to Bolo, he said, "Some disciples from Gargara and Sualkuchi are coming. As always, my father wants you to arrange pigeons and papayas for their meals, and one more thing! The next month's paddy will be harvested on that bothersome Marabhitha land. My father would like you to go there with me. We'll go on our bicycles. I'll take my old one. To tell you the truth, I'm not at all keen on going but how can I say no to my father?"

Bolo admonished him sternly.

"Saru Gossain, you'll have to go! You must show them your power and authority! And you'll not take your old bicycle. You'll go on your elephant! With the *howda* on its back, all polished and shining! You are the son of an *adhikar*. That land is yours. Since the time of Jenkin, when it became *kheraj*, you've paid tax on it. That land came out of water, rich and fertile! It's Goddess Lakshmi's boon! So you'll go there on your elephant, in the *howda!*"

Indranath kept silent. How can Bolo understand his innermost feelings? This piece of land, out there at Marabhitha, has become the focal point for his trial of conscience.

The old Gossain from North Bank continued, "You're like my son. Your father and I played *mughal pathan* together. We used to go to Janardhan, play harmonium and sing together. Both of us learnt English together and read *Life of Nelson* together. Listen, son! More catastrophic than the ceiling will be the red wind that will soon blow this way and take away everything with it! To fall down low from high up, do you know what it means?"

... No, no! time is running out for him! He, Indranath, is not in the right frame of mind to listen to all these admonitions or sound advice and mortal lessons!

Bolo said, "I know. There are many reasons why Indranath is sad and dejected. His sister died not long back. Durga went back alone to her in-laws, even though none came from there to escort her. His favourite elephant had to be shot dead. And in Marabhitha, there's this communist threat! How can he remain calm under these circumstances?"

The face of the old Gossain registered sympathy for Indranath. He got up from his chair, put his hand on his shoulder and consoled him.

"Indranath, don't let these things bother you. Have faith in God. My blessings are with you, my son, always!"

The old man and Bolo came out to bid farewell to Indranath.

Bolo walked with Saru Gossain for some distance. The sun's rays were now pale. The cowherds were returning from the pastures with their cattle, raising clouds of dust. They were carrying plantain leaf containers of temple offerings. Bolo said, “Saru Gossain, don’t worry so much. In the old days, my ancestors came to the aid of your forefathers whenever they were in danger. Now I’m here to help you in the best way possible!”

Indranath nodded his head.

“I know, Bolo, I can reveal the innermost feelings of my heart only to you and only with you can I breathe a sigh of relief.”

“Why don’t you tell me everything? On both the banks of Jagalia, people say that you have become a stranger to normal life. Believe me, in no way can that girl of the Rajapukhuri priest meet you.”

Indranath hung his head and did not say anything. Deep inside him there was tussle. How could he disclose what he felt so agonisingly?

Both were now walking over the newly laid gravel surface of the road. Teak trees rose up on either side. The sun’s rays fell on them in a peculiar pattern of light and shade that created an illusion of leopard skins covering the trees. Indranath said, “We’ve played and grown up together. I want to confide in you. Honestly!”

“Come on then. Tell me!”

“I’ve no desire for land, you know that already... and the girl you mentioned; I tried my utmost, but I couldn’t forget her! I cannot forgive myself for this! Dreams hardly turn into reality, do they? Giribala gave up her life; Durga had to go back to her unwilling in-laws; and Saru Gossainee, you know all about her... In my mind, I really don’t know what to decide! What to do! I just want to sort of detach myself from everything. I am only trying and believe me, it’s all very agonising.”

Bolo said in soft, low voice.

“I understand you, Indranath. I can imagine what

you're going through. This is a kind of test, a supreme test for you. In the hands of fate!"

"No, no Bolo! It's not a test or fate or whatever. It happened naturally! Now, my only consolation is that the girl, Eliman, exists. She is there! That's what cannot make me forgive myself..."

"Indranath, your love is noble. You've not touched her, probably, nor have you ever spoken to her with an open heart. If, even in your state of extreme distress, she is a source of consolation to you, I can only express my admiration for this love."

"Listen, Bolo, I have expressed a desire to my father."

"What's this desire?"

"They have insulted my father by shouting that he should plough his own lands. It has been unbearable for him. He called me to the sandal room and told me to proceed to Marabhitha at once. He too wants me to go on the elephant. He has asked me to call the workers from Gargara and make the *howda* fit for the journey. He pointed to the attic and said, 'Take out those old tusks to adorn the *howda*. You must go there like our old *adhikar* ancestors, attired in turban, silk *punjabi* and *shantipuri dhoti*.' When my father and his father used to go to Marabhitha, the disciples would welcome them with drums and cymbals. They would alight from the *howda* and walk on a long cloth laid out on the ground. Later the disciples would cut this cloth into strips and distribute them amongst themselves. Whenever a member of their family fell ill, the strip from that cloth would be tied around their heads as a talisman.... Today the same people are threatening us. I've heard that the Brahmin opium smuggler from Cooch Behar, who was caught in Jokram Bhagawati's house, has joined them after coming out of the prison. It's also said that a boy from the family that was hostile towards the old Gossain, has also become one with those communists and he is now strutting about like a leader shouting slogans against us. They are all shouting—Gossain come, plough your own land!"

Indranath and Bolo reached the wooden bridge. Indranath said, "Bolo, go back now, the old Gossain must be waiting for you...."

"Oh, it's all right! He'll stay the night. I've made arrangements for him in the portico, so that he can cook his own food and sleep there."

They continued walking on the newly laid gravel surface of the road. Two trucks, roared past them. Indranath said, "When our people went there to plant rice seedlings, they talked amongst themselves in whispers and didn't resist them. But now-a-days the whole place reeks of gunpower smoke. A young man who is said to be an illegitimate child of my grandfather—I've heard that he is now one of the leaders roaming around that place. But Bolo, I haven't yet told you what I want you to know."

"Yes, tell me, Indranath."

"I'll certainly go there, to challenge the insult thrown at my father. I'll ride on the elephant in the *howda*. I'll see that the paddy is harvested. But do you know what'll I do once the paddy is cut and tied in bundles?"

"What? What?"

All of a sudden, there was loud report of gun-fire, and with a chorus of "gok, gok, gok" a flock of wild ducks flew over the Jagalia West Bank. Bolo resumed.

"Oh, it must be the young Gossains of North Bank, out for a bit of duck shooting! But go on, Indranath, tell me what you'll do at Marabhitha."

"As soon as the bundles of paddy are loaded on bullock carts, I'll make a proclamation."

"What!"—Bolo exclaimed.

"Yes, I'll proclaim that henceforth the land will belong to those tenant farmers who have been cultivating it for so many years."

Bolo was aghast.

"What are you saying? You've been paying tax all these years. Those rascals are abusing your father and telling him to plough his own land. You still want to give them the rights to the land! Really! I don't understand your mind!"

After a long pause, Indranath said,

"Our *bandhas* are already there, staying in tents, prepared for harvesting the paddy. Those rowdies have not resisted them yet. The Bengali Inspector of Palasbari has come to us again and again, saying that he'll arrange for police protection. He said that grabbing land by force is like playing with fire. I declined police help and told him that there won't be any bloodshed or rioting at Marabhitha. When the women were planting rice seedlings, those people didn't make an uproar or stop them. It seems that again the drums and cymbals will beat in welcome for the Gossain. The cloth will be laid out and as in the old days, the Gossain will walk over the cloth and the disciples will bow down to him with reverence. All as it was in the good old days!"

Bolo started laughing. Indranath also smiled. They were now on the elephant yard. Indranath again urged Bolo.

"You go back now. That old Gossain must be waiting for you, and your house is full of guests."

Bolo replied, "After lunch, the ladies have settled down with their *golokdham*. As for the Gossain from North Bank, his main purpose is to purchase land here, taking advantage of the land sale going on, due to the ceiling act. He is a bachelor. Made quite a bit of money doing *jajamani* in Cooch Behar. But Indranath, what you said about making *kecha patta*[17] in the names of those insolent rowdies, your tenants... are you serious?"

"Yes! I have made up my mind! I'll remain firm in my resolve."

"For God's sake! They've insulted your father and in return, you'll reward them! I've never heard of such behaviour from any Gossain of South Bank! Are you out of your mind?"

Indranath remained silent. They were now standing near the old banyan tree. The spot where poor Giribala had met her tragic death was clearly visible from there. Bolo turned to Indranath and said in farewell:

"All right then, I'll leave you now... don't worry about the pigeons and the papayas. I'll arrange for them. And ... out there at Marabhitha, I'll be with you like your shadow ... yes .. like your shadow!..."

Indranath took a short cut to the manor. A pale crescent moon hung in the sky. Again he imagined that a hazy net shrouded the moon's surface, which had also caught in it all the trees and shrubs, the *urium* and the teak and the *sonar*, the entire landscape!

Suddenly his eyes fell on the flimsy wall of Jokram Bhagawati's house. He could see, through the chinks in the wall, the glow of a hanging clay lamp. Ah! In the dim glow, a fleeting glimpse of arms and a slender neck, shining like fresh sugarcane juice. Whose vision was it? Has she really come back? And why? Has that opium-eating Brahmin completed his jail term and come out? Is he threatening her again with engagement gifts? But this is not the time! Oh! Let it not be now! He was going through one long agonising ordeal,—and her arrival? At this moment? No, no! Not now!

Indranath resumed walking towards the *sattra*. Near the *batghar*, a *dinkana*[18] suddenly flew out of a berry bush and passed over his head. He was startled. An inauspicious sign! Morose and sullen, he entered the courtyard. A kind of pain shot through his bosom. Only some days back, whenever he returned from Bolo's den, Giribala and his mother would be waiting for him in anxiety, mixed with inquisitiveness. In winter, they would be seated on the verandah with a fire before them; in summer, they would have palm-leaf fans in their hands. But now there is no one, the verandah is empty.

At this moment, Gossainee, his mother, must be in the small dark room smoking her *hookah*. Earlier Guimeni used to give her company in daytime, but after the death of Giribala, she spent her days alone in the small, dark room. Nowadays she did not even fill up the bowl of the *hookah* with water, so that it would not make a bubbling sound and disclose to others that she was smoking...

Human life, Indranath reflected, goes through such phases and transforms itself. Nothing is permanent. In this process, human relationships become a sharp, piercing weapon, hurtful and acrimonious to near and dear ones. No, no! He must not torment himself and become restless. The hour was not far away, and the place was also marked for him, when he would face the supreme moment of the test of his conscience, of himself!

Suddenly he recalled the scriptures of Mark! "Those who desire to follow me, must sacrifice their own self, and each one must carry his own cross and stand behind me...!"

Will he meet Mark again? If so, where? Beyond the far bank of Brahmaputra?

Indranath went to the well and washed his hands and

face, and poured some water over his feet. His eyes were drawn towards the backyard of Bhagawati's house across the road. Nothing! The view of the wooden pillars and the verandah, was blocked by overgrown *dhatura* and *lantana* bushes. Even the *kathana* tree, under whose branches Eliman used to stand, was not visible now. Darkness shrouded the place even in that twilight hour. Why had she come? That crooked Brahmin! He must have harassed and threatened her, no doubt!

The "chuk, chuk, chuk" of the *dinkana* rent the air again.

That night Indranath dreamt that he was lost in a wood of dry, thorny bushes. All around was arid, desiccated space. He wandered on and on, aimlessly. Then, unexpectedly, he espied Eliman, standing in a barren part of the wood. He rushed towards her, but all of a sudden she turned into a red flower, the red flower became a pool of blood! The blood splashed on a thorny bush, and drops of blood dripped down from the sharp thorns…

Indranath woke up with a start.

* * * *

A month passed by. It was now time for the paddy harvest at Marabhitha. The tuskless elephant was taken for the journey. Brisk preparations were going on to make the *howda* ready, and tie it on the elephant's back. At last the *howda* was up in place, tightly secured. But this tuskless elephant lacked the majesty of Jagannath. There was a long white streak on his ungainly trunk, with white spots all around, like a leopard's skin. He was also headstrong. He would try to dislodge the *howda* from time to time with his rolling gait. Then the travellers had to get down, the ropes would be tightened again.

The Bengali Police Inspector had sent word two or three times, saying that Indranath would need protection and urging him to take some policemen with him. But why the police? The time for the test of his conscience had come. Indranath's mind was gripped by mysterious thoughts and emotions.

Bhagawati, the priest, consulted his charts and calculated the exact auspicious hour for commencing the journey. The Gossainee had already despatched two of her most faithful disciples at night to Marabhitha. They performed the first ritual, traditionally done to launch the first harvest of rice paddy, and brought back five heads of *shali* rice ears. They were placed on a plantain leaf and kept in front of the granary with a mustard oil clay lamp. The Gossainee prayed in a clear, loud voice.

"Oh, Gods of the four directions! Protect this boy! He is going to take possession of his own land ... Take care of him!..."

....Many people had gathered in the *batghar* to bid farewell to Indranath. The Gossainee had also come out and she stood there with the *gatala* covering her head. On seeing her, two or three women remarked.

"Oh, Gossainee, why are you sending this tender boy to that cursed place? In the midst of those fox-like *mandals*[19] and those terrible men who make gun-powder? Why are you sending him there?"

The Gossainee remained silent. Guimeni, who was standing beside her said, "Ahh, what gibberish! He's going for the paddy reaping ceremony. All the tenants will receive him with bowed heads and folded hands. *Bandhas* will carry his sandals and horn players and drum beaters will lead the way! Just wait and see! Everything will be as it was in the good old days!"

The elephant was made to kneel down. Indranath stood beside it, all prepared to start for the journey. The Gossain *adhikar* had also come upto the gate. Indranath was wearing a silk *punjabi* with *shantipuri dhoti*, and over his shoulder, a silk *chaddar*. Someone cried from the crowd:

"Ah, he's looking like a god come down from the heaven! Who can defy this god? After all, a Gossain is always a Gossain!"

Indranath touched his father's feet and then went to his mother.

But what's this? What has come over Gossainee? She hugged her son tightly for a moment, and then rushed to the inner verandah, losing all restraint, and sobbed convulsively.

Everyone in the crowd was stunned to see the Gossainee break down like this—this lady who could hold back her tears with great effort, even under the most tragic circumstances! They whispered among themselves.

"Poor Gossainee! After Giribala's death, she has lost control over her mind. Tobacco, tobacco, tobacco! Always smoking tobacco! Her fingers and lips have become dark with tobacco stains."

Meanwhile, three open carts passed by the road. They were loaded with long poles pointed at both ends, sickles for cutting paddy, ropes for tying sheaves, boiled and dried rice, ripe tamarind in earthen pots, salt sacks and clay jars of jaggery. Six or seven reapers were perched on each cart. They were all in a jovial, festive mood, singing harvesting songs amidst laughter and, exchange of banal jokes...

The *makhana* had already traversed the path leading out from the *sattra* and he was now on the main road. On both sides of the road, crowds of men, women and children had gathered, jostling each other to have a better glimpse of the procession. They were mostly from the families of *kahars*[20], *kamars*[21], *badhais*[22], *napits*[23], *dhubis*[24], *dhulias*[25], and others, belonging to the *sattra* and the surrounding villages. In the year 1813, when the great earthquake had struck Garaimari and razed it to the ground, the then Gossain had shifted the *sattra* to the bank of Jagalia and brought with him all these families. Now after more than one hundred and fifty years, their roots and branches had spread out and many of the descendents had even gone as far afield as the North Bank to seek suitable work.

Underneath the banyan tree, the old Kowria blew on his *kalia* a farewell tune vigorously for his master, Saru Gossain. He was clad only in an old dirty *gamucha*, wrapped round his waist. His dark back glistened with sweat like the wet mottled skin of a frog.

On the elephant's back, in the *howda*, Indranath's heart was fluttering like an agitated bird trapped in a cage. On the way, the top of the *howda* brushed against a low mango tree branch and some leaves got stuck on it. There arose a cry from the men following the elephant.

"Ahh! That's good sign! Everything will turn out well! Just wait!"

The crush of humanity along the road had swelled manifold, as if all the people had spilled out of their dwellings, leaving them empty like abandoned beehives.

From the *howda*, on the elephant's back, Indranath could look inside the courtyard of Bhagawati's house. Yes, there she was! Standing beneath the *kathana* flower tree! Her hair was dishevelled, her *gatala* soiled. He could somehow sense that a storm was raging inside her. Yes, undoubtedly, she had something crucial to convey to him, which had compelled her to come back! But this was not the time! No, no, not now! Her voice seemed to call out with anguish,

"Oh, Listen! That Brahmin has come out of jail. Do something! And quickly. Or else I'll jump into the river! There, in Jagalia! Do you hear me?"

... Indranath's reverie was shattered all of a sudden by the shouts of people invoking divine blessings. They bade him farewell at the outer limits of the *sattra*.

As the elephant ambled along the road, Indranath diverted his attention to the scenery all around. As far as his eyes could see, nature was draped in green on both the banks of Jagalia. On the right, fronds of betelnut palms and bamboo groves were visible. They were like a green roof stretching out over the *sattra*. All these scenes were to him very dear, very precious. They were a part of his childhood and the years of growing thereafter.

On the other side, he saw long-legged yellow-beaked herons wading through tall *kachidariya* grass in search of fish. They have long been a familiar sight to him...

A strange experience of Kaltu the *mahout* flashed into his mind. He was fishing, one day, with a rod and bait. He had caught a big one and just when he had unhooked the fish, a heron grabbed it. Kaltu lashed out with his rod in sudden anger and hitting the bird in a vulnerable spot, killed it by accident. Then, to his utter surprise, he saw a live, non-poisonous snake crawl out of the slashed pouch beneath the dead heron's neck!...

Ahh! How beautiful are the green banks of the river! He felt as if he had seen this lovely scene after a long lapse of time. All these days past, he had moved about in abstraction, brooding and lost in thought. His eyes were open, but unseeing... Indranath feasted his eyes on the landscape with its many shades of green. There it was dark hued, almost black! And there, it was soft green like silk! And over there, green like a parrot's feathers!

Bolo followed at a leisurely pace on his bicycle behind the elephant. He was, in turn, followed by two or three disciples, also on bicycles, The pointed bamboo poles loaded in the carts ahead were rattling with the jolts and jerks of the carts. The reapers began singing lustily:

Are bhai patalar pere bhuynkap
ahil har har kari
Tiri chali hatat dhari kare
Lara lari
Ghar khahil, bera khahil
aru khahil kanthi!
Duwar mùkhat, puti thala
Gahenther hathi.

(From deep below came the
earthquake. Women with children
in arms fled here and there. House
crashed, walls collapsed, verandahs
disintegrated. And near the gate, the
Gossain's big elephant got buried
alive!)

The sound of cart wheels and the rattling of the pointed bamboo poles could be heard a long distance away. Indranath glanced behind him. Kowria was also following the elephant, still blowing on his buffalo horn. Behind him, walked Birohu, the elderly *bandha*, Guimeni, and other women of the *sattra*. The woman were singing away happily, the same songs they usually sang when a Gossain was on his way to visit his disciples. Indranath felt that all these women, Kowria and the others continued to follow him, with a strong desire to catch a glimpse of his face, just as the people of Ayodhya were reluctant to see Rama depart for exile and followed him a long distance.

Never before had any Gossain of a *sattra* gone in person for harvesting paddy, with reapers and all the accompanying paraphernalia in tow! Never before had this happened!

They were all convinced that Indranath's presence in person at Marabhitha would be more effective than even the most powerful weapon on earth. The disciples and the tenant farmers there were basically pious and faithful. The influence of the Communists would be like words written with water. They would dry up in the heat of Saru Gossain's presence. This was the conclusion in the minds of most of the people in the *sattra*. The priest, Purshottam Bhagawati, the *mohura*, *jajmani* Brahmins of Borharamdo, Saruharamdo, relatives from Khatiamari, Machkuchi, and as far away as Jhalimabari—all approved of Indranath's decision to go personally for the task of taking possession of the land...

Indranath wiped off the dust from his eyes and face. Except for the short sojourn at Gauhati, he had spent the rest of his life at the sattra. He now recalled his childhood. Many times, he would dodge the rigid routine of a Gossain's son, and run away to play with the children of fishermen, potters, cobblers, and the like, clad only in a *gamucha* tied round his waist. Durga would run after him, to catch him, with scolding words.

As soon as he was caught, she would march him off to the well and wash him, muttering and scolding him all the time, "What a naughty boy! I've never seen anybody like you. Always playing with those low-caste dirty children! Don't do it again, son."

...And Kowria with his buffalo horn following the elephant. As a small boy, Indranath would go running right up to the cooking stove of Kowria's ramshackle hut, and the latter's wife would cry out in horror,

"Oh, my God! That boy of the Gossain has come right inside! What'll people say? My goodness! What'll they say? Oh, dear!..."

And Kowria would urge her, "Go on! Give him a piece of hard jaggery! Nobody'll know!"

...He used to visit, even as far away as Tallapara, a potter's place and watch with fascination the potter's wheel, revolving fast, with the lump of wet clay on it, taking shape under the potter's skillful fingers. He would playfully fling his arms round the potter's neck and climb on to his back. The latter would chide him—

"My goodness! My boy, you'll have to take a bath now! Get off my back, will you? Oh, is anybody in there? Give little Gossain here one cucumber from the backyard! Oof! He's standing on all that rubbish! Oh, I say! Are you listening? Bring one *peerah* for Gossain!"

The rickety, pot-bellied, half-naked children of the potter's village used to gather round him and stare at him silently. Normally when they were by themselves, there would be a noisy scuffle for getting hold of the cucumber. But in the presence of Indranath, they stood quietly as if they would give up their everything to this son of the Gossain. They were struck dumb by the sight of this fair boy, with an undefined feeling of utter amazement that they themselves could not fathom.

He would even run into the ramshackle hutments of

shuris, ignoring playfully the consequences. He remembered eating, with great enthusiasm, *chunga pitha*[26] offered by these poor souls.

They would shout as soon as they spotted him in their midst.

"Oh, look! Larua Gopal[27] has come! He has dropped from the heavens into our courtyard!"

Yes, they really thought that the Gossains had descended from heaven. They dared not touch a Gossain, even a mere boy like him. And when they were on the threshold of death, they had a keen desire to touch a Gossain's feet. All of them, these untouchables, were bound by chains of humiliating and debilitating poverty. On top of that, they were in the clutches of that demon, the opium! Nearly half of these people, who were so dear to Indranath, would be struck with night blindness even before they reached adulthood!

There! They followed him riding resplendent in his *howda*, on the towering elephant! Should he tell them, "Go away! Go back! Go back!"

His eyes filled with tears....

What has he done for them?

Yes, now is the time! This is the occasion! The *mohura* had already brought, according to his directions, all the *nathi patras* and *pattas*[28] with him.

Yes, he, himself, would go to each of the tenant farmers' houses in Gargara, Khapegaon, Nargaon, Goraimari and other places. He would stand in front of their *harkala* (a bamboo pole placed horizontally between two vertical posts serving as a gate) and ask:

"What ails you? What's your problem? Has your granary collapsed? Is anyone of you struck down with *khenrog* or *kalazar*? Are you in urgent need of money to purchase bullocks?"

Yes, yes, he will try to find out everything from them about themselves.

He would go all alone. There is no need of another person. Because only the one who goes alone, who walks alone, can find out whatever he wants to know.

Indranath's eyes were drawn to the marks of *khurpee*[29] behind the makhana's ears. Some of the wounds caused by the *khurpee* had festered and later healed, leaving discoloured patches. Some wounds were still unhealed. An odour like that of boiled rice soup rose up from these *khurpee* wounds.

Ah-h! How green it was! How beautiful it was on both sides of the road, as far as the eyes go! The green vegetation was full of trees and bushes of various kinds—*ejar, kotahi jamun*, *bijulee* bamboos, in various shades of this dominant colour, as if the colour green was attired in ceremonial dress!

...Indranath's mind went back to his ancestors. Four hundred years ago, perhaps lured by the sight of such natural beauty, his ancestors from Kannauj, had pitched their palm-thatched huts at Garaimari and started tilling the fertile soil.

Yes, it was here, in this place, that his father and his grandfather had played *mughal-pathan* and *bagh bal* in the open fields and among the trees.

The bullock-carts, bearing the *hulabaris*[30] and other accessories along with the reapers, had galloped ahead and disappeared from view. The elephant was now moving quite fast along the road. All those who had followed it from the *sattra*, were now left far behind. The only sound to be heard was that of Bolo and the disciples of Gargara on their bicycles, talking among themselves.

The *howda* was mounted on this *makhana* elephant for the first time. Even then he bore it quite well. The *makhana* had not dislodged the *howda* so far by his rolling ungainly gait, and moved ahead briskly. But there was no peace in Indranath's heart. It fluttered like a fish caught in the net. He felt as helpless as a man tied firmly to a wooden frame, like Jesus on the cross.

✯ ✯ ✯ ✯

...As if nothing was wrong! The reapers were cutting the rice paddy in the fields. The *bandhas* were tying the harvested paddy into sheaves, and in turn, six of these slender sheaves were tied into bigger bundles and stacked on one side. All this work was going on in enthusiastic spirit, without any hindrance.

Indranath got down from the elephant and stood beneath the branches of an *urium* tree. Bolo and the disciples from Gargara alighted from their bicycles and watched this peaceful activity in stunned silence.

Bolo exclaimed.

"Just see the impact of your glorious presence! Leave aside coming here and fighting with your men, they haven't even come out of their houses!"

The disciples from Gargara said, "So what if the Communists have instigated these people! Their fathers and grandfathers belonged, after all to the days of the old Gossain. Can a banana become ripe all of sudden?"

Indranath remained silent. The work was going on smoothly, but his mind was still in turmoil. Happiness or peace of mind eluded him. His heart still fluttered with that nebulous pain.

These tenant farmers from the days of the old Gossain. Yes, but their lands had been eaten up by the river, and they had long dreamt, and hoped fervently, for this land that was once underwater. The Communists had incited them, saying,

"What does it matter if the Gossain has paid tax on the land all these years? If it had remained underwater, could he have done anything about it? How can he just grab this land? He must come here with a plough on his shoulder. He must plough the soil with his own hands!"

A little distance away, the reeds whispered and their whispers mingled with the sound of the sickles cutting paddy.

From the village, further way, no sound! ... Not even the noise of pounding rice. Only the rustling, susurrous sound of reeds..

shsh, shsh, shsh
shsh, shsh, shsh

Nearby was a big stump, flat on top like a wooden stool. Probably a big tree had stood there once upon a time, and somebody had cut it down. Indranath noticed this stump and thought it would make a good platform for addressing the farmers and the village people.

The reapers were laughing and shouting to each other.

"Ha, Ha! Ho, Ho! See what's happened! Gossain comes here on his *howda*, and these people are shivering and hiding in their houses like wet cats! Ha! Ha! Ha! After all he's a Gossain! Only some lucky ones can have his attention. But those people! Their bad luck has mucked them up! With those Communist devils!"

Again that acute pain! Indranath walked slowly towards the tree-stump, climbed up on it and stood erect. Suddenly everyone heard his loud voice, and was stunned to see him standing on the tree stump with one hand raised skywards. He addressed them in a clear, loud tone,

"Where are the peasants who first cultivated this land? Call them here immediately .. right away!"

The reapers, taken aback by his words, questioned him,

"But Gossain! Why are you calling them here?"

"Why, Gossain?"

"You have cut the paddy. You have done your work well! Now the desire of Adhikar *Mahaprabhu* has been fulfilled. Call those peasants! I want to give them their *kecha patta*!"

Pin-drop silence. Even a leaf falling down on the earth could be heard.

Indranath was standing there in the same posture.

Suddenly a fierce, full-throated cry powerfully rent the air.

Oi! Oi! Oi! Oi!! ...
Oi! Oi! Oi! Oi!!...

Everyone listened with alert ears.

Oi! Oi! Oi! Oi!!...

All of a sudden, men, armed with pointed bamboo poles and iron spears, jumped out of their hiding places behind various haystacks! They were bearing down on the field, running swiftly, arms raised, clutching their weapons!

"Yes! Yes!! There! Spears!!"

"Yes! Yes! Pointed bamboo poles!"

"No! No! No drums or flutes in their hands! To greet the son of Gossain!"

"There! There!! The spears are shining!"

"Run! Run! Run!! For your life!!"

"We're so few against so many!"

"Run! Run! Run !! For dear life!!"

"Quick! Quick! Grab those hamboo poles! From the

cart! Take those spears! Quick From the carts!!"

The *mahout* shouted from the back of the elephant.

"Beat the drums! Bang the cymbals! Drive them back!"

"Gossain! Shall I let loose the elephant?"

"There! They've come!!"

"Run, Gossain, run!!"

"They've entered the field!!"

"Run, Gossain; run!!..."

"They've entered the field!! .."

Then, in a fraction of a second! Oh, horror of horrors! Right before their eyes, someone plunged his pointed bamboo pole into the back of Indranath's head!! He collapsed, that very instant, and lay sprawled on the ground...

"He's killed! He's killed!!"

"Hold him! Hold him!!"

"Oh, who's there? Hold him!"

"Oh, blood! Blood!"

The earth, the sky, the whole world was reeling before Indranath's eyes. He tried, with all his draining strength, to sit up, but just then, someone dealt two more blows on his head, and he collapsed again, face down, on the earth.

A dark haze arose in front of Indranath's eyes. He saw, in a daze, many faces. There! His father! Standing in the sacred sandal room! But his feet are bare! There! His mother! Who never went out beyond the *batghar*. She has now come running to the banyan tree! Who's holding her? Who's holding her! Is it Durga! Ah! Ah!! Touching him and pressing his arms, she's crying. "Who's has hurt you? Who has killed you? My son! My life!" Ah! Is that Giribala? Who was burnt to ashes? Who's now standing there? In a clear voice, she's saying, "Come! Hold my hand and come with me!" Ah! Those people! *Mohura*, Guimeni, the priest, those women! Whom are they holding with their hands? Is it Eli? There! She's running, her hair cascading! Eli? Eli? The Jagalia has dried up! As if it is a river of desiccated bones! No! No! It's not a river! ... It's a forest of bones and thorns! And drops of his own blood are falling on those thorns and bones! Yes! His own blood! ...

⭑ ⭑ ⭑ ⭑

Nineteen eighty-one!

The land ceiling act came like a hailstorm. There were many amendments added to this ceiling act. The sons of Gossains had to spend many days and nights on the steps of the courts of justice. Some sons of landlords were thinking of opening book-shops or even butcher's shops, after losing their lands permanently! One or two Gossainees, involved in land fraud cases or cheated out of their precious land assets, who had never crossed the *batghar* earlier in their lives, not only went to Gauhati, but were even on the verge of being locked up behind prison bars!

In nineteen eighty, electricity came to the *sattra*. But it illuminated only a few houses. The rest still burnt mustard oil or kerosene oil lamps. Now, on the banks of Jagalia, girls from Gossain and Brahmin families go to low-caste houses and tie nuptial knots with the low-caste boys. Most households are free from the opium habit, but even now, the odour of frying *pan* leaves comes from one or two houses.

Nowadays Bihari traders or Kabuli merchants hailing from Kabul, sometimes make a round of the *sattra* conspicuously. They lure some low-caste girls away with dreams of marriage or even marry them with due ceremony. But alas, these girls either come back ruined and disgraced, or they are sold in the flesh trade.

The high school has expanded. Now a college has also come up at Mirza, near the *sattra*. Girls and boys commute to and fro and study there. A few have even become important officers.

In nineteen eighty-one, after thirty years, near the site of the old wooden bridge, which is now a brand-new bridge of steel and concrete, Bolo came face to face with the Communist leader who had instigated the murder of Saru Gossain. He had come out of jail long back.

The pain that this man felt for the poor and the downtrodden was no less than the pain in the heart of Indranath. Moreover, he was the illegitimate son of the old Gossain. His mother had been cast off by the latter after he had showered her with gold ornaments.

Bolo met him after many years, but they could recognise each other. Both had beards and moustaches with streaks of grey. Both had shrunken physiques, where their skins hung loose. Both were in the last phase of their lives.

Bolo motioned him to stop. The other man complied willingly. Bolo said to him.

"You seized the land after shedding a river of blood. Could you distribute the land properly among the poor peasants? Are they contented and well-fed now, after thirty years?"

The leader remained silent. Bolo gestured with his hand and continued.

"Near this very bridge, we consigned the dead body of our most beloved Gossain to flames."

He broke down for a moment. Then he took a step towards the leader and shaking his finger at the latter's forehead, said haltingly,

"You! you killed him! You were the one who cut him down!"

The leader burst out,

"The peasant's bellies were empty! ... And ... .And your Gossain came in his *howda*, to get the paddy harvested! No other Gossain had played this kind of farce!"

Bolo said, "Did you look at that *howda* closely? That *howda* was moth-eaten. Only I knew what went on deep inside his soul."

Even in this old age, Bolo could not restrain himself. He took out his handkerchief and dabbed his eyes with it. He said again:

"Before breathing his last, the Gossain told me, the experiment I wanted to try is successful! but now you say that nobody has a full belly! Thirty years have passed and nobody has a full stomach? But the Gossain went away thinking..."

Bolo broke down completely. He wiped the tears from his eyes and continued—

"Believe me, he had no desire to sit in that *howda*. I knew the storm that was raging in his mind!"

The leader, who had passed his whole life in bitter vengefulness, was not a man to give up easily. He followed Bolo for some time. Then he asked:

"Are you telling me the truth? Was that *howda* really moth-eaten?"

Bolo turned and said :

"I had, with my own hands, helped in tying the *howda* to the elephant's back. That *howda* was moth-eaten..."

References

A NOTE ON THE SATTRA :

1. Sattra is a Vaisnavite monastery founded by the Vaisnava saints of Assam. These monasteries were sometimes spread over vast lands donated by Ahom kings and in one case, even by a Muslim nawab. There are hundreds of sattras scattered throughout Assam, on both the banks of the Brahmaputra. They have become centres of religious as well as cultural activities of the region. Though many of them are on the verge of being shut down or disintegration, the rest of the sattras are still very active and they have protected and preserved traditional Assamese culture. Prof.M.Neog writes in his book *Sankaradeva and His Times*—"An Assamese Vaisnava *sattra* proper consists of a square enclosure wall. Varying according to its strength, with four openings or gateways called karapat (corruption of Skt. *kapata?*) and containing four rows of huts or four long houses, each divided into a number of rooms at the sides and the central temple,composite of a shrine called *manikut* or *bhaj-ghar* and an assembly hall. The four rows of huts or long houses with sets of rooms on the sides are each called a *hati* (Skt. *hatta,* a fair with rows of shops). The individual huts or rooms are generally of an equal size except those on the eastern row which are somewhat bigger, being the residences of the

superior or abbot called *sattradhikara* or *satriya* (also *sattradhikari sattariya* or *sataniya*), his deputy called *deka adhikar* or *deka sattriya* and the principal office-bearers of the establishment."

The adhikar or the Gossain, recognised as the formal head of the *satra*, combined spiritual sanctity with social authority and commanded extensive feudal landed property. He was almost a minor God in human form. S.C. Goswami writes in his book *Introducing Assam's Vaisnavism*—"The *adhikars* are held in the highest respect not only by his disciples, but by persons of all ranks and creeds. In case of some of the most influential *sattras*, the administrative head of the province has on many occasions exchanged ceremonial visits; and Lord Chemsford,as Viceroy received them in a big durbar, during his visit to Assam."

Chapter One

1. A game of dice. In the dice board, portraits of various abodes of Hindu Gods are drawn. As the final goal, a *Golokdham*, which is known as the abode of Lord Krishna with his consort Radha and the gopis, is depicted. The dice player who reaches it, crossing all the hurdles wins the game. It was a popular game among the women of South Kamrup in those days.
2. A kind of white-coloured sweet-smelling indigenous flower. Its flowers and leaves are used as vegetables.
3. An itinerant group of theatrical performers, mostly in the villages, enacting plays from *puranas* and Indian classics.
4. A body of persons appointed to decide a case either by the parties themselves or by the order of the authorities.
5. A kind of loose shirt for men.
6. A kind of thickly clustered green bamboo.
7. The fork-tailed shrike.
8. Assamese woman's long raw silk skirt, tied at the bosom or round the waist.

9. Any foreigner, particularly the white-skinned European and Englishman.
10. Cane baskets.
11. Driver of elephants.
12. Helpers of mahouts and noosemen during the capture of wild elephants.
13. A hanging oil lamp.
14. Assembly of opium-eaters where they sit together and smoke opium with areca nut leaves.
15. Decorative gate found only in the houses of Gossains.
16. Wife or widow of a Gossain.
17. A veil or shawl used as the upper garment of Assamese women.
18. The junior Gossain's wife.
19. Bonded labourers.
20. A theatrical performance peculiar to South Kamrup where the stories are selected from the *Puranas* and the *Mahabharata*.
21. Four days in *Asarh* (July) when the earth is supposed to be unclean and the digging of earth is forbidden. A ritual observed mostly by Assamese widows. It is believed that the earth menstruates during this period.
22. Evil stars or planets.
23. A business deal in connection with elephants between two parties of elephant merchants. The money earned by catching and selling wild elephants is shared between them equally.
24. A land measure in India; 5/8 of an acre.
25. A kind of thin bamboo.
26. A room where rice is pounded with a wooden contraption.
27. Sweet smelling lime.

CHAPTER TWO

1. A kind of indigenous Assamese silk made from a species of silk-worms which feed on the leaves of castor plant.

2. Very fine muslin lower garment for men made in Shantipur in Bengal which was popular in Kamrup among the aristrocacy and upper class.
3. Bailiff.
4. A species of paddy which is reaped and gathered in the month of June or July.
5. A kind of hard wood tree.
6. Young mistress. A term of endearment used for a young daughter of a Gossain.
7. The priest
8. A piece of cloth draped over the shoulders by Assamese women. Especially from South Kamrup.
9. The onset of menstruation often dreaded by young Brahmin girls in those days. If they did not get married before the first flow of menses they would be made outcaste.
10. Elephant depot.
11. A pointed iron prod used for taming and driving elephants.
12. A shooting platform up on a tree generally used for hunting wild and dangerous animals in jungles.
13. A festival in which all the images of gods and goddesses are taken to the river bank where they are worshipped with due rituals and ceremonies.
14. A festival in connection with Goddess Basanti, another manifestation of Goddess Durga.
15. An Assamese manual of obligatory daily rituals and customs for Kamrup Brahmins written by Lakhi Deva Atta.
16. A kind of plate made out of banana trunk.
17. A ladle made of coconut shell with a wooden handle.
18. A kind of acid fruit which is prepared with fish.

CHAPTER THREE

1. Vermillion.
2. An old maidservant sent with a bride to the groom's house.

3. During shraddha (a religious ceremony for the dead) ceremonies, live goats are buried headfirst and sacrificed by suffocation, in this part of the verandah.
4. A customary expression indicating outrage.
5. The District Magistrate's court.
6. Those Gossains of South Kamrup who are followers of Damodar Deva, disciple of Saint Sankar Deva.
7. Chandi is another manifestation of Goddess Durga.
8. Stale rice soaked in water, kept overnight and eaten with baked fish or potato.
9. An ornament of the ear shaped like pomegranate flowers. This ornament is worn only in the South Bank of Kamrup.
10. A merchant.
11. A Brahmin who earns his livelihood by carrying out religious ceremonies and rituals for various people. The people who employ the Brahmin are known as jajmans.
12. A common expression of horror and shock among women of South Kamrup.
13. A married woman whose husband is alive, supposed to be auspicious.
14. Rehearsal for a theatrical performance.

CHAPTER FOUR

1. Manor house.
2. Granary.
3. Friends and relatives.
4. Coarse cotton cloth imported during the Second World War.
5. Portrait and horoscope.
6. An auspicious gift of rice, cloth and other offerings.
7. A room where the wooden sandals of dead ancestors are kept for worship. It is a common custom among all Gossain families of South Kamrup.
8. Rice pounder.

9. A kind of citrus fruit.
10. A division of a district in Assam in charge of a fiscal officer called maujadar.
11. Woman of loose morals. One who has slept with twelve men literally.
12. An indigenous tree. Its leaves are used for making canopy cover on bullock carts.
13. A sweet scented hair oil.
14. A kind of white flower.
15. A kind of village theatre which originated in Bengal.
16. A kind of indigenous flower which blooms in the evening.
17. Leaseholder of an elephant depot.
18. Lord or Master.
19. Priests.
20. Betrothal gifts.
21. The family or race, mainly founded by different sages like Kashyapa, Bharadwaj, and so on.
22. Policemen or army men.
23. Royal land grants to learned and pious Brahmins were tax-free. But the British made them taxable, only reducing the rate to 50%.
24. An employer of a priest at ritual and sacrifice.
25. A term used for addressing a learned Brahmin or priest;also a term of endearment.
26. The era of Salivahan which is used by the Assamese in their calender.

Chapter Five

1. Unpaved road.
2. A work believed to have been written by the composer of the *Mahabharata*, Vyasa.
3. An indigenous citrus fruit.
4. A kind of gourd.

5. A power given for settling light criminal cases.
6. Traditional Assamese tray.
7. The great saint of Assam, Sri Sankar Dev.
8. Lowest of the low caste people.

CHAPTER SIX

1. Vaisnavite religious festival celebrating Lord Krishna's birthday.
2. Brahmins who act as agents for temples in the main piligrimage centres of India.
3. A kind of wild berry tree.
4. Brass or wooden tray.
5. Please see ref. no I, ch. Two.
6. A pendant shaped like a drum set with red stones, worn in Kamrup.
7. A typical Assamese necklace of heavy gold.
8. An elephant without tusks.
9. A kind of yellow spotted snake.
10. A book of incantations and spells for curing snake bites etc.
11. Purification ritual for atonement in which twelve quarters of a rupee and other gifts are given to the officiating priest.
12. An Indian measure of weight.

CHAPTER SEVEN

1. Please see ref. no 6, chapter 6.
2. An Indian measure of weight: one tola is approximately ten grams.
3. A necklace in the shape of a new moon.

CHAPTER EIGHT

1. First step of marriage ceremony in which an offering of silk cloth, vermillon powder, oil, betelnut, etc, is made.
2. Please see ref no. 5 chapter one.
3. Large cushion or mattress.
4. Please see ref. no 4, chapter 6.

5. A kind of yellow-skinned banana, much favoured in Assam.
6. Great master.
7. It is a term used for Muslim inhabitants of Assam.
8. Sacrificial fire.
9. Nature with all its three basic traits.
10. A kind of thorny bush found in Assam.
11. Tobacco.
12. A container used by opium-eaters, which is made by breaking off the top part of an earthen pitcher.
13. Bengal before the partition of India.
14. Those women who remain in the house throughout their life without having any menstrual cycle.
15. British soldier, generally any soldier with white skin.
16. Little daughter.
17. A dangerous frenzy in male animals such as elephants.
18. A tree bearing white flowers.
19. A kind of hard wood.
20. A kind of heavily clustered bamboo.
21. A ceremony before the daughter- in- law enters the kitchen for the first time and starts cooking.
22. Sultan Gazi was a legendary dacoit.
23. A ceremony for a young girl after her first menstrual discharge.

CHAPTER NINE

1. A shawl worn by both men and women.
2. Low wooden stools.
3. Trays.
4. Handkerchief.
5. Decorative handles of a palanquin.
6. Incantations for women which were very much in vogue in the Nagaon and Kamrup districts of Assam. They were invoked for charming and seducing men.
7. Blacksmiths.

8. A container made from plantain trunk.
9. A coarse cloth imported in the time of World War II.
10. A British lady's style at the time of World War II, imitated by high class aristocratic Indian women. The blouse had puffed sleeves which looked like pistols.
11. A kind of lentil.
12. Mixed vegetable curry.
13. A kind of yellow pulse.
14. A very fine variety of fragrant rice. It is compared to slender tooth-picks.
15. Clarified butter.
16. Traditional Kamrupi towels.
17. It is a part of the memorial service for the dead after the prayers and rituals. The house holder washes the feet of the Brahmins. They are then given a feast and afterwards gifts of money or household articles. Later the Brahmins sell or exchange their gifts among themselves. Sometimes it leads to a bitter quarrel and scuffle among them!
18. Relatives and friends.
19. Disciple of Damodar Deva, the Brahmin Vaisnavite saint.
20. Various kinds of spices.
21. Expiation.
22. A wind instrument made from buffalo horn.
23. Potatoes were always called 'vilayati alu' in Kamrup because they were never grown locally in Kamrup, and the people considered it a foreign product.Vilayati is anything hailing from London.
24. A very fine variety of rice.
25. A kind of river fish without scales. Many people in Kamrup do not eat it as they believe that it consumes human corpses thrown into the river.
26. Eel.
27. It is a well without any plaster on the inside surface.

28. A kind of spotted arum plant, which grows everywhere during the monsoon in Kamrup.
29. Alms - auspicious gift of rice or cloth or any other offerings.
30. Land lease given on periodic basis with tax.
31. Brahmin knowing all the Hindu scriptures.
32. Purification rite for expiation in which eight quarters of a rupee and other gifts are given to the off ciating priest.
33. A pulse of red colour.
34. A sacred book where the codes of rituals are written.
35. A brass container for water.
36. An auspicious feast for the newly-weds.

CHAPTER TEN

1. A nooseman who helps in capturing wild elephants, or elephants in frenzy.
2. A holy man. A votary of Lord Vishnu, residing in a sattra.
3. An elephant specially trained for capturing other wild elephants.
4. An arrangement between the landlord and tenant in which the latter has to give half the yield of the land to the former.
5. An arrangement between the landlord and the tenant in which the tenant has to give the former half the yield of the land or equivalent value in cash or kind.
6. Elephantine fool.
7. A flowery canopy.
8. Big cotton shawls.
9. Temple agents.
10. Hibiscus flowers.
11. Merchants hailing from Marwar region of Rajasthan.
12. A land lease given on periodic basis payment of tax.
13. A kind of raw silk of golden colour.
14. People of a particular low caste who carry the palanquin of Gossains. They also make and sell country liquor.
15. An elephant without tusks.

16. A sacred mantra to be taken by the bride and the bridegroom immediately after marriage, so that the bride can enter the kitchen and take charge.
17. A sweet-smelling flower.

CHAPTER ELEVEN

1. A kind of creeper shaped like bones.
2. Witch doctors practising Tantrism. The word ojha is also used for the leader of a group of Assamese chord singers.
3. Yellow spotted, long and slim snake.
4. A process of catching wild elephants by running them down with tame elephants.
5. The king.
6. A very rigid atonement.
7. Paths.
8. These are common command words for elephants.
9. Common command words for elephants.
10. A jute rope used as a lasso for catching wild elephants.
11. A kind of sword.
12. *Jaharbat, mit khara, churangi, karih* —these are the names of various diseases associated with elephants.
13. A village of people ostracised by the Ahom kings, for adultery or sexual crimes. Later the Muslim Fakir, Shah Amin, converted them to Islam.

CHAPTER TWELVE

1. A fragrant rice.
2. An indigenous tree.
3. Traditional Assamese towel.
4. Agbiyas or Agchaul Diya are couples who have lived together secretly in sexual intimacy without marriage and who have been later allowed to live as man and wife within the society by performing a ceremony which is not according to Vedic Shastras but sanctioned by the community.

5. Purification rite for expiation in which four quarters of a rupee and valuable gifts are given to the officiating Brahmin.
6. Purification rite for expiation in which six quarters of a rupee and gifts are given to officiating Brahmin.
7. White skinned Australian soldiers in base camp near the sattra during the last war.
8. Dancing posture representing the God of Love.
9. Dancing posture representing a crane's perseverance.
10. Dancing posture representing the speed of a mongoose. These are all parts of an Ojha's dance performance.
11. A rare handbook of information and instruction with illustrations for the Ojhas or the village chorus parties.It was originally written on the bark of the sanchi tree.
12. A kind of indigenous tree. Its wood is used for making furniture
13. A major Assamese festival.
14. Young ladies.
15. A spirit residing in bamboos, as per a belief. The tantrics of South Kamrup tamed this spirit with special mystical incantations, for carrying out their bidding, mostly to crush their enemies.
16. An incorrect rustic version of Inquilab Zindabad.
17. Land surveyor.
18. Stale rice.
19. Advance given in connection with land sale.
20. A land measure in India. 1/3 to 2/3 of an acre.
21. Cultivated land.
22. Land Deed.
23. Offering of mashed ripe bananas with rice.
24. A widower or an estranged husband bringing a girl, without marriage, to stay with him.
25. Brahmins brought to Assam by Ahom kings from a place called Kanyakubja (Kanauj)in U.P.
26. Boys acting as dancing maidens in a travelling drama group.

27. A biography of Saint Damodar Dev, the founder of the Damodariya sect of Kamrup.
28. All the images of gods and goddesses are taken to the river bank and kept there for worship and performance of certain rituals.
29. A person who leaves his native soil and visits a foreign land, thus becoming impure.
30. A Sanskrit grammar book.
31. A kind of wild flower.
32. Another name of Lord Krishna who is supposed to have a bluish complexion. Neel means blue.
33. Fire torch.

Chapter Thirteen

1. Tuberculosis.
2. A manual describing Hindu rituals.
3. Ascetics who follow rigid rituals and live naked in the caves.

Chapter Fourteen

1. Sub divisions of a district.
2. Fisherman's caste.
3. Opium eaters.
4. A small measure of weight. One tola is approximately ten grams.
5. Soldiers from the British Army.
6. A secret mystical ceremony.
7. A narration about Dhruva.
8. Unregistered land deed.
9. Owner of the elephant depot.
10. Low caste, particularly applied to an unknown foreigner.
11. It is a part of the worship of Devi Basanti (another form of Goddess Durga) which takes place in the month of October-November. In this ritual, goats are burnt in a straw hut made specially for this purpose. In later years, as it was considered

too barbaric, a small opening was kept in the wall of the hut to give the goat a chance to escape.

12. Village level trial of a man who seduces a girl and abducts her.

CHAPTER FIFTEEN

1. Residential school in villages for teaching Sanskrit where the teacher and the pupils stay together.
2. Book of lyrics on Vaisnavite religion written by the saint, Madhava Deva, the well-known disciple of Saint Sankaradeva.
3. Bank draft.
4. A pitcher-shaped cane basket for fishing.
5. A kind of small river fish with lots of bones and spikes.
6. Adoption of an adhikar from outside if there is no suitable successor.
7. One who recites the Bhagavat, the holy book, in which Lord Krishna's life and deeds are narrated.
8. Followers of Sri Chaitanya Deva of Bengal.
9. Bride price. Assam is probably the only state of India, where dowry system is not prevalent. On the other hand, many Gossains of Kamrup gave cash or kind as a gift to the bride. Many poor Brahmin boys from South Bank had to remain bachelors due to this custom, and many of them had to go to Cooch Behar to work as priests, leaving behind their parents, to earn money for the bride price. This was known as going to Vilayat. The custom does not prevail now.
10. A game brought to Assam by Mughal invaders.
11. A bush resembling bamboo.
12. Rice powder taken with curds or milk and jaggery.
13. A kind of tray with a stand.
14. In upper Assam, three baskets, and in Kamrup, four baskets of grain or four bighas of land.
15. Land granted to Brahmins free of rent by Ahom Kings.
16. A landed estate granted to a Sudra priest.

17. Unregistered land deed.
18. A kind of bird, resembling the cuckoo.
19. A land surveyor.
20. Makers of brass and copper utensils.
21. Blacksmiths.
22. Carpenters.
23. Barbers.
24. Washermen.
25. Palanquin bearers.
26. A sweetmeat made of jaggery and rice powder, roasted in hollow bamboo pieces.
27. Child Krishna.
28. Old papers of land deeds.
29. A goad: a sharp pointed stick with an iron tip, used for controlling elephants.
30. Long bamboo poles, pointed at both ends.